The Witch at Sparrow Creek

# THE WITCH AT SPARROW CREEK

## A Jim Falk Novel

**Josh Kent**

Hippocampus Press

New York

Published by Hippocampus Press
P.O. Box 641, New York, NY 10156.
http://www.hippocampuspress.com

Cover art © 2015 by Jason C. Eckhardt.
Cover design by Barbara Briggs Silbert.
Hippocampus Press logo designed by Anastasia Damianakos.

First Edition
1 3 5 7 9 8 6 4 2
ISBN: 978-1-61498-123-7

The Witch at Sparrow Creek

# PROLOGUE

James walked along the path with his father. His father had his hands on Jim's shoulders, pushing him along. There was no moon that night, and the woods around them were black. James couldn't tell if his eyes were opened or closed. The woods were so quiet. Their feet crunched along in the snow. Sometimes, ahead, he thought he heard a laugh or a whisper from the trees.

Soon he could see a dim and dancing yellow glow—the small, fluttering light of Old Magic Woman's fire that he'd seen so many times before of an evening. This night, at the sight of the glow, James's stomach twisted and his head filled with a stuffy heat.

Ithacus Falk felt his boy hesitate on the path in front of them.

"James," he said, "do not be afraid. You must do this thing." He pushed him along.

"Pa," James whispered as the light of the fire grew orange and spread through the snowy trees, "what happens?"

"No one can say, but you will soon see," Ithacus said, and a small smile came to his face in the dark.

"And you did the same—you did the same?"

"Yes, boy, the same, but it is not the same for everyone. Now hush."

James could see the fire reaching toward the dark branches in the clearing ahead now. This fire was much, much larger than a normal camping fire, and there was a special kind of shape around it made by logs. The logs crossed one over the other, forming a crooked circle that went around into the center of the bright fire. A tall shadow was standing there, the flames curling and flowing behind it.

Jim stopped all of a sudden, and his father nearly pushed the boy face first into the snowy path.

"I don't want to," Jim said.

"James, you will, you will see, you must pass through this."

James didn't understand any of this, but he didn't know what to say or how to say it. He only knew that he wanted to go back, back through the forest, back up the mountain road, back through the field and into his warm bed at home—yes, but that wouldn't be far enough away. James wanted to go back into the past. He wanted to go back before the witch, before his mother died, to sit again on the woven rug in his parents' home while his father stoked the fire and his mother boiled water for coffee. He wanted to run so fast that no one could see him anymore. If only there was a hole out there somewhere in the moonless forest, a hole that he could dive down into and go through to the land of the past, if only he could . . . Especially if it meant that he would never again arrive at this place, this moment, this shadowy fire in the night.

He peeped open his eyes through his hands and squinted at the blaze as his father moved him forward again. The figure standing by the fire was not Old Magic Woman. The figure was too tall to be any person and had long, crooked arms that reached from the shoulders nearly to the ground. The flames showed that the figure's face was like a mountain cat's, but from either side of the head came long, twisting antlers.

James felt a cold come into his chest.

"What is that, Pa?" James asked as the dizzy feeling came over him again. Beside the figure he could see now were standing four old men, Old Magic Woman's people, the Katakayish people of the woods and rivers, those people sometimes called the First People or the River People. Four Katakayish men stood around the fire, each one in a shiny costume of leaves, beads, feathers, fur, and jewels, each man's beads and jewels shining out in a single color of his own, black, yellow, blue, and red. They were all wrinkled with graying hair, but they looked strong and fierce because the Kataka-yish people were strong. It was also said, however, that they were passing away.

When they saw little James and his father approaching, Black and Red got out their drums and Blue put a flute made of bones and sticks to his old lips. The drums pattered and then started into heartbeats beating as the flute twittered high and low, winding its way around and through.

Then Yellow began to sing in the language of the River People, the language of the Katakayish people, which Jim had learned from Old Magic Woman and from his father, but the words were terrible and the man's voice grinded in the fire and snow.

> When Eyabé came to the mountain
> Kitaman with flaming teeth
> Set upon him to devour
> Flesh by flame
> Flesh by flame
> When Eyabé came to the mountain
> Kitaman with razor rocks
> Set upon tear to pieces
> Skin from blood and blood from bone
> Skin from blood and blood from bone . . .

James entered the circle around the fire with his father. The drums pounded ever louder, ever faster. The four old men started to dance with jagged, jerking motions, twirling and bending, fol-lowing one another around and around the fire in a right-handed circle while Yellow sang his song of Eyabé and Kitaman.

The beast with the antlers and the cat's face could only be Kitaman! James remembered Kitaman from the stories Old Magic Woman had told him and his father. Kitaman was the one who came at the end to take you by flame into the dark world forever. Suddenly its arms moved and rose high with flaming claws. Kita-man took two wide steps aside, and behind him was a kind of table made of grasses and ropes and sticks. The table was in the same shape as the base of the fire, the crooked circles inside of circles made from the ropes and branches.

The creature set its flaming hands to the table, and licks of red and yellow fire started spitting out from the sides and spilled up into the trees.

James knew that the grass table was for him and that he was going to the flames and that Kitaman would feast upon him.

James's body felt stiff and he tried to scream, but only a harsh whisper came out of his mouth.

Then he managed to wriggle out of his father's grasp. Ithacus raised his hands and then reached them both out to his son. He looked at his son's wide-open eyes as they looked about this way and that, first at the dancing men, then at the fire, then at Kitaman, then at Ithacus. But little James didn't look his father in the eyes.

"You must not fear!" his father shouted over the drums and over the flute and over the singing of the terrible song. "You must not fear!"

But little James looked at the fire and the big monster and saw teeth and eyes glitter in the firelight and heard the old man voices singing the terrible song.

"Skin from blood and blood from bone!"

His father reached out to grab him, but little James was quick and he spun and ducked and left before his father could turn. Little James Falk was wailing and tearing off down the path, disappearing from the light.

"No! No! No! No!" James was shouting into the night.

His father stood staring a long while as the men began to notice the object of their ceremony was missing. Yellow stopped singing, and then the drumming stopped. He looked at the others; Blue started to smile and giggle. It wasn't the first time he had seen a little boy run off into the forest, afraid to become a man. But Yellow fiercely shushed him and waved his arms and pointed to the boy's father. Blue put his hand over his mouth, but his eyes still smiled.

Ithacus looked down the path, waiting, waiting for his son to return. The fires on the ends of the arms of the cat-beast dwindled, and then the long arms folded and broke in the middle and dropped to the ground. The beast collapsed in a slow way, and two human hands reached up and took away the face and antlers, and Old Magic Woman stepped out of the shaman trappings she wore and walked to Ithacus's side.

She looked into the darkness with him for little James. "Another day, maybe, another day."

Ithacus looked at the ground, watching as the flames made their shadows dance in the cold, black night.

"Another day," he said.

# CHAPTER 1

Spencer Barnhouse pushed his glasses back up his nose and wiped his forehead. He knew Jim Falk had got him into a place that he was probably not going to get out of alive.

Maybe if someday he saw Jim on the other side, maybe at the very end, or maybe in the Straightway . . . maybe they'd let old Spencer Barnhouse give this boy a good one in the jaw. That would make him happy. He'd owed many things to this boy's father, but now that his father had disappeared, what was he doing?

Spencer rolled the barrel of powder slowly and quietly into the shadows of a storehouse and waited among some left-around crates. He was sure someone was watching him from the far end of the docks, but if he kept quiet long enough, maybe they'd go off. Or maybe they'd figure he wasn't up to much but drinking and wandering about looking for trouble. Especially if he acted none too worried about watchers and concentrated on a flask and a smoke. He did just that. Sitting on top of the barrel in the dark, he rolled some tobacco in paper and lit it up. He took long slow puffs and then produced a silver flask from his coat and pulled a long drink from it, screwed the cap back on, and stuffed it back into his breast pocket. He shifted a few times in the moonlight, making sure to keep his eyes out over the black water and away from where he sensed his watcher stood. Then Spencer stood and stepped slowly out to the edge of the dock where the ship was. He leaned on a post and smoked, making sure not even to glance in the direction of whoever it might be that was eyeing him.

Moments ago, Jim Falk had grabbed a mess of special weapons and other items off this boat and stolen off into the dark corners of Hopestill, just as they'd planned. Now Spencer hoped to explode the little cargo boat into pieces: maybe they'd think it was done by good, common thieves and that the weapons had been lost in the blast, not stolen. Maybe.

But who was this watching him? Jim Falk had finally got Spencer in a spot. Sure, there were plenty of others around who might take up the task of exploding one of Varney Mull's ships in the dock, out of spite or even for sport. To some folk in Hopestill, Varney was just another villain in power—a man who gave out work and money, but a man whose generosity was thin compared to his greed. There was a high price for any favors granted, and Mull had no issue with collecting his tolls.

Spencer sucked on the glowing little roll of paper between his fingers. It was then he figured one of Varney's men had stepped out of some hiding place at the far end of the docks and begun to walk not too quietly in Spencer's direction. He was coming straight at him. Spencer was going to have to acknowledge him, look up and make some greeting, and that was just what the man needed. He wanted to see Spencer's face so if he ran into him on some other night and in connection with some other slightly questionable events . . . some other night when there'd be more than just this one man against Spencer.

He'd hurried to get it done. He could have thought this through and been long gone before the boat exploded, he could have done so many other things, but Falk appeared out of nowhere and was in such a damned hurry. Spencer cursed his luck and cursed Jim Falk. He'd hurried to get this thing done for Jim. It was weapons Falk needed and right away, but these were Varney Mull's weapons he'd stolen.

"Why can't you make it a business of forging your own, Falk? You've got time on your hands. Learn a trade, for the love of your father . . ." Spencer spoke in a plain, calm way even when he was irritated.

"No time, Barnhouse, no time," the outlander said. "No time now. No time before. Especially not now. There's not time enough in the world to do all the things. You do the things you must while you have time."

"You seem to know just how to twist the words of your father to fit your design," Spencer said and finished the bottle of whisky they'd been sharing. Falk had said "no time," but Spencer knew there was a lack of ability and an utter lack of patience and discipline that was more than likely behind Jim's helplessness and urgency. There was something else too.

"You know what's at stake here," Jim said and peered with his strange blue eyes deep into Spencer's own pale ones.

"Do I now? Better question yet, do you?" Spencer asked. He stood, pulled another bottle from the shelf, and poured a full glass for himself. "Jim, it's been so long since I've talked of any of these things—these things we're talking about. Sometimes I doubt if I ever saw them in the first place. If it wasn't for your father and, well, what he's left us . . . Now you're having visions of red-headed women and ghosts and birds." Spencer laughed, but not very much and not very hard. "Maybe I think you've chewed too many of those green leaves of the Katakayish people, Jim. Maybe you spent too much time with old women in the woods. Maybe your father was more of a storyteller than we think." Spencer again tried to laugh, but couldn't. Even as the words left his mouth, he knew that he did not mean any of them. In a way he wished it were true that he didn't believe. He wished that he didn't believe in spooks or witches. He wished that he didn't know there was that certain darkness that Varney Mull used to control the ports and pubs of Hopestill. But Spencer Barnhouse had more than belief. He knew. He knew because he had seen. He knew, but he wished he could be like those who didn't know and only believed. If he only believed, maybe there might come a day when he forgot, or when he doubted enough to forget. But for the memory of Ithacus Falk . . . and here was little James Falk, not so little anymore. Here was Jim Falk and not for the first time. Here was Jim Falk asking some fool favor.

Asking Spencer to put his life in danger. He wasn't sure why he didn't just turn this fool out into the night.

Spencer gulped the whisky and smashed the glass into the fire. He spat and shook his head, leaning forward with his left hand out touching the portrait of Ysabel Barnhouse. He looked at her picture, her black hair and half-smile, and the cold pain of her loss churned inside him.

Jim sat there watching the old bookkeeper walk about in the dirty library office. He tried to keep his head up on his shoulders and his eyes open and reached slowly for the whisky Barnhouse had poured for him. He took a sip and then downed the rest, worrying a bit that he might slip into that place where his memory went out entirely, but he was really not too worried about that.

Barnhouse turned to Jim. "How many of them are left?"

Jim said, "I don't know. I told you I don't know. I can't remember everything all the time like you. These visions I've been having don't allow for a lot of exact measuring. Also, they're not exactly about them. They're focused on this redhead woman and a church on fire. Last I can think though and remember, there were more than enough that my pa knew about. He'd catalogued them somehow. But those things are supposed to be all lost, now aren't they?"

When he said that, Spencer moved forward waving his hands a little, as if to silence him.

Jim kept on. "It's harder and harder to remember or see since I can't find the old woman. Can't find her. My pa's voice is fading from my head too, especially without the leaves. But they can't exactly reproduce as I remember, and as they say, the Evil One can't create, so they gotta go around eating life to live, isn't that the things? But there wouldn't be any more of them. Making life somehow. I don't know if that's a thing they're able to accomplish. Right?"

"You'll kill them all, then, you alone?" Spencer said and unwrapped the long green leaves from their wax paper wrapping. He started counting them out.

"I don't know. You could come with me. We might do better."

"There's too much keeping me here. If I leave with you, there'll be no one to keep an eye on Mull and keep an account from Hopestill."

Jim Falk scratched his cheek with his thumb. "Emily might be safer somewhere else too."

Spencer's face was stone. He wandered back to his desk and pulled out a parcel, wagging it in the air. "It takes a long, long time for me to grow these. You'll have to go through them more slowly. Or find your old woman again."

Jim nodded and took the roll of bright green blades from Spencer's hands and leaned back in his chair, "How old is she, Emily?"

"I can't believe it, Jim, but she's fifteen years old."

"If I come back, you and I together can rid out Hopestill, make it safe again."

"If you come back."

"If I come back."

Spencer smiled, and his teeth and glasses caught the firelight in the dirty room. "If you come back, Jim Falk, you and I will rid the earth."

Spencer looked out over the black water and then down at the planks of the dock. The man who'd been watching him was taking his time, the lazy steps of someone with nothing but time and no cares. He was coming up on Spencer now, but Spencer kept his head bowed low, sucked down the last good puff of his smoke, and, turning away from the dark figure who'd approached him, flicked the tiny spark into the black water and said, "Evening."

The man said nothing as Spencer casually leaned his elbows on the railing that separated the walk from the water and Varney Mull's weird little boat. For a moment, Spencer Barnhouse thought that maybe the man was just a passerby and hadn't noticed him. Maybe Spencer shouldn't have said anything at all.

But then the footsteps stopped and the figure came slowly up alongside and settled into leaning on the railing right beside Spencer, who stared straight ahead into the water.

A raspy, whistle-toothed whisper from beside him asked, "What's he looking at? Is he looking out into the dark water?

There's no moon out tonight, so he's not looking at the pretty moon. Maybe he's looking at this boat. Here's a boat docked all alone on a cold night, so near to winter. What a funny little boat. Is that what he's looking at?"

Spencer was quiet, then reached in his coat and started rolling another smoke. "You want one?" he asked the stranger.

"How courteous," the rasping voice came back. "I don't care for it."

Spencer rolled it quick, popped it to his lips, and lit it up with a match.

Spencer told the stranger, "Ten years ago, my wife was killed. Murdered. Viciously. I loved her. I don't know who did it." Spencer tilted his head a little to see if there was a reaction from the dark form beside him. "There was no moon that night either."

Spencer Barnhouse set a knife about the size of his forearm out on the railing. He just set it there lengthwise, and it glittered dimly in the starlight and the dim lights of Hopestill.

Spencer took a slow, deep breath and listened close for that first rustle of movement that would mean the stranger's strike, but instead he heard the soft boots of the stranger retreat slow and then quicken.

He put his big knife away and turned to walk home. He left the barrel of powder among the crates and junk around on the docks. Maybe, if he could, he'd try to retrieve it during the day when he'd be more likely obscured by the obviousness of his activity and other commotions on the docks, and maybe a different hat.

Spencer Barnhouse went to his empty home in the middle of the night. He'd picked out a place for himself and Ysabel right among the bustling shops and markets of Hopestill. When they'd bought the place with the money he'd inherited, Hopestill had been a bright and new hub with shiny stone streets and smiling vendors and street performers. They'd stolen even the stones off the street to build the walls that Varney Mull required around this town. At this late hour, coming home through the muddy walkways of Hopestill was treacherous.

Spencer spent time looking back over his shoulder for the raspy-voiced figure. The drizzling rain that had started up muffled the noises in the dirt streets, and time and again he whirled about to the sound of footfalls or whispering only to see rain-splattered streets and the leaning walls of uninhabited homes.

Yes, he'd helped Ithacus Falk before. He'd helped Falk do some less obvious things. Turn up some books, or find some old maps, get a translator of the old tongues or Katakayish and Ahmen tongues that had been needed by Falk. He'd helped Ithacus Falk read the books and taught him some reading and writing too. Ithacus Falk was good at the older ways of writing. His son, though, was something else altogether. Jim Falk's mind blurred when Barnhouse tried to teach him, and he became forgetful when presented with newer vocabulary no matter how simple. It was as if, somewhere along the line, Jim Falk's mind had become full and it was hard to pack anything else inside.

Spencer pulled his coat tight about him. He missed Ysabel fiercely, but at times like this, knowing that Varney's men couldn't get to her was comforting to him. The worst was over for her and she waited for him somewhere.

These weapons that Jim was after were something special, though. Jim made it seem as if even Varney wasn't sure of their worth. They'd been fashioned far off, and Jim said that what Varney didn't know was that they'd been made for killing demons.

"Varney doesn't know what you and I know," Jim said. "He doesn't know what it is exactly that he's dealing with. He looks at everything as though they're just things. He's taken these weapons because he senses there's something special to them, but he doesn't know about any of it beyond money. He thinks he can sell them to the right buyer and make money. And maybe it is that he can, but I'm not going to pay money for them."

Spencer was glad, though. Glad to take from Mull who'd ruined his hometown. And glad to help Jim get on with finding and ridding the world of these things. He'd wished he could go along with Jim. He'd wished for a way to get revenge, but if not vengeance, he wished for some way to remove from his heart the sick fear that he felt in place of peace.

He shut the door behind him and went in quietly. He walked down the hall before he removed his coat and looked in Emily's room. She was asleep, curled under the blanket with a serious look on her face. He closed her door.

Sitting down at his desk and lighting the oil lamp, Spencer walked to his fireplace and poured another glass of whisky and poked around in the fire. He paced, turned back to the fireplace, and, reaching out at an odd spot on the right-hand side, wiggled a stone and pulled it. He set the loose stone on the mantelpiece and reached into the wall. From the wall, he produced a black tin box.

He sat at the table and pulled several rolled scrolls and a black, leather-bound codex from the tin box. Picking up a quill pen and putting it in his mouth, he got out an even smaller black book.

With the quill pen, he wrote:

> Jim took these things to kill the killers
> The whole lot of specials
> The whole lot of simples
> The Dracon pepperbox and slugs
> The hex-hatchet of his father's making
> The leaves
> The Longshooter (disassembled)
> Other books and papers which I have not yet accounted for
> Maps of the southern river lands

# CHAPTER 2

He walked in.

Bill took a look at him and figured who he was from the looks of him. He'd wished his wife would have not told him many, many things.

Bill nodded and adjusted his belt around his waist and said, "Well, she says there's a spook in back a them woods."

"Where at?" he said.

"Up, way up there," Bill said, "and he comes down."

The room in Bill's house was cold and brown. The sky coming in the windows was white.

"When do you see him?" he asked.

"He's got a long, gray face, yellow eyes, like egg yolks." Bill said. "I dunno, he comes down at different times."

Bill's wife came in. "Oh, my . . ."

She looked at the strange man in the hat, and her mouth moved as if to say something, but then she said, "We have company. You should tell me when we've got company. We have coffee."

"Ma'am," he said and glanced at her quickly, but didn't look at her, and then turned back to her husband. "I'm Jim Falk. I'm here to talk about the spook."

"Well," she said and looked quickly at Bill, "you tell 'em. I'll just get you some hot coffee."

"I'm tellin' him," Bill said.

She went off. She was pretty, with red hair and high cheeks, and she was younger than her husband. Jim Falk didn't look at her, but he wasn't sure that he had to look at her to see her. It must be her.

Jim said, "This spook—he comes down in winter or in summer?" Then Bill looked at Jim and opened his eyes a little wider, but not very much, and he pointed at the wood chairs and his square table in the room. Jim saw that Bill's fingers were crooked from work with busted knuckles.

They sat. There was a book with a leather binding on the table and a couple of candles. The candles were dirty. The book was a book of the scriptures.

Bill went on, looking at the candles and the table. "He comes down every season, I suppose, maybe once a season, maybe more, but there's no certain time."

"When does he come?"

"He comes at night in summer."

"In fall?"

"In the fall he comes at night, and in the spring."

"In the spring he comes at night too?"

Bill nodded, but looked at the backs of his hands and not at Jim.

"What about in the winter?"

"In the winter he comes at night. He came during the bad blizzard, and it seemed like he came twice that winter and came during the day."

She brought out two white cups of dark, hot coffee. She set them down in front of Bill and Jim and then leaned in the doorway listening.

"Twice in the winter?" Jim continued.

"Yes. That's how I remember it. Violet?"

"Yes, Bill?"

"Tell Jim Falk what you said when the spook came down out the woods during that bad winter."

"Well," she started. She moved around, recrossed her arms, and stared at her feet in black shoes on the wood floor. "That winter was a bad one. That winter was about four years ago, and when that spook came down outta them woods, well . . ." She talked as if she was bored, arranging herself against the door frame. "Well, that's when the baby Starkey went missing . . . and I think that spook got hold of that little baby."

"For what?" Jim asked.

She blinked and looked at Jim sort of sideways and squinted, whispering, "I think that particular spook's a baby eater."

Jim Falk looked at her. There she was. She leaned on the doorway with her pointy shoulders and her ruddy hair. Jim saw no lie in her eyes, but he caught something else there, playing. It was like a jewel or a sparkling thing. Jim looked away. He wondered if somehow or another she knew—if she knew that he had seen her, or someone that looked like her, in his mind.

"That's right," her husband said, "that's right." He picked up his cup with a clink and blew off the steam. "A baby eater."

Jim Falk flipped open a little leather book to a blank page. Bill Hill watched the pages of black symbols go by, words he didn't recognize. Violet shifted again.

Jim asked, "Who is the baby Starkey?" and got out a little black stick that looked a little oily.

Violet said right away, "That was Dan and Elsie Starkey's baby. Their real baby together. They lived up the road." She sneezed a short sneeze and looked at her husband. He looked down at his coffee.

"That's been a few years back now," she said, pulling a small rag from somewhere in her shirt and wiping her nose. "Dan's moved on."

"That's right," Bill said. "Dan's supposed to have moved up north somewhere and Elsie lives with her other boy now, that Simon. It ain't right by the scriptures, him leavin' her alone like that, just walking away from her, leavin' her with that boy. That boy, Simon, he takes care of her, they say I guess on account of she's been sick."

"Except he ain't her boy," Violet said and went back fast into the kitchen.

Bill looked at Jim and watched him write things in the book with the oily stick. He shook his head and said low, "That boy's not from around here. He's from some other place across the sea or some such place. Like them people from the Far East that they took out west to make 'em build the towns in the West. Them Starkeys raised him up from young. Guess they found him all alone."

"You mean you think he's from the Far East?"

"A foreigner of some kind. Maybe a one from the Far East."

Jim drank some coffee. Violet was off in the kitchen making noise, and the wind was blowing against the little house.

They drank some more coffee. Jim closed his writing book and looked around the little house. It wasn't too different from the one he grew up in. A wood-burning stove in the kitchen filled it with that fire and coffee smell he remembered from times long ago. He didn't want to think about that. Jim glanced at the stack of fire-wood in the corner.

"These woods are the woods the spook appears in right here in back of your house?" Jim finally asked.

"Yes," Bill said. "Yessir."

At the bar down in Sparrow, they were drinking beer—Hattie Jones, Benjamin Straddler, and Simon.

Simon, the Starkey boy, was telling them about a trick with cards. The trick was called the moving hole. Hattie was laughing at the idea, and beer was jiggling out of his mug.

Hattie said, "I need me one o' those, a moving hole." He looked down at the little boy, who was playing with some papers on the floor by his stool. "Show us!"

Simon did the trick, and everyone was taken aback. He punched a hole in an ace of spades with a knife. Then he took the hole out of the ace and put the hole in his hand. He held up his hand and showed the hole all the way through. Then he took the hole from the middle of his hand and moved it to the king of hearts. He showed the ace again. It was okay. He showed his hand again. No hole.

Hattie Jones just about swallowed his pipe.

Benjamin Straddler was too serious to smile, but he said, "That is some trick."

Then, Jim Falk came in the front door.

Everybody looked at him for a second or two, but he looked honest and plain enough. They looked back at their beers and their friends, but they listened close in a sideways way.

Huck Marbo was the owner of this bar, and he had one leg and one daughter. Many years and many trials were upon his brow, but his smile was still bright and quick because of his daughter. May ran the table service for Huck, and though she was not generally thought of as pretty, she had a brighter, bigger smile than her father and her simple hands were quick to service.

Jim Falk came and sat down at a table by the window, and Huck nodded for May to serve him.

Jim felt good to sit down. All that afternoon, after talking to Violet and Bill Hill, he had gone tramping in the woods. A gray light was on everything, a fog. The sky was white and cold and the trees stuck out over the loam black as hairs. Everything was dim and solid. The woods got colder and harder to see as he went up the mountain. His black boots crackled on the leaves.

Even though the fog was thick, he focused his eyes on everything, and that wore him out. His mind and eyes got tired, but the pictures might stay forever—or at least if he couldn't see them in his mind's eye when he was awake, when he slept tonight the dreams might show him the details. Maybe he would see something he didn't see. It happened.

"We have beer and whisky and coffee," May said and looked at the table when Jim looked up at her face. She didn't talk loud either.

"Beer," Jim said and meant it.

He looked past her and out the window. The night was black. It made him think. His mind rushed through the forest. There was a funny thing about this one tree that started fiddling in his head. There was some wiry shape, writhing. It faded out.

The bar came back in his vision. It was a nice place; maybe it was even pretty. It wasn't exactly a bar either. Jim Falk had stopped in many such places. Small settlements like this one usually had some spot that doubled or tripled as a store and a bar and whatever else. Some of them even had pianos. This one did not have a piano. There were some oil lamps, candles, and even a picture on the wall of a boat going down a river. There were other things that they were selling—rope, nails, mallets, marked bottles, and other such things on shelves.

He saw this Simon Starkey kid, from the Far East (so Bill Hill supposed), doing card tricks for the men with hats and red faces. Then they laughed, and the kid from the Far East made a noise like a bird and flittered his hands around. Then they all laughed again and started to play poker for money.

Just as the game started, Hattie Jones tapped his fiddle-bow four times on the wood table. His pipe blew smoke as a song began whining out of the fiddle, and a little boy with wide eyes stood up beside him and hummed exactly what the fiddle whined.

Hattie sang a song. His voice was cracked and old, and it made Jim think of the sounds of cold birds in the mud. The little boy stood up and started singing with him.

> Old them woods was, shiver, shiver
> Filled her boots with snow and silver
> Shiver, shiver! Shiver, shiver!
> Little darling by the river.

Jim took a drink of beer and smiled while the mug covered his mouth, but stopped smiling when he put the beer down.

Jim could never remember all the words to that song because for some reason he had started to focus in on this Simon Starkey, but the song was something about a lost little girl in the snow who was loved by the fairies. He wanted to write it down, but he didn't.

It was this Simon fellow who had got all Jim's focus. When he was over at the Hills' earlier, Violet was saying some things about this kid, Simon.

"He was raised up by them from a little baby, is what they said," she had said from in the kitchen.

"Violet," Bill said, "you open up that window if you're gonna be smokin'."

The kitchen window squealed and there was a pause as she tinkered with something. She continued, "They came here with the baby, but that boy was full-grown sixteen years."

"That's right," Bill said and pushed away his coffee cup a little.

"He spoke perfect too, just like me or you or Bill, remember? Even better than some around here speaks their own," she called in.

Bill said, "Most foreigners have an accented speech." And he eyed Jim with a half-squinted eye.

Jim gave a quick nod and called in to Violet, "Violet, this is very good coffee, thank you."

"Thank you, Mr. Falk," she said and came back in the room with a smile and looking a little flushed and fiddling with her necklace.

Jim Falk gazed at her and then back at Bill. Bill was staring out the window at a fog rolling in from the woods. Since Bill's eyes were looking out the window, Jim took a second glance at Violet Hill. She was looking right back.

"How you get such a thick fog when it's cold out like this?" Bill said, and Jim looked out the window fast.

Violet's green eyes drew Jim back to her. "Dan, who was married to Elsie—he moved outta here about four or five years ago now, I guess, whenever that spring was right after the real bad winter and the awful snow." Violet swallowed, put her left hand to her throat, fiddled with a silver chain, and then went on. "Elsie's older than me. They come up here from some river town. They used to talk about that big river that comes down from the town they were in, River Top, River Den, River something." She squeezed her eyes real hard as if that might help her remember. "See, Mr. Falk, Elsie might be older than me, but she's still young, and that

Simon boy isn't at a right age, where they . . ." She wagged her finger at the empty coffee cups and raised up her eyebrows.

Bill said, "Yes, we're done."

"The right age?" Jim said, watching her hands take the cups.

Violet looked him straight in the eye, and he saw again that strange, moving jewel behind there. This time it slithered. "Well, I just mean that he ain't the right age to be really raised by her. Since Dan's gone, gone who knows where, she and that foreign boy that ain't her boy have been shacked up in that house, if you catch my meaning."

✦

"Hey! You! Stranger!" Simon yelled over Hattie's wiry fiddling.

The little boy who had been singing there along with Hattie stopped singing suddenly and started working at drawing pictures with ink and a feather on some yellow papers. He was working hard.

Jim had been staring at Benjamin Straddler's hat and had faded out. It happened when he was thinking.

"Hey! Stranger!" Simon stood up now. He was a strange-looking kid for sure and he was strong, had strong arms. His eyes had an uncomfortable effect on Jim. "You wanna play?"

Benjamin Straddler tipped up his hat brim and laid his eyes on Jim Falk. He pulled on his stogie. The cigar breathed an orange light on his face and on his one raggedy eye where the eyelid was torn and the eye was whited over behind.

Jim didn't like this look, but while he'd been faded out thinking, May had brought him another muddy-looking beer. He looked at the beer in the glass mug, picked it up, and drank some, trying to see if maybe Benjamin might look away.

Benjamin Straddler was looking at him harder now; Jim could feel that raggedy, busted eye poking around in his head. Straddler was looking in there for who Jim was. Jim patted at his pockets as if he were looking for some tobacco.

"No, thank you," Jim said finally and raised his glass to the group. "Thank you very much, but I'm not a card player."

"I guess he's not a card player," Simon said and grinned way up with only half of his mouth.

Benjamin Straddler just shook his head and said, "Outlanders. What? They don't play cards where you come from on account of the scriptures?" Then he forced a laugh out of his throat and looked around at everyone, but no one else was laughing.

Hattie Jones squealed the fiddle and put it down all of a sudden. His lips puckered up and his brows went together and he took his pipe out of his mouth and said, "Hey! Who are you anyways?"

Jim had his nose back in his beer cup and wasn't expecting such a straightforward question. He felt the urge to bark at the old man, but instead he held his eyes on the table and slowly drank the rest of his beer in one long drink. He stood then, and May and Huck and all the rest of them who were in there took notice.

Jim Falk made a thin silhouette in a long, dark coat. His hair, which before had looked blond, they could now see was gray as ash. His hands were strong and bony, but his face was lined and honest with eyes blue and strange. He tipped his hat, but did not take it off.

"My name is Jim Falk," he said. "I believe that around these parts, you might call me a ghost killer or maybe even a hunter. I rid spooks."

All the folks looked around. Huck Marbo looked over at May, who was pretending not to listen. When she caught his eye, he twirled his finger fast in a little circle in the air. This was to tell her to clean her tables and clean the kitchen and go to bed.

That night, after more beers and some kind of talk and excitement with the rest of them, Jim made his way along a dark path back to the Hills'. He couldn't remember whether he'd made friend or foe at Huck Marbo's bar, but he couldn't care. His head was filled with whatever this little town's good beer was and it gave his mind a soft, wooden feeling.

Back at the Hills', Jim fell straight to sleep. His legs went up on the table in the Hills' backhouse and his chair leaned back against the windowseat in the little room.

When he woke the next day, he had no memory of when Violet had come in and moved him out of the chair and onto the bed. She laid him there, right by his sack of gear, which he reached out for. He hugged it and snorted.

She stared for a long time at his drunken face all snarled and snorting. She looked over her shoulder and out the window and could see that the lamps were still burning where Bill had been up looking at his plans for fixing up the storehouse. Her hand lifted because she wanted to touch the outlander's forehead to make the wrinkles go away. Instead, she left quickly and quietly shut the door behind her.

Jim sniffed and rolled around in the bed. "On that one tree," a face in his dreams told him, "there was a black spider eating another black spider that was exactly like it." Again, the lips said to him, "A black mirror eating a black mirror. Which one is the black mirror?"

That same night, Benjamin Straddler hurried through Sparrow mumbling to himself. Mumbling to himself past the shuttered windows, mumbling and stumbling along the rickety bridge over where Sparrow Creek ran through the middle of town, pulling his coat close to him and huffing along and looking from side to side with his one eye in the black and fog. He wanted to go talk to the preacher's brother, John Mosely. He figured that if he went straight to the preacher there might be a lot of trouble all of a sudden and it might come toward him.

He came up two steps and onto the flat porch and knocked fast. John's wife answered the door with a mean face, "It is very late, Benjamin Straddler. John is sleeping. You smell drunk. Go away."

She started to shut the door and he put up his hands. "Ruth? Uh, how is John?"

Benjamin wasn't the kind to drop by here at the Moselys' late at night, drunk or otherwise. In fact, the only other time he'd been by was during the big snow a few years back.

"It's cold and black out there, Benjamin Straddler. You could lose your way on a night like this. Come in and sit down. Should probably have some coffee before you're back out in the night."

She squinted and looked him up and down. Watching him as he pulled at his coat and looked this way and that, she helped Benjamin bump through the door. He slumped down and propped himself up very slowly, but neatly, in a soft chair in the foyer. He smiled at Ruth. "No moon, no moon out. Coffee . . ."

She turned to him before disappearing into the little kitchen. "John's asleep nice and sound. Let's try not to wake him. He doesn't often get good sleep these days."

Benjamin Straddler remembered this foyer. He had dug snow out of it with John Mosely and John's older brother Vernon, the preacher. Vernon had his ears all burned up with the frost. Them preaching folk, like Vernon, they were always somehow finding bad trouble. Benjamin didn't understand a bit of it. He didn't understand how a man could believe stories and old writings so strong to think that others should believe them too, and he especially didn't understand why good folk like these Moselys who tried to do good would run into such bad problems all the time. But when Vernon and John and this here Ruth had come to town, it just seemed as if their own special trouble came with them, might have followed them here. Just the way a special trouble had come for Notham Taylor, who'd been the other preacher, trouble, trouble, trouble.

It wasn't long after the Moselys showed up that the bad winter laid hold of Sparrow. Yes, Benjamin had surely saved Vernon from frozen death in the frozen night.

"I dragged him outta the snow and back up the church, and Pritham worked at him," Benjamin said.

"Benjamin Straddler, are you talking to yourself?"-Ruth said as she reappeared in the foyer entryway with a white cup.

"Ruth?"

"Here's your coffee, now drink it fast and let's out with it. What's so important that Benjamin Straddler comes knocking around the Moselys' in the middle of the night? We haven't seen you around the church in a long while. So what's the trouble that's finally brought you along?"

Benjamin opened his mouth and then shut it and then opened it again and then said, "Well, Ruth, there's a man come to town called Jim Falk, and, Ruth, he says he's a ghost-killer." He swallowed. "You know, a spook ridder? He rids out spooks is what he said, if you know what that might be . . . and he's here on account of he wants to get rid of a spook. That's what he says. I told him that there ain't no such spook and that Violet and Bill Hill are a couple of troublemakers. He's stayin' up their place, he says. A spook!"

"So *who* is this now? A spook ridder? And try to sit yourself up, Benjamin."

Benjamin drank a fast half-cup and said, "Well, that's what he says. I don't know. He says he comes from a town around down South. I can't remember now the name he said, it was a plain name that you can't remember well, but he talks like he comes from up North from one of the big cities. He's got a real straight-like voice, like he's done a lot of book reading, almost kind of sounds like a preacher, but he also kinda sounds like one of them natives from the backwoods; you know he's got that sound to his voice, like them old people. He said that he's crafty with ways of ridding out spirits. And, Ruth, you know, I think he may have got . . . He did something. I don't know how he did it. But, Ruth, well, we got to thinkin' that maybe he's got a power."

"A power," Ruth said to him. "You're sure?"

He nodded, but then looked into his cup for a long time and then looked back at her and back at the cup. "He did something. I don't know how he did it."

Benjamin Straddler's eyes began to close.

Ruth was older and looked tired too, but she also looked at him with her mouth pulled down and one eyebrow up. She must have understood something of what he was saying.

She said, "Let's get you headed toward home. I'll tell John all about this in the morning and we'll need to go and see about this. This stranger is staying up with the Hills?"

"Well, yeah." Benjamin drank the other half and swallowed hard. "He's staying with the Hills is what he said. He told us Bill's got him roomed up in their backhouse back there."

"Well," Ruth said, "I'll tell John and in the morning, well, we'll need to see about this."

Her hands passed something small back and forth between them. Benjamin could not see it.

She let him out the door with a few encouraging words and looked up and down the crooked street that led up to their home. It was so dark.

She closed the door behind her and looked into her right hand. In it, a long, black spider curled wispy legs.

Benjamin got home somehow and laid down his head by his wife's head. Lane was sleeping deep and soft, but her face looked concentrated. The coffee Ruth made for him had given him just enough energy to get home and dizzy.

He blacked out. In his mind he saw Jim Falk, though. He saw the way he looked at all the men in Huck's place. He saw how those eyes held some secret. Then he saw Falk in Benjamin's own kitchen. He was eating Benjamin's bread at Benjamin's table, laughing with Lane. Lane was laughing and Falk was pouring dark wine into a golden goblet in her hands. There was an emerald light growing and jumping between them.

He sat up quick in his bed in the dark.

"Spooks!" he yipped and squeezed his temple as the blood rushed forward.

Lane woke up then and put her hand on his shoulder and climbed herself up on his back and hugged from behind. Hopefully he wouldn't be sick tonight.

She pressed her long nose into his fat cheek, kissed him, and whispered, "You smell very bad."

"I'm sick. I feel sick."

"Go back to sleep," she said and kissed his ear. "There'll be eggs in the morning and toast with butter."

This thought of the hot eggs pushed away all the other thoughts, and he fell asleep smiling with his head on Lane's chest. He dreamed of the little horse. The little horse was running through a pumpkin patch. The little horse licked his hands and he could feel the hot tongue. The little horse kicked and started dancing with him in the amber light of October. Red and gold leaves floated and swirled around them, and in the sunset was the black shape of a stranger with a beat-up hat.

# CHAPTER 3

Her husband was already headed into Sparrow to pick up another bucket of nails, some glue, and some other such things. He was pretty near finished fixing up the busted storehouse.

Jim Falk rolled out of the small bed and washed up quickly. Violet was knocking on his door right away.

"Mr. Falk!" she called through the wood.

"Yes?"

"Mr. Falk, I've got breakfast."

He opened the door. Violet had a tray, and on it was a decent breakfast with milk and coffee. Jim, for the first time, saw she was about half-a-head shorter than he. The trees reached up behind her gray silhouette in the white morning.

"Thank you," he said as she handed over the tray of food.

She gave him a little half-smile. "You'd better get to your work soon. The last thing this town needs is another lazy drunk." She might be serious, but there was a smirk on her mouth when she said it, and turning quickly, she invited his eyes on her neck and waist. "I've got some extra rolls and butter. When you're done, put the tray out the door."

Jim ate the eggs and toast and thought about the spook and this woman. Did she know? Did she know that she'd appeared in his head?

Last night, at Huck's bar, Benjamin Straddler told him there was no spook.

35

"Ain't no spook up in them woods or up in any woods," Benjamin said, looking slowly, one at a time, from Jim to Simon to Hattie. "Those Hills are troublemakers and they want to have some kind of importance in this town, and so they make up tales and become a part of them. Bill Hill was a good man before he fell into marrying that Violet. She comes from the Gray family up the Ridges. The Grays are known for their insanity."

Jim thought about that and looked over at Simon. "Simon, then, what about that baby? The Baby Starkey?"

Simon's eyes grew dim and his smile faded out. "What was it that they told you? That the spook come and got her? Sorry, stranger. That baby died because of the cold and we ran outta wood. We ran outta wood and we were all huddled up close, but it just got too cold. It just got too cold one night and all of us all fell asleep. It was like the winter cast a spell on us, a deep spell. When we all woke up, we could not wake up that baby, and then Elsie started in something awful. Screaming at that baby. It was worse than the cold or the whole winter, or even that little dead baby—Elsie's screaming."

Benjamin said, "You see, now? The Hills will tell you it was the spook that got that baby, and that it was the spook howling in the night. It was Elsie in her grief."

Jim Falk listened to it all, but he remembered especially "a deep spell."

He shoved the tray on the table empty.

Today was the day to do two main things.

The one thing to do was to go into town and see. He had to see what kind of a town this was, and how many people were in it. Maybe he'd ask around a little bit, a few questions, but not a lot. People don't like outlanders. People don't trust outlanders. Outlanders, if they don't wind up dead, at the least get sent back out, out into the outland.

He had to make it all very natural, gentle, and piecemeal. You can't ask all the questions to one person, or it gets their blood up. You spread the questions out, take it slowly, and be patient. You be patient and you look and see what their eyes say. You have to watch the light in their eyes. Or the darkness. A lot of times people will say what they want *you* to say. They'll also say things without saying things, so that's why you look in their eyes.

The other main thing was getting up behind the Hills' and finishing up to try and memorize the woods. He'd slept already late and had to hurry. In town, he would need to get some oil for his lamp for when the sun goes down. He had some burning oil anyway, but he needed lamp oil too.

Violet said when she came to pick up the tray, "It's a little while's walk to get there, but if you need anything else there's Huck's shop as you know on the north side by the main road. You gotta pay for it there, though. But we might not have some stuff as you might need."

She left with the tray, walking back down the lumpy hill that led up to the house where she lived. Jim watched her go. She walked sometimes with her head looking as if it was about to turn and look at him.

Jim stood on the steps to the backhouse. They were sturdy and made of blackwood. Blackwood was hard to find and harder even to build from. Bill Hill must be a good woodman, and a strong one. Jim looked over where the storehouse was going back up; the morning light came down in through the places where the walls weren't so done yet.

He looked at the shafts of white light against the black insides of the half-done building. He squinted. Was there a shadow leaning in there?

Jim wondered at this while some birds chirped and rustled. At times, he was sure that his father was out there watching him. Sometimes he sensed it like a wind or a tone in his soul—that he was watching him. It was the only thing that pushed him forward. To come to a town like this, to follow a dim dream down from the north. Only to hope to see him again, to find him. Jim didn't know where his father was; all he knew was that his father was not dead.

He blinked a few times, and some clouds moved to let the light open up in the shed. Jim saw the gray blanket that Bill Hill must have thrown over a nail on the wall. No one leaning, just a tricky shadow.

Maybe he wouldn't go into town. Maybe that Straddler fellow and Simon were right. Maybe Violet Hill, with her bright red hair and her cigarettes, maybe she was just another crazy Gray from the Ridges. He reached into his pack and felt the little satchel that held the leaves and looked back into the half-built storehouse. A wind picked up and blew the little blanket like a cloak.

Barnhouse warned him that he shouldn't eat them too fast. He squeezed the package and ground his teeth. It was an important day.

Today was the day to do the two main things.

# CHAPTER 4

May Marbo woke up in her bed and curled her toes. She was tired and it was real warm in her bed. She didn't want to get out. She got out.

Downstairs, her pa was up and walking around and making breakfast. The smell of hot eggs was rolling around in her room.

She put on her slippers and went down in the kitchen. There was her pa, Huck Marbo, stumping around on his leg made of wood. His blond hair was thin as a winter fire on his head now, but his muscles were still hard and strong. The look of him made her feel safe. She had seen this man, even with his leg as it was, come galloping through waist-high snow to bring them victuals from the shop. When her ma died, she watched him carry her beautiful body out the front door.

Now he was making eggs and coffee with his broad back to her.

"Good morning, May," he said without turning around. The smell floated about the room and the eggs crackled away in the black skillet on the wood stove.

She sat down and rubbed her brown hair around and pulled it around her face.

"There's eggs," he said.

She scooted up her chair.

He put some eggs on a big plate. "You want eggs? These are straight from Mosely's chickens, from them chickens that the chicken man brought through here last spring."

"Yes, please," she said. She hated the chicken man.

"And coffee?"

"Yes, please, and thank you."

He fiddled around, got out the coffee powder, put the kettle on, and lit a fire under with a snap of a match and a whoosh of flame.

He set the eggs down in front of her and sat down across from her at the long brown table. The morning came in the big window all gray and white with crow sounds.

May started eating.

Huck regarded his daughter for a moment, her nose pointed at her eggs. He placed an empty cup in front of her and said, "May, I want you to stay away from that Falk fella at the shop last night."

She didn't answer. He set another cup down in front of his plate and sat down.

He picked up some eggs on his fork and put them in his mouth and swallowed. "Ya hear?"

May wasn't sure what to say. "I don't know what to say," she said.

"I'll help you." Huck looked at her straight in the eye and she looked away quick at her eggs. "You say, 'Yes, Pa' and that's the end of it."

The kettle whistled, and he got up and tended to it while she moved her eggs around on the plate.

Huck poured boiling water in the two white cups, "That Falk," he said. "That Falk is some kind of trouble."

He sprinkled now a portion of brown, powdery coffee into each cup, "He's an outlander. No one knows where he's from, and he won't say." He dropped a spoon in each cup. "But I'll say for true that nothin' good's ever come from outside Sparrow and nothin' ever will."

She looked up at her father. His voice was strong when he said it, but something about his eyes looked worried, soft, tired.

"What about those church people?" May asked.

Huck put the mug in front of her. "Now wait on that and don't sip it up right away, it'll burn ya."

She nodded. "What about them people?" she came again. "The Moselys? They came from up north, right?"

Huck got quiet and sipped his coffee. In the middle of each of his brown eyes, right near his deep pupils, there was a ring of grass green. This was in each eye and gave him the impression of having a kind of deeper, greener self behind the first one. Sometimes, when he went deep in thought, the green would shift until it was dark as autumn grasses. "Them folk is God's people. God's people are never outlanders. God's people is God's people. Folks like that Jim Falk, they're the ones from the outside."

May got a little scared of her pa and went back to eating her eggs.

They sat eating then in a long, speechless breakfast while the crows cawed in the gray sun.

At last May said, "May I be excused?"

Huck kept his eyes off her and replied, "When you finish up around here, I want you to come straight into town. You don't talk to anybody. You don't stop. Not even at Vernon Mosely's to see the chickens and rabbits. Don't stop at the creek bridge either. Not to-day. You come straight to the shop. Nothin'. No excuses."

She said, "Yes, Pa."

Down the path back to town, there was a house Jim could now see from the road. He couldn't see it last night in the dark. In fact, he remembered very little about the walk home last night in the dark. That was a mistake—a mistake he couldn't make again.

Crows flew up in the air from near where the house was.

He looked up at the little white house as he was coming around the bend and saw there was a girl running down to the road from the house with a basket on her arm. She wore a plain old tan dress and a long cloak with a hood on it. She looked almost like some little thief.

It was May Marbo. "Mr. Falk!"

She ran out of the gate and came up close to him and then took a step back and looked at her basket. She only thought briefly of what her father had said to her.

Jim was a little surprised by her rushing up and just tipped his hat and smiled.

She took a quick look at him, then looked back up to the house and then down the road toward town. "Well, good morning, Mr. Falk. You wouldn't be heading into town this morning, would you?"

Jim tipped his hat back a little and said, "Why, yes, I am, and I would be honored to escort you—Miss Marbo, isn't it? If you will allow it."

She smiled again, wide and toothsome, and said quietly, "I will allow it."

They started walking.

The path was barely wide enough for a carriage or a cart drawn by horses, but one might be able to squeeze through. In most places, the trees bent in and darkened the white sky. They were close. The sound of their shoes on the path was muffled.

They walked in the cold quiet for a while and then May laughed. Even the sound of her laughter stopped short and fell in the road. He looked over at her. Her brown hair was damp and flat and just as she laughed, a breeze blew through the tunnel of trees and whipped here and there strands of hair around her head.

Jim asked her, "What's funny?"

"Oh," she said, "you remember at my pa's last night when you showed everybody that magic trick where you broke the glass by staring at it?"

Jim had forgotten. "Oh, I did?" Then he remembered. "Oh, I did."

For a moment, a fear gripped Jim Falk. What had he done? A damned fool he had been to go getting so drunk, so drunk that he put the whole of it in danger, as he had in Batesville. Maybe when he got down into this little Sparrow town, the men of Batesville would be waiting for him, following him all the way down here, and ready as ever to string him up and burn him. That was the kind of trouble he was always pulling behind him. Barnhouse well knew it. He wondered what would happen now. Someone in this town might soon get the same kind of ideas the men of Batesville had.

"I don't know how you did that trick," May said, her cheerful voice breaking his thoughts, "but even Simon Starkey's mouth was wide open and,"—her voice got quiet—"it's known that he's some kind of magician."

It came back to him then.

He'd been drunk on Huck's whisky, and Simon was in his face with more card tricks, and then he made that mouse appear right out of a handkerchief. Jim was filled up with the sad whisky energy.

"You hear me, Simon, Son of the Starkeys, you are nothing but a fraud . . ."

Simon laughed and grinned, and his face looked darker and his smile looked sharper. "A fraud? A fraud? You should be more careful, outlander, coming into town and casting about accusations!"

Jim spun up out of his chair and then swayed around to keep from falling and slumped back into his chair at the little table. He said something that none of them could hear and began to trace something with his finger on the table top.

"See here!" Simon shouted and waved his arms and walked over to Jim's table. Simon grabbed the mouse that he had just pulled from the red handkerchief. He placed it on the table right in front of Jim. Under the handkerchief, everybody could see it scrambling under the cloth. Then, his other hand came down hard and smashed the mouse under the red cloth.

He looked around at everyone smiling. "I lift up my hand . . ."

He lifted up his hand and there was a completely flat handkerchief. When he lifted that up, out of the handkerchief fell, red as rubies, rose petals. The little crowd in the bar made a gasp and men looked around at one another to see if the other men had seen what they'd seen. May was looking at her pa, but then she looked over at the outlander and then back at Simon. Everyone else looked back at Simon.

Then, as if the little thing knew just the right moment, clambering onto Simon's head came the mouse sniffing the air, its tiny eyes sparkling. There was a boom of laughter and clapping from the crowd.

Jim got hot at all the applause, and from his slouched position in his chair he pounded the table and shouted, "Tricks, only tricks!"

Jim's face was red and sad, and he took a very deep breath which everyone could hear him take. The people all looked at him. He looked around the room, pulling each person in with his eyes, and then he fixed those sunken, whisky-drunk eyes on his beer mug. His blue eyes widened up their pupils.

Nothing happened.

Everybody standing around thought this outlander might be frozen, maybe even dead. Then the room got so quiet that the outside noises of the wind seemed to stop. Everybody watching felt a kind of pressure in their heads that made them squint a bit, and then there was this whine, high and quick, but barely audible.

They looked at the mug that Jim Falk was glaring at. There was a dull pop. The mug cracked up its side and beer flowed out. It cracked right up the middle like split wood.

Nobody talked while the beer ran on the table.

Jim looked around at everyone. Everyone was amazed and stunned. May was smiling with her mouth open.

Jim about stunned himself. He staggered out of his chair while the beer began to drip on the floor. He tipped his hat. "Good evening," he said and left out the front, left them all standing dumb.

It all came back to him now, mostly. May was stepping along beside him, stealing quick glances at his face here and there, but looking forward mostly.

"I forgot," Jim said to May as they turned a slight bend. "I forgot I did that trick."

"How did you do it?" May asked.

"It's just a trick, May, that's all," Jim said and began scanning the close woods again. "Just a trick, like Simon turning the mouse into rose petals."

"It seemed different," she said. She was bashful around Jim, but outside of the Hills, Bill and Violet, she had been the friendliest one so far.

They walked a way without talk. The trees in places grew out into the path. "It doesn't look like a lot of horses come up this path," Jim said.

"No," May said, "ain't a lotta folk keep horses here. In fact, nobody does anymore. They come into town sometimes on horses from other places to bring stuff through."

The path then came to an upward slope that rose for about ten feet. On the other side, it went clear down, about a half-mile, all the way to the end where Jim could see the tiniest boxes of the houses in town.

"Why not?" Jim was looking way down on the path now. Ahead of them, he saw a figure in the road standing near to the woods.

"Don't know," May said.

Jim set his eyes way ahead on the figure and felt a tremor that started in his gut and raised his hairs and still, something more than that. He felt the jitters. Then he saw the figure move, and Jim's breath quit. It was a dark, crooked thing with long, curly spines. It was still quite far off.

He stopped walking and said, "May, stop, May."

She wasn't scared until she looked at him and saw how serious and faraway his eyes were.

"What . . ." she started.

"Shhh," he whispered, "don't talk. There's a spook up there on the road."

May got closer to him and started shaking. The jitters were heavy and rolling along the path now. It was feeling around for them.

"Stay close and don't budge," Jim said. "They can't see so good, but they can hear and feel things that men can't."

Jim saw it cross back and forth, back and forth across the road. It flickered at the left edge of the path and then disappeared into the trees.

"May," Jim said, "I want you to stay close by me now. We're going to pass on into town, and once we get there I don't want you to tell anybody what we saw. I just want you to say that we walked into town together and that I went off and you went about your business."

"Okay, Mr. Falk," she said, but she never did see anything.

They passed in silence along the road. May stuck close by. Now he could feel the jitters constant. The jitters he'd first felt left a permanent signature in his mind, a pulse. He could feel the spook now, but it had moved far up into the hillside somewhere. It seemed unconcerned with them.

May whispered. Her eyes were darting from side to side, and she would turn once in a while in great fear to look back up the path. "What kind of a thing is a spook?"

Jim said, "May, it all depends. I don't know for sure, but none of them are good."

"Mr. Falk," she said as she looked up at him. The fear was bright in her brown eyes. "Does the Evil One send them?"

Jim Falk looked at her long, square face and saw softness in her features. He wanted to comfort her, but instead he told the truth. "Sometimes," he said, "sometimes the Evil One does send them."

He felt her shudder with her whole body when he said it. Then he said, "Let's get you into town and then I'll come back out here and maybe, after that, we won't have to worry about it anymore."

"What will you do?" May asked.

"My job," Jim said and meant it.

Jim got May into town.

She squeezed his arm pretty hard and ran off toward her pa's shop without looking back at him.

Jim unrolled his gear bag and got out his gear and checked it. He laid down his coat. Then he geared up.

His hatchet he slung over his left shoulder on a long, tightly braided leather strap. This hatchet had been his pa's, and his pa had executed many evil things with it. He adjusted the strap around his waist so that it wouldn't drag along as he ran.

Then he fed the Dracon pepperbox pistol with six shots of silver-lode and holstered it. This was the weapon and ammo Barnhouse had secured for him. He wished he had packed better ordnance; he wished Barnhouse was along with him; but this was it, and it was time.

Finally, he put on his leather shirt and collar. This protected his neck and chest from claws and spines and raggedy teeth.

He hefted his hatchet a moment in his right hand, straightened his hat, and plunged into the woods.

He moved fast.

Outlined in his memory, punched like a stamp, Ithacus Falk stood. This was his pa. "When you're trained in on the jitters, the jitters is trained in on you. That's the thing, boy."

These woods were thick, and it wasn't long until all he could hear was the noise of his breath and his boots crunching on the dead leaves. Once he got in a ways, he stopped again and unraveled his pack. From inside a small pocket deep in, he pulled out a leather pouch. Out of this, he got two green as grass leaves. He put them in his mouth and chewed them. Then he swallowed them with his eyes closed.

He took a good drink from his flask, rolled his pack up, and then started back slow up the hill. The leaves opened up the colors a bit.

Where there had been only black and gray, now there was brown and some red, even some purples and a lemon yellow.

Then his nose opened up too. The crisp, black smell of mud and the raspberry and smoke smell of the moving wind filled up his nose. He heard now too the sleeping insects waiting, buried, for spring. Mostly, though, he could feel the jitter-trail now, heavy as wet rope, leading him through the trees.

The hill rose up and up and up, and Jim walked slowly. This served to conserve his energy as well as keep the noise down.

The two main things he was going to do today were completely out.

He marched and stopped and ran and stopped and looked through the woods and ran and stopped again.

Finally, he came up over a crest and saw it. There it was. Hunched over a log. It was an ugly, messed-up thing and Bill was right—its eyes were like egg yolks and its face was gray.

It kept using one of its mangled claws to push its drooping bottom jaw up. As if it couldn't keep its own mouth closed for the weight of its lower jaw.

The whole beast looked built from the throw-away parts of other animals: goats, horses, fish; scales glittered under fur, antlers twisted out of its back and head, and horns sprouted from its legs and thighs.

What's it doing scrabbling its lopper-jawed self all over that log? Lookin' for what?

Jim hunkered down behind a lightning-cracked tree near the edge of the clearing. The wind was mercifully still so the thing might not pick him up right away, but Jim knew it was just a question of time now. When the attention came off the log its full focus would be on him.

The spook paced now, back and forth, its wet eyes staring at the log.

There must be something alive in there.

He could see the log shaking a little, and it was just wide enough for maybe a rabbit or a mole or a skunk.

And then there was a skunk, and, just like that, the wind shifted the stink his way.

"And the little skunk said, 'Well, bless my soul,'" he mumbled.

Now up came the skunk skittering through the woods and straight past Jim. Jim looked up and the spook caught him in the eyes and held him in its pinhole pupils.

Jim heard a voice in his head. It was the low, sinister voice of the spook. "Jim Falk," it asked, "do you want to die?"

Jim said, "No."

The thing rambled forward shaking its massive head and wheezing, a few pincers emerging on long, black stalks from under its mane.

Jim stood and steadied himself.

It stopped by a tree and cocked its enormous head. Its jaw lolled against the ground. It froze. Its gaze fixed on him. It gathered itself. Jim watched its muscles bunching.

Jim threw his coat's left breast open. The Dracon pistol glinted mutely in the gray forest.

The spook lunged at him, and Jim Falk drew the weapon and popped the trigger in one move.

His hand went numb with the blast, and a singing entered his ears. The flash of the weapon left red, sunny swirls on his vision, and his nose burned with the blue smell of powder smoke.

Six balls of the special silver-lode erupted from the gun and met all at once with flat, wet thuds against the spook.

One in the thing's head below the left eye, one in the center of the chest, one in the pooch of the thing's baggy stomach, one in its wrinkly neck, one in its left leg and one in its right.

"One says good morning and one says good night," Jim Falk said and watched it drop dead. The eyes in the head still moved.

Jim holstered his gun and pulled his weird hatchet. He could see the silver-lode sinking away into the beast, producing gray twirls of smoke.

He leapt on its molting back and hacked full force at the muscular, convulsing neck of the spook.

Forged to the purpose, his hatchet rose and fell and stuck and sawed and rose and fell and twisted and pulled many, many times before the neck was severed enough to permit him to wrest off the head.

The forest floor was matted then with black juice and offal. Nothing would grow here in spring.

Jim used both hands and tossed the wide, ugly head to the side. The eyes, though dulled in luster, still blinked slowly and watched, the mouth yawning in despair, as Jim doused its separate body in the special burning oil and, as with flint and tinder, set it ablaze.

The smoke billowed black and thick.

Jim looked at the head and the face of the thing. It was cruel, he thought, that something so utterly pitiful, false, and evil-bent should be alive.

Then Jim wrapped up the head in a woven blanket and tied it with a cord.

He headed down the hill and, at the bottom, back toward the road. He headed for Violet and Bill's place.

The sun washed through the white sky. It waved and flickered through the creaking black trees. It reminded him exactly of golden wheat and warmth—a time his father had dunked Jim's hands in warm water when he was a boy and rubbed his big coarse hands over his own. "Get all the dirt off for dinner."

Jim got a little smile then and slung the head of the thing over his left shoulder and walked onto the road as the rays of the sun disappeared back into the clouds.

Violet was out on the porch. She was up on a stepstool and trying with a rag and water to clear out the rest of a wasps' nest that had been long abandoned, but stuffed in the corner under the roof. A little whistling could be heard coming up the road. It was an old song. Violet knew it, but she couldn't quite place the words.

Soon she saw Jim Falk's brown hat and gaunt frame marching up the dusty trail with a woven bag over his shoulder. Whatever was in the bag she didn't know, but she felt a heavy chill in her heart when she saw it. Was it moving?

She was about to run down to meet him when she saw him, but the sight of that sack kept her back. She stood on the porch as a sudden, harsh wind picked up her orange hair and whipped it out of its bun and blew over her water bucket.

"Hoo-wee! Wind's pickin' up!" Jim called through the sudden gale. "Gonna be a bad storm tonight! Gonna get cold! I killed your spook!"

He was at the porch now. Standing there, he looked shorter than her and he tilted his head to look up at her. It was then the wind gusted up again and caught his hat and floated it out into the road.

She smiled then as he scrambled after his hat in the wind—first left, then right, trying to catch his hat, then back up the road, then back down. At one point, the hat spun right in front of him as if an invisible man was twirling it on an invisible cane.

This got Violet to laughing and when she laughed she really cackled loud, which brought Bill out from the back somewhere where he had been working.

He didn't see much that was funny. By the time he got there, Jim had got his hat back on his head.

Jim smiled a little and licked his lips and looked around and hefted the sack from off his shoulder and onto their little front yard. The grass was all dead here.

"Well, you folks don't need worry anymore. I killed your spook, and here's its head in my woven sack."

He raised the sack, but the couple just stood there.

He raised it again and pointed back toward the woods.

Jim didn't know what to say next, so he said, "As for any kind of a fee, I am going to waive it on account of I guess I expected this hunt to take almost a month and be hiking in snowy woods next week or two. Since I did none of those, I just figure a good meal and a night's rest before I head on my way will be payment enough."

Violet smiled wide, but Bill's eyes were fixated on the woven sack. It was of checkered cloth, red and black and yellow and blue. It was also seeped with a blackish, oily blood.

"Mr. Falk," Bill said, "I would like to see this thing's dead head as proof."

Jim looked at Bill and then looked at Violet. The wind grew still and now the shadows of evening crept in on the edges. Jim looked down at the sack in the dwindling light and said, "It may be best for Violet to go inside, then."

"What will you do with it?" Violet asked quick as though she didn't mean to.

"Do?" Jim kicked it a little. "You do the same thing to all of them. You burn them and scatter the ashes in running water."

"You do all that later." Bill took a step toward the bundle. "Violet, you go on up inside."

Violet looked at the two men who were looking at each other. Then she went up the steps, over the porch and into the house. She closed the door and stood right behind it with her back to it, turning her green eyes toward the door as if she might see through it.

Jim hunkered down and flipped open the blanket. Inside was the severed head of a pony.

Bill Hill winced and jerked his head.

Jim's eyes darted over the stinking pony head, searching for the ugly face he had seen in the woods. Where was the great maw and the yellow-yolk eyes with the black pinhole pupils? Where was the grisly neck that had taken thirteen hatchet swings?

Bill said, "What the hell is this? Some kind of trick?"

Jim mouthed something.

"What? What did you say?" Bill asked again. A power, an angry power was growing in Bill's voice and throat.

Jim could suddenly feel how close he was standing and saw Bill's fists clench and tighten.

Jim mumbled again.

"I suppose you come up around here to play parlor tricks for me and my Violet." The anger burned in Bill's every word now. He stepped in toward Jim and stared him straight in the eye, nose to nose.

Bill's voice got low to a whisper. "My wife . . ." He put his hand on the back of Jim's head and pulled his ear closer to his mouth, and whispered now, even hoarser, even lower. "My wife can't sleep. She's going crazy with fear. She has night terrors. She cuts the sheets with her toenails trying to run from this thing in her sleep. Sometimes she mistakes her own husband in the night for the beast, and curses me in God's name . . ." His voice had become a rasp; his clutch on the back of Jim's head was desperate now.

"Stranger," Jim said calm and clear, "I don't know you and I don't know your Violet, and I don't know why I would play such a trick, unless I was charging you money and planned to run off with your money. Which I am not and do not. Now, if you would, please let go my neck."

Bill did let go and Jim said, "The tricks of the Evil One are not new to me, nor to anyone who was schooled in the ways as I was." He walked in a slow circle around the pony head. "Sometimes the Evil One, by means of a metamorphosis, will transform one of his fiends into a fair form in order to . . ."

He stopped and looked at Bill and then he rolled the pony's head from the blanket. "What I killed in the woods was not a pony, Bill. But the Evil One has made a mockery of my good deed."

Bill looked Jim Falk over. Jim looked fine and honest, but Bill sensed something wasn't right. The Evil One? Did he mean the Evil One? He thought of Violet, his beautiful Violet.

"Leave," Bill said, "Leave Sparrow and don't come back. If you come back I will kill you dead. My wife has no one to turn to now."

With that, Bill Hill walked back up in his house, leaving Jim Falk with a checkered blanket and a pony head.

# CHAPTER 5

Bill paused inside the door and looked back out to see what Jim Falk was doing out there. Violet was standing with her back to him.

Jim was wrapping up the dead head.

Bill was looking. He was looking and then his belly got ill. Looking at the pony head, watching Jim roll it back up into the woven blanket, he started to turn away and shut the door. But just then, did he see the eyes move? Did they? Did they roll around in the head and look right up at him? Did they turn yellow?

Bill swallowed hard and shut the door. He looked at the back of his wife's head, the way her red hair draped down her neck and back. He remembered that once she had been young and that her smile had been bright and that she danced with her arms linked with the others girls in a circle. He remembered that there had once been a laughter that came out of her that made his own hard face brighten, that made him think of clear skies and good wine.

He looked around at his home: that wood table his pa made, the book of scriptures, the dirty candles.

Maybe he didn't see those pony-head eyes looking at him. He shook it off and pinched between his eyebrows together with his thumb and forefinger, as though he could squeeze a better vision by that. He looked again around his front room: that little table and chairs and the hard, brown wood of the floor.

When he looked up, Violet was gone. He heard Violet shuffling around in the bedroom off to the side and the wind blow against the side of the house.

"Nahhh," he said aloud and went back in his bedroom to talk to his wife.

She was in there changing the sheets on the bed and she had a look in her eyes that he hadn't seen in some time.

"Where's Mr. Falk, gone off so soon?" Violet said when he walked in. She was looking at the bed.

"He's getting to his stuff. He's all done now," Bill said and looked away from her. Out the window of the bedroom he could see the worn-out side of the back house.

"He got the spook, Violet." Bill said.

He looked at her and saw right away that she wasn't sure she believed that.

"What did it look like?"

"Violet, I don't want to say." Bill wanted this to be the end of it.

She finished up the pillow and looked back up at him.

Her eyes were hungry for specifics. "And then will he burn the head?"

Bill leaned up against the wall by the window. "I suppose he'll take it off somewhere and scatter its ashes in the water as he said. Maybe he'll take the old path down the creek to the river and do it there. I don't know. Tonight, maybe. All's important now is that you don't need to worry anymore."

She patted the pillow.

Some of the settled hardness lifted from her pretty face, and she walked toward him and squeezed him close with thin arms. "I knew it would work," she said. "I was scared at first what Vernon and Ruth and all the others would think if we had around a man like Jim, but now . . ."

She let go of her husband and went over and sat down on the bed, looking out the window and then up at the ceiling. "Now, whether they believe me or not, we know what we saw and what he killed and now it's over. Whether they ever believe us or not, now we can know."

She stared at the window. "Those whispers and those things I saw in the snow."

Bill stepped in front of the window.

She stood a moment with her hands in fists at her sides and then swallowed and ran to him and kissed his balding head and then his mouth, hard.

She kissed him again and again and again.

Bill didn't kiss back.

Outside, Jim was finishing up.

He knew what he had to do, but he had no idea what to do; but he had to do something.

He wrapped up the head again and looked at the blanket. He looked at the colors on the blanket and thought of long, long ago. He thought of his father talking with the old woman. He remembered the fire and the dancing men of the river tribe. He was getting bothered and he reached into his pocket and grabbed his little book. He flipped about in it and looked for something, glancing back at the blanket that was still sopping with the gross blood of the spook or the pony head.

The thing about it was that he didn't know for sure now if he had killed the spook and killed the spook right. He paged furiously through his notes.

Never before had he seen one of these metamorphoses. He talked about them because he heard his pa talk about them at Old Magic Woman's tent. He'd also read parts of it from a book that his pa had showed him—a book that Barnhouse didn't have.

Also, there was another thought. He hadn't taken too many of the leaves over time, had he? Old Magic Woman said you could eat too many leaves and that they might have some permanent effect of memory loss. Or the leaves might get too potent and burn your mind up in an instant.

"Them leaves'll help you out as soon as they mess ya up," his pa said to him around the fire one night. "Now you take one now, and you sit here with me, and I'm gonna take one, and we're gonna sit here together, and when the world starts changin' around you, you just sit tight. Keep still and then there's no problem. That's the key. Keep still."

He tried. He tried to keep still.

Old Magic Woman, though, after that, she tried to teach him the art of growing the plants just right and making it so that they didn't get too powerful, and told him when to pick 'em so that they didn't turn to poison. But he didn't listen well and he couldn't re-call any of that anymore. And she was gone.

He relied on Barnhouse now. But those sources were back up north. The decision was that he would go on out alone.

But hold on. Jim was sure he hadn't got too many leaves in him that day to believe that a pony was a spook. And besides all that, the pretty Marbo girl, May, she said there were no more horses around. So why would there be any ponies at all?

That thought stopped him for a second. No horses. Somewhere in his mind he remembered a story that Old Magic Woman had told him. A story of a great warrior who had been killed by the horse people and because of how he died, the people in the village no longer were able to keep horses. It was hard to remember. He tried remembering too, another story of a baby born of the Evil One with horse's hooves and a tail . . . he couldn't remember.

He hadn't a lot of time, though. He moved to the back house to snatch up his gear. He got the feeling that Bill Hill's rifle snout might come poking out of one of the windows and drop him like a duck. He resumed his urgency.

He got in the door and put down the woven sack and got all his gear. He rolled out his gear on the bed and checked to make sure it was all there: the long rifle, all his pouches, his bullets, extra sil-ver-lode, the powders, the hatchet, and the other pouches with specials in them. He glanced it over, his eyes picking out each de-tail. He rolled it back up and strapped it on his back.

Once he got it all together and strapped up on his back, he turned to go out the door. He'd decided to take the old trail all the way to the river and then burn and distribute the ashes of the head there. It was a strong river.

He reached down by the door where he put the sack and pulled it up.

It was empty.

Jim whirled back around and scanned the room across—table, chair, bed, window. There, just in time, a dark form, a watery shadow in the corner of his eye, slipped out through the half-cracked window, and he watched it float lazily off into the woods.

Then, once it melted into the thick woods, he felt immediately the eyes staring at him. His neck, chest, and belly got heavy again with the jitters.

The eyes of something waited just beyond the edge, out the window, just up in the tree line. Something he couldn't see, but something that could see him. The eyes winked, bright with evil.

He wanted to run back down to the Hills'. To run down there and bang on their door and scream at them to get out, get out! He'd dump his special powder in a circle around the house; he'd catch up Violet over his shoulder . . .

He didn't budge. His gut told him that Bill was not a maker of idle threats. He fully expected to be shot and killed if he came down by that house again.

No.

His word was his own to keep. He said he'd leave Sparrow and he would.

He'd leave Sparrow, but he'd go by way of these woods. He'd go right at those killer eyes and find out.

He looked back in the corner by the door where the woven sack sat. He looked at the space where the dead head used to be and knew beyond doubting that the Evil One had taken an interest in Sparrow.

Then he looked out the window into the woods.

Through the night, the howls came again and again.

Benjamin Straddler sat at his table with his wife and listened.

They were eating some pork chops, and both of them were looking at each other.

"Do you want another pork chop?" Lane asked.

"There haven't been wolves in Sparrow since I was a boy." Benjamin watched her fork over a chop.

Lane got up from the table and went to the stove. "There's two more sitting in here, and I won't be able to eat another."

"I might go over to Huck's tonight." He waited for her to reply, but she busied herself. "There'll be men over there talking about the wolves, and there's a bright moon tonight too, Lane. A bright moon," he said and turned his head a bit toward the window as another round of baying struck. "And there's wolves." Something far away caught his memory for a moment.

"Well, what am I supposed to do while you're there?" she snapped suddenly with a flick of her long, brown hair. "Lock the doors?"

Lane turned back to the sink and then back to Benjamin. She didn't care how many men got together to sit around and drink and make decisions. A few years back, when the snows had come and the wolves came down from the mountains looking for food, those men sat around drinking and deciding and nothing came of it then except some decisions about who would get what house in case the other died.

She looked in Benjamin's good eye. "What if while you're down there talkin' something comes through here? What if a pack of them gray wolves comes through here? Or what about what if the Hills are right?"

She looked down at the floor and then back up at him. Her brown eyes were watery. "Benji, what if them wolves are bringing with 'em what they brought before? What if the Hills are right?"

Benjamin Straddler held closed a place in his mind that kept a memory. "Lane, no one really knows what all happened back then.

This is a different time. Things aren't just like they were back then just because we're hearing wolves in the night. I'll come back. I won't be far off, and I won't be long. I am going to go and see and then I'll be back. I'll come back and we'll sit together."

She paused in memory and squeezed her eyes together and remembered all those years ago.

All those years ago, Benji came home one night during that big blizzard, that big blizzard that froze off Vernon Mosely's ears, and Benji was screaming and carrying on something awful. Usual times when he was doing this sort of thing, Lane would either run out the back and wait it out, or yell at him until he was shut up, or even please him until he was shut up depending on how it was he reacted to things.

He came in.

It was cold and he was standing there and his eyes were red and his skin was white and blue. He went forward and backward.

She ran to him and threw a blanket on his body and he slumped down on a wood chair and she started some hot water in a pot.

He stared at the floor of the house and, after a while, a long stream of vomit came up his throat and slapped at the floor of the kitchen. It stank, it stank bad.

She started to clean it anyway and he started to talk.

"There was a way they could find animals," he slurred and stood teetering looking out the window and shaking his head. Almost sobbing, he sat back down only to stand again, his eyes wide, his finger pointing at the window. Then he sat down again and mumbled something and was still for a long time.

Then suddenly he shouted: "Did *they* know it? No!" He moved his hands around as if there were a lot of people listening. "*They* didn't know the way! I knew it!"

"I know, Benji," she whispered. This was an old story to her. She'd heard it from all angles—sober, drunk, asleep, and in prayer.

She kept cleaning, and small, hot tears traced her cheeks and dangled from her chin.

"Them stupid, greedy animals!" He pounded his foot near her head, pinching her long hair.

"Them stupid, dumb-as-dogs-and-pigs animals!"

When her finger, through the cloth, got warm on the vomit, she gave up. She retreated to the kitchen table. She put her head on the table.

"I was just a little boy! 'I don't care!' I said! 'I'll tie you up! I'll eat you alive!'"

Lane was sobbing now, surrounded by her dark hair, sucking in air over the table.

"Tie 'em up. Tie up their mouths!" Benjamin Straddler stood up in his kitchen and took off his coat and his shirt and his pants.

"Lane!" He looked at her sad and poisonous. "Don't look at me. Go to bed. Go to bed! You can't see me! You can't see me!"

Now she was done crying. Her fury was bright, but her words came in a whisper. "You'll die this way, Benjamin Straddler. You'll die like this! There's nothing on this earth can save a man so poisoned!"

Benjamin reeled in hot, drunk anger. The door to his bedroom clapped shut and locked as Lane fled from his swinging arms.

He wet himself and fouled the kitchen, all the time thinking about the black, hot heart of the wolf filling his mouth.

This night, Lane waited, standing in the middle of the kitchen. Benjamin didn't return from Huck's this night.

She held her rifle straight at the window until she could barely see light coming up through the woods. The thing that had been rasping just below the window seemed to fade away as the dawn rose. Whatever it may have been, she was glad that she didn't have to find out. She fell asleep in the chair with her shoulders hunched up around her neck, the weapon across her lap.

The sun rose and played in the dust of her kitchen and brightened her face, but Benjamin didn't come back.

# CHAPTER 6

Nobody was at the bar because everybody left, except for Simon and the chicken man, and Benjamin Straddler who just came in.

The wolves had been going on for a while and the place had emptied out. Huck and May stayed, though. May was asleep in a safe place and Huck had his gun close.

"Tell him," Simon said and looked at his friend, Benjamin Straddler, and then looked at the chicken man.

Benjamin looked at the chicken man and winked his eye at Simon. "Them chickens you sold way back is still around here," Benjamin told him and looked at his half-cup of whisky, "or at least the sons and daughters of 'em."

"Yup," the chicken man said and took a bite of an apple. It was small and green and far from ripe.

Huck watched the three men. Huck was tired and leaned on the wall. Sometimes his wooden leg still hurt his knee. The chickens were good, Benjamin was right, but the chicken man himself had an eye for May. On top of that, Huck knew the routine of the wolf story. It ended in Benjamin Straddler getting kicked out of his shop. He'd hoped that Benjamin had maybe had his fill at home tonight, or that maybe Lane had helped him get to sleep or convinced him to stay home.

Benjamin Straddler had that wolf story about his pa and the wolf, yes. But there was also something that had happened to old Benji during that blizzard. Huck had lost his beautiful wife, Vernon

Mosely had lost his ears, but Benjamin Straddler had lost his mind. Something had happened to Straddler that night that had set him to drinking and drinking hard. Harder, Huck thought at times, than he'd seen any man ever to drink.

"Them Moselys that run the church? They been takin' good care of them chickens you sold 'em. Sometimes the church does up a meal and them chickens is good eating chickens too," Benjamin said.

"Yup," the chicken man said and gnawed the hard apple. His eyes focused on Benjamin and on something far away at the same time. It seemed as if he was more spitting out the apple on his chin than really eating it.

Outside there was a yipping and then the wolves joined in together. Because of how the wind was blowing that night, everyone had trouble telling which direction and how far away the wolves might have really been.

They all listened, though, looking up into the air. The chicken man, Simon, and Benjamin all looked up and left and right, as if, through the roof of Marbo's Bar, they could see the wolves' howls moving across the night sky.

"The chicken man knows his chickens are good," Simon said after a moment. "Don't tell him about his chickens. He knows about his chickens." Simon smiled and took his shot of whisky too. "He's the chicken man."

Benjamin Straddler scratched at his stubbled chin. He was red and wet looking.

Simon listened to the howling, and it seemed somehow to please him. He looked over at Benjamin Straddler and chuckled a bit and said, "Tell us how you killed them wolves."

"What's the chicken man wanna know that for?" Benjamin put some reddish coins on the bar and tapped on the bar with his forefinger and leered at Huck, who leaned his gun against the back counter as he grabbed the bottle.

Huck poured more whisky in Benjamin's cup.

Benjamin drank it right away, all of it. He looked the chicken man up and down. The chicken man was bony and pinkish with a spiny fin of white hair on his head.

"Huck!" Benjamin shouted suddenly.

"Yes, Benjamin?" Huck said.

"Huck, where's May?"

Huck placed both his hands on the bar and leaned into Benjamin Straddler. "There's no need to bring her name into this conversation." Huck looked at the chicken man. The chicken man's eyes were pink too. Huck looked back at Benjamin. "And if you ask me one more question tonight about her, I will make sure you never come in here again without walking like I do."

Huck was dead serious and hinting at his leaning shotgun. Benjamin leaned back and the chicken man looked around stupidly.

"Well, chicken man," Benjamin Straddler said and smiled but wiped it away quick with his thumb, "when I was a youngun, and I was workin' for my pa, we was horse raisers and had us some horses." Benjamin blinked and looked up. "All them horses is gone now, but we raised 'em. Ponies too. Folks are superstitious about raisin' and keepin' horses around here these days, but this was back in the early days, when Sparrow wasn't much of anything except a place to stop between here and there."

Huck Marbo went back to being far way and standing by his gun.

Benjamin leaned into the chicken man. "But see, my pa had to go out and get wood for us in the woods. See, they used to have a thing in this town that you had to go out and get wood for a preacher. And it come up his turn, so he goes out." Benjamin squeezed his eyes for a few seconds as if he saw something far away. "Then he didn't come back for a long time."

He squeezed again and took a little more whisky from his glass. The chicken man, who was sucking on the core of the apple now, locked his pink eyes in on Benjamin Straddler's eyes.

Benjamin kept on. "A few days passed and then we started looking. It was a group of men from the church that first headed it up. Old Marley Upton, Bannings Driver, Wise Moore, and Donny

Trim and his boys. Huck, you remember some of them, don't ya? They've all passed now. Trim's boys moved up to the Ridges. But they looked six days for my pa up there in them woods and never found him. Strangest thing. I thought he liked t'fell in the river, or been killed by a man from over there on the other side of the mountainside, maybe even by a bear out from the country. Sometimes, too, there were certain men would come down and they were killers and they killed a lot of folk in the early days when us Straddlers first got here. Weren't none of them first people either, so I thought maybe one of them killers killed him. Maybe too, I thought a native coulda killed him, like one of the River People from the other side of Make River."

Benjamin Straddler's eyes got a little wetter. His one bad eye was especially red and twinkling. "I thought a new thing about my pa about every time I blinked. I saw a new way for my pa to get killed. I even thought about him killing himself with his buck knife"—he was whispering now—"but couldn't think of a reason why."

The chicken man was squinting hard trying to figure out what Benjamin was trying to tell him.

Simon's teeth were white, smiling there over Benjamin's shoulder.

Benjamin took a pause and got a smoke. He lit it with a match and started smoking it. "So, a young boy as I was, I hated all the waiting. I waited for three days, and I went to the men in the church and asked them why my father wasn't looked for, and they said that he was found. 'He is dead,' they said, 'he got killed by wolves.'"

Simon waved a hand at Huck. "Give us all some shots, on me. Whisky."

Huck was quick for Simon, and the chicken man noticed how much they smiled as the money went back from Simon to Huck, even though Huck looked as if he didn't like smiling right now. Somehow that Simon had a lot of money. Since no one was really sure exactly what it was that Dan and Elsie Starkey had left behind or how they came into it, there was always a kind of rumor that the walls of Simon's house were stuffed with treasures.

They all shot the whisky down.

"Them men from the church, I told 'em all how stricken with grief I was. Stricken! I sat in that little church and bent my head and told 'em. They told me that things were in mystery and how God's ways was God's ways. They sat there and tried to explain to me the way one world crossed into another world. You know all that nonsense they start to say when they don't know what to say because they don't know what to say. They start in on telling you there's a purpose for this and a purpose for that. Ain't no purpose! Ain't no purpose! There's just cold, evil death. That's all! There ain't no purpose! Spells and stories! Ain't no purpose!"

Simon had not ever heard that come out of Benjamin before, and a funny look came over his face.

"How?" Benjamin said and looked down at his empty shot glass in his hand.

Simon filled it up for him.

Benjamin looked around and around. "You tell me. How does a good God cause a little boy's papa to be eaten by wolves? You tell me!"

There was a sudden and small breeze through the place that they all took notice of. Maybe someone had opened one of the latched windows. They all looked in different directions, almost expecting to see that someone had passed by them all sitting there.

"My heart was sick for my father." Benjamin looked up at them.

They turned back to Benjamin.

"For a man like my father," he said, drawing them back into his memory, "for any man to be eaten by wolves." He clenched his teeth, the little glass of brown liquor shook in his fingers, his face twisted and pinched into an awful grimace. "For a little boy's papa to be eaten by wolves!"

# CHAPTER 7

Pretty sure that Bill was looking out his bedroom window and up at the back house, Jim slid out the same window where the dark shape had gone through.

He dropped low on his knees as dusk was coming in over the yard and cleared his head. It was really cold out now. The winds had earlier brought in a cold that would turn to frost by morning. Due to the cold, the feeling of the eyes and the heavy jitters were lifting. Jim's body and mind were closing up. The cold had a strange way of covering up those things that lived in the shadows.

Seeing that he was about to go hunt, he couldn't afford this cold snap lifting away of his sense of the thing.

Jim crawled around to the backside of the back house where he was sure he couldn't be seen by Bill Hill. There he unrolled his satchel and got out more leaves and chewed them. He remembered again what the old woman had told him and what his pa had told him. He remembered again what Spencer Barnhouse had told him—that it was taking longer and longer to make the batches. He chewed and chewed and swallowed the bitter juice and the spiky strands.

He looked at the woods and remembered more things about being at Huck's the night before. He remembered how he'd caught eyes with May Marbo, how her brown eyes had glinted with deep greens just as her father's, how she'd taken his arm. In his memory, when he looked down at the arm of the girl, he saw instead his mother's arm, the hand grasping, grasping.

Jim shook his head, reached into his pocket, pulled his flask, and gulped to help him swallow down the chewed leaves. He straightened his hat and listened and watched the woods. There was nothing now—just a cold breeze that seemed to bring the darkness from back over the hill, covering the bent and crackling trees. If Bill came tramping up the back way with his rifle, Jim would hear that for sure. Then he'd be able to slip right up into the thicket, the same way the shadow had.

He saw Violet now in his mind, her hair ruddy as autumn, crossing and uncrossing her skinny arms, patting her own shoulders, twiddling her little fingers. Bill said she tore up holes with her toes in the sheets. Running from the spook in her dreams.

Her eyes were deeper somehow now in his memory. He worked them out in his mind so that he could see each separate, tiny jewel of her eye. Something moved behind her eyes, a shape, a sign. Something curled and twirled there like a smoky, dark flame.

He wished he knew where the old book his pa kept was now, or could call its pages up in his memory. If wishes were horses . . . but this town didn't keep horses.

What was a spook doing down here in Sparrow? In some ways it might make more sense if he saw one of them lurking in the shadows of the docks in Hopestill, but he still wasn't ready to think of that.

Then, in his chest, he felt something move.

He squinted, and the trees seemed to take on a watery, glassy quality, shifting dim windows. Through the trees, he could see a dark shape up there in a piece of the woods way toward the top. It swayed this way and that. His heart beat as the leaves and the whisky grew strong in him again.

The dusk was almost complete now; only the thinnest gray light came in through the rickety trees.

There, between some low branches, just almost out of sight, he could see the eyes, winking, yellow, round as eggs.

The jitters jumped in him. Even in the cold, the leaves broke through and helped him to feel. He moved slowly. His gear sack was unrolled by his knee; with one hand he slid out the butt of his long gun, nice and slow and neat, into the cold grass by his leg.

The eyes winked.

Now, with nimble fingers, he attached the chamber quick and squeezed it locked with a quiet click.

The eyes lowered and thinned and bobbed.

Jim knew the thing could feel him too. That's the toughest part to get by on one of these beasts. More than sight or sound or smell, the spooks had a way of feeling what it is you're meaning to do. Jim was pretty sure the thing wouldn't have full command of its special sight until pitch dark.

With a silent slide and a few twists, he assembled his long gun and then brought the long silver bullets from his satchel and slipped them into the chamber; he held still and breathed slowly and let his mind begin on the wander.

The wander was a trick his pa had taught him.

"Once," his pa told him, "there were an evil kind of people in this land. Long before even the first people lived here. And these evil people were in league with the Evil One. Bendy's Men is what they still call 'em in stories. And they used to live up high in these woods and way back on old roads and in the hollers where folks don't go anymore. But folks like us, James, we travel in the Old Paths—the paths that are almost now forgotten. We're the ones who were born to see. You and me. Bendy's Men have a different kind of seeing; they could see what was on your mind. That's a power the Evil One give 'em. Maybe they couldn't even see you. Maybe, maybe they wasn't even near you, but they could see thoughts that was in your mind. Old Magic Woman showed me a way of making your thoughts wander, or even go blank and black. She said that you shouldn't learn to do that when you're so young like you are now, but I'm gonna show you how. I am going to show you anyway."

Jim fired.

He lost his own sight for an instant in the flash, but the gun made only the smallest sound of a sneeze.

The spook made another noise, a hoarse, empty whine that started low and went high. That noise meant that the silver-lode had hit the spook deep. The whole of the woods seemed to shiver with the noise—and then, then started the wolves.

The howls came first from the north and then the wind picked up and whirled the noise around. Answers came from all directions now, covering up whatever yowling the spook might be doing.

Jim watched the yellow eyes falter and then lurch off into the ever-darkening trees. He slung his gun on his back, rolled up his sack quick, and gave chase.

The jitters were hot in Jim's heart now; he could nearly see them waking out behind the fleeing beast. Through the darkling trees, he could see here and then there, its hulking shadow stopping to turn and bray at him, flashing its strange, curving teeth, whipping spines behind as it whirled and fled.

One eye, Jim could see now, was completely blacked out.

"I hit you good," Jim said to the thing, running behind it. "This time I'll burn every piece of you to smoke and let the river wash you away."

It was night and the wolves were howling. Doc Pritham opened the door, and in walked William Wade.

"John," William Wade said. The moon came in the door behind him, putting his face and messy hair in a shadow.

"William Wade," Doc Pritham said.

"I'm getting too old for these trips," William Wade said. He had with him a big leather case and some black bags that tinkled as he passed through the doctor's door and into his office.

"Too old?" Doc Pritham said, and a small smile started on his face. "You're practically a baby." But Pritham stopped there; he could see now by the oil lamp on his wall, he could see in Wade's eyes a kind of blankness that comes with fear. "Something the matter, Will? Here, here, it's only wolves," the doctor said and started moving around all the papers and empty bottles and scribbled writing that were cluttering up his table. He cleared a spot just enough for William Wade to set down his carryings.

William Wade took a deep breath. "Have you got something to drink, John? I'm parched." William Wade looked up at the ceiling as though he could see the howls.

Doc Pritham went to his shelf and grabbed a brown bottle and a heavy cup. He poured and gave it to William Wade. "Wine," the doctor said. "It will bring the color back to your face. It's a dark wine from the south."

A smile came up on William Wade's face when he took a gulp. "It's sweet."

The two men stood there quietly while William Wade drank the rest of the cup. Doc Pritham quickly refilled it.

William Wade went to the leather case and began unbuckling it. He breathed heavy again. "There's an issue," he said.

"An issue?" Doc Pritham's hands went to the back of his scalp and he scratched his old head with both hands.

"A problem," Wade said.

"A problem with the shipment?" Pritham asked.

Inside the case were many small dark bottles, some with labels, some with strangely shaped stoppers, some filled with liquids, some with powders. There were also paper-wrapped packages bound with coarse string and some smaller lidded boxes.

"Yes," Wade said, "a problem with your shipment, but more than that."

"Just tell me, Will."

"I couldn't bring everything you ordered."

Doc Pritham went to his desk and shuffled around in the papers there and picked out a sheet and laid it over the items in the opened case. "Well, fine, it's not the first time. Here's the order, what's missing?"

William Wade said, "It's not exactly what's missing from your order as it is what's missing. Rootfire, Apoplexy, Inhere."

"I don't order Rootfire or Apoplexy. What would I want with those?"

"Someone took them from the inventory. Last month. I count every week. I had to leave Hopestill and go to Woodmeer to get extras of some of the usuals. The new man in charge up there in Hopestill, that Varney Mull's demanding to take all the firsts of the goods that come off the ships now, so I had to head up to Woodmeer. When I got back, someone, somehow, had gotten into the storage. I don't know how. I couldn't see how they got in. They took those, but they took something else too, John, they took the translated pages."

Doc Pritham raised his bushy eyebrows and patted around in his jacket for his pipe and paced back and forth in the little room.

William Wade sat down, taking another drink from the cup. "Your order is incomplete."

Doc Pritham started up his pipe with a match and said, "Who would take, who would even know that you had those pages? Who could even know to take them?"

Wade said, "You know what could be done with those ingredients and those pages. It's been strange in Hopestill for the past few months. Shipments come slow from the east, slower and slower, supplies are less and less. Some of the captains are telling me it's on account of the weather, others say a war at sea, but they only mumble these things to me and don't look me in the eye . . ."

"Wade, the only person to know about the translated pages other than you and me would be he who is translator of those pages," Pritham said.

"That's the worst part of it, Doc; they're saying he's been killed. Not only that he's been killed, but that he was killed in some strange way, by a poison or something of the kind. There's a rumor that a strange man has come to town, been visiting Barnhouse, and that when they found his body, it was burned up, as if it had been burned from the inside out."

Doc Pritham took in a deep smoke and sat down at his cluttered table and then blew it out. This moment was one he had feared since he had been shown the ancient writings that Wade was talking about. There were very few people who knew about them, and even some of those who knew about them didn't believe in the power contained inside of them. If it was the truth that Spencer Barnhouse had been burned up from the inside out, it would mean not only that someone had stolen some of William Wade's ingredients and stolen the papers, but that it was someone who was somehow able to read the papers and use what was contained in them. There were no people on this earth who knew how to do such things outside of himself and Spencer Barnhouse, and maybe, just maybe . . .

William Wade fussed at the fasteners on his big coat and took it off. He hung his jacket on the doctor's coatrack and took a seat at the table.

"Well," Wade said, "it's a strange set of events. I can't get Rushwater or white pollen for nothing, so if you even wanted to derive a simple from those, you couldn't get one. And there's less and less gunpowder coming off the ships. I only brought what I had to bring, which I haven't measured. So I only want you to pay for what I could bring."

"Why would someone kill Spencer Barnhouse?" Doc Pritham said and closed his eyes.

"No one else has the abilities that he does."

"That we know of," Pritham said.

"That we know of," William Wade said.

Vernon Mosely ate a piece of chicken off the end of his fork. He looked at his daughter, Merla, and she smiled at him. The morning sunlight came through the kitchen window and lit her cheerful face. She was a happy girl and good at chores, but she was always so very quiet. Vernon had imagined his daughter to be more like him, cheerful, sharp, and ready to talk. She was cheerful and sharp, though.

Vernon smiled on days like these probably more than some might think a preacher should. He couldn't help but feel that his life had been spared, that there were things in this world that one should enjoy. Even if there were joys beyond measure to come in the heavenly kingdom, there were certainly some measurable joys in front of him just now. He also knew how quickly things could change.

But his younger brother, who was in front of him right now, didn't often bring along much joy. No, John Mosely had been something other than a joy on many occasions. There had been so much hope in Vernon that once John had married up with Ruth Eavan, this would somehow create a way for his little brother to grow up all of a sudden—to become a little bit more of a man of his age. Unfortunately, almost the opposite occurred. He grew down. This Ruth woman was one who assumed some role over him so that John fell into a kind of servitude with her and turned into something of a combination of her little boy and her little servant. It made Vernon angry, but still, here was his brother, and his brother was his brother.

After a moment he looked up at his brother, smiling, and swallowed, his brow pinched.

John Mosely looked at his brother and raised a cup of water to him.

Vernon wiped his mouth, "Well, go on."

"Well," John said, "Ruth had a . . ." Merla put a plate in front of him. "Thank you, Merla. Ruth had a talk with that non-believing Benjamin Straddler last night."

Vernon smiled and considered this and his brother's thin face for a moment, waiting. He waited longer. "Yes?"

John Mosely eyed Merla. She was a talker. Sure, she was quiet enough now, but he could tell by the way she held herself—she was a talker. John Mosely didn't like talkers. He didn't like girls who went on talking at all.

John looked at Vernon and sort of nodded his head to the side. Meaning for the girl to get out.

"Merla," her father said and tipped his head back to catch her eye, "give your father a kiss and go mind your mother."

She kissed him and was off through the house to her mother's room.

Vernon bit into another morsel and looked at his plate and not at his brother as his brother spoke to him.

John said, "So she said that Benjamin Straddler had come by the house and said strange things."

"Not a surprise."

"That he was drunk."

"Not a surprise."

"Well, she said that there was a man come to town and he said some strange things and that this man may be some kind of"—John whispered now—"may have some knowledge of the craft as you call it."

Vernon Mosely stopped chewing for a moment and looked at his brother. Then he started chewing again and looked back down at his plate. "Explain."

"Well," his brother said, his fingers twitching at the table as he talked, "she said that Straddler said that the stranger stood up and announced to everyone—they were at Huck Marbo's, of course—that he stood up and announced his name to everyone there, and said he was Jim Fox, or some such name, and that he had some kind of powers to cast out demons."

"Powers?"

"Well, yes," John Mosely said and his hands stopped playing. He looked at Vernon with a serious face. "That's what Ruth understood from Benjamin."

Vernon started back in on his chicken.

John picked up his knife but didn't eat. In the knife he could see his own eye. In the other room, he heard a shrill cackle. Vernon's wife, Aline, laughing.

Vernon smiled, but wouldn't look at his brother. "Benjamin Straddler," he swallowed, "has been hanging around a long while with that Simon Starkey, am I right?"

"Yes."

"Simon was said once to have a book of magician's tricks, and a lot of folk say that they seen him do tricks, making things appear, and the like."

John was surprised at his brother. "So you already know?"

"Know already what? There is no already about it, brother. This has been going on for a few years now—am I right or am I wrong? I heard that the preacher before me, Taylor, before he passed, had even spoke directly to Simon about this. Am I right?"

"I think so," John said. "That sounds right. But this is something serious. Something needs to be done."

"What, brother? What needs to be done?"

John Mosely's face was red. He didn't like outlanders. He didn't like them one little tiny bit, and neither did Ruth.

"Well," John finally said, "I ain't the right person to say what needs to be done. I guess that should be up to you and up to the doctor and up to the other men of the town that run the town meetings."

"Well, anyway," Vernon went on after nothing was said for a while, "all this stuff with magic and the Starkeys and Benjamin Straddler and his drinking and the wolves and all, all that was before my time and yours in Sparrow. But if he's been up to it again, and he's been bending on Straddler's ear about mystics and magic, and Benjamin's been taking to drink, there might be a little less to this story. There might be a lot less to this story. You know, the chicken man is in town. The chicken man always brings out strange stories for Benjamin. What's his name? I can't remember. Everyone just calls him the chicken man. It's good chicken!" He waved his fork in front of his face with a piece of white meat dangling from it.

"I suppose, Vernon, but Ruth is awful concerned about this, and she wanted me to come over right away. Benjamin wanted to wake me up last night and tell me, but Ruth wouldn't let him, seeing as how he was drunk and all, and she didn't want to wake me up for that, but she was awful concerned this morning about it."

Vernon put his fork down. "Go home, John Mosely. Tell your wife that I will be by shortly."

"Well, okay," John Mosely said and left his food untouched at the table. He went out the door and closed it.

Vernon Mosely stared at the closed brown door for a long time. A darkness came across his features and his hands ever so slowly made themselves into fidgeting pink fists.

"Powers?" he whispered and worried.

Soon he was back in his den. His wife and daughter were in the other room talking, making plans for the big winter feast in three months. He stood in front of the fireplace and stared at a little white brick in the mantel. He went to the window and drew the blind. He could hear Aline joking about the paper dolls that Merla had made for the winter feast decorations last year. He was glad to hear them laughing together. He pulled the blind tight and went back to the mantel.

He used his fingers and thumbs to ease the white brick out of its place in the mantel and from there drew a long silver and flat box. He sat in his chair and opened it.

Years ago, Spencer Barnhouse had given this treasure to him. It was one of only a few—how many he didn't know, except that there weren't many.

He opened the box, and there, on the flat yellow paper, was the strange handwriting. The ones who'd written the stories, the ones who'd written the stories of the coming of the great Hunter. The ones who'd seen into the future and said that he would bring the power to heal and to kill. These papers were papers that Barnhouse himself had spent years translating into the common tongue. There was no one that Vernon knew of who could speak and translate the old tongues anymore except for Barnhouse.

Powers. The Craft. The Hunter. So many thought that these were only rumors, or the leftovers from old stories, from times long, long ago.

Closing the heavy silver box, he began to think, think of the next place he might hide them, of the next town he might take his family to, of the next step in their journey so that he could keep them safe. If there was such a step.

Truthfully, Vernon didn't believe them so much either. Except that if they weren't true, why would there be so much danger in keeping them? If they weren't true, then why, when his brother came by to tell him that there was a man in town who seemed to have powers, why was it that his hands had gone cold and his mind was set to whirring?

⊞

In the dark, Jim could see up ahead the thing's good eye go wide, disappear, and then dip low.

Jim had given it a good shot in the head, but the thing kept going. It was strong.

The moon came out from behind the clouds and the forest turned a cold, bright blue between the black shafts of the crooked trees.

Jim stopped and hunched and watched. He wasn't ready for a face-to-face fight now; he wanted to get the spook when it was tuckered out, or wait until it had stopped along somewhere thinking that it was hidden. Then he could have a chance to hit it again good with his long gun. Another deep shot of the special silver-lode in its head would make for a quick and easy end to this.

The wolves howled as the moon appeared. They sounded closer, as if they were moving in. Maybe it was the wind.

Jim saw the beast's bristling, sharp shadow ahead in the moonlit trees. It lumbered down into a valley and came to a stop. The eye appeared, probably looking back, but now it was winking, blinking. It was turning from yellow to pink. Maybe another shot might not be necessary. Maybe he could go down and get in there and drop it with his hatchet. The special lode that Barnhouse had procured for him was doing its trick.

After that would be these wolves to deal with.

Old Magic Woman had showed Jim and his pa ways to calm and speak with the wolf she had, but he hadn't seen a single one since then. Jim pushed around in his mind to remember. He remembered his pa speaking quietly with Old Magic Woman, the two of them sharing a pipe.

Old Magic Woman never looked old.

It was her hands and the way she moved and her voice that made her only to feel old: her deep, pure voice, her palms covered in lines, rough as dog's paws at the ends of her floating arms.

Her face was young and brown with a wide nose. Her eyes were pure and black.

Jim couldn't see the spook's eyes anymore.

He waited.

The howling stopped.

At the edges of his vision, shadows began to flicker.

He could smell them now and hear them passing in the underbrush.

Knowing that these were the wolves and that somehow they had homed in on him and were packing up around him, he thought to fire his long gun to scare them off. But this gun didn't make any noise and wasn't going to do him any good in the close quarters of the dark woods.

He slid away his long gun and, in one motion, pulled his curving, special hatchet in the one hand and his Dracon pistol with its six barrels in the other.

The moon began to move behind the clouds, but not before Jim caught the reflection of a creek moving along just down at the bottom of the valley.

The spook couldn't pass through water. He knew that. It would have to move along the creek, back up into the hill, or down towards Sparrow.

Jim breathed slowly and took in the hot feeling of the animals that were closing in on him. In a way, the leaves he had taken allowed him to feel the movement of the creatures. In the dark wood like this one, it didn't matter whether he had his eyes open or closed. Around him, they made a kind of wave in his feelings, so that when groups of them moved one way or when one of them moved another, he felt a kind of tug or a push. He had to rely on his eyes, though, because these wolves were many and they meant to tear him to bits.

White spots flickered now and again as clouds passed over the moon.

Branches crackled.

One shadow, at Jim's right side, showed its teeth.

May was lying on the little bed in the safe room at the top of the shop. She could barely hear the chatter of the men at the bar and sometimes the low, brighter sound of her pa's voice.

Over everything, vibrating the room, she could hear the wolves howling, howling, howling.

She was glad to feel safe, though.

The last time she had ever even seen this room was back when she had to come in and clean it with her mother. The jarred tomatoes that were there then were still here now. Still jarred.

She'd never had to stay up here in the cot. She'd heard wolves howl before, when they'd come down from the mountains in the bad winter. She remembered her pa saying that he wondered why the wolves just didn't stop up in the Ridges and eat up all the folk up there instead of coming down into Sparrow and bothering all the good folk down here.

May looked at this cot. She wondered how anyone would sleep in here. There were no windows, there were no pictures. It was just a box with a door.

The door locked from both sides.

There was a roll-up staircase leading up to it. Underneath the safe room was a big, wide hall where her pa didn't really keep much around. There was just the wood floor now and some empty crates around. There was a book of scripture too that the former preacher had given her pa.

It was just a space. The only time he'd used it was back when John Mosely and Ruth Eaven got married—they used it to decorate the hall. It was her mother's idea to have a flowerfall, little white bellflowers and redvines to spill out through the hole in the ceiling and wind down to the floor. Pastor Mosely stood in front of them with his little pulpit set there and the messiah's sign on the front.

Ruth looked old enough to be John's mother just about. She did look pretty, though. That was three whole years ago now. But God's ways is God's ways and they are united.

That's what her pa would say.

She tightened the sheet around her as the wind kicked up now, blowing around the shop. She heard the chicken man's horse whinny outside the shop. Somewhere the wind blew open a shutter with a clack. She didn't like being in here at all. What if something happened? What if something sneaked in here with her? Like that thing, that spook that Jim said he saw out on the road. What if that thing was real like he said and that it was from the Evil One like he said? Couldn't a thing like that just come slithering in through the cracks in the ceiling? Couldn't a thing of the Evil One just move like a mist?

# CHAPTER 8

Jim sensed movement on every side and the shadow in front of him growled and bared its teeth and bowed its head.

This was the thing: his mind was stuck on Old Magic Woman's wolf, Fenyra—"Fennie" as Jim called him, the trickster chief, the friend of his father, the friend of the people.

These wolves tonight were not like Fennie at all. They had a poisoned way about them. They were gnarled and scared things.

The moon came out from behind the clouds and the forest flickered alive with the pale stars of the wolves' shining eyes. The eyes roamed through the forest, twinkling, hollow, and mean, until the clouds hid the moon again. The animals yipped one to the other and crooned low in the flickering darkness of the trees. The clouds were moving fast and the wind suddenly blew all cold. Jim turned and turned in a circle. A storm was coming.

The pack was closing in.

Jim knew what to do and held up his Dracon pepperbox pistol.

Maybe, maybe if he could blast it once into the air, the report alone would send them all bounding back into the shadowy hills.

The woods went dark and the eyes disappeared. A big wind blew the trees.

The shadow leapt at him. Snarling with wild strength, it clamped on his right arm. Jim's skin tore like cheese under the teeth and his gun dropped into the dirt when his hand came open with the pain. His blood ran hot and sopped the sleeve of his coat.

He fell. He fell down into the dirt and grass, he felt their rank bodies sliding underneath and about him.

Another wolf was at his left ankle, tearing with vicious power at his boot. Then another pulled at the long flap of his jacket, trying to drag him back into the brush.

He knew that they were waiting. They were all were waiting for this moment. He was on his back. The clouds raced across the sky and the woods lit blue. The hot breath and blank, round moon eyes whirled around him.

He could hear the cloth of his jacket ripping and feel a kind of bumping at his side. He thought he saw his Dracon pistol glint somewhere in the wet weeds. The ragged paws of the beasts ripped at his forehead.

He focused on the moon. Bright as it was, its clear surface was split by gray clouds. Then it disappeared.

He felt teeth puncture and shake at his left boot, and he gathered all his strength into his good left arm with the curving hatchet in his hand.

The clouds burst and the forest was rushed with the sound of the rain.

Jim muttered as fresh, dark rain spilled onto his face. His eyes became clear and bright. "I didn't come to Sparrow to be killed by you crooked dogs!"

He gripped his hatchet with his left hand and swung. The hatchet arced and connected full with a wolf's snout. Jim was no kind of kidder when it came to keeping his weapons sharp. The wolf lost its whole nose and fangs from the swipe and let go, bucking wildly backward and mewling into the darkness.

Jim choked when he heard the wolf's gargled breathing. Even though they tore at him to kill him, his memory of Fennie swelled. There was no spit for him to swallow.

He chopped hard then at his right. The back haft of his hatchet cracked the skull of a wolf that was ripping at his right forearm.

That one yipped out then and let go.

Jim tried to get up and slid a bit on the soaking floor of the wood. He wondered if he lay in rain or in his own blood or in the blood of the wolves, and figured probably all three. A picture flashed in his mind that he had seen in one of Barnhouse's books: it was a scratchy drawing of a man with a wolf head holding a hatchet. There were words underneath the drawing: "Vryka had turned."

He tried again to get up and he was able to half stand now.

The woods got murky and he thought he might have seen the wolves running off, but others, many others stayed. They were staying, waiting. Why weren't they killing him? He saw some snouts go up into the air as if they suddenly had a scent, even in all the rain.

Jim's right arm felt flat and ached. He tried to move it.

In the gray and blue light, blood rolled from his fingertips and mingled in the black water. But his hand only shook.

The woods around him faded in and out. A huge wind blew the treetops. The sky went dark. Thunder rolled. The rains poured on. The wolves looked as if they were traveling around him in a circle, a spinning circle, that soon was one long wolf with a thousand hollow-lit eyes.

He couldn't feel his right arm. He felt around for himself. He grabbed his belt with his left hand; he couldn't feel it. His hatchet seemed to float in front of his face.

Heaviness came to him.

He staggered and tumbled back to the ground again and thought about May Marbo. Her teeth were white and then crooked, like warm ivory vines. He felt he could remember her from somewhere else—if he could only reach out to her. She was right there, holding his pistol out to him.

He struggled just enough to sit up again, and then he half stood. He was going to make it. If he could just get at his pistol . . . Through the blurring rain and the wind, he thought he saw May holding it up to him in the rain.

Then it happened. A wolf, he thought, leapt from behind him and took his neck in its maw. As he flipped, he saw the wolf that had come for him. He was certain that around each of its silver eyes he saw other eyes, so that the wolf's face had four eyes on each side of its head and that from its fanged mouth extended something that looked like flexing spines.

He saw May turn with a wide mouth, covering her eyes as this monster wolf dropped him to the ground and, as the forest faded from his vision, May faded too. The sky became the trees. His head banged on a rock. The raging of the wolf at his neck became quiet now, a tickling stream in his ears.

He saw another shape then. A hulking form passed onto the trail, waving its thick arms. It lurched from the corner of his vision.

There was a flash and a noise like a thunder-crack.

He was wet with his own blood as the giant wolf leapt over him, wildly dashing away. The figure leaned over him.

The night faded out.

May put a cloth on his head. His skin looked soft and white and there was a fever running in him fierce.

"Make sure to keep those bands tight and don't let him move his arms," Doc Pritham said. "He may wake up soon. When he does, come and get me immediately."

Doc Pritham stood. May looked at his old face and his transparent blue eyes. He talked with some kind of heavy accent from the North, but May could understand him very well. In fact, most people could understand him fine; some people just pretended not to.

She nodded.

"This collar he wears around his neck—I am not sure where he found such a thing," the doctor said and pointed at it. "This is what saved his life. Otherwise, crunch! The wolf would have had his neck and his head would have come right off." The doctor coughed and looked at May's face. "I'm sorry."

May shivered, but the doctor was right. He had removed the strangely ornamented leathern collar and breastplate from off of Jim and hung it on the wall near the chest of drawers. There, in the neckpiece, and all about the shoulders of it, were the puncturing and tearing marks left by canine teeth bearing down into it. Here and there too, were marks that looked to be made by knives or razors slashing at his neck and chest.

May looked at Jim's face. He looked at peace. Here and there, long red scratches zagged and flecked. His face was square and thin and handsome, and May did not notice this, but as she was looking at him her body had begun to lean forward and closer as she inspected him.

Huck came in and looked at Jim Falk and looked at May.

"Doc," he said, "I don't like this. I don't like this outlander being laid up here at my place of business. What if he dies?"

May turned away from the convalescing stranger and looked at her pa with raised eyebrows.

The doctor closed his bag. "I have given your daughter specific instructions and bandages. This man appears to have some fever from the wolf bites and the scratches. He also has lost a good deal of his own precious blood. He will be weak for some number of days. He may never regain full use of his right arm. His fever, if not kept in check, could bring on a delirium; but, with proper care and attention, he will not die. I will come by often, but he should not be moved and I cannot have him in my home right now."

Huck looked at the doctor and frowned. He looked at May, who was wringing the wet cloth in a basin. He looked out the window. It was gray. The chicken man's cart was out there—busted, horseless, chickenless.

The doctor put on his hat and said, "He should not be moved."

He tipped his hat to May and turned his back to them to leave.

He said without turning around, "I'm expecting another shipment of medicines shortly. More that might help this stranger. If he wakes up, come and get me straightaway. There are diseases of the blood and of the mind and spirit that can be caused by the bite of a wild animal. Especially the wolf. Come and get me straightaway should he wake."

The doctor left.

May looked at her father. He was incredibly unhappy. He walked over and watched the doctor go out through the front of the shop. Then he closed the door to the safe room where they were.

"This used to be where your mother napped after dinner," he said.

"He'll wake up soon and we'll get him on out of here, Pa," May said and stepped toward him. She could see in his eyes that deep green ring growing ever deeper. He was thinking heavy thoughts.

"May," he said and moved toward her, placing his big hand on her little shoulder, "I don't know what you heard or saw last night. I don't know what all I heard or saw last night exactly either. But from what I can tell . . . from what I can tell, there's a chance that, well, I think I might be wrong about this here outlander, Jim Falk. I don't know, May. I don't know for sure, but things in my mind are starting to change, and I don't know for sure."

Big tears were dropping out of May's eyes now and her head was down. The sound of wolves raised up the worst and darkest of her mind. What she had heard last night had shaken her up. Her face grew pale. While she couldn't remember exactly everything she had heard, her mind turned the words into pictures, wicked things, spiders, spooks, witches, and wolves swirling about in the snowy tornado of her mind.

She said, "Stop it, Pa. Stop it. I don't like it when you talk like this. I don't like you being in a way where you can't make up your mind. What is it that you don't know?"

"What did you hear?" he asked, lifting her chin up so he could see her eyes.

"Pa, I don't know exactly. Noise. Noises. I heard a lot of noises." May didn't want to say. "I don't want to say," she said.

"You heard noises," he said low, "and you heard all that filth coming out of Benjamin Straddler's mouth. And all that talk about spooks and the Evil One and all that."

May looked at her feet and thought about what Jim Falk had told her as they walked along the path. She saw a dark, sparkling shape in the corner of her mind.

"Well, Benjamin Straddler is a sick man, and he isn't right in the head. He's the one you need to stay away from, May. He's got something awful in him."

May wiped her face and her nose. "Benjamin brought him back, though."

There was a quiet moment between the two of them.

From the little room, they could hear Jim's breathing coming steadier and deeper now. The town of Sparrow was very, very quiet outside.

"Pa," May whispered, "do you think that Benjamin really did all those things? Do you think he ate a wolf alive like he said?"

"I believe that he did, May," Huck said. "I believe that he did."

# CHAPTER 9

The men were hollering at each other in the fog.

Vernon Mosely was with Doc Pritham down by the creek. They were sweeping the creek on the Sparrow side. Huck was up by the wood's edge near the hill.

Hattie Jones was spending a lot of time looking at the chicken man's cart. Samuel sat in the mud beside him or twirled around in a circle looking at the white sky.

The ground was dark and muddy all over and it was cold because it had, somewhere between evening and morning, frosted. There were marks in the ground all over, paw prints where wolves had been running around Sparrow all night. Here and there were darker places in the dark mud as well. These darker spots were caused by blood. There were strange marks too—long, deep ruts that weren't caused by the wheels of any wagon.

Chicken feathers flitted about in the foggy air. Save for the occasional shout of someone when they came across a ravaged chicken or more of the strange marks, hardly a noise could be heard.

Hattie Jones's boy, Samuel, looked to be enjoying himself, his face lit up, his smile wide as he looked into the sky. Around him the grim faces of the men of Sparrow, the frowning jowls and the crossed brows, appeared now and again in the fog. The boy smiled and smiled so that some of the men shook their heads when they caught sight of him. Even if some of the men wanted to smile at his sunny face, they didn't.

Everyone was looking in the fog.

Bill Hill and Violet appeared, shambling out of the misty morning, and Hattie saw them and came up to them, pulling Samuel along. Hattie frowned a bit when he saw the sight. The sad thing about the Hills was that Violet was so pretty, but Bill had worn her out. Too many mornings started with Hattie seeing the two of them arguing here or arguing there; sometimes Violet would hide her face as she walked about. Hattie was sure he knew why, but he couldn't figure out why such a tough and pretty lady would go on staying with a rude-tempered man like Bill, except that he had built up a lot of the town and probably had some money on him.

"The chicken man's disappeared. All his chickens too. And his horse," Hattie said.

"Horse," Samuel said.

Violet was holding on to Bill's arm and wasn't looking at anything in particular. Maybe she was staring at his belt buckle or his chest.

"We just come in to get some things at Huck's," Bill said and looked at Hattie.

"Well," Hattie said, "everyone is looking. You should help us look. We're all out here and we're looking."

Bill Hill looked down at Violet and said, "Why don't you go on to Huck's and get the things that we talked about? Are you feeling well enough to do that?"

Violet nodded her head and he let her go, but only after she looked and looked into his eyes and then he nodded his head to tell her to go on. She looked shaken, rickety. Bill coughed and patted his chest and rubbed his left arm with his right.

"Violet hasn't been feeling all too well. Now what's happened here?" Bill asked Hattie and put his hand on his hips and looked around. He looked real tired. His eyes were red and his face unshaven. "The wolves have had their run of the town, it looks like to me."

"Well, Mr. Hill," Hattie said and turned around in a circle. His little white beard flapped on the end of his pointed chin. "Not just the wolves." He stopped in his turn and looked on up the east side of Sparrow. He squinted his eyes as though he could see through the fog and up into the dark woods on the east hill. He whispered, "There's somethin' evil been loosed on this town. Yessir. Some kind of evil spirit has passed right through here. There, look at this."

Hattie directed Bill's face to a spot in the mud where there was a long mark, all crooked and long. "That's where the thing's long and crooked tail went draggin' across the ground."

Bill didn't look right at the mark. He looked near it and his eyes didn't focus. Bill looked exhausted. When he bent to look, his weight brought him down on one knee into the cold, wet mud.

He bent there for a minute glassy-eyed surveying the mud; tendrils of fog floated by his blank face.

Hattie came up to him and put his hand on his shoulder. Hattie could see now on Bill's back a bandage that had been wrapped tight around his chest and under his shirt. Blood was leaking through it down his back. Bill's eyes were getting wide and distant.

"Doctor!" Hattie screamed.

"Doctor!" Samuel screamed. "Doctor!"

"No." Bill choked up some dark spit. "No doctor. I don't have doctors and I won't have them putting their hands on me."

"We're getting the doctor!" Hattie hollered. "Come on, Sam, we're getting the doctor!"

Hattie pulled his son along behind him by the hand hollering into the fog. "Doctor! Pastor Mosely!"

Bill winced and raised himself. He felt his stomach get sick as the blood ran thick down along his spine. His heart jumped a few beats and he fell face down on the muddy road into Sparrow.

Soon Doc Pritham, Vernon Mosely, Hattie, and Samuel were dashing back through the fog, their feet slipping on the ground. The doc's pack was banging on his thigh as he ran.

They found Bill face down in the mud. The blood spread black across his back and shoulders under his blue shirt.

"Turn him. Help me turn him!" Doc Pritham shouted.

The men reached and grabbed him. "Gently now," the doctor whispered. "He's alive, roll him gently."

"His wife's gone off to Huck's," Hattie said.

"Don't touch me," Bill said. "Get your damn hands off of me."

"You will bleed to death if you don't do as I say," said the doctor. "Now that's enough, men. Did the wolves do this? Have you been bitten by the wolves? Leave him on his side. You, Jones, get the stretcher, and you, Mosely, take this man's hand and lead him in a prayer."

Mosely looked at the doctor and his mouth came open as if to say something, but he said nothing.

The doctor took a knife and cut Bill's shirt away. His chest and shoulders were wound tight with a thick bandage of cloth. It was soaked and crusted in blood. The wounds were terrible underneath.

"The creek smelled funny to me. The water looked dark and rusty," Mosely said to the doctor as he knelt down beside Bill. "There was a strange quiet down there all along the bank. Was that your experience?"

Doc Pritham opened his bag. He snatched out a dark brown bottle and a glass funnel and blue bottle with one hand, and with his other hand he clutched Bill's face and squeezed the lips open. "Yes, it was," he finally replied to Mosely.

Bill mumbled through his clutched mouth, "Stop touching me. Get your hands off of me, you. I don't want no doctors."

"Who is this—is this that Violet Hill's husband?" the doctor asked as he assembled with one hand the blue bottle against the brown with the little funnel between, poured, and then moved his right hand to Bill's throat, causing Bill to say "Ahhh" and down went the mixture.

Bill Hill choked, but he couldn't help but to swallow.

"It sure is. This is William Hill, from out at the end of New Road. He and his wife Violet live out there and they were coming to church for years, but in recent years they stopped coming. As you can see, it was especially because of us starting to accept medicine along with prayer." The pastor lifted Bill's quivering hand into his own and began his prayer.

The pastor's hands were pink and white and the purple veins stood out.

Down by Sparrow Creek it was dark. The sun was barely coming up over the mountain and it was cold from all the rain that had come through. The chicken man was running. The chicken man was running for his life.

He'd been back up at Huck's place a few hours ago and it felt like a long time ago now. He'd like to be back even there now. He'd like to be anywhere. He'd like to be hammering together a chicken crate or feeding his horse, Cousin.

All that racket got kicked up outside Huck's, and then there was all the howling and that shuddering loud noise and all his chickens went missing. And Cousin had galloped off. God knows what that was all about. Then that Benjamin Straddler went wild and went running off into the darkness of the woods. He was wild. His eyes had gone, all gone, and he took off with his shotgun.

And then, there was that Simon kid, calm as a cow. His eyes were funny too. They were shiny—shiny as if a happiness was in them deep enough that nothing could get to the bottom of it. It was the kind of happiness that you see in the eyes of a gloated dog. Simon had been knocking back the whisky and not saying much at all. The chicken man was just eating apples and listening. Every time the wolves would howl or the wind would blow against Huck's shop, Simon got this settled look in him, a look of satisfaction, really a look of peace.

Who could that be chasing him? It wasn't a wolf. It was too big to be a wolf. It wasn't a bear, it was too sneaky to be a bear. No, this had to be a somebody. But if it were just a somebody, then why did the fear clutch at his heart and run up and down his back the way it did?

The chicken man's boots slid in the mud by the creek and his ankle turned funny and he toppled. Someone was chasing him hard. He started shouting in the cold, black air, "Whoever you are, I just want my horse. Just don't take my horse!"

He was yelling and pulling himself back to his feet. He wasn't sure if he had hurt his ankle or not.

The chicken man wasn't sure what scared him so awful bad. He could sense something, though, about whoever was running after him. He felt dreamy about it, as if whoever it was, they were evil and wiry and they meant to do away with him, do away with him in some awful way, some way that made his knees shake.

He kept running. The chicken man was completely out of breath, but he pushed on. He pushed on through loose rocks and over mossy banks. He pushed on through deep, thick mud that sucked at his boots in the dark. He pushed on, splashing his soaked feet through veins of ice water that ran into the creek. After a while, he'd cut himself on so many of the tall reeds and the whipping branches and the sand stones by the creek bed, his lungs felt as if they'd blow up, his vision blurred in the darkness. He had to stop.

He stopped.

He couldn't hear anything but his own breathing. His breath came out in front of his face in little white smokes. He couldn't hear anyone around. He was thirsty and his body, now settling still, began to burn and sting from all the cuts. He'd twisted up his right ankle a lot worse than he thought. He realized this and the feeling in his ankle joint was hot and sick.

His mouth was parched. He sucked cold air.

His eyes were wide in his thin little head.

It was lucky that his legs were so strong from all the chicken runnin'. He coulda rode Cousin far and away from here, though. Where'd he gotten off to? If he hadn't that horse, he couldn't make a decent living. Of course, he might always find and buy another horse, but he'd raised Cousin up from a foal and he and Cousin were like cousins.

It wasn't right.

Them wolves might have got to him too.

But, now, who was this? Who was this following him?

He got himself down by the creek side and scooped up a cold handful of water and slurped it. It felt good going down his throat. It was icy. He could barely see anything around him. He could hear now the trickling of the water licking the banks. He felt the stings of the cuts on his hands bright as fires.

The moon was coming out from in between the clouds now, and the creek bed got lit up with blue and green lights from the sky and from the moon. The green moon played in the water.

There was someone standing there. There they were right there, right there behind the big tree. For a flash he saw their shape and then they disappeared behind the tree. It was a big person, maybe hunched over.

"Who is that?" the chicken man whispered into the thickening darkness. "Come out of there."

A feeling crawled up his spine, that same feeling from before.

"Come out from behind that tree," he said. "Come out here and let's see who y'are! Causin' an old chicken man to run like hell." He paused and took a few steps forward and lowered his voice a little. "You're giving me the jitters standing back there. And where's my horse. Where's Cousin?"

There was no answer, though he thought that he might have heard a whisper.

"What?" he called and stepped a little closer.

Again no answer, but something in the wind that sounded like a whisper.

He moved in closer still to the tree. It was a wide tree that looked as though it had twisted itself over a big, heavy stone. It's funny how things can grow and live even in places where it seems they aren't supposed to.

He saw something.

"Who is that?" he whispered.

There was a crackling noise and something heavy shifted in the mud. "Get out here! You're making me mad! Get out here and show yourself, or I am going to come back there and whop you one!"

The chicken man hardly ever in his life had felt so angry. All that fear inside him had curled itself up in the back of his neck and he was ready for a fight.

The moon came out from behind the cloud again and there it was.

He could see now there was something behind the tree, it looked like an animal carrying another animal on his back or something like that. It reminded him of something he'd seen many years ago at the docks in Hopestill. Men had brought something in from deep out on the ocean, something with horned whips for arms, something alive that seemed that it shouldn't be.

He raised his fists and squinted up his eyes.

But the chicken man hardly got a look when his legs went out from under him and the breath was knocked out of him. Soon he was upside down and his face was wet and hot and he tasted blood in his mouth. Then he was tired and he jerked back and forth. The world felt soft and far away. He thought he could see something looking at him in the dark. He thought he saw yellow eyes, like a cat's, spinning around. Maybe it was a mountain lion had got a hold of him.

He could feel something pushing into his neck and heard what must be the bones in his back cracking. He knew without a doubt at this moment that he was being eaten and that he was going to die.

He had a feeling of relief, and an ease settled into his mind as his vision darkened and all went black.

The doctor and Vernon Mosely took Bill Hill up on the stretcher and took him into the church. Hattie Jones tried to poke his head in the door, but the doctor shooed him out and started into dressing Bill Hill's wounds. Bill's back had been torn up pretty bad. It was a strange place for a wolf to bite at someone.

"That's a strange place for a wolf to bite at someone," Vernon said. He took a seat beside the cot they had him on.

The doctor had redressed all his wounds on his back and had him lying there on his stomach. He was asleep. Whatever that elixir the doctor gave him was, it was something that put him to sleep right away, and with a smile on his face. Medicine is a funny thing, and normally Vernon wouldn't allow it so openly. He'd allowed it, though, and when some folk found out they'd left the church. Just as the Hills did. Someone in his position could get into a lot of debate and even be put out of the church for allowing a hand other than God's to touch the life of a person like this. Vernon let his own ears fall off to protect such a principle; but now, since he had been in Sparrow, there had been some changes in his mind about certain things. He knew too that the doc was a man who didn't go around telling about things. He'd seen the old doc pretty close-mouthed about a lot of things.

But this here—this here with Bill Hill, this was something else. The doctor hadn't said much yet. He'd cleaned him up good and stopped the bleeding. They'd lifted him up and set him down on his stomach. Bill was smiling in his sleep. That was nice.

Water had passed out of a cup and over Bill's lips many times. No one had come in or out of the church. There was quiet all over the town. Bill breathed shallow breaths and his face was white.

No words passed out of the doctor's mouth and no words came out of Vernon. In his head he saw, over and over, a shadowy stack of wolves, their black gums and yellow teeth . . . five, six of them gnawing on Bill's back bones.

A crow cawed outside suddenly. It came to roost in the top of the small church there in the middle of town.

There wasn't too much to this church. A few wooden chairs were arranged neatly and looked clean. There was a wooden pulpit with the messiah's symbol on the front, the arrow pointing down above the arrow pointing up. Then there was Bill Hill, lying there with a smile on his face and his eyes closed.

"Wolves . . ." Doc Pritham started into the cold air.

The crow went on. They both crooked their heads and listened.

"Huh?" the preacher said when the bird quit. Vernon moved in his chair a little. The chair creaked. His mind had gone far away, turning over the things in his mind that had gone on. He was staring at the symbol on the pulpit, heaven touching the earth, wondering when the day would come, wondering when the promises would be answered, among other things. Where was the chicken man? Where was the chicken man's horse? Where was the chicken man's chicken? If the powers of darkness were moving again in the world, why did the writings say that they were all but gone? Were they all but gone? Did the writings say that? He put his face in his hands.

"The wolves, preacher," the Doc kept going, "the wolves are coming down off of the hill and looking for food near this town. Which shows to me that there is a shortage of prey in the hills. They're starving and they are coming down out of the hills to feed. They will return." Doc Pritham folded his hands together as if he were praying and brought them up under his nose as he spoke calmly. "Knowing the cannibal nature of the wolf, they're now likely feeding on those of their pack which Mr. Straddler killed with his gun. Then maybe they may eat the horse and then maybe they eat the chickens, and then, maybe . . ."—he frowned at the fact—"they will return in time."

Bill Hill was breathing quietly now. It was getting dark outside and the church inside started getting dark too. They were both looking at Bill's face now and they could see a little color coming back to it.

"The wolves came down from the hills back when the blizzard hit too. That's when all those things happened. That's when Brother Taylor froze and when all the other things happened too, before you were here," Vernon said.

"If the wolf is hungry, it will come back. As I said, the dead wolves and maybe the chickens will feed them for a time, yes. But they will be back. Other animals will come too. Bears. Others . . ."

"Others?"

The doc stood up and stretched his legs out. He was bothered. He patted his pants and straightened his jacket. He thought of the wounds on Bill's back. He picked his hat up off the floor and beat it on his leg. The wolves hadn't gone for Bill's neck. It's not like a wolf. His face was wide and healthy and his eyes were light blue, almost bright-looking as he said, "I'm having a pipe. I will be just outside the door. If he wakes, call me." He put on his hat, "I will be just a short time."

Doc Pritham got outside and closed the door to the church behind him. He looked out through the little town. Nobody was out. All the doors were closed up and smoke was coming out of the chimneys. The tracks were around still in the mud. The dusk was coming in gray and windy. He packed his pipe. Then he lit it up with a match and a few puffs. His serious face lit up in the darkening evening. Red and yellow flickered in his eyes as the smoke floated away into the air.

He said, "Others," and looked around, squinting. He thought of the church and man lying there in a coma. He thought of the long, puncturing wounds on Bill's back—wounds that were not made by any wolf. He looked at the coals in his pipe and watched as the wind passed over the bowl and made them glow all the brighter.

Down by the creek, Hattie Jones and little Samuel were standing beside each other.

Hattie Jones didn't like taking his son around to look for dead people, but he did it anyway. He knew that he was a good man for taking care of this little one whose parents died in the big freeze, he knew he was a good man for playing the fiddle over at Huck's and letting the men of Sparrow smile and clunk around dancing just for a little while, he knew he was a good man for never taking a wife and never cheating at cards, he knew he was a good man. He wondered why such evil things could befall a town where such a good man was. It wasn't just him, though, there were other good men and women in Sparrow. Brother Taylor was a preacher and he froze to death. Only God and the angels know what happened to that little baby, Starkey. He looked down at this little boy, whose eyes were wide and darting, whose smile went on and on. It made Hattie smile too, but only a quick, grubby smile that he wiped from his mouth, and then he took off his hat and scratched his head and then put his hat back on.

Hattie and Samuel kept on staring. The creek was getting rough as the wind was coming down through the little hollow. The trees were all dead and winding around everything.

"That's blood there," Hattie said. "And there's blood there and some there. Them cowards up in the town are going to run hither and thither and have all kinds of conversations and philosophies. In the meantime, an old man with a fiddle and a boy with his drawings can clear out the Evil One!"

He barked a laugh and clapped Samuel on the back.

They were staring at a pile of white on the ground in front of them.

"Sticks?" Samuel said.

"They're not sticks, Sam." Hattie said. "Them's bones."

Hattie got hunkered down close and looked good at the bones. "They're white," he said finally. "These are the horse's white bones." Hattie got back up and reached in his sack and grabbed his whisky and took a long, meaningful drink from the brown bottle and looked around and snorted and spit, adjusting his pants. It was getting dark.

He looked back up at the town and looked at Samuel who was just standing there staring at the pile of white bones in the muddy bank.

"Lord," he said and hunkered back down, "there's no head around here. These are just the bones and there's no head."

Then a feeling came over Hattie. It was deep and it was no good. It shivered him all over and came crawling up his neck. It was like something was looking at him. He got out his fiddle from out of his bag. He hadn't tried this in a long time and was scared of the results, but he was more scared of not knowing than he was afraid. He put the bow to his fiddle and whined out a long low peal into the woods.

Nothing happened at first, but then the birds, which he hadn't noticed chirping before, immediately stopped.

He looked at Samuel and then walked in a slow circle around Samuel and around the horse's bones looking into the dense woods.

He put his bow to the strings again and pulled another note that started low and rose and rose and, this time, at the highest pitch, he scraped his bow across loud three times.

Then, from the woods he heard a noise that raised his hairs. It sounded a bit like a man, but it wasn't a man, and it sounded a bit like a wolf, but it wasn't a wolf, it sounded like something that wasn't a person that was in pain and was asking why.

"Samuel, stay close and don't look back! There's a devil down here! We gotta get!"

Hattie grabbed Sam's arm and whipped the both of them up the bank and up they went, both thumping their feet against the ground at the same time, up the path back to town.

# CHAPTER 10

Simon Starkey could never sleep very well. His nights, even the nights after he'd had too much whisky over at Huck's, were long, fitful, and full of nightmares. Nightmares of his little sister, nightmares about his real parents, nightmare about the killers.

He moved in and out of his mother's room, always scared that he would find *them* in there. Sometimes he could see on her the blotches where they had been feeding. Other times he told himself that they were caused by his mother's illness. He had often wanted to call on that doctor, Doc Pritham, to come and tend to her, but he feared that almost as much as he feared seeing them in her little room.

Too, he could tell that, at least as of late, ever since that outlander showed up in town, someone had been watching him. He didn't know who, but sometimes in the night he would see a shadow moving this way and that among the trees outside his little house. He would poke at the fire and drink and doze and stare. He thought he would have the strength to fight them off when they came for her. He thumbed through the grimy pages of the black book, hoping he could read the words, hoping he would find something inside those pages that would open up the power to him, hoping that somehow this dark practice would give him the power or the right spells he needed to overcome them. But he would fall into a deep sleep and awake to find that they had been there without his knowledge. Sometimes he would wake up and find himself seated by the fire, when he'd last remembered that he had leaned up against her door. Or he would wake up to find that much of his furniture had been knocked around or someone had put the fire out with dirt in the middle of the night. He'd found one morning that someone had come in the night and wrapped black hairs around all his fingers.

He knew they would come for her one day.

This night, Simon stood on his porch and stared into the patch of woods that was just across the muddy road that leads up from Sparrow to his home. He was sure that he'd seen someone move back and forth between those two big trees that were just across the way. With the moonlight coming through the clouds and the woods, it was hard to tell what was a branch and what was an arm, what was a clump of leaves and what was a hunched figure. He squinted and bobbed his head up and down and looked into the dark. Much time passed and the moon traveled across the night, but he didn't see any more motion that he could discern apart from the wind blowing the trees in the dark.

He sat on the rocking chair and thought of smoking and was turning to head in to get his paper and tobacco when he saw it again, as if all this time it had been waiting for him to turn away.

"Who's there?" he called into the night. Nothing happened.

He stepped down from his porch and looked and looked. Just there, he thought he saw a figure, a hooded figure standing beside a tree.

"I see you," he said. "Who are you? What do you want?"

A whisper came to him. It wasn't a whisper that he heard, though. It was a whisper in his head. The voice was not unpleasant. In fact, it was almost soothing. The voice of a kind old woman.

"The preacher will come," the voice said, "and you must give him the token."

"Who are you?" he called again. He was frightened even though he felt no threat from whoever was there.

"You must give him the witch's thumb," the voice said.

An image appeared in Simon's mind. He saw Ruth Mosely

passing something between her hands. The witch? A thumb? The preacher?

He knew of the witch. He'd heard of the witch. Never seen her, but knew that she lurked in the dark woods. He knew that there was something in her that was against even the killers, but that she was not to be trifled with and that she was indeed very, very old.

"Who are you? Are you the witch?" he asked and looked through the darkness to the edge of the woods. Whoever was standing there had noticed that he'd noticed and now the figure stood next to a large tree, almost to the edge of the muddy road. It was tall and shrouded in a hood, but nothing about it felt menacing.

"What are you doing here?" he asked. It occurred to him that whoever was standing there wanted to help him somehow, that he was being pointed to something. This was not one of the killers; this was not one of Old Bendy's Men. But who?

"You must give the preacher the witch's thumb," it said again.

Suddenly Simon was waking up on the rocking chair and the moon was coming up and out from behind the clouds, casting long shadows of trees over the muddy road. There, where he was sure the hooded figure had been, was a bent, young tree whose leaves had turned brown but not fallen, so that a clump of them appeared to be something like a figure in a hood, leaning against that other tree.

He would not fall asleep again that night, but instead he went back inside and stoked up the hot fire and stared into the bright flames. A witch's thumb?

The preacher was in the dark. The moon was moving in and out of the clouds, but the preacher was still in the dark.

What did that doctor really mean? Mixing elixirs and talking about weird wounds.

Though there was something to what that doctor said. There was a weighty kind of light in the doctor's eyes when he said, "There are certain mysterious diseases too that can be caused by the bite of a wolf. And some of us are more susceptible than others." Then, "I'll watch him. Huck Marbo and his daughter are watching the other."

*The other.* That outlander who came in, Falk. The one with the supposed "powers" that his brother had come to him about. There was another here in Sparrow with supposed powers. So the preacher left the doctor at the church to watch over the sickened and broken body of Bill Hill, while the preacher went into the dark.

The preacher rolled it all around in his head; he remained in the dark. Maybe the outlander had brought these things with him. Sparrow didn't make much time for outlanders, but in recent years they had let Doc Pritham come along and make his stay. It was a slow realization and a sad one to reconcile when simples and elixirs looked to do more work than prayer. Some had lost faith altogether, others went to live up in the Ridges with those who'd left Sparrow since before him. Importantly, they'd accepted the whole lot of the Moselys when he'd come with his wife and daughter and brother and sister-in-law down from Miriam.

In the end, maybe Pater Mingus and Gunny Foder had been right to get their folk on out of Sparrow and move half the town up to the Ridges. Maybe. He'd heard through the wind and rumors that many had died in the Ridges soon after the move on account of a skin blight.

Throughout all this, the preacher wondered about his fireplace, about the brick that moved and the metal box that contained the parchment upon which the secret writings were written.

Soon, though, he was close enough to the house he was headed toward. He could see something of it through the trees—the roof and a long curl of white smoke reaching into the purple night.

The evening had finally rolled itself down into a wary kind of stillness. Sparrow was closed up, but not sleeping. He pushed his scriptures to his chest. The trees were thick on the side of the path. As he was rounding a corner, the wind blew and the timbers creaked.

He stopped and turned.

"Who is it?" he whispered into the trees.

No answer, but the preacher was suddenly inspired to speed it up. He sped it up, ambling along the path now with his shoulders bent forward, pressing toward the dull orange light at the path's end ahead.

This light was coming through the latches in the windows there at the Starkeys'. It flickered bright for a minute, and the sputtering curl of white smoke coming from the chimney went dark and gray.

Someone was poking up the fire.

It was late and the clouds were still trailing across the purple sky and the moon was still pretty full. He looked back down the path toward Sparrow; maybe he should head back. Patches of green light grew here and there in the town, opened up in broken patches. The wind whirled. He turned back toward the house.

Maybe Elsie Starkey was up to stoke the fire and keep the little house warm on this night, if she was even well enough to do things like that. He hadn't seen her since the blizzard.

He would stop by and assure her that all was well. Tell her he wished he'd come to visit sooner, laugh with her over how long it had been. He would tell her that good men were watching over the town tonight. He would tell her all those things if she were the one poking the fire, but Vernon couldn't shake the feeling that things weren't all that well, especially with Elsie. There was something sickly and strange about the fire in the house; there was something hunched and crooked about the house. The shadows and lights that came from the windows and cracks in the home looked too long and too alive.

The other one who was rumored to be with powers—that magician, Simon Starkey—was in there, waiting for him. How could he know? How can men know the hearts of other men?

This was not the way.

He stopped in his tracks and dropped his hands to his side. The scriptures in his right hand dropped to the mud, and he bent immediately and snatched them up.

The latched window ahead seemed to open a little wider.

Vernon Mosely stayed on his knee and started to pray. He said a quick prayer and stood back up, turning to leave.

He took three steps.

"Preacher?"

Vernon turned and saw that Simon had the shutters open and was looking out at him. The fireplace behind him was going and his head and shoulders showed black and orange.

"Preach! I heard they couldn't find the chicken man, Preach."

Vernon's mouth turned down tight on both sides, and his eyes squeezed shut.

His heart throbbed in his chest. "That's right," he said.

"What are you doing out there, Preach?" Simon called. "It's not safe being out there."

Vernon said nothing back and didn't move at all; he wondered what he was doing out there himself. Somewhere, between Simon and the wind, Vernon thought he could hear something else. Someone else was close by. Someone was whispering in the dark.

Vernon opened his eyes and rolled them slow left and then back to the right.

"It's cold and dark, Preach," Simon said again. "You should come inside."

Vernon heard for sure now. His gone ears could still hear, and this time he heard for sure. Somewhere over on his left, just beyond the edge of his vision, right there, right there in the shadow.

His feet came suddenly alive and moved him straight to the Starkeys' door and right up inside. The door snapped and clicked shut behind him.

It was warm in here.

Simon was behind him at the door, fooling with the lock. Vernon actually felt a bit relieved and somehow welcome.

The Starkey place was simple. He remembered a bit of Dan. Dan had been a very good man to come with Elsie to church, though they couldn't seem to get their "son" to come along. Dan didn't really talk much. He was simple and he worked hard. Sometimes he worked with Bill Hill, but he mostly kept to himself and would clear out trees and keep up the roofs in town and some other things. Vernon looked about this simple man's home and saw where Dan's winter coat still hung by the fire. He squinted a bit.

"Shhhh!" a voice came from the bedroom.

Simon appeared wearing a robe, whispering, "Mama's sleeping. You don't need to wake her."

It was more than warm in there suddenly. It was hot.

Simon's face had a sheen on it.

"Staying warm tonight?" Vernon asked pleasantly.

"I never much liked the cold, Preach. Try to keep your voice down. We don't need to wake Mama."

"Yes. Right. Sorry," Vernon said low.

There was a wood table here and three chairs. The fire kept a steady heat and flickering light in the room.

"Sit down. Can I offer you some coffee, Preach, or a bit of whisky to take the chill off?" Simon said and poured some from a bottle on the table.

Vernon shook his head no and waved his hand. He set his parcel down on the table.

"How is your mama, Simon?" the preacher asked the man in the robe. "How is Elsie?"

Simon looked back at the door and then at the floor. "It's a terrible thing, Pastor, it's a terrible thing."

A wind blew around the house clattering the shutters and then dying as quick as it started. The fire snapped and Vernon took a seat at the table across from Simon.

The two stared at each other. Simon was smiling in a friendly way.

The preacher adjusted himself in his chair.

Simon drank whisky from a little black cup.

The fire blazed, lighting Simon's face. Vernon had never really got the chance to look at Simon or talk to him much.

Now, here Vernon was, to ask this thing.

And there Simon was across the table, sipping whisky. Vernon figured, as everyone else did, that Simon was born in the East and that Elsie and Dan had found him somewhere and had raised him up. But no one knew, and no one was impolite or brave enough to ask for the truth. But there was something not exactly right in the story. Simon was much older-seeming, but he was younger-looking. He looked not unlike a boy of the River People or the first people with high cheekbones and a smooth face. His eyes were big and dark and there was even a certain kindness about them. Too, there was a deepness in them. Those eyes were sparkling and black and there was a sense in them of other lands, places that were very, very far away.

"Someone's out there," Simon whispered and looked toward the shuttered window, gesturing with his eyebrow.

"What?" Vernon said, but really he had heard.

"He's quick and quiet," Simon whispered, "and whoever it is seems to have a knack for staying just on the edges of the light so you can't exactly see him." He raised his thin eyebrows twice.

"Who is it?"

"Can't tell," Simon said. "Maybe it's whoever might have killed the chicken man. I heard the chicken man's been killed. Maybe it's that outlander."

"Who told you about the chicken man, Simon?" Vernon asked and looked him in the eyes.

"Just something I heard from around town. Mama," Simon said, motioning with his head over his left shoulder to the dark room he had just come from, "said that those wolves must've killed him, but I heard too that they couldn't find him." Simon looked into his cup and lifted it to his lips and took a long drink. He cleared his throat and said, "I heard Hattie Jones said there's a demon wandering down by the creek."

Vernon stopped breathing for a moment.

"Do you believe in that, Pastor Mosely? Do you believe that demons are alive?"

Vernon's face slackened. A lot of folk in town were asking him the same kinds of questions. A lot of people in the square were looking to him asking him questions of all kinds. People wanted to know what they had done to make the Lord punish them or the devil to send demons. People wanted to know if it was the devil that was after them. That's what people who are afraid want—they want details, and they want certainty. What could he do? Some folk were saying that they were fixing to leave Sparrow altogether, maybe head up to the Ridges where they heard there was never any trouble because folks didn't change up there, so they said. Bill Hill's condition worried him. Hattie Jones was spreading news of a monster and the chicken man was missing and who was this Jim Falk that had passed through claiming to have powers? Why had this outlander come at all?

"Why are you here, Pastor Mosely? What's got you out here tonight to see me?"

Vernon cleared his throat. He knew that what he was doing was somehow wrong, but he felt he couldn't stop at where he was. He felt drawn into it without his own will. He thought momentarily of the metal box containing the secret writings and wondered about the ways and the paths and how it seemed in the scriptures that no matter what some did, they were bound to a path, even if it led into darkness.

"I'll, uh," he cleared his throat again, "I'll have a drink of that whisky, if you will."

Simon looked at Vernon and then looked closer at Vernon. Then he laughed loud and shut up quick, casting his eyes toward the door of his mother's room, "Here you go, Preach." He set out a black cup and poured a little whisky into it. He set the bottle between them and said friendly, "If you want more . . ." and gestured with his open hands.

"Thanks." Vernon raised the cup to his lips and dropped the whisky in his mouth. It tasted terrible, like fire. He swallowed hard and his gullet came up. He held back a vomit and swallowed hard again. As soon as the heat hit his stomach, it spread through his body. He felt suddenly a bit stronger. His vision seemed to sharpen.

"Simon," the pastor said and looked deep into Simon's deep eyes, "I know that you do magic of some sort."

Simon looked at the aged pastor. Vernon's face was serious, wrinkled and squat as a tree trunk; his hands were wide and pointed, and his brown eyes were lost, looking as if they didn't belong to his stout frame and tough old face.

"Magic? What is magic? What I do is my business, Preacher. You are a man of the Word, a man of the Way; what do you care about magic and tricks? Magic is nothing when compared to the Way. Right?"

"What I am saying to you, Simon, is that I know that you do magic and I hear some people in the town, like Benjamin Straddler for one, believe that you have some powers beyond tricks."

"What is it exactly that you want from me, Preacher?"

"The town is in a bad way. There's all kinds of talk." He nodded. "Demons, as you say, devils and monsters, spooks, wolves. Everyone in Sparrow's got it that there's an evil about the town."

"An evil?"

"Like you said, Simon, demons alive."

"Demons alive?"

"Yes. And the thing of it is, I don't know for sure that they're wrong."

Simon leaned back into his chair and looked away and into the fireplace. "Neither do I."

"What I don't want, Simon, is for these people to start looking for the cause of these things."

"The cause?"

The preacher looked at Simon.

Simon was quiet. He looked at his feet sticking out from underneath his long robe.

"When these folks start talking, what they say and think can change men into monsters and women into witches whether you think it or believe or not, and quick. You know as well as I do some of the things that are happening in the north."

Simon rubbed his forehead and turned his eyes toward the fire. "You mean the burnings? Why are you here, Preacher, what do you want?"

"I need to know if you have a way from your books or your mixes or whatever it is that you do. Can you tell the future?"

"No," Simon said.

"Can you tell if there's an evil come into this town? A demon or the devil or a spawn of the devil?"

"No."

"Or a curse? Are you able to tell if a curse has been put on this town?"

"No, Preacher, I just do tricks. I am no mystic or medium or witch or warlock."

"Do you know where I can find one who has such—such powers? One who might be able to help?"

At this, Simon stood up. He adjusted his robe and walked away from the table toward the fire.

He had his back to Vernon when he said, "Yes."

Vernon's eyebrow went up.

When Simon turned about, he had in his hands a little black box—something that immediately made the preacher think of a tiny coffin.

Simon walked over to the little table and set it down and sat down.

"You do not know me, Preacher. You do not know my people or where I come from." He traced a circle with his finger around the box. "Neither do I, Preach. Do you know what that's like? Do you know what it is like not to have a people? Do you know what it is like not to know the voice of your real father or to remember your name? Do you know, I have dreams, Preach. Sometimes I dream of my people. I see their faces clearly, but when I wake up I cannot remember. I see their homes and their lands, but when I wake up I can't remember. What I can remember, Preach, is pain. I remember the hands that dragged my true mother away. I remember my father screaming after her and the men in black robes holding him back, I remember the silver knives that stabbed him, but I cannot remember his voice. I can only remember the feel of the scream."

Vernon Mosely looked at the long face and the watery eyes of this man, Simon, and he put his shaking hand again to the cup of whisky and brought it to his lips. Now he was sure that whatever was in the box, it was something that would not lead to good.

"I don't know how I escaped, but I have an idea. There was someone in the woods, Preach, who I think saved me, brought me here to be taken care of by a person of Sparrow. But I haven't seen her in a long time and I think that this is why."

Simon opened the black box, and inside the black box was a brown cloth. Simon unrolled the brown cloth and inside the brown cloth was a long white thumb. The thumb had a nail on the end that nearly looked like a yellow fang or a bird's talon.

"I believe," Simon said, "she is being held captive somehow by means of this thumb, which is hers. If you take the thumb into the woods, it will lead you to her door. By no other means can you find her."

Vernon Mosely had absolutely no idea what to do or what to say.

"If you can find a way to release her, please set her free."

"Where did you . . ."

"I cannot and will not say any more about this. If you tell anyone, you will die."

# Chapter 11

Huck woke up.

He heard May talking to Violet. Violet's voice was small and creaky, not like usual. He straightened himself up in the chair and stretched his neck right and stretched his neck left. He listened some more.

"Some of those wide bandages, the big ones, and more alcohol and any medicine you have for wounds," Violet was saying and clearing her throat.

Huck looked out the window of the little room. His knee was hurting him where the leg was gone. He'd fallen asleep while he was watching the outlander.

It was October, and October was getting colder. It was gray and bright out the window. Leaves were stuck to the edges of the window, black and curled with the rain. This bad cold snap came through right when this outlander did. He looked at Jim there lying on the little bed. His hookish nose, the thin cheeks—there was something about Jim Falk that was sickly and pale, and yet, there was a strength in him too. Huck Marbo wasn't sure what unsettled him more, the strength or the sickliness. What bothered him most about Falk's features was that they weren't familiar to him at all. He didn't even look like any of the faces or the faces of the families from up at the Ridges. He didn't look like any of the Mantres, the Bildooks, or the Westerlies, any of them at all. He certainly didn't look like a Mosely, a Marbo, a Jones, a Hill, a Straddler, a Pritham, none of them. In fact, there wasn't a man alive that Huck had seen that had such a long and sharp face. The only other faces that Huck knew of that had such high cheeks and sharp noses were the faces of the natives and the River People.

"You brought this rain with you," Huck said to the outlander lying on the cot. "Among other things." Huck's eyes wandered about the room. What other things the outlander had brought he didn't know; he didn't believe in what they even might be anyway.

Huck looked back at the outlander, Jim Falk. At some point Falk had fallen into a deep, peaceful sleep and he was drawing long, relaxed breaths now. His eyes were rolling around quick behind the lids. The health had come back slightly to his thin face. Huck leaned in a little and squinted. Despite all the things that looked wrong about the man, and especially in his sleep, Jim Falk looked kind. His face was narrow, but soft and lined. His closed eyes were deep-set and his gray brows were raised in a sincere way. He almost looked worried, but not quite.

Huck leaned back up and sat down. He strapped on his wooden leg.

He heard nothing now from the front room. Maybe he heard May creaking up the rungs of the ladder to get some bandages off the top shelf. Maybe he didn't. Violet was out there buying bandages. Huck took a deep breath as he made his way down the hall. What happened? The night had been something terrible. Huck was going to ask questions. Vernon Mosely should know something about this. Vernon Mosely would know what to do beyond praying. John Taylor had been a good man. He had been a good preacher, but he never knew what to do beyond praying and waiting. Religion can keep your children in line, but it won't keep you from freezing to death.

"What are we supposed to do, John? What are we supposed to do? Just sit here and pray?" Huck asked.

The shaking preacher looked at him in the snow bank and closed his eyes as the blood seeped dark below his legs. His blue lips mumbled prayers. The snow covered his face slowly, surely.

Jim Falk snored loud and smacked his lips and Huck came back from the memory.

For unknown reasons, Benjamin Straddler had dragged this outlander through the rain back to Huck's. This was the man, stretched out here on this cot, this cot where his wife had napped so many afternoons. Now this stranger lay here, snoring.

Benjamin Straddler was not the type to really give a hoot about anything until it meant life or death, and then Benjamin seemed to give a hoot about everything.

"Pa?" It was May's voice calling him.

"Pa, Violet wants alcohol for wounds, Pa. Pa?"

Huck appeared in the big hall with two flasks.

Violet was sitting at the bar on one of the stools. Her head was laid on its side on the bar, her arms crossed under her head. Gray sunlight splayed in through the shuttered windows of the front of the shop; all around her shone the dusty shafts of light. Her hair spilled as red vines over her pale face. Somewhere behind the red locks those dark eyes sparked.

May stood behind the counter, high up on the ladder, looking over at her pa.

"Come on down, May," he said.

Huck came into the front room all the way now and set the flasks on the bar. Violet didn't budge. She was all hunched over on the stool. She didn't look so good.

"What's happened to you, Violet Hill?" Huck asked her.

Violet sat up, arching her back and pulling the hair from either side of her face with both shaky hands. "Bill's been attacked," she said and closed her eyes and steadied herself in her seat with her left hand on the bar. "My husband's been attacked."

Huck took a few more steps toward her. She was real rickety, with her eyes half-closed there, and the way her lips stayed together when she spoke . . . What was that smell coming from her?

"Attacked?" Huck asked quietly now and limped a few more steps toward her.

May came down from the ladder and over by her pa.

Violet opened up her eyes. The pupils were black, wide and glittering, "Attacked by the spook," she whispered.

Huck turned to May and slowly, in his warmest voice, said to her, "May, you go on upstairs and let's see if we can't find some more help for Violet here."

"Like what, Pa?"

"May," he returned slowly in the same fashion, "I am sure you can think of some things that a woman like Violet here might need. Can't you see she's in a state, here? Something to calm her? Go on up and start pulling some things together and I'll be up in a minute."

"Yes, Pa," May said and went off.

When May had cleared out, Huck said in a whisper, "Violet." He went over to her and caught her up in his arms.

"Huck, I'm tired," she said loud, breaking her whisper.

Huck brushed the red coils of her wet hair away from her white face. She was in a cold sweat. The freckles on her cheeks were darkened, flushed. Violet's pupils were big and sparking, as if she'd been in some kind of darkness or a trance. And what was this smell? It was something that smelled sweet and heavy. It wasn't liquor, but what was it?

He kissed her wet forehead.

"Don't," she said.

"What's happened?" he whispered in her face. "What did he do to you this time?"

"Nothing. Nothing. Put me down," she said weakly.

"What?" His eyebrows were raised.

"Let me go, put me back on the stool. Anyone could walk through that door and see how you're looking at me. See what's in your eyes. Let me alone."

She wriggled free of him and stood unsteady a moment. She found the stool and settled back on it.

She whispered and pressed her fingers and thumb against her forehead. "See, Huck, it's me."

"It's you—what's you? What's going on, Violet?"

Huck grabbed up a pitcher of water and poured some in a

brown cup and gave it to her. He could hear May rummaging around in one of the cupboards. He remembered suddenly the out-lander who was knocked out on the cot and wondered if he shouldn't get Violet out and on her way, but she said again, "It's me, Huck."

He turned off his tenderness. Things that had happened in the past were just that. They were things that had happened in the past. For some folk those things go away; but for Huck, for Huck Marbo, those things somehow stayed close, and sometimes they were brought closer.

"It's you what?" he asked and put the cup in her hand. She brought the cup, shaking, a little to her bluish lips.

"It's me"—she looked down in the water in the cup—"that brought the ghost killer."

"The ghost killer?" Huck wondered what she was even talking about.

"The outlander, Jim Falk."

"The outlander."

"It's me that called him here."

"Called him here? What do you mean, called? On account of what?"

"On account of I wanted him to rid this town of the spook."

"Violet, you and I know . . ."

She burst out at him, "You and I don't know! Huck Marbo! You and I! There is no you and I!" She grabbed his face with her hand and whispered, "And we don't know!"

"Pa!" May came running in the room.

"May! Everything is all right here." Huck turned quick around to his daughter, who had come running from the back. Her hair looked messed up.

"No, Pa," she said, "no, not you and Violet." She suddenly shut up.

Violet sipped her water and her eyes looked around.

Huck stood there and May stood there with her eyes fixed on him. Violet continued sipping, looking back and forth between the two, darting her sparkling dark eyes.

"What, then?" he asked after that went on too long.

May cleared her throat. "Our guest," she said, "is awake."

Something made of glass fell and broke somewhere in the shop.

"Who's your guest?" Violet shot the question quick and took a big sip from the brown mug.

"May?" the outlander's voice came from the back of the shop. "May?"

Violet froze with the mug in front of her face.

A hole of some kind had opened up in Vernon's mind. He felt empty. His head felt so empty and he felt alone. He put his hands on his belly. He put his hands on his face. He thought of his home and his fireplace. He thought of his wife. Something had left him, something important and vital, but he couldn't quite figure out what it was.

The old woman's eyes were blank, though there was a spark alive, twinkling as if her black pupils were filled with water. Her crooked and clawed hands stretched out in front of her at the fire, the palms wide open at the end of her strong, wiry arms under the brown cloak.

The house smelled bad. There was a sweetness to the stink, but it was the sick sweetness of rot. Vernon could almost get used to it, especially with the fire burning, but it was powerful and thick and the slightest disturbance of the air in the room opened the smell up fresh again.

"Some nights," the old woman said, "the spirits are harder to get to. That's just the way it is. Sometimes there is a great power on the other side which blocks them from coming through."

Vernon felt a sick feeling. "Why can't you just tell me?" he asked quietly.

"The power to tell is not in me, Preacher. The power to tell comes from the other side." She craned her head up in his direction, her eyes glinted. "I am just the hollow. It comes through the hollow."

The fire in the middle of the dirt floor swelled and crackled up to the ceiling. The witch's eyes reflected the fire as her shadow went jerking up behind her.

Vernon felt a shudder up through his bones. Something crawled up inside him; something dark and cold as creek water spilled up into his neck and his back and his shoulders. The air in the room got somehow thicker and colder too, and there was a tingling in his skin. The hairs on his arms stood up.

The fire bloomed and curled and lit the room. Wylene's face was bright with the firelight flickering in and out, the shadow of her pointed nose stretching and disappearing across the creases in her face. An arm of fire moved and licked toward Wylene's outstretched and sharp nailed fingertips.

Another funnel of flame poured out from the fire and swayed toward Vernon.

The witch reached forward and let her fingers play in the flames. "You must do the same, Preacher. You must do the same."

Vernon shut his eyes and reached out, feeling the tickling fire with his hand. It didn't burn, but it didn't feel right.

Vernon could hear a dark voice in his mind now. He couldn't understand it. It came in like many voices at once, but one all the same, some whispering, some crying. There was one main voice, though—a strong, throbbing voice that stood clear from the rest of them. He couldn't understand what it was saying at all, but at the same time he felt he'd heard this voice before somewhere. Somewhere in his life . . .

The voice took him wandering through his own memories—somewhere back into his mind. He was just a boy. He was just a boy and that night his mother was crying so hard somewhere in that little house on the hill. In the middle of the night, his mother was sobbing. Was there a voice then too? Was it this voice? That night he got up and went to the window and looked out over the field and saw, through the shadows of the field, a dark shape, something writhing its way to the little house, from out of the woods and to the house and for his mother. His little legs were locked and heavy. It came through the purple darkness, a wicked shadow, to consume him.

"Wylene!" Vernon found himself shouting. A terrible noise, loud as tornado wind, had started up in the room. He was shouting her name over the noise: "Witch!"

The old woman had fallen over on her back, flat out, her arms winged out on both sides in the brown cloak. Her eyes still wide open, her breathing quick and in a panic. Her sharp fingers clutching into the dirt floor of the house.

The fire sparked and shot up and went straight out, embers and all. The room went completely black and still. The noise hushed away. Now Vernon could only hear the quick raspy breath of the witch on the floor.

Then he heard a whispering in the corner of the room. There, in the pitch black and quiet of the house with no windows, in the night, he heard the whispering and saw something glitter there: two tiny pinhole sparks of light where the whispers were coming out of. Eyes.

Vernon prayed to God.

The witch, Wylene, said, "Beside the stool is flint and tinder. Light the fire! Light the fire, Preacher! Light the fire quick!"

Vernon snapped up the flint and tinder and clacked them together. The fire sprang up and he looked in the corner and yelped.

An image was there, burned into the wood of the wall. The image was broken, wild, and raggedy with claws at the end of each arm. It moved. Vernon turned his eyes to Wylene, who was sitting up now and staring in the direction of the weird image.

Vernon's mind was in a whirl.

"Preacher," the witch said and straightened herself up. Standing now, she stumbled and leaned against the wall. "There's an evil here in this place. There's an evil in the land of this place. It's woke up. It's woke up and it's looking for something. Something that I cannot see. It's waking up to find it. It's old, Preacher. This evil thing is old, older even than these woods, or this mountain." She paused and looked far away off into a distance somewhere beyond the walls of the dark house. "Older even than me."

Vernon was at a loss. He sat down in the dirt and pulled out his book of the scriptures. Wylene looked at the strange bundle of papers in his hands.

"You may find a way in those writings," she said and moved toward the stool. She plopped down on the stool, exhausted. "You may not."

Vernon started to cry.

"Find the stranger, the outlander, and tell him what you saw here tonight. Tell no one else. No one. Not even the magician."

Vernon screeched at the woman, "Can't you do something?"

"Nothing," she said and poked at the fire with a stick. She chuckled a little. "There's nothing I can do. This thing, the evil thing, it will destroy us all. There is nothing I can do."

She smiled a sad smile and put her right hand to her mouth to cover her smile. She had no thumb on that hand.

She ran in with a cup of coffee for him, shutting the door behind her. She could hear her pa talking quick and quiet to Violet Hill in the other room.

His right hand was wrapped up in the bandages, and another bandage was around his head. He was sitting up at the edge of the bed, and his shirt was dirty with mud and the blood was crusty on his bandages. She wanted a clean shirt for him.

His eyes were clear and deep and blue when he looked up at her and said, "May."

"Yes," she said and handed the white cup to him. "Pa wanted me to bring you a strong cup of coffee."

Jim Falk took the cup with his left hand and before taking a sip asked, "Who saved me?" He took a sip. It tasted good to him. "This tastes good," he said. "Thank you. Who saved me?"

"Mr. Falk, Pa can tell you everything as soon as he's in here," she said.

"My hand," Jim said and looked at his right hand—"who put the bandages on me?"

Jim tried to stand up, but there came up a dizziness in his head. He saw in his mind the canopy of the rainy forest again in the night and felt for a moment the hot breath of the wolf against his face. He sat back on the bed and looked around the room, his mind wandering over the events that occurred.

"Who was that?" He looked at May. She was there, sitting on a little stool by the bed stand. On the bed stand was a bottle. She looked clean. Her square face and her high cheekbones looked strong, her eyes were wide looking, thoughtful.

"Well," May said, "the doctor who came to take care of you, his name is Doc Pritham, and he put the bandages on you and left with me specific instructions for your care. One of the main ones is that you shouldn't go trying to stand up so fast right away like that." She looked at him and couldn't help but smile, but then she hid it fast. He was back to looking at this right hand with the bandages on it. Then he looked up at her again and they were both quiet for a bit.

"Pritham?" Jim said and blinked and looked down at the foot of the little bed.

It was late afternoon. Some birds outside were chirping in a gray and muted way. There were no windows in this little room and the light came in from the main hall and from the little oil lamp on the side table. There was a warm feeling in the room, a comfortable heat, and the smell of medicine was coming from the brown bottle on the side stand beside May. May's eyes flicked between Jim's and the bottle, and the oil lamp, and a little brown cup there with it.

"What's in the bottle?" he asked, motioning toward it with his left hand.

Questions began burning up in the back of his mind. Where was his pack, his gear, the leaves? "Where are my things?"

She looked at the bottle and then back at him. "Your things? All your things are safe. We've got them here. Your gun and everything. Benjamin Straddler brought everything back with you."

"Benjamin Straddler?"

"Mr. Falk," May said and her big eyebrows came together, "Benjamin Straddler is the man who brought you out of the woods and down in to here. He brought you straight to us. He's the one got the doctor along to get you all bandaged up."

Jim blinked slowly, taking that in. "What's in the bottle?" he asked again. A stinging pain had started in a gentle way in his right hand. He could tell that it was only going to get worse. Too, he was having troubles in his memory. He couldn't remember certain things.

Just then, Huck Marbo appeared in the door. "Mr. Falk," he whispered, "you should lie back down. You should be resting. Once you've had your coffee and taken your medicine, you should lie back down and I'll fetch the doctor."

"Where's my gear?" Jim said loud.

Huck put his hands up as if to shush Jim and said, "Now don't get excited, it's not good for your condition, you've been attacked and had a hard fall. Your gear and things are safe and they're here in the shop. I'll have May fetch them for you, but please, for now, just lie back down and rest."

"Huck!" a woman's voice called from somewhere in the shop. "Huck! I don't have any time to wait for you!"

It was clear that the woman was angry. Jim Falk looked sideways at May. The voice sounded like a voice that he thought he remembered from somewhere.

Huck Marbo shot a look at his daughter and off he went in the direction of the voice.

"He's quick," Jim said and smiled a little smile—something about that woman's voice though, and he was tired now. May was looking at him. He should lie back down on the bed and rest his head. Violet, he thought—that was Violet Hill's voice.

May stood up and quietly shut the door back closed.

"The doctor told me to tell you to stay on your back and to rest as much as possible." She paused and rolled her eyes to the left, trying to remember. "And you have to drink a jigger of this medicine three times a day. The doctor said that if you have a prayer that you know, it would be a good idea to say it each time before you took the medicine."

"A prayer?"

"Yes, he said that is important to the cure."

"The cure?"

"That's what he said."

"That's what he said?"

"That's what he said."

She poured the elixir into the tiny brown cup. She handed it to him and he sat up again and took it in his left hand.

"It's good medicine," she said and a smile appeared on her square face.

"I want to talk to this doctor."

Jim smelled the medicine in the cup. It wasn't pleasant, but somehow it smelled strong and safe. He'd heard of this Pritham, but he couldn't remember where or when. His head was cloudy with dulled pain. Something of the smell reminded him of Old Magic Woman. Something of the smell touched his spirit. He took it in one swallow and looked at May.

Her eyes were so deep.

Violet saw Huck's back in the door. He was gesturing, making some sort of quiet talk, but it looked like something important. Violet's eyes narrowed and she tried to see through him into the room.

What lost her was how Bill and most everyone else in the town could be so blinded to the spook, the demon, whatever it was. She turned to her cup of warm whisky and took a drink. He was a good man and he was a smart man, but she couldn't understand.

He'd seen it. He'd seen it for sure, and for that matter, so had some of the others. She thought of Jim Falk's strong face—that light that was coming out of it as he rambled up the road with the spook's head in the bag. He'd seen it. He said he'd killed it. Had he seen it?

Bill hadn't seen it, even when it came at him, shuddering across the kitchen and taken him by the head and back.

"There's a bear in here, Violet!" Bill shouted and blasted shot from his shotgun, shattering wood and glass in the little kitchen.

It was too much for her mind right now. She was pretty sure that it was him—that it was the outlander, Jim Falk, in the back. It was too much for her to think about right now, and she had to get these items back to Bill and she had to get back up to the house. She slid off the stool and steadied herself. She thought of the stranger in the woods who had given her the powders. "Take these that you might use them against the foe, to call the one who is to save you."

She went back behind Huck's bar and poured herself some more whisky. She drank it and swallowed it heavy and fast.

She staggered more. The color left her face and she coughed a bit.

She went down on her knees.

She clutched at a leather strap around her neck and pulled up the locket that she wore around her neck. She opened it. It was empty. Her hands suddenly trembled as she stuffed it back in her shirt, but not at once, and not without taking a serious look into it and licking it again to be sure. She was sure and it was empty.

"Huck!" she cried at his back. For a moment she choked quietly and then called stronger than before, "I don't have any time to wait for you!"

Jim swallowed the medicine in a big gulp.

"That customer sounds impatient," he said to May.

The doctor's medicine warmed his stomach and his mind. He watched May getting up and smiling at him and getting ready to leave. There was something he wanted to say to her. He felt so grateful. The throbbing in his hand faded away and soon he found himself floating along a green sky, a cool wind breathing over his body, and then stars and smells of campfire. He was seated by Old Magic Woman's warm fire outside her tent. She was telling him a story.

"My grandmother was Matrune and she told me of the Big Flood when I was just a girl. My grandmother was said to be misshapen by her past and frightening to look upon. She wouldn't come out of her little cave when she talked to me. She made me stand at the edge away from her. She made me burn sage all around me. She wanted to see me. She wanted to sing me her song. She wanted to sing to me her life song, to tell me before she faded from the world. She did not want me to see her, but she wanted to tell me her story. I stood with my back to her. She told me how the big water came crashing and how many were destroyed."

Old Magic Woman's hands and fingers waved and rippled out in front of her. "All of them killed by the big, running waters. There were two enemies, though, that came and protected her. It was hard for my grandmother to tell this story." She stopped and looked deep into the fire, her eyes changed and lazily closed as though she nodded, as though the fire told her something, and continued.

She sang:

> "When the morning stars were shining
> Shining were the people's faces
> Shining faces by the River
> Shining water in their eyes
> When the Pishta came from Wydder
> They who brought the dying hunger
> They who made the brothers sickness
> They who made the forest sickness
> They, the Pishta from the Wydder
> Weak we were the River People
> When we called out to Sky Father
> When we cried will no one save us
> From the sickness of the Pishta.

"But when the water came, when the great one, the Father, sent the waters, Matrune was protected. She had special favor with the Sky Father. Those who protected her took her to a safe place and she slept for a long time in the darkness. She would wake in the dark where it was hot and they brought her food. She said the food was dead things and that it tasted of fear. 'Matishne,' she would say, 'It *was* fear.' Her voice was very old, but it was strong and sweet."

She sang:

"The water rushed and crashed and pounded
Many Pishta drowned in waters
Crashed their bodies into nothing
Water monsters ate their insides
Yes, the water monsters ate them
Many Pishta drowned in waters
Many of the people died there
Many dead were in the water
Sky Father when he saw the terror
Heard his children's blood cry Father!
He cried tears the more and flooded
More and more with tears of sadness
All the world was drowned in mourning
Mourning Father for his children
Mourning for the world beneath him
Mourning for his little children
Katakayish of the River.

"Matrune did not know how long she slept, but the hole where she was grew smaller and smaller and, as much time passed, she began to see a little light. The colors in the hole changed. It was dim and dark, and then it became purple and then blue and then green and then, after that, she was able to see where she was. Deep in the rocks in a cave. And her once handsome and strong protectors were there, but they had become misshapen and hideous monsters. They stood at the cave's entrance. They were demons. They became that way from eating all the dead fear in the darkness. Matrune saw her reflection in the black waters. Her skin was white and her hair was black. So long in the darkness, she had forgotten her own face. She had forgotten almost how to see light. She had grown and she was naked. But she saw her own face and she saw that it was beautiful. She took her protectors and stepped into the light of the new earth. The light hurt their eyes and their skin, and so they went and hid in the shade of the woods. They hid from the One who sent the terrible flood. They hid and waited for people and children to return to the earth. Lonely and hungry, they waited in the darkness and she longed for her people to return, knowing that they never would."

"Your grandmother is Matrune?" James, the boy sitting by the big fire, asked.

"Yes, Matrune, daughter of the black moon," Old Magic Woman said. "My mother was called Matishne, daughter of the black river."

"Your name is Matishne too?" James asked.

"Yes," Old Magic Woman said and smiled, "but my true name is Mate'eya'ishne'mate'rune. Which means dark fire, daughter of the river and daughter of the black moon." She smiled and her smile was bright.

"Why does my father call you Old Magic Woman?" James asked.

"Because . . ." Old Magic Woman said and smiled. Her teeth white and perfectly square glimmered in the firelight, her dark eyes twinkled and crinkled. "Because, James"—she raised her voice up loud and held her hands over her head—"I am! I am Old Magic Woman!"

As she shouted, a cool breeze passed across their faces and flapped the big fire back and forth. She laughed, her eyes locked on James's eyes. He laughed loud and big into the pines, looking away from her eyes in shyness and then back again, laughing bigger, bolder right along with her.

When she left him in the empty home, he was left with terror. He felt that he might have known the same terror that Matrune felt in the cave, all alone with terrible monsters eating fear. That is exactly what the loneliness felt like. His mother gone, his father disappeared, and Old Magic Woman saying to him, "You will have to pass through the world now alone, little James Falk. I cannot carry a child who will not listen to his father. I cannot teach a student who will not learn. You will have to pass through alone."

She said these things to him in the empty house of his parents as he cried on the floor beside the stove where his mother had made so many breakfasts while his pa sat scribbling in papers and trying to teach Jim to read. Now they would all be gone, they would all be gone.

She said these things to him as tears fell from her own eyes and she handed him a warrior's satchel, a woven blanket, and a pack of medicines. She said this to him and turned and stepped out the door and she did not look back in the open door, even as he called for her. Even as he screamed her name, she did not look back. She did not look back because her face was shining with tears.

# CHAPTER 12

Benji Straddler's father was standing at the door.

The sun was rising behind him over the pines. All around him, the morning was quietly singing in orange and green, wet and new. The woods smelled good in the cold breeze.

Benjamin Straddler's father was dirty. In fact, that's what they called him, Dirty Straddler. He never got clean and his skin was red and black with dirt, and his knuckles too were black with dirt, and in the cracks of his red face, black. Dirty Straddler was dirty all right, but he was strong and good, and he smelled like fire.

"Come on, Benji!" his father hollered at him. His teeth shone like light out from his dark face. They matched his blazing, white eyes in the morning. He grabbed at his son's hand and it disappeared in his dirty grip. The two went galloping together through the high grass, down the bank of the river, then up the river, the sun breaking through the pines here and there in sparkling spots, down past the garden full of pumpkins.

They came up to the barn.

"Now, here!" Dirty Straddler said, and whisked Benji up on his shoulders. "Now here! Are you comfortable up there? Look in here! Look who's had a foal!"

Benjamin could see in there. He could see that big, black, wild horse, Dandy. She'd had a foal for sure. The little thing looked shiny and it was being licked and licked and licked.

Benjamin said, "Oh, my, Daddy, oh my, look at Dandy's baby."

He woke up saying that now and again. He woke up in the night, sometimes with tears splotching up his vision, reaching out for the bottle he kept under the nightstand, fumbling in the dark, trying not to wake up Lane.

Most of the time, though, she heard him.

She would wake up when the sobbing started and listen only. That was all she could do. Once she had tried to comfort him and he had reacted violently—obviously in a sleeping state, but violently. So the sobbing would start and she would lie there listening and then the mumbling and the words came out; sometimes he said different little sayings, some of which were nonsense, but she couldn't remember them all. Always, though, he would get up at some point, sobbing. Sometimes the sobbing led to all this coughing, but always then, scrabbling around for the bottle. The drinking and the crying.

Finally, after he'd had enough, he would pause for a long time and she could feel his eyes on the back of her head. She could hear him open his mouth. He stretched out his hand and put it on her shoulder. "I love you, Lane," he would say, and she would mumble something, as if she half heard in her sleep.

"I am so sorry," he would say and then, a few minutes later, he would pass into such a deep sleep, soundless, that she worried sometimes he would not wake up.

He did, though. He always did wake up.

This morning, Benjamin woke her up.

Coming in the door, he went straight up to her.

She was sitting in the chair, asleep, with the gun across her lap, the morning light coming through the shutters, playing in the dust around her sleeping form.

"Lane," he said quietly in her ear.

She opened up her eyes and jumped.

"You're covered in blood!" she yelled.

"Lane, something is happening!" he yelled.

"Are you all right?" she yelled.

"I'm covered in blood," he said.

"But are you all right?" she said, and set the gun aside and stood up. Her hair was kind of messy and her eyes were puffy, but she was beautiful to her husband just then.

"I'm all right," Benjamin said, "I'm all right, but something is happening. Something's happened in the night."

He looked odd to her. There was a weird light in his eyes. Something that she hadn't seen before at all, ever.

"What is that in your eyes, Benjamin Straddler?" she asked.

Benjamin didn't know either, but he could feel it, and had an idea. "I'll tell you," he said, "but we need to keep this between us. We need to keep this between you and me. This is something for us Straddlers only, and we need to keep it just between you and me."

"Well, my goodness," she said.

"Make some coffee and some breakfast, Lane. I need to wash all this blood off of me and then when I come back. I'll be clean and I'll tell you what's happened."

"Well, my goodness," she said and started the coffee right away.

"This thing you saw, this thing in the night, what did it look like?" John Mosely asked Hattie Jones. John had been out in the fog looking with the men. Now they were all out in front of the church.

"It wasn't in the night, John Mosely, it was just now!" Hattie said and looked at his son, Samuel, who was looking around and twirling a feather. "I didn't get really such a good look. I was only able to see it from the corner of my eye. I don't know if I saw anything."

Some of the other men of the town had heard Hattie hollering and started to gather around the three of them standing there in the fog. The fog was going around them in gray ways.

"It was something, though. I don't know," Hattie said, and John Mosely saw Hattie's eyes darting back and forth, as if he was searching frantically for something in his memory. Hattie took notice that the shadowy shapes of the men were starting to gather around him. He wasn't sure what he had seen at all. Maybe he had just been scared because of the bones and the way the wolves being around made him feel, which was scared and uneasy. Maybe when he'd used the special call with his fiddle; maybe someone just called back at him that way to make him scared and run off. Maybe it was just a tree that he'd seen in the fog and that had been blowing in the wind—just the crooked black limb of a tree sticking out there in the fog. Or was it a long, reaching, wicked arm?

"I don't know," he said again, "but more than the look of whatever that thing was, there was this feel of it. The feeling that comes . . ." The men pushed in closer to listen to his words as he said, "The feeling that comes when you're around something like that."

The men froze. John Mosely froze too, and in his mind a mist was forming into shapes. Pieces of a strange puzzle were coming together in the mist in his mind. The fog opened up just enough to see the front of the church. The steps were empty, the little windows were closed. He thought of Ruth and the things she had told him, all the things she had told him about what would start to happen if Sparrow let outlanders in.

"The feeling," Hattie continued, looking the men in each of their eyes, one at a time so that he could see for sure that each of the men was looking at him. He moved backward toward the steps. "The feeling that you get when something wants to kill you and drag you down into Hell."

The men mumbled.

Someone whispered, "'Into Hell,' he said."

At this, something happened in John Mosely's head. He caught a flash, a picture, a vision in his mind of a man—the man that Benjamin Straddler had described to Ruth, whatever he said his name was, Jim Falk, the outlander. The one who'd been doing the tricks at Huck's with Simon—he stood there in John's mind against the dark night sky. John's mind blurred the memory of Falk with imagination. A tall, pointed hat like a witch's with its wide, black brim. In John's mind, Jim had a moldy armor laid upon him, fearsome with shining spikes and strange symbols etched in red on its mottled surface. In one hand he hefted a heavy double-ax for executing the victims, in the other a leather-woven lead for the Thing in the Night, a knife-mouthed monster, a lizard and a wolf at the same time, breathing its poison-hot breath, ready to swallow him up. Ready to drag.

John Mosely grabbed Hattie by the shoulders. "The outlander!" he whispered, but very loud, right in Hattie's face.

John's eyes popped wide open and he looked over Hattie's shoulder at the mumbling men. "The outlander's brought the beast! Benjamin Straddler knew it! My wife knew it. He told us, Benjamin told us! He came and warned my wife last night!"

John's skinny frame was tittering around, still holding Hattie by the shoulders. "The outlander's brought this beast and it means to kill us all! I told you, I told you those from outside would bring nothing but evil! We've got to keep these people out of our town and out of the church!"

He stopped yelling and looked at Hattie Jones. He swallowed hard with this new fear and conviction he had found. "And it's like you said, Hattie, they've come to kill us all and to drag us into Hell."

It was night. Most of the people in town were still inside the little church. Some of them had gone home, but a lot had stayed up at the church because of the goings-on. They stayed around to talk it out. The doctor had got Bill Hill all comfortable with whatever he'd got in those little bottles, and then he left. Some of the folk were frowning and talking fast and quiet about the doctor being allowed to bring such things into a place of worship. Others were standing near Bill saying prayers. There were plenty of folk about, but not Violet. Violet was not there; she had gone home to rest.

Doc Pritham wondered about that. But he had to get on with things and leave these people to take care of Bill Hill. With the outlander being attacked and the chicken man disappearing and now Bill Hill, the preacher had gone to look for answers and the doctor needed some too. Doc Pritham was not sure that he wanted to know the answers because he was afraid that he already knew the answers.

Now, Doc Pritham was sitting in his office drinking some liquor with Jim Falk. There was a big bunch of candles on the table in the middle of them. Their faces were tired and serious in the flickering light. Falk had gone from Huck's when May had given him the last of the medicine. He wanted more medicine. He was healing fast.

The doc looked at Jim's eyes and felt his pulse. "It's fast, the medicine is fast, but you're healing very fast."

Then he sat down and started fooling around with his pipe stem. He was rolling around the events of the past few days in his mind. It was coming together pretty well, but he didn't like what was shaping up. What was shaping up was dark and like a bad prophecy coming into being.

"Most of the people are staying up at the church right now, waiting for the preacher to come back with some kind of answers," the doctor said.

Jim had his right hand on the table near the candles. It was completely wrapped up in a bandage. There was no blood seeping through. Underneath the bandage, he could feel his hand. It felt as if it was humming. It seemed as though the doctor's medicine was working. His body felt warm and supple, too. He was looking at his bandaged hand and then back up at the doctor. He was thinking about the church and thinking about the medicine that the doctor had given him. "It might help, being in the church might help," he said and took a drink from his cloudy tumbler. "It might not." Jim fiddled a bit with the bandage. "Where's the preacher gone off to?"

Doc Pritham said, "He's gone off somewhere. He has an idea about a way to find the truth."

"The truth?" Jim asked.

The doctor made a grunting noise and banged the bowl of his pipe on the table.

Jim Falk said, "Doc, we're going to have to help each other."

The doctor said, "I know." He turned up his pipe and got some good tobacco and started putting it in. "These people—these people here in Sparrow. They have good hearts and some of them have good minds to go with the hearts. More than this, though, the people have fear. Too much fear. Even among themselves."

Jim took another drink. He watched the doctor for a while. The doctor had white hair and big eyebrows. His face was wide and strong, and his mind was strong and his eyes were clear. Jim said, "That cure I took. The medicine. It was a special from the Old Way. Can I have some more?"

The doctor puffed his pipe and frowned.

"Doc, my father and my old grandmother, they taught me the Old Ways, the Waycraft, the Path. . . . I can take more medicine. I can handle it. I've been taking these medicines since I was a boy. It won't harm me the way it might someone else."

The doctor took a long pull on his pipe and for a little while he sat with his face in a rectangle cloud of blue smoke. The candle fire did some licking away of the smoke, and from behind the cloud Jim could see the doctor's eyes twinkle a bit. The doctor took a little drink then and put it down again and smiled. He was looking at Jim right in the eye now.

A little smile grew on the doctor's face underneath his fat nose. "Jim Falk, what exactly is the thing that has brought you here?" he asked him.

Jim Falk looked across the table at the doctor and said directly, "It wasn't a certain anything as such. It was something, though." He took a sigh and his hand lifted up and waved in a dismissing way. "I was called to come here in dreams by the woman Violet Hill. She called me here by vision."

The doctor puffed again. "Well, Falk, you are right, of course. About the cure that I gave you, the medicine—and there is something else that I know." He set down his pipe. "I know that a man such as you, such as you are, does not come along a certain way for the simple reason of a vision. If you have visions, you must have them all the time and you can't follow each and every one to its thread's end."

The doctor raised his left hand and made a motion with it. "Perhaps you do. Perhaps a man such as you are does such a thing. Wanders around, this way and that, following every breeze, chasing every notion. Perhaps." The doctor paused a moment and put his long-fingered hands together as if in prayer and brought them to his lips under his nose. "But I know. In your mind, in the way that your mind likely works, I know that there are many such visions that come to you and how you use a way of finding the path to take. You should, at least, know a way to find the right path among the paths. But I see you, Mr. Jim Falk, and I see into your eyes and I see that your paths are twisted by the darkness."

Jim's face, which had looked pale and worn, hardened, and suddenly a fierce light glowed in his eyes. He was concentrating on what the doctor was saying. The doctor said two things that were a kind of code among men and women who knew of the Old Ways, the "paths" and "darkness." These were pulled out of the pages that Barnhouse had translated and the writings that were lost and his father's journals.

Jim opened his lips to say something. Just then a great wind blew at the side of the house, in through the open windows, and the candles smoked out. There was a noise following the wind—screaming and hollering. People were wailing and crying out for help.

"That's coming down from up at the church," Jim said and leapt from the table, seized his gear bag up under his left arm, and flashed out the front door. The doctor stumbled about in the dark of his office. He grabbed up his medicine bag and scooped in an armful of tinkling bottles. He darted out into the night after the outlander. In his mind, the doctor saw two tangled spiderwebs.

It was dark for sure and the fog was still heavy on the town. Jim could hear the people wailing in the church, but he could see nothing but moonlit fog.

They were crying out, but he could not understand. The wind was whipping the noise of them this way and that way, twisting their words up in the fog—making it so you couldn't understand a thing. The fog was thick enough that his own hot breath came back against his face as he ran.

Things clicked and flashed in Jim's mind. When he'd left Huck and May Marbo behind they'd waved friendly-like in the doorway, the light of dusk blending them into the dark of the wood. He wanted medicine. He wanted to chew the leaves. His boots pounded on the dirt road. Behind him, he could hear the doctor catching up to him. The old man was fast. He heard the bottles clinking.

Jim thought about the people in the church and he thought about his pa. The doctor reached his side, jostling with a sack full of his vials and medicines.

The doctor said to him as they ran toward the church, "I know you are looking for your father."

"Give me some medicine," Jim said and stopped. "My hand is on fire with this itching."

The doctor stopped too, turned, frowned, and shook his head, but was quick with a brown vial to Jim's mouth. "We don't have time for this."

Jim grabbed at the bottle in the doctor's hands and gulped eagerly.

"That's it," the doctor said, pulling it away. "That's all for now. I've never had anyone to take so much."

"Or to heal so fast?" Jim asked and under the bandage, the doctor saw a wiggling in the wounded hand.

They turned together and ran again.

As they ran together in the fog, a smile broke out on Jim's face. This was definitely the Pritham that he'd seen on Barnhouse's inventory sheets. Barnhouse had mentioned him in a throwaway way a few years ago, pausing, his eyes stuck in a point in the air and then looking at Jim and shrugging his shoulders.

It was coming to Jim that the circles were closing. In his mind he saw himself moving along a map, a dark and dirty map with changing lands and scribbled buildings, strange claws jutting from messy trees—Jim was moving, paths were crossing, closer and closer to his father. . . . Pritham was a kind of proof of this—the paths crossing, closer and closer to the conjunction of all paths.

Jim slung his pack on his right shoulder and, with his left hand, he pulled his hatchet. They could see the lights from inside of the church through the fog putting big circles of yellow up in the gray clouds. They could hear the people hollering, but they couldn't see much of anything but moving up near the church.

The light from the church came through the fog in yellow spots. The two men walked slowly, quietly toward the dark shape of the building.

Jim saw the doctor walking next to him out of the corner of his eye. Was this the man? He'd started to remember. Barnhouse had told him, "There are others, Falk. There are others who are realizing the danger. There are others who know that the Evil One seeks to destroy the Way. They will come. They will come for me and for you."

Jim smiled and smiled. He saw the church up ahead. He saw its little roof, the hand-worked walls, the glowing windows, the smallness of the place that made it look like a smoking stove in the middle of the road.

He remembered his pa teaching him about places such as this, places hidden away in the mountain where time stood still, where the people were God's people, and where evil from the old days came to dwell.

"Old Bendy's Men lived in these hills at one time," his pa had told him. "That's why these places become such places. That's why no one is too much interested in passing through these places anymore. Maybe they don't even know why they don't go through a certain way. They just get a sense of it. The thing is that there were these men here. Long before the River People came to know this place. Long before even a lot of these animals. There were these evil men here and we seen 'em. We seen 'em in visions and in the land, back in the waves of time, and sometimes we just plain out seen 'em."

They stopped in front of the church.

A few low voices could be heard from inside.

The doctor looked at Jim's silhouette in the fog. Jim was tall and thin and his hat was on and his coat was raggedy and worn. In the fog he looked a bit like a scarecrow made out of outlaw clothes. He had an axe in his left hand and the pack on his back where he kept what else the doctor didn't know. The doctor had an idea, but he didn't know. Jim Falk was a man of the Way, though. The doctor knew that now for sure. Jim Falk was a man of the Way and what else was in his pack was for the ridding out of spirits or for destroying evil.

Jim Falk looked at the old doctor. The old doctor was thick in the chest like a barrel and his glasses twinkled in the church light. The doctor had brought along with him a little pistol and he was holding it out in front of him and to the side. Jim saw the doctor's eyes flickering about keenly in the fog. He could see the light in the doctor's eyes. He felt sure that there was something much, much more about this old doctor that Jim was supposed to find out and know. There was something deep inside the doctor that was beyond Jim to see right now.

Now things were quieted down. There were voices in the church, but they were hurried whispers. It was still outside the church and someone was whimpering on the inside.

Jim and the doctor walked in a small circle with their backs facing the other's. Nothing happened.

The wind blew a little and the fog swirled. Jim felt the tug and dull moving in his chest. The jitters, just like that, started up.

Jim nodded to the doctor and jerked his head in the direction of the stairs to the church door. The doctor, pointing his gun out into the darkness, made his way backwards up the steps.

Then there was a noise from somewhere beyond what they could see in the dim swirls of fog. It was a dark sound, an intake of breath that made the fog twist and race out of sight and then shift and move back.

Jim whispered, "See who's in the church and get inside there."

The doctor turned to try the lock. As he did so, he saw one of the shadows near the church crouch.

He didn't move. His left hand, reaching for the iron latch to the door, began to shake.

Jim was facing the other way.

The doctor did not want to look back. Doc Pritham had never seen anything like what he had just seen. Whatever was crouched down there, it was inky and thin and wicked-looking.

He froze up.

Then he saw Jim moving quiet and fast behind him. "Get inside, Doc!" Jim said in a low voice. "Get inside!"

The doctor heard something else too. Something close to him, whispering to him, calling him. Whispering something twisted into his mind.

He rattled the handles and heard the folks inside holler. The door was blocked and he couldn't move it. Behind him he heard a sudden noise like a grunt, and he looked to see Jim battling against something in the darkness.

He pointed his pistol at what he thought he saw.

There, in the shadow beside the wall of the church, something had its pointed, long fingers dug into Jim Falk's back. There was hair on the fingers, shining black hairs. Something of it made the doctor think of a horsefly. He got a sick feeling and drew back the hammer on his pistol. He saw the thing's black eye roll and twinkle. It was looking at him. It was tearing away at Falk, but it was looking with one dark eye right at the doctor.

Then the doctor got a sense of stillness about him. He felt he suddenly was filled with a power. His hearing and vision sharpened, and he stepped down the steps without fear toward where Jim was being whipped around in the shadows. The doc's gun trained in effortlessly on the dark spot where its head must have been.

He saw the thing's eyes now, black and twinkling in the darkness—its face something like a man's face without a nose, the gray spotted skin on its neck, the broken glass teeth in the black maw glittering and something like tubes reaching from inside toward Jim's face.

Jim's hatchet shone in the church light as it shot up into the air and then landed heavy and cracked on the thing.

Jim sprang backward, away from the creature and toward the doctor, and the doctor pulled his trigger.

The powder flashed them both blind for a moment. He'd missed the thing's head, but the shot must have met a mark somewhere in the creature's body. The wiry shape of the thing shuddered and toppled back into the shadows with a squeal and then a deep, sawing groan.

Jim and Doc Pritham stood in burning anticipation for the next mêlée, squinting into the blackness about the little church. Then they saw its wild and crooked form scampering off into the edges of the fog. Somehow, it appeared to spread and expand into the edge of the woods as it went into the fog.

The fog rolled back into the surrounding woods, and the moon broke from the clouds and suddenly shone bright onto the church. On the ground by the stairs were steaming little pools of some liquid.

The doctor broke open his bag and dropped to the ground. This might be the blood of the thing, he thought. He pulled a glass dropper, put the tip in one of the little pools, and began squeezing the bulb.

The doctor was busy collecting when he saw Jim's left hand snatch the brown bottle again from his satchel and take it to drink.

"You're going to reverse the effects and lose your memory permanently if you keep on!" the doctor shouted up at him.

Jim put the bottle hastily back into the pouch. The night looked like day to him now. Sparks leapt from the edges of things, the door to the church glowed red like a warning. "Step aside, good doctor," Jim murmured.

Jim knocked at the door of the church. He'd thought the jitters would have gone, but they hadn't and yet they weren't exactly the same. His breath was coming out now in heavy white wisps. He looked down to see that his bandage had been ripped asunder in the struggle with the creature. He could see the blood spotting on his tattered bandage and the puffy white flesh of his healing hand.

He knocked again, ignoring the red glow of the door becoming ever brighter.

He could hear someone move up to the door and through the red light, could see a black mass.

"Folks? Folks? You can open the door now. We're here to help, the doctor is here with me."

Jim turned to the doctor. "Why are they all in there?"

The doctor said, "Sometimes they go there when they're scared."

Jim put his ear to the door. He heard whimpering and whispering; no answer came to him from inside the church, but he could feel the people on the other side. He could feel the fear. Jim wondered if Bill and Violet might be in there. He wondered if, when they came and opened the door, Bill Hill might level his rifle at him and blast him. He wondered if May was inside. He thought of how her face looked when he woke up. He saw her sweet hands pouring the medicine into the cup.

"It's Jim Falk!" he said louder now at the door. "The outlander. I'm out here with the doctor and whatever there was to fear out here in the night, it's gone. It's run off. Now you don't have to open the door if you don't want to. You can keep it shut if you're safe in there. But if anyone is hurt in there, the doctor can come in and give them a hand. Can you open the door?"

"Doc Pritham?"

A young girl's voice came through the door, but Jim didn't recognize it.

Jim said, "Hey!" to the doctor, who was carefully squeezing droplets of the black liquid he had collected into a tiny glass vial.

"Who's that?" the doctor yelled at the door, barely looking up from the task at hand. "Is that you, Merla? It sounds like Vernon Mosely's daughter," he said to Jim.

The doctor put his things away quickly and ran up to the door. "Open this door!" he yelled. "Open this door!"

Jim saw the black mass getting bigger and bigger, coming toward the door.

"Get back!" he shouted at the doctor and pushed him sideways as the wood of the shattering door burst into the night. Something came running.

Vernon Mosely didn't have a memory of how he'd got back to Sparrow. He stood on the steps of the church and looked around. The sun was coming up through the cold trees. He could see his breath in front of his face, floating and disappearing.

He was even too confused to think about the witch and what had happened. He just felt tired—too tired for his own mind. His head shuffled through all kinds of things but couldn't stay on one thing long enough to form a real thought.

Why had he come here to the church? He should have gone home. Were there people here, maybe waiting for him? Home to his wife and his daughters. He couldn't see their faces. His mind felt terribly heavy. He could have curled up in his bed and forgotten everything—his life, his learnings, his parents. Forgotten about Simon and the box with the thumb inside.

"This is the key," Simon said. "This is the token. Otherwise she won't even be there to talk to you. Her house won't even be there. She knows you're a man of the Way, Preach. It's your kind that drove her out here. She won't see you unless she knows that you're not of the kind that want her dead. But there's a real kind of magic that's been put over her. I don't know what it is or where it came from. Only with this piece of her can you find her."

Why had he come here to the church? What was it that he needed? To tell someone something? The old hag had sent him on his way. She'd said something. He couldn't draw it up. When he tried to remember her words, he was stricken suddenly with the twinkling eyes of the shadow thing that had burned its mark on the wall.

Here at the steps of the church, he felt warm. He started to feel safe.

"Everything is all right," he whispered to himself and sat down on the steps. Something had happened. He shook his head. He put his hands up to his face and put his palms into his burning eye-sockets, rubbing. He was tired. He put his left hand down in something sticky.

Something had happened here at the church. There was blood on the steps. There was blood on the steps and splintered wood all around. The door was destroyed.

He heard the Starkey boy talking in his memory: "A witch like that spends a lot of her time saving up energies for keeping herself young and alive. Who knows how long she's been around? Even with the thumb, she can't even always be found, Preacher."

He got up and looked. Nobody was around. There were black spots in the grass out here, as if something had burned the spots; the grass was black and crisp and dead. He went in and looked. He looked in the corner where Bill's cot was. Bill's cot was there, but Bill wasn't in it. Nobody was inside.

Vernon Mosely walked slowly up the aisle, step by step, looking into the pews on either side of him. Expecting to see someone there. Someone sleeping or someone hiding; he didn't know. He felt, though, that someone was there. There was a heavy feeling on the back of his neck, as if someone was watching him. He was tired and his mind ached. His heart fluttered in his chest and a heavy dizziness started to flush his face.

He walked against some force, slowly up to the pulpit, underneath the plain sign of the meeting of heaven and earth. His hands went cold.

A little sunlight had begun flickering in through the windows. It lit the dust in the church. It caught him across the face, but his eyes didn't catch the light; they held a darkness about them.

He got up there by the pulpit and leaned on it, looking around the church: all the empty pews, the blanket on the cot pulled onto the floor, blood on the floor, mud on the floor, an abandoned glove on the front pew. Something's happened here.

Weakly he called out, "Hello?"

The use of his voice caused him to get dizzier, and his vision started to blank out.

Nobody answered him.

There was nothing around but the broken door and the smear of blood by the broken door. Strange spots of blood, sharpened, red marks, as though made by hooves, drying in the sun through the windows.

He turned to the Sign, the sign of the meeting of heaven and earth, hoping for an answer from the touching arrow shapes.

Vernon's heart was fluttering again in his chest. A nausea came up in back of his throat; the feeling in his hands and arms and chest disappeared so that he only felt a floating and his knees buckled.

He fell. He curled around, away from the podium, and tilted his head so that he could look up and see the Sign, the two planes touching. Heaven touching earth. "When? Oh God, please soon," he said.

He reached for it with his hand, but he could not feel his arm.

He was curled up there in a ball on the floor as if he'd been struck. Then he felt a burning in his arm and face and in his mind.

The things that had happened at the witch's crawled up in the back of his throat and stuck into his neck and head like pins. What would happen to him now? He frowned and bit his lip. Somewhere in his body, from where he could not tell, pain fired and twisted. His left arm tightened and twisted crooked in an unnatural way.

What of his wife, his home? What of his daughter, Merla? He saw again the black eyes, the spiny horns, the curved claws. They would come for them all. His hand seized up at the end of his gnarled arm.

They would come. He gasped again at the pain. Maybe not to-night, maybe not tomorrow night. But they would come. He knew now. He knew what was happening. The writings, the teachings, his parents, his whole life it seemed, bubbled and frothed with an oily poison in his mind. No, it hadn't been the outlander at all who had brought these evils to these innocent people. It was him that had done it. It was him and his damned pride. That he could keep old secrets hidden, that he could . . . Again he saw the curving teeth and ripping spines, twitching in the darkness, hungry.

But how could he stop it? The outlander? The witch said to tell no one, but . . .

"Preacher?"

Vernon heard the voice, but he didn't recognize it straight off.

"Preacher, is 'at you back there?"

Now his eyes popped open, and he recognized the voice. He found a strength to grab hold of the side of the pulpit with his right hand and begin raising himself up.

He was trembling as he raised his eyes over the pulpit.

"Boy, you're in a state," said the voice.

The preacher looked at who it was, and there, standing in the middle of the little church, was the chicken man.

The preacher couldn't look right at the chicken man because it made him sick to look. But he had to look anyway. The chicken man was all mangled up, torn, stretched too far. Mangled up in a way where he ought to be dead, but he wasn't dead. He was standing there talking.

"Something else here last night, Preacher. Something else," said the chicken man.

The preacher locked his eyes on the wood of the pulpit in front of him. He was frozen and he couldn't look up at the broken thing that was talking to him. It wasn't the chicken man, but it was. The chicken man spoke in a hoarse and lisping way. Something changed around him and the room got colder and felt darker. The preacher felt as if someone was putting out the light in the back of his mind.

He heard the chicken man sliding his twisted legs toward the pulpit. He smelled the sweet stink of rot coming off of the chicken man.

"You're in for trouble," the chicken man's voice came, somehow deeper-sounding now. "You're in for trouble." There was sweetness in his voice, a sweetness like sleep. The church swirled away into a white pinhole.

"How long did you think you could hide from me?" the chicken man asked again angrily, but it was no longer the chicken man's voice. "Look at me, old man! Look at me!"

The preacher deeply dreaded what he would see, but he rolled his eyes up toward the voice.

It was not the chicken man who stood there. It was a terrible man, a terrible man he'd never seen. A terrible man with eyes that seemed both black and hot, and a sharp, bent way about him.

"Vernon Mosely," the terrible man said, "you are found. You are all found at last. We have awoken to find you all and you will all die. You cannot hide in hollows and behind the walls of this wooden hut that you call a place of worship, this shamble of rotten wood and dying faith. Your people will disappear from the earth along with the nonsense scribbled on the tattered animal hide you call scripture. We will find it. We can see it now."

Then there was a hand on his shoulder. "Preacher!" a voice shouted right into his ear now.

He was lying under the pulpit and looking at the ceiling feeling pain, but also relief. He was twisted up and he'd fouled himself, but the terrible man was gone.

Hattie Jones grabbed him up and propped him up on a stool and put his whisky flask under the preacher's nose. "Wake up, Preacher!"

Vernon opened one eye. His face felt numb. He couldn't see right.

"Morning, Preacher!" Hattie shouted in his face and laughed a little. "What a scene, what a scene! Where had you gotten off to? What did you find out?"

The preacher reached out and put his hand on Hattie's flask and Hattie stopped talking. He watched as the preacher put his hand on it and drew it close to his lips.

Hattie pulled the flask away from the preacher's snarled mouth and twisted the cap back on. "There's no need for that, is there, Preacher?"

Hattie helped the preacher over to one of the front pews and sat beside him.

"Here, Preach," he said and pulled a cloth from his pocket and began dabbing the preacher's forehead with the cloth.

Vernon tried at some words, but they wouldn't come. Out of the corner of his open eye he could see his left hand and arm, curled and gnarled at his side like a burnt stick.

Hattie started talking. "Something awful happened, Preacher. Where was you? Something came after us all when we was waiting for you. At least a lot of us did. We was all up in here with Bill Hill like you told us. Bill Hill started talking to everyone in a deep voice, but his eyes was closed the whole time. He was talking but nobody knew what he was saying. Then he got quiet for a real long time and then someone outside the church started whispering inside to Bill. It sounded like something was on the roof, like a big animal, and everyone was scared. Then when the doctor and Jim Falk got here, Bill stood up and told everyone that we shouldn't answer them if they called for us. But see, it wasn't like it was Bill Hill anymore. There was blood coming out of his mouth and his eyes were all white. Where was you at?"

There was a long pause between the two of them. The preacher was moving his mouth and kind of moaning something.

"What?" Hattie asked him.

The preacher groaned, but his mouth moved in a way that didn't make words.

Hattie looked at the preacher's face. It looked as if Vernon had been hit by a lightning strike. "Preacher!" he shouted. "Looks like you got hit by lightning strike. Your face is all black and your eye! My goodness, Preacher."

Hattie sat there looking at the preacher for a minute. The preacher didn't say anything at all. He was just staring straight ahead at the pulpit. Hattie took a drink from his silver flask. He took another drink. He stared at the pulpit for a minute with the preacher.

"Yeah," he finally said. "Yeah, Preacher. Who would believe it? Who would believe it?" Hattie took another drink and then screwed the cap back on and slid it away into his inside pocket.

"Who would believe all this? Wolves and then a monster in the night. A monster in the night, crawling on the roof, Preacher. Then a dead man wakes up and looks like a demon is inside of him and breaks down the door and runs off into the night. You should have seen it, Preacher. Monsters and dead people. Monsters and dead people. I couldn't believe it. I'm sittin' there lookin' at Ruth and she's lookin' at Bill Hill's body. Bill Hill's body is layin' there and he's not breathin'. And I'm sittin' there lookin' at it. He's dead. Dead as dead. And he ain't movin'—and then that thing outside starts in a whispering and this moan comes up out of Bill's body like he's groanin' or something and this terrible stink comes out of him. It was awful and some of the women got sick and started to cry and some of the men got sick too. Then he was totally still for a long time. Then the thing outside, or whatever it was, starts scratchin' at the walls. We thought it was a wild man at first, like one of the River People, except that all of a sudden we could hear it up on the roof scratchin' on the roof, like I said. We were waitin' for it to burst through the windows. It must not have been very strong, or maybe it wasn't smart, or maybe there was something about the church that it couldn't get in, but it couldn't get in. Who would have believed it, Preacher? Who would have believed it? Then it was pounding at the door and whispering into the cracks in the door and I swear, Preacher, we could see Bill Hill's mouth moving as it was whispering in here. It would whisper and then one of the women noticed and would say, 'Look at Bill! Look at his mouth! It's movin'!' We could hear kind of what it was that was being said, but all the time too, we weren't sure what we were seeing or hearing. We thought Bill Hill was dead, but then there was the possibility that maybe he wasn't dead at all. I mean, maybe he just wasn't dead at all. Maybe he was totally alive and maybe outside, this thing. This thing in the night. This monster or whatever it was, Preacher, maybe it was just something like an animal scurryin' around. And maybe the whisperin' in the door, maybe that was just the wind. Yes, I guess that coulda been. Or maybe that was the doctor and Jim Falk. That might be true, Preach. That might be the real truth of it, because I don't know how else a dead man could get up and tell us all to be quiet with a weird voice and not to answer the doctor and the outlander and then he up and run at the door and broke right through that door and knocked down the doctor and knocked that outlander off the steps and then tear off running out into the night like that. Preacher, are you even listening to me? Are you even listening to me? Preacher?"

Hattie looked into the preacher's face, but the preacher didn't seem to see him. The preacher was still breathing, but he just didn't seem to see him. He put his hand on the preacher's hand, and the preacher's hand squeezed his hand. From the preacher's open eye came tears, glistening in the sunlight that was coming now through the windows.

Huck was sleeping loudly. He was leaned up against the post.

May had no idea how he could sleep that way, "I have no idea how you can sleep that way," she whispered in the room.

Huck snorted a bit and then fell back into a deep sleep. May looked out the window of the shop. The sun was coming up. The fog had cleared outside and the sun was coming up. It lit up the muddy ground and shined through the trees.

She could see, from the window, the front of the church. She could see Hattie helping the preacher down the steps. The door looked as if someone had torn it into pieces and threw it all over the yard.

She was tired, but she didn't want to wake her pa. She was glad to see him finally knocked off to sleep.

May sat down on the window seat and watched the sun lighting up the crooked trees. She put her face against the window and tried to feel the heat of the sun, but the window was cold as ice. She rolled her eyes along the frame of the window and jumped. There on the window, on the outside of the window, two fat, black spiders wiggled in the wind. They both looked the same. They were frozen dead with the night's frost. They were facing each other as if they were looking at each other.

She shuddered and got away from the window and moved to the other one.

From this one, she could see the side of the church and the edge of the woods. She sighed and put her forehead up against the glass. A raccoon, a big one, was pacing back and forth at the tree-line, stopping now and then to stand up on its back legs and smell the air. It took its time, pausing and sniffing, figuring it all out. She smiled as its round body wobbled off into the autumn trees. She could hear the birds.

She was tired. Her pa had been up all night pacing back and forth just like that raccoon. Pacing back and forth in front of the windows and looking out into the night. He was sure that it wasn't safe to go out. He thought all those folk that had run up to the church had gone crazy.

"So what?" Huck said, looking out the window and up at the church. "So what? The wolves can't go in the church? Is that the idea? Wolves is natural, May. They're running out of food up on the mountainside. They came down here. They ate all the chickens and now they're moved on."

He patted her on the head. "Now they got talk of all kinds of things. One thing happens and the next thing you know, the town's full of monsters and magicians. So what? I tell you what, the people that believe in this nonsense about spooks and demons are more dangerous than the wolves."

Her pa was right. The night passed by. The wind blew. The fog curled, but no wolves came back, no monsters showed their faces.

Now Huck Marbo was snoring, his face smushed up against the beam in the middle of the big room.

He smiled a little and said something in his sleep. His smile was something that May loved to see, and he didn't do it but quick when he was awake. Since her ma was gone, if he did smile it usually got followed by his eyes getting tears in them.

So this was nice. He was there, smiling for a moment, saying something in his sleep with the sun coming in the windows.

She didn't know it, but he was dreaming of his daughter in the water and she sure was having some kind of trouble out there. She was having a time trying to stay stood up in the creek.

The dream was part memory and part dream. He laughed, watching her wade out into the middle, slipping here and again with the net in her one hand. Tumbling forward, almost dipping her tanned face and honey hair in the water and then somehow bending herself back, flashing her white teeth in her big smile.

"Lord, watch yourself!" Anna called from the creek bed.

Her voice shone into his mind. He could feel her fingers laced in his.

May sure was having a problem out there in the water.

Anna jumped in the water after her, laughing now and then turning toward Huck, scolding him, wagging her finger. "You'll ruin her yet."

She turned back to steady her daughter with her one hand and slipped and fell in up to her shoulders.

"You're no help!" Huck shouted through barking laughter. He jumped in now. Wresting them both, one in each arm, carrying them out of the cold waters, squealing and kicking.

Both of his feet, bare, digging into the mud and rocks of the banks of Sparrow Creek.

When he woke up, he could still feel her fingers laced in his and looking down at his hand, he saw that a shaft of sunlight shone through the icy window right on his hand, warming it. The sensation of it drifted away.

"You're up," May said. She was tinkering with the stove, getting it going, making some hot water.

"You been watchin' up at the church?" he asked.

"Yes," she said and yawned and stretched, "and the fog's cleared up and the sun's come up. I saw the preacher leaving the church with Hattie Jones, and the preacher looked like he was hurt."

Huck was tired for sure and after squinting out the window for a few and bobbing his head up and down, he sat right down in a chair and May came and sat with him at the little table by the post.

They sat there together in silence for a while and Huck looked at his daughter.

The reason for the way that his daughter could find a way to be happy and smile even in the midst of all this strangeness was because of her mother and the fact that she was like her mother. Her mother had shown May ways to be strong, but May had a streak in her that was no good. Not no good in a vile, awful way, but no good in a mischievous way where she just wouldn't listen and she had to go and find things out herself. To her father, she was lovely—a square face and straight, big teeth with deep, round eyes that had that same green tone as his. She was short but strong-shouldered, and now, though he still did not believe it, she was a woman.

And yes, even with all this strangeness about, she smiled in the sunshine. That was her mother's way too. Why are you smiling, Anna? Just because.

Now they were both up and drinking coffee together.

Huck looked across the little table at his daughter.

"May?" he asked and took a little sip, not looking in her eye, "let me ask you a question. What do you think is going on here?"

May looked at her coffee swirling around in the white cup. She looked out the window toward the church and squinted. She remembered Jim's words that she wasn't supposed to tell anyone what she had seen.

"Pa, I walked into town with Jim Falk the other morning," she said in a cool manner, still looking out the window.

Huck didn't make a sound and he didn't move his eyes from off his cup.

There was some quiet at the table.

May breathed.

Huck scratched the back of his neck and thought of Violet and what she said about the look in his eyes.

"When I was coming out of the house," she went on, "Mr. Falk happened to be coming down the road and he asked if he could escort me into town. I know you told me to stay away from him, Pa, but there didn't seem to be anything else that I could do at the time except for accept and go with him. Besides, with the strange things that the Hills were saying, they had me kinda scared."

Huck didn't say anything. He took a drink of coffee, then he said, "May . . ."

"Something about the way he asked me, Pa, the way he asked me is what made me think that it would be okay and safer to go into town with him. So he walked with me a while and it was strange out. It was strange and quiet out and things seemed muffled around us. Then we got to a point in the road and he started squinting and looking on ahead and he grabbed hold of me and told me to be quiet and we crouched down together."

Huck looked up at his daughter now. His eyes had gone into a deep green and were moving quickly back and forth. He was searching out her face to try and see if she was scared. She wasn't. He didn't think of it often, but sometimes he wondered what would happen about this. Since the bad winter, so many had died. So many of the young kids, they hadn't made it. It wasn't right. There was no one in Sparrow May's age except for Vernon's daughter, there were no boys for her to go chasing after or to be shy and coy around. The closest man to her age in town was that damned Simon, and he was still her senior. He shuddered at the thought of her wandering up to the Ridges to court.

So he listened. His blood boiled, but he listened.

"Pa," she said, "I could see something. I couldn't see exactly what it was, but it didn't look right. It looked like something dark and like a thing, not a person and not an animal. It gave me chills just looking at it. It was far away too, so I couldn't really make it out exactly except for the fact that it gave me these chills to look at it. Then it was off into the woods."

Huck sat up straight in his chair and calmly took a sip of his coffee. "What did the outlander do?"

"He brought me all the way into town and protected me from whatever it was. He said that it was a spook and that it was possible that the devil sent it."

Huck sipped again at his coffee. He said, "The Evil One."

"Pa, that's what Jim said."

Huck said, "That's what the outlander said. What do you think?"

"I don't know, Pa," she said. "What do you think?"

"I don't know, May. I just want you to be careful, May. That's all I want you to do. Be as careful as you possibly can."

He looked out the window. The sun was playing in the frost and in the wet pools of frozen mud. The birds were chirping.

May turned her head and looked out the window with her pa. Some of the sparkling of the outside came in through the window and gave her big, round eyes a twinkle.

Her pa looked at her face, glowing in the light.

"May," he said, "I think the sunshine was made just for you."

The doctor unwrapped Jim's bandages very slowly.

"You're healing so quickly," Doc Pritham said as Jim winced.

"How does it look?"

"Better. Your wounds are already closed."

The doctor did some wiping and smearing on of some other kind of stinking paste.

"I can still feel them," Jim said and stretched his thumb out a little. He stretched his index out and his middle.

The doctor half smiled and looked at Jim, who was looking away and out the window. The sun was coming up.

"When I move them," Jim said, "I can still feel the other two. How can that be?"

The doctor looked at Jim's hand, but said nothing. A wolf had taken away Jim's pinky and ring finger along with part of the hand. There was no getting it back.

Jim's face was fresh-shaven and the doc's medicine burned at the back of his throat. He didn't feel bad at all. He felt an energy inside him and maybe it came only from the medicine, but he had in him a certain hope as he watched the sun lighting up the little town outside of the doctor's place.

His eyes glinted as the doctor started slowly wrapping his hand.

The sun coming in the window lit up Jim's face, revealing the healing scars on his right cheek and the two long slashes below his left eye.

Jim sensed the doc looking at him.

"Lucky even that I have my eyes," Jim said and put his left hand on the fleshy marks there under his eye.

"You are right," Doc Pritham said, "you are right. If you believe in this thing called luck, then you are lucky." The doctor laughed a little, but Jim wasn't in the mood for laughing. Whenever he drank the doctor's medicine, it seemed like after the initial rush of feeling better, there came a time when memories kicked up in his mind. The medicine dragged his mind off to somewhere else.

Something was bothering him now about these things that were happening in the town of Sparrow. His mind reeled back in his memory, seeking for connections. His father, his mother, Old Magic Woman. His mind opened into a place he did not like, a place that had been sealed. It was the medicine, but he couldn't help himself.

Jim put the cup of medicine to his lips and took another drink. "There was an old witch that killed my ma, Doc."

The doctor finished up and sat back in his chair, looking at Jim, his eyes suddenly kind and deep. "Yes?"

Jim stared into the sunshine drinking the medicine. "Came right down from somewhere in the woods one night, dark and slippery. All the chickens had died just the day before, Doc, and we didn't know why. But I think my pa knew why. They were all dead and just rotted, like they'd been dead a long time. It put the fear in my ma something awful. That old witch. She'd been comin' around lookin' for me, like they often do children. Turns out, my pa had been keepin' her away with his craft and special barriers for years, which he knew how to make against her. But see, her power was growing somehow. Somehow the barriers weren't taking like they once did. My pa started lookin' to kill her. And to kill her, he knew he needed a special image of her. But she always kept her features and body in the darkness. One night, though, my pa tricked her by having me there in the barn like I was asleep. Had my ma out callin' for me like I was lost."

The outlander swallowed and his eyes danced around the edges of the window. He went on. "This was his plan to kill her. Kill that witch. My ma was out there hollerin' around for me like she couldn't find me." Jim stopped talking for a moment and lifted the cup to his lips. He tilted the cup back and it was empty. He stared into the empty cup and a desperate look came onto his face. He remembered.

His father, Ithacus, stopped screaming her name and fell down on both his knees in the wet grass. It must have rained, because water dripped from his coat and his shirt and his hat were drenched with cold water. He was just now starting to feel his skin burn with the cold. The next thought was of his little boy. Was he still in the barn? His voice was rough as he tried to call out to James. The rain wasn't in the sky any more and the October dawn came through the dark clouds in orange and blue over the grassy field. The barn was still in the shadows.

Ithacus turned and dashed toward a patch of downed grass and found the boy shivering and pale. The boy stared up at his father, but his eyes didn't see him. His eyes saw something terrible. Ithacus removed his long coat, which was still mostly dry inside, and wrapped his son inside. He picked up the boy in the bundle and tromped through the field as the dawn rose.

"Sarai!" He was out of breath, but he managed a cry and held close his boy. Wandering through the dim field in the rain, holding the boy to his chest, screaming. Screaming her name.

Ithacus's heart and mind drowned in confusion as he carried the heavy boy home. He wanted things. Odd things, like warm honey and whisky, like a fire and a fist fight. He wanted anything that would keep him from wanting her back, and yet part of him didn't believe she was gone. He wanted to kill the witch.

And then he thought of the witch and deepest hatred burned in his chest and arms. He held the boy tighter and looked to his left and right and up into the air to make sure her black, shivering shadow wasn't twisting at him from some unexpected angle. The hate made him sick. His mind moved to the barn again as his boy coughed and spat. He thought of the book and the instructions he could remember. What if it worked?

That book, that bundle of old pages that Spencer Barnhouse had given long ago to Ithacus's father. The book had long since been lost in the caves south of Rhymer, but he'd remembered in detail the pictures he'd memorized as a kid on how to build the flash box and how to make the special paper for catching the image. Maybe the witch thought he still had those pages; maybe that's why she'd finally come all the way down.

Bendy's Men had chased him all through the swamps and caves for those pages. Then again, maybe the witch wanted to do with little James just the thing that witches do. He thought of the sketch of the flash box and the words that were penned in the black ink in a square around the drawing. What if it worked?

He got James up in the house and got him out of the wet clothes and, after a while, into a warm bath. They looked at each other throughout the process but did not speak. Both Falks had blue eyes. Though Sarai's eyes were brown, her son had eyes like his father's and his father's father's. Ithacus looked at the boy in the washtub and saw something different from what was there. He saw the boy in Sarai's arms. His wife's eyes gleamed in the setting light of the sun as she too looked upon the new child.

He was little more than a red and pink and wriggling bundle of wrinkles, but his eyes blinked and caught light under the long blond lashes. Sarai Falk held the boy out with both hands and for the first time Ithacus grabbed up that life in his arms, that life so alive.

Sarai's face was soft and sharp with the high cheekbones and broad, black eyes of her mother, and now her dark lips burst into a white smile of small, square teeth. "What will his name be?" she said and immediately with strong hands and arms pulled him back to her. Ithacus's gaze leapt from her eyes to the bundle in her arms and back again.

"James," Ithacus said. "His name is to be called James."

They had waited to name him. Waited to be sure he would live.

Sarai beamed at her boy and then reached out with her hand and traced along Ithacus's cheek and ran her finger down the long scar that ran from his temple to his chin. "He has your eyes."

At this, Ithacus's own face grew dark, the deep lines creased about his brows, and his eyes narrowed. He took a step toward his young wife holding the child and placed his hand on her back. With his other hand he drew her head close to his and leaned her head on his shoulder, looking at the boy. The child's eyes opened for a moment and his wide pupils rolled lazy in the center of blue irises. Sarai was right: his eyes were like his father's, and what would those eyes see? Crooked and dark images sprung up in his mind, and Ithacus shuddered at what those young eyes might grow to see. What scenes of joy and dread might play in front of those bright and tiny eyes? Ithacus kissed his beloved's head and walked to the edge of the fire.

They'd been on the move for too long.

The New Land held a kind of vicious bounty—offering as much food and shelter as danger. Too, Ithacus could feel the jitters at the crest of every hill and along the edges of every river, every stream; and at night, as his wife slept, he watched the shadows moving in the darkness.

There was an evil in this land, an older but familiar evil that Ithacus did not expect to find here. In fact, he had expected to escape it forever when he took his young bride and what few items they could and climbed aboard that strange boat in the dark.

Yet here they had found, high in a cliff bank, this winding cave that held no animal's lair and no stench of death, and that would serve well, if only for a short time. Until he had time to get what he needed to build a place and get some animals and do some planting.

From the little mouth of the cave Ithacus could see up and down the river, and there was only one path that lead up to the opening of their cave. Over and behind them were nests and coils of a thick and almost impenetrable thorned vine, and among them

were thorn-covered trees, the likes of which Ithacus had only vi-
sioned in tales and bad dreams, yet there they were. Tall and
mean-looking with hard, barbed leaves, an animal or man who
dashed into those trees for cover would sooner bleed to death than
escape a pursuer. It was a fit spot for safety.

So here they had come to rest and here this boy had been born
in the deeps of the cave. Perhaps this would be where they would
make a new home, but only time would tell.

Already the cold October winds moved the pines along the long
and muddy river. Already the leaves of other trees began turning to
gold and red. While out past the thorns and brambles, Ithacus
hunted in the rich forest behind the ridge and brought home rabbits,
deer, and many small, cold fish which he prepared special and
which gave Sarai and the baby strength. They drank the bright water from the streams that rolled down the mountainside, and Sarai
and Ithacus told stories of their parents and the old country, and
they laughed in the warm sun at the cave's mouth and the baby
laughed too.

Sometimes shadows crept to the river's edge—the long, lean,
odd shadows of living things, maybe mountain cats, maybe wolves,
but they were soundless. Ithacus and Sarai kept the fire back away
from the mouth of their cave, but still the smoke rolled into the
sky, and sometimes at night Ithacus would watch the gliding
shadows at the water's edge. At times they were fast and liquid-like
and seemed to rise up into the pines, but other times they hulked
and paced at the water's edge. Stopping and unmoving they seemed
to be feeling through the dark, or looking, looking through the dark
for Ithacus and his woman and the baby. Sometimes Ithacus
thought he saw long, thin shadows, like snakes, twisting from the
wood's edge and toward the cave, but when he looked again they
were gone.

Ithacus knew that if these were what he feared—and were not
men, or cats, or wolves—it would mean they were something
darker. Darker things than he expected to find in the New Land. It
also meant that these shades and shadows could not cross over the

water and would have to find and wind some other way along the water's edge until they came to an end to the river, a bridge or fallen tree, or some other place that was strange and would let them pass over.

He grimaced at the thought of that darker power giving them a way to cross and letting them come slinking up the Ridges to the cave. Even along the pass where he could see, he stayed up nights dreading that the shadows would come and that they would have teeth.

But for a long time the shadows did not come.

The shadows did not come for a long time, and the boy grew strong and wild and his mother taught him well the ways she knew.

Ithacus woke up from his dream of the old days. The memories passed out of his mind, a warmth giving way to a cold wind. She was gone. Sarai was gone.

Neither James nor his father knew how much time had passed. It seemed to them that the sun was moving in a different way. At times the light would dim through the windows and darken until both were sure that the night had fallen; and yet, through glittering tears, they would watch as their little house lightened again. Too, the hard rain of last night had changed to a strange dust of snow that came even when the sun shone and blues broke through the gray clouds until time seemed mixed and the day or night no longer mattered. The boy didn't get out of the warm water of the tub for a long time. His father would wake from a heavy sleep now and again and put wood in the stove and get the water boiling and pour it into the tub.

Later, James's mind might stab at him with the memories of the witch. If it hadn't been for this plan, his mother would have lived. If it hadn't been for him, for his wretched father.

But then, his mind immediately removed itself from those thoughts as if the thoughts were flame and he would sink into sleep and younger memories.

It wasn't enough that the little pig had learned its way out of the pen, but it would stick its nose in the air now and buck its snout, laughing. James ran in the mist. Again and again he heard the wet drumming of the little pig's feet going along this way and that, and he turned again this way and again that way to follow. His own bare feet slapped hard the cold mud. He couldn't see it, but it was out there.

Soon he heard his pa holler from in back of him somewhere. His pa was mad. James wanted to train up the little pig; he'd seen its own special pig smarts and liked how it laughed at its own smarts, jutting its little face up in the air, proud and looking around.

An open patch in the fog appeared and he could see the fresh little hoofmarks dug in the mud, skittering off one way or the other. This went on, zig and zag, his pa hollering, the tiny thumping of the hooves, the fog swirling and clearing with the sunshine.

James stopped short, his head pounding, his feet burning with the cold mud. He listened. He closed his eyes and listened. No noise. No hooves. With his eyes still closed, he tilted just a bit to his left and then burst, disappearing into a heavier patch of the fog. Emerging with the squealing, kicking piglet. Laughing with little Eli in his bare arms.

And then he woke in the warm tub in the strange weather. His father was standing by the stove, looking out the front window out toward the barn.

"James," he whispered, "get your clothes on and go feed the pigs."

Hot tears came from the boy's eyes, but he splashed water in his face to hide them and clambered out of the basin and headed to his room. Pulling on his pants, he heard the front door open and shut and knew that his pa had walked out into the strange weather to see about the witch trap.

James came into the hay barn to find his pa standing at one end with the weapon. He'd only caught sight of the ax once before. The strange ax with its shining, waved blade and curved and heavy handle. His pa stood with his head down. There were candles lit on a path in the dirt all along to a post in the center of the barn. There on the post was a pale square of paper. Upon the pale square of paper was burned the image of the witch. The face on the square was even more hideous than what James had imagined as he lay there with the thing breathing over him. What made it so terrible was that the real face of the witch was a person's face. It was a dead face and filled with broken shards of teeth, slashed with cuts, bruised, the eyes even seeming to be squeezing from the sockets. The thought that there could be any life in that face was what made him sick. Anything that looked like that ought to be dead, but there was no mercy in the Devil's Way.

"If you're not going to feed the pigs," his pa said, "stand away."

He did as his pa took a deep breath and then a deeper one and then his pa's body seemed to go limp as if he were about to fall over. Without warning his pa's arm whirled, the post thudded, and the silver blade rang as it marked deep in the post and right through the wicked image with a whistle. The candles blew out and off somewhere in the strange weather of the morning a howl went up that pitched into a wail and then into a screech that made the hairs on James's neck rise up. His pa looked toward the barn doors and then back at the post.

The picture was bleeding.

The doctor was sitting there looking at him and when he saw the medicine was all gone and that Jim had stopped talking he said, "Falk, I can't give you any more of that medicine until tomorrow."

Jim frowned.

"It'll poison your blood permanent," the doctor completed.

"It doesn't matter. She's dead. There's no getting her back."

"I suppose not," the doctor said.

"If I can't have any more medicine, give me some whisky."

The doctor nodded and, getting up, clinked around for a few seconds and then returned with a little mug of sweet-smelling whisky and put it in Jim's left hand.

Jim sipped it and coughed a bit and said, "That creature, that thing, the witch, whatever she was . . ." He turned and looked at the doctor. "There I was, lying in the hay, my eyes shut, and that thing came slinking in by way of the high window and she came right down close to my face. Like a spider, Doc."

He looked up at the doctor's eyes. "She eased herself down through the air like that." He made the motion with his good hand, the hand floating down. "And only the devil knows how."

Jim drew in a deep draught of air and looked back out the window. "I kept quiet like I was sleeping, but I could feel her there. I could smell her cold, terrible breath. I wonder. I think sometimes I wasn't convincing enough. Why did she leave? Why did she go after my mother?"

Doc Pritham watched him close to make sure his eyes stayed alert and his face didn't turn blue. This was a side-effect of this treatment, memories and truths sometimes uncontrollable rolling out of the patient. He could see Falk's eyes were fading in and out of here and now and were floating off somewhere else. Falk's eyes would roll and then close and then open and roll again.

For a moment the doctor thought it was all over. Falk nodded and was still. Then Falk's head jumped up and started talking again. "I kept my eyes closed tight, but she was there and I could feel her black eyes moving over my body. I could see her face in my mind. A wrinkled, white mask with shining black eyes and sharp, broken teeth. My pa was hiding and flashed a powder trap on her that caught her image on a special plate . . . but she grabbed me in her raggedy hands and stole me up toward that high window. It banged my head against the ladder and I went out. Just like when the wolves got me in the woods, Doc. Just like when I ran from the fire. Just like when I ran from Kitaman. Just the same as that night."

Falk reached out with his left hand without looking and, picking up the small cup, drank the rest of the whisky. His eyes came back from that faraway place where they were and focused again on the doctor.

The doctor saw it then in Falk's eyes. He saw the light. It almost appeared as if far back in Falk's head somewhere there was a tiny sky and in that tiny sky there were stars, stars like when the lake is still and the night is black and the stars are strewn across the blackness. It twinkled there and disappeared as if it had never been and Falk yawned, not seeming to take any notice of anything but that he was tired and wounded. Made it seem certain the light had never been.

The doctor opened his mouth. "What was that outside the church, Falk?"

Jim looked down into his cup. "I wonder if it matters. Does it matter if we know? If it is evil, if it's the evil we think it is. Maybe there is nothing to be done. Maybe we can't stop it. How can we stop it? What did you see, Doc? Did you see a monster? Did you see evil? If you did, if it is that evil, do you really think we can stop it? A doctor and a drunk ghost-killer?" Jim asked, turning his face back toward the window and the sunlight. "I've been running so long."

The doctor stood and, rubbing his chin, walked to the window and looked out the window with Jim Falk. In the doctor's little yard frost was over everything, the grass, the mud. The sun was bright and yellow and the sky was almost blue for the first time in a while. The sun sparkled in the frost on the grass and brown mud.

The doctor and the outlander looked at the morning together. Neither of them talked. Even as the pink sun slowly lighted the sky and the birds twittered in the cold air as though spring had come early, no words. No words for a long time, just the sun growing orange and melting the silver frost on the window.

The doctor grunted uneasily. He turned away from the window and reached into his front pocket for his pipe. He got it out and packed it with tobacco and lit it and started smoking it.

# CHAPTER 13

Benjamin rubbed the soap chunk furiously over his hands. Lane was making hot water on the stove to bring to him.

Though the night had been cold and strange and lonely, her husband had come back with something different. Something there was different about him, but she couldn't quite know or say what it was. There was an energy to him that wasn't there before and she could see it in his eyes and it felt like an energy that was good.

She watched him now with his shirt off in the sink working hard to get the blood off. His massive frame and white skin with freckles all over was charged with effort. He looked like a large boy suddenly to her, and was he smiling? He turned and looked at her and there was a wonder of sorts in his eyes. She brought the pot and poured the warmed water into the basin where he worked the blood off his skin.

"The outlander," he said. "The outlander was in the woods and the wolves had him. It was exactly like what happened to Dirty, it was exactly like what happened to my pa."

She handed him a fresh shirt and he put it on.

He turned to her and she sat down in front of him on the chair.

He started talking and waving his arms as he talked.

"I went up after I was at Huck's; they had me deep into the telling of that story of my father." Benjamin Straddler looked down, a frown growing under his nose. "They wanted to hear it. I didn't want to tell it, Lane, but they wanted to hear it, Simon wanted me to tell it again, so I told it. When them wolves were howling and everything was going on, I grabbed up my gun and ran out the front door. There was howling coming from everywhere. I ran out. I ran out with my gun and just ran everywhere. I wasn't sure where I was going. I ran around everywhere and wound up in the woods with the wolves and the outlander. There were so many, though. More than I've ever seen before. Something different about them. The smell. There was a smell, it was awful. I can't hardly believe now when I think about it that it's possible for there to be so many wolves up in them woods. And they just kept coming. I was going to shoot, but I didn't know where to shoot, and if I shot, then I'd have to reload soon enough and what if one jumped on me? There were so many! Soon enough, though, I was up on a path and I saw his body. I saw his body lying there in the mud in the path and I could see the wolves that were tearing at it and so I fired, but I fired up into the air and all around. There were some wolves on him, but I didn't want to hit *him*."

He sat down at the table because he had to. He touched Lane's arm and then let go and started stuttering and looked at her and looked back at the table with his arms spread out, looking into the table as if it was a mirror. A tear came straight down his left cheek and hit the table.

"I guess I scared them off. I scared those wolves off."

She reached across the table and put her little, white hands on top of his big, red hands.

"Lane," he whispered her name, "when I walked up to the body"—he shook his head and squeezed his eyes closed and opened them again—"I saw the face."

He was looking directly at something that wasn't there. He went blank and far away and another tear came.

Lane patted his hand. Her eyes were wide and expecting and looking seriously at her husband.

She saw his hard wrinkles softening, a gleam rising up in his eyes.

"What is it? What happened?" she asked.

Benjamin's mouth opened. "My father," he said. "It was my father."

Lane didn't know what to do. She squeezed his hands tight with hers. Some birds chirped outside in the rising sun.

"Your father?" she finally asked and then pressed her lips together.

"That's why I picked him up. I picked him up and slung him on my back because he was my father." Here Benjamin paused again and his eyes moved from the wood of the table to meet his wife's gaze. Her mouth was shut tight. Her eyes were watery with the effort of holding back.

"But I looked at his face, Lane. I looked at his face." He put his hand out into the air over the table between them and patted it a bit. "I touched his face and it was my father. It was old Dirty Straddler laying there in the mud. I picked him up and slung him over my shoulder and ran him back down to Huck's because I couldn't believe it. The whole way I was yelling at him that I had him and that it was going to be okay. I don't know how exactly I believed it, but I believed it because it was real. And I ran into town. Ran through the fog and got him back and banged on Huck's door and he opened it and everyone's gone and May is locked away still and there's some kind of commotion out in the fog. I sling the body out onto one of the long tables. Huck is yelling at me, 'Not in here!' 'Don't bring him in here!' and I laid into Huck something awful with curses out of my mouth and filth that I have never heard before."

Benjamin put his head down on the table.

"When I looked at his face, Lane. It wasn't my father at all."

Lane was about to speak when Benjamin said, "It was Jim Falk. It was the outlander."

The journey down from Hopestill had not allowed Jim Falk much sleep. Some days he was sure that he had found a way to sleep and run at the same time. Other times, he ate the Leaves so he could see in the dark and for the extra bursts of energy they gave him to run on through the night.

They were after him, though, he was sure of it. Whoever they were. They were coming.

Barnhouse had not known enough yet to explain it all to him, but he had explained enough of it. Barnhouse was good at keeping secrets, but he said, "These men are not from around here, they're cruel men and they're good at finding out secrets."

Sometimes he thought he saw them through the trees, their hats distinct and square among the moving black branches. Sometimes he swore he heard the dogs barking over the horizon. Sometimes the pounding of his feet and the thumping of his heart in his chest were the only noises on the earth. The days came shorter and the nights cooled and stilled. The frost came onto the mountains. Still he ran. He thought of his father and of his mother. He thought of Spencer Barnhouse and his hidden books and papers. He wished for a clear path.

Now he rested under the sun and the pines around him. It was cold and winds blew harshly in the tops of the trees, telling him that snow was coming. He didn't build a fire for fear of them, but he had found a warmer patch where the sun was gazing through the canopy. He brought out a piece of stale bread and ate it. He drank warm whisky from his flask, and as the sweet metal taste of it hit his throat, he felt alone. Maybe thankfully he was alone, maybe something else had drawn them away. Something in his head told him that they would find the trail again, though.

He felt at his new weapons in his pack and wondered if it would be worth it all. He wondered if there really was any way to rid out these things that had come to the land. He wondered if he hadn't lost his mind long ago when his mother died and his father was dragged into darkness. Maybe he was just crazy. Maybe the things that happened were just a group of things that had happened all at once and terribly and his mind had no other way to put them together. Maybe the dreams of the red-haired woman and the dark figure and the little town with the arrow-shaped church were the visions of a madman. They were his visions, though, so he had little choice.

The sun came in on him and he ate and breathed. He thought of his father. He thought of his mother. He thought of the dead face of the witch and the thing that had grabbed his pa.

He saw his father disappearing into that black space . . . the hideous arm reaching out, the evil hand clutching his father's head.

He groaned as his mind took him back to that place. The memory, when it came, clouded out all his other senses. The smell of the rain and dirt in the grass, the sick smell of the witch's decayed body on the fire spit. Those creatures turning the spit and whatever they were saying to one another, and then, that blackness, the hole—disgust came over him in waves like a heat.

Jim saw the wicked hand with curling black veins clutching the back of his father's head. Ithacus's eyes were wide, his mouth open, but he did not look at his son. He looked up, up as if he had been praying. He did not speak or cry out. He waved his arms wildly around him, grasping for his hatchet. He grabbed it and threw it, but toward Jim. Then he was gone into the hole and then the hole was gone. It didn't shrink, it didn't disappear in a puff of black smoke. It was just gone. Gone as if it had never been there before, and so was Jim's father, only the strange hatchet lay on the ground.

Ithacus had brought James along and he was sure that the two of them would at long last be rid of this witch. Jim wished they had not gone. Jim wished he could have been brave.

"Boy," his father said to him, "we must do this thing. We must. The witch must die. The hatchet trick may not have been enough to kill her."

He handed his son a silver pistol. "You point this end, see? And if she comes at you, you point this end at her face, right at her face, it has to be at her face. Do you understand?"

His son nodded.

How his father knew what way to go through the dark woods; James did not know. He held the heavy pistol and followed.

Soon they were crouching at the edge of a hill. There was a sickly sweet and pungent roasting smell in the air and a fire smoked and lit the clearing below them. His pa said something to him that made his skin cold. "Old Bendy's Men."

It was just a few of them, but they were there.

"Look, look!" he said. "They're burning up the witch and eating her! They haven't noticed us. They're so consumed."

James did not want to look. He heard crunching and chattering.

"They must be weak because she is dead, they're trying to eat up her powers."

James did not want to look.

His father pulled the hatchet. "There are only two of them. Remember, aim right at their faces, right between their eyes. Don't be afraid of them, just breathe deep and aim between their eyes. Right where the nose should be. Do not be afraid of them."

Suddenly his father was rushing at the fire, but James was frozen.

He whispered, "Pa, no, I can't."

"Shoot!" his father was yelling now. "Shoot them!"

When James stood up, he saw the black hole, he saw the hand pulling his father in, tossing the hatchet.

Jim Falk hated the memory and sometimes hated his father too: why would he take his little boy to do something so terrible, so dangerous? But deep down, he knew his father only wanted Jim to become who he was meant to be.

He got out his whisky and drunk deep. He counted his leaves and put them back. He opened his rifle case and glanced it over. He took another drink. Wherever this rifle had been made, it was one of the lightest long guns he'd ever seen and it was a deep blue and black. It reminded him something of a fish in murky water. There was something like a dragon on the handle, tiny with its mouth curled toward the muzzle. The blues and blacks of the rifle looked to change so that it hid from the sunlight through the trees and even in his hand, when he turned it this way and that, it would not reflect the light. These men in Hopestill, that Barnhouse had taken the weapons from whoever they were, they were stocking up special weapons and other things for a reason. Where were they coming from? He didn't know why, but he knew that it could not be for good. He shined his father's hatchet and put it back in his belt. He took a bit more whisky.

He thought of his father's face.

"Trouble in all shapes and shades," he mumbled, reciting the old words he had often heard his father say. "Trouble in all shapes and shades," he said again to the woods around him and rolled up his gear sack, getting ready to move again. If he moved just right, if he ran fast enough, maybe he could leave the memories behind him.

But suddenly, pain was on him.

He bent down on one knee. He squeezed his temple with his right hand and blood ran from his left nostril and over his lips. This happened sometimes before a vision came. He got dizzy and came down on all fours. The world around him faded away. The sunlight faded, the trees faded, his gearsack faded away.

He saw the little town again—the little town nestled on the creek. He saw the woman's red hair, like vines, flickering and winding around her face. Behind her was a shadow with glimmering eyes and a shape behind her, a dark shadow shimmering and making the woman speak. There was something so familiar about the shadow, yet it was a sinister thing.

Then the church appeared. It was in the shape of an arrow, pointing straight to the sky. It was gold and then it was black and then it was the shape of a sparrow and then it was gone.

When he woke up, it was night. The woods were dark and in the distance he could hear something crunching through the woods and leaves. What it was he couldn't quite make out. Maybe a bear, a dog? His mind was cloudy, overlapping with the visions and the world around him. He wasn't sure if the visions were over yet or if the real world had been given a chance to come back. What was the difference? Would it make a difference if he knew? Sometimes he didn't know if there was a difference at all between the real world around him and the world of the other side, where the visions came from. Maybe that was where his father went. Old Magic Woman might call it the realm of Kitaman. Spencer Barnhouse called it the Wyddershins. His father might have called it a splitway. Jim didn't know about any of that.

Jim knew the world only as it came to him; the pain in his head and the world came to him split in two.

His flask was nearly empty. He had to get somewhere soon. He knew he had to go to this little town, this little town called Sparrow. He also knew that something was coming toward him through the woods. He picked up his bag and he ran into the shadows and trees. He ran on through the night and he never looked back.

No one could see her face, but she was talking clearly and quietly and they all leaned their faces and ears toward her. There were just a few of them in the little room, but there were enough of them. She made it clear, as she always did, that no one could know. No one could know about the meeting; if it was your first time, you had to go off with one of the others and take a special oath.

After she said these things, she lit a candle and her pointed face appeared over it. The few that were there brought their faces into the light, and one by one they each looked one another straight in the eye and nodding heads.

Ruth Mosely set the candle down on the little round table in the middle of the room, and the few that were with her took their seats.

She spoke softly but surely. "A few nights ago, Benjamin Straddler came to our home and told us of the arrival of this James Falk. He told me that James Falk had come here looking to 'kill a spook' and that this man claimed to be what the River People call a 'ghost-killer' and that he had powers. Those of you who are with me tonight, who were with me last night when Bill Hill's dead body came to life"—she swallowed—"those of you who saw the face of the thing in the window, you are the ones who can make testimony."

A man with a brown hat on, his face in the shadows, said, "Bill

Hill died. He was dead and there was an awful stink. Then the thing in the night, it came and somehow made Bill's body start to talk. We all heard it. We couldn't understand it. It was like a bunch of nonsense. But one thing we could understand is the name it kept saying, it kept saying 'Do not answer, Faaalk.'"

A woman's voice said, "It was horrible."

A man's voice said, "It was awful."

An old man said, "These things came to town when the outlander came to town. It was calling for him. He must be the master of the things. I knew we shoulda moved up to them Ridges. Them people was right and I knew it."

Ruth said, "We knew this town has been headed in a bad direction for a while. It was God's will that the blizzard came on us. Was it not? It was to punish us for straying from the true path. Was it not? You could go up to the Ridges, but I will tell you this. The folks that live up in the Ridges have strayed from the path even farther than Sparrow. There's no good up there at all and this thing has come on us all. This James Falk is kind of a sign. He is a kind of warning. He has brought this evil with him; of that there is no question."

Now she swallowed again and stretched her neck up and down; her arms came in and rested on the table with their long fingers at the end. She put one hand on top of the other and looked around at the people at the table. "I spoke with my husband last night on such things as have been happening. We are in agreement that this Falk is what is written about in the writings as one of the killers of the Way. He has come to our town seeking to destroy us, to destroy the true teachings, rid out what's left of our good folk, send demons for the rest of us—and that's what he's brought with him. Called by Bill Hill's wife, Violet Hill, by way of some spell, as an act of revenge against us all and against this town. This is shown by the evil outcome of their acts. Powers to control the dead, powers to control wolves, and drawing demons from the dark places."

There were intakes of breath and clearing of throats.

Ruth continued, "James Falk is practicing the craft, Violet Hill is practicing the craft, the doctor has made a way for them, and

John Mosely and I have decided that we will deal with it as those in the North have been dealing with such things. We will have to deal with this according to The Old Law."

The man in the brown hat with his face in the shadows asked, "The Old Law? What? How?"

Ruth closed her eyes ever so slowly and said, "We cannot allow them to live. They may have the craft and the Evil One on their side, but we have God on ours and we have many. They are few."

A woman said, "But . . ."

There was silence for a long while. Ruth looked around at the people until she had caught the eyes of each of them and stared deeply into them.

"The Law," she said, "is The Law."

"But we don't know . . ." an old man said.

"We will take it up with my husband's brother, seeing that he is the preacher, but we will do what God says is to be done," Ruth said and looked at the woman next to her.

People's heads turned slightly as they peered at one another out of the corners of their eyes. Each one was searching for the re-action of the other, looking for doubt, or for a shaking head, but all the faces were strong with fear and their faces were like carved stones in the flickering candle light.

One of those faces was the face of the preacher's wife. Ruth was staring at her.

Aline looked into Ruth's eyes in the candlelight. They were gray and dark, even with the light reflected in them. Aline's eyes were squinting. Her right hand moved over toward Ruth, and she put her right hand over Ruth's hand and squeezed it.

At that moment, from above them, they heard a commotion. A door was flung open and smacked heavily, and someone above them was crying out: "John! Ruth! John! Ruth!"

It sounded like Hattie Jones.

"Now what?" Ruth barked.

The candle went out and the people in the darkness scuttled about. There were harsh whispers: "The back way! The back way!"

Ruth flew up the lightless staircase and appeared outside the shack in the back yard. She dashed around the side of the house toward the noises.

Yes, it was Hattie Jones yelling, "Ruth! John! John! Ruth!"

*Where was John?* she thought as she came in her own front door, behind Hattie Jones who had her brother-in-law, Vernon Mosely, draped across the little chair—the same chair Benjamin Straddler had slumped into only nights before.

There was Vernon and he looked crumpled.

"What's happened?" Ruth said, running to Vernon's side and pushing Hattie away from her brother-in-law.

Then, up from the cellar and in through the front door came Vernon's wife with a wide mouth and watery eyes. "My dear! My dear!"

The rest of the people were coming around up from the cellar, their bodies pushing into the little room, their faces peeking, mumbling to one another.

"You stop shouting!" Ruth barked at her.

Aline Mosely tottered about trying to see her husband's face, her hands flying around in the air. "This evil! This evil! This evil Falk!"

"You stop shouting, Aline Mosely!" Ruth snapped again, and this time she smacked Aline's face. The people who had rambled up from the cellar looked at one another.

Ruth knelt down and looked at Vernon Mosely's face. It was puffed up and green-looking. His arm, his left arm, had turned a sickly black and purple color as though it had been burned to a crisp. Ruth huffed and puffed and looked at the open door to the cellar. How did they know to come back around here to find her? Now she was sure. She was sure that someone in her group was talking about it with the others.

"Ma'am," Hattie said, "looks to me like he's got himself a snakebite somethin' awful. I found him in the church, lyin' by the pulpit just like that."

Vernon's eyes twinkled and he suddenly drew in a ragged, wheezing breath. He struggled for a moment trying to talk, pushing the air out of his dry lips, trying to make a sound, but all that came out was invisible air and white foam.

Ruth suddenly leapt to her feet and brought the back of her hand so hard across Hattie's old face that it knocked Hattie's hat off and he fell back. Ruth shouted at him, "Why did you bring him here? You stupid, stupid man! Grab him! Grab him!"

With another strange burst of strength, Ruth lifted Vernon's legs and was motioning now with her pink face and pointy head for Hattie to grab Vernon's shoulders.

Hattie picked up his crumpled brown hat and put his hat on his head.

Vernon wheezed again and they pulled him forward from the chair.

They picked him up and Ruth shouted, "You're a damned fool, Hattie Jones! You take a man with venom right to the doctor, you don't bring him around for prayers and coffee, you don't bring him home to die, you take him right to the doctor!"

Hattie was hurt. His face was red and his eyes watered, but he carried the preacher all the way to the doctor's house with Ruth, not looking at Ruth the whole time. He couldn't get a word out of his mouth at her because he knew what he said would be awful, and even after being hit in the face he still refused to say anything awful about this woman.

This woman Ruth had never done Hattie Jones a lick of good. He knew it. Samuel knew it too. Samuel knew it too in the special way that Samuel knew things. You can look into that boy's eyes and you know he knows. He might not tell you, but you know he knows. That woman Ruth came to town and started right in on all the good people. Married up with that John Mosely, the preacher's brother, and then started in on all the good people. She didn't understand. It was like she didn't know. How can she not know, a woman like that? She was smart and old, too, but there was something in her that was mean, something in her that was all pinched up. But she was God's people and that's the twist about it because it was like she didn't know. Or maybe it was that she didn't know for others and she only knew for herself. Somehow, though, she had got it in her head that she was some kind of way more of one of God's people than the rest of them and she didn't understand, plain as it was, that God's people is God's people and that's the end of it. How could she not understand that? But anyway, she didn't. She had this way about her and started in something awful on all of us about how we was doin' things that we shouldn't, praying and waiting on miracles and the like. Got so bad with her and her judging everyone that Benjamin and Lane Straddler up and left out one time and never did come back to church.

But right now, he was helping her but he couldn't even look at her.

For an old woman to hit an old man, an old man like Hattie . . . Hattie realized that he had made a terrible mistake and that she was right, of course; he guessed she was right, he should have dragged the preacher straight to the doctor's and then come and got his brother even though his brother didn't seem to be around.

John Mosely came running up alongside of them just as he came up in Hattie's mind.

He grabbed his brother right out of Hattie's hands, and Hattie was left standing in the morning sun on the hill. He watched the two of them struggle with the preacher, taking him down over the low hill down to where the doctor's little house was.

Hattie stood there by himself on the hill. He thought about the broken door and the things that he had seen at the church. He thought about his son, Samuel, he thought about the chicken man, and he thought about the horse bones. He started plodding back to his little house at the edge of the creek. Samuel would be there waiting for him, feeding the chickens, maybe.

He turned again and saw John and Ruth Mosely pounding on the doctor's door and the door opening and them carrying the preacher inside the door.

Hattie prayed a little prayer in his heart that the preacher would be restored to health and that the Mosely woman would stop being mean.

Hattie Jones walked home with his hat on his head, mumbling to himself, "I'm sorry, Ruth, sorry about the preacher."

When Ruth and John came in the front of the doctor's place, they weren't expecting to see Jim Falk sitting right there with the doctor.

Ruth's eyes came wide open and she almost dropped her husband's brother straight onto the ground. If John hadn't been holding him tightly by the shoulders, she would have.

John hadn't seen the outlander yet, and the doctor was staring straight at Vernon's withered arm.

Jim Falk watched them all come in together, but didn't budge from his chair. He looked at the preacher. The preacher's face was contorted and his right eye had gone squeezed shut. It looked as if the right side of his face had been somehow burned and his left arm looked exactly like a burned-up and twisted stick.

The doctor stood up and put down his pipe. "What is this here?" he asked in a quiet voice. He walked quickly to the back of the room and clicked open a door there. "Get him in here and lay him down on the bed."

John Mosely and Ruth carried him in the door just as the doctor told them to and put him down on a neat little bed in the little room.

As John Mosely set his brother down on the bed, he noticed that Ruth was not looking at him or at his brother's mangled arm. She was looking out the door and into the main area where they came in. Her eyes were wide. He could see she was kind of afraid.

"Ruth!" he shouted at her.

She turned and looked at him. "Did you see?" she whispered. "Did you see in the front?"

He shook his head.

"The outlander," she whispered, and just as she did, she put her hand up and her long index finger over her lip to shush him from saying anything.

John Mosely's eyes got big and then bigger. He arranged his brother quickly and was set to rush out the way he came when the doctor came in through the door blocking his way. The two almost collided in the door frame.

The doctor adjusted himself and asked, "What's happened here?"

Ruth said, "Hattie Jones found him up at the church"—she said it quietly—"said he was curled up at the pulpit just like this."

The doctor eyed the preacher. The preacher was still breathing. In his left eye, the only open one, there was a glimmer of fear. The doctor could see that the intelligence in the preacher's eye was trapped, trapped in the frozen and paralyzed face.

"Can he speak?" the doctor asked John; and seeing that John was occupied only with looking out into the front area, the doctor called out to the preacher, "Can you speak?"

A noise like a wheeze came from the preacher, and John turned and looked at his brother.

When the big snow had passed through Sparrow and it got so awful cold, John's brother had stayed out too long in the snow and got so cold that most of his ears had come off and they had turned a permanent grayish-black. Along the side of his head, they looked like an animal's ears now, pointed and curled. Vernon's face was pinched on the right side, a black and purple bruise ebbing out from his right eye, which was swelled completely shut now.

His left arm was the worst thing that John Mosely had ever seen happen to a human being. It was black and crisp and the fingers looked as though they would flake away like a husk; and yet, they somehow looked molded together too. The arm had lost its human qualities. It looked like something that, long dead, began to resemble earth and roots.

Doc Pritham pushed past them both and out into the main area. "Falk!" the doctor cried.

And then they both appeared in the room and the four of them were in the room together with the preacher lying there on the bed between them. On one side of the bed were the doctor and the outlander. On the other side of the bed were Ruth and John. In the middle, on the bed, was the preacher.

Ruth said, "Oh!"

John Mosely said, "Ah!"

Jim Falk said, "What's happened here?" His keen eyes went over the preacher's body fast, and when he saw the curled and twisted arm and the eye that was slowly sinking into the preacher's head, he looked at the doctor. He looked at the preacher's brother and the preacher's brother's wife, who were both looking at him with wide eyes.

Jim said, "These good people should go."

The doctor nodded in agreement.

John said, "What do you mean? This is my brother. I'm not go-ing anywhere."

Doc Pritham said, "We have to move fast. We can't argue. His life is at stake. If we do not move fast, he will die."

The doctor moved fast and bent over the preacher and soon the preacher's coat and shirt were removed exposing his old, gray-haired chest and the rolls of fat of the preacher's soft belly. A blackness was running along the side of the preacher like little streamlets underneath his pale skin.

Ruth looked at this and said, "What is happening to him?"

The doctor sped out of the room.

Jim looked at the two frightened people and said, "I know spe-cial ways of medicine, and so does the good doctor. We can save him, but we have to move fast. You must let us do this. You may go into the other room and pray if you wish. But you should go into the other room. It's going to be gruesome." As he was saying this, the doctor came back in the room with a book with old pages and strange writing in it and a bag.

"We're not leaving," Ruth said. "Prayers! If it's God's will that he die, he'll die; if it's God's will that he live, he'll live! Prayers! This man was bit by a snake, he needs the anti-venom! Not prayers! Prayers and miracles and false hopes, do you see what you've taught the people?"

John Mosely said to the doctor, "And this man cannot be in here! This man probably called the snakes up out of the Pit to bite my brother!" John pointed at Jim Falk, wagging his finger at the end of his thin arm.

The doctor looked at John Mosely. "There's not time for all this!" the doctor shouted suddenly, his face becoming red behind his bushy white brows. "There's not time for this!"

The doctor pulled from his black bag a long and silvery blade.

The preacher groaned loudly.

"Vernon!" John shouted.

"Stand back!" the doctor yelled at the two frightened onlookers.

Jim Falk moved around to the other side of the bed, using his glare to try and move John and Ruth out of the way and into the corner of the little room.

"We're not moving!" Ruth shouted in his face. "We're protecting this man of God from your evil, from your spells and your"—she almost spit when she said it—"prayers!"

"I am not here to do evil, woman!" Jim suddenly found himself shouting. "I am here to rid it out!" Jim had not noticed it, but his left hand had pulled the hatchet.

Ruth and John moved out of the way.

"That's my brother!" John shouted.

Jim reached out with his left hand and grabbed the broken preacher's twisted arm. He tried to remember what Old Magic Woman had shown him about clearing up the demon rot. He knelt down beside the preacher. He looked at the doctor. He started to remember. He quietly started to say the things that he remembered to himself, and where his hand was touching the preacher's arm, it looked as though the air around it began to get smoky.

"What are you doing? He's saying a spell! He's calling the devil!" John shrieked. His eyes were flashing around at the scene.

Ruth had closed her eyes. No one could see that she was not afraid. She was hoping. She was hoping that what she saw in her brother-in-law was a sign. A sign that he had been found. A sign that her time was coming and that she would receive her reward.

She just kept closed her eyes, though, hoping. She had been doing her own kind a praying, a practical kind, a kind that she knew one day would bring results.

Doc Pritham positioned the long, flat blade just at the crux of Vernon Mosely's shoulder. He inserted it with a thrust. No blood came from the wound, but the blade's color appeared to turn from a silver to dull yellow.

"You're killing him!" John shouted and rushed forward.

Jim Falk yanked sudden and fierce at the preacher's arm and a moist popping sound came from the blade. The preacher's arm came off in Jim's hand and the preacher sat up in bed, suddenly fully awake and squirming. John Mosely crashed into Jim Falk, but Falk was a stone and John tumbled into the corner.

The preacher's face lightened and turned its usual pink and the swelling eye and right side of his face deflated and settled to a gray and yellow bruise. He opened his eyes and a light came into his eyes and he looked around the room blinking.

"Thank God," Vernon said and he looked at the outlander who held the twisted arm in his hand.

Tears came from both the preacher's eyes, and John Mosely got up and pushed past the outlander. Jim looked at Ruth and caught a strange look in her eye, a flutter that she was disappointed at her brother-in-law's recovery. She looked at Falk and scowled.

Jim shrank quietly out of the room with the thing that used to be a preacher's arm.

The doctor was at the other side of Vernon with a cool cloth dabbing his face.

Ruth was still in the corner, still scowling.

John Mosely grabbed his brother's head and kissed it.

"He'll need rest," the doctor said. "He will live, but he will need rest."

"How did you?" John asked.

The doctor looked at John and then at Ruth. "Prayer and medicine."

"Ruth," Vernon said and looked up at her grimacing face, "Ruth, my arm. My arm. My arm." He began to sob now.

The doctor laid him back, and the preacher almost at once stopped sobbing and fell into a sound sleep.

After a few moments of looking at his brother sleep, John said to the doctor in a whisper, "What is that witch-man doing here?"

He motioned toward the main area where he had seen the outlander go.

The doctor did nothing to answer. Doc Pritham grabbed the long blade that he had and took it into the other room. The door was closed and the outlander was not around.

Ruth came out into the main area. The doctor and her husband followed close behind her.

The doctor was wiping the long blade with a cloth he had dipped in something clear and pungent. Ruth stood there. John stood there too, watching the doctor and looking around the room to see if the outlander was hiding anywhere in the room. Maybe he was hiding in the corner. Maybe he knew a trick where he could hide in plain sight. There were many things that a man in league with the Evil One would be able to know how to do. What all they were, who knew?

The doctor lit a match and touched it to the dripping blade. A bright flash of blue fire shot up the side of the long blade, and a flame jumped from its tip and hung in the air above the blade, twisted and vanished.

"What is that you're doing?" Ruth asked the doctor slowly, her eyes narrowed now, her courage had come back to her.

John Mosely said, "The outlander. Where's he gone? What was he doing here?"

"Yes," Ruth Mosely asked. "What was he doing here?"

John added in with a shaking voice, "And what about my brother? What about my brother's arm?"

The doctor slipped the long, weird knife into a black pouch. He then turned toward them and looked them both in the face.

Ruth was getting angrier every time the doctor didn't answer a question. Her arms came up and crossed, her shoulders came up closer to her long ears, and her chin came forward more and more. She took a slow step toward the doctor and her voice came out in a low pitch. "I am sure the people of Sparrow would be very interested to know that somehow you are involved with this Jim Falk. Prayers and medicine? Prayers and medicine? That would be a very interesting thing for them to hear about. They also might be interested to know that you have an old book on your person, an old book with strange writing in it. Don't you? Don't you have something like that around here? Wouldn't that be an interesting thing for them to know?"

The doctor's back was to her. His eyes went wide, but then he turned, smiled at her, and reached into his pocket and got his pipe. He turned around and pulled out a chair from the table. He turned around and looked at them both and smiled. He turned back around toward the table and pulled another chair away from the table and turned it a little bit toward John. Then he went around to the far side of the table and pulled out a chair for himself and sat down and began packing his pipe with tobacco.

"Please," he said, "please, won't you sit down. We have a lot of things to talk about, I think. Why don't you sit down and we'll talk about this?"

The two made glances at each other.

"Please," the doctor said in a very calm voice, and his match came to his bowl and he puffed blue clouds of smoke, "please, won't you sit down and we'll have a talk about prayers and medicine and old books."

The two moved forward slowly and each, in their own time, sat down, never taking their eyes for a moment off the doctor's wrinkled, mysterious face.

The farther up she went, the uglier the trees got, thorn-covered, twisted, and cracked. Violet was thirsty; her mouth was completely parched. Time and again she would drop beside one of the gray trees and pick up a batch of wet leaves and suck on them, getting any moisture she could. Then she would spit the leaves out and wipe her mouth. Her eyes were tired and she couldn't focus on much.

The sun was going down in the west. The trees made long shadows. Where was the stranger? The stranger that had given her the powder.

The morning had been beautiful. The sun's light had melted some of the ice and warmed the little streams that ran in the back of her home on the hill, but she found no comfort in that. She had to keep going.

She couldn't return to her home now because he was there. Whatever it was that he was, he was there now. If she could just find the stranger, again. She fingered the necklace with the tiny vial inside.

Bill had come home in the middle of the night.

At first, she thought that maybe she'd taken too much of the powder she'd been taking and that she was having a dream of some sort that was mixing with the wind that had been swirling around her home in the dark. She couldn't keep the fire lit because the force of the wind had somehow forced itself right down the chimney, and each time she would start up the fire it was almost as if a giant person were standing over her home and blowing cold breath down into the chimney to put out her fire.

She was cold and the wind was blowing and there was nothing for her to do but mix an extra portion of her powder over the stove fire and drink it down and crawl into her bed. She had the covers pulled all around her as the wind banged and clapped around the house. She could hear too that the door of the back house where the outlander had been staying had blown open and was now banging and banging in the night.

She wrapped the covers around her even tighter as she began to drift off. She could see Huck's round face close to hers—feel his warm breath on her cheek. She could feel his strong hand take a hold of her shoulder. Her mind reeled backward to the days following the big blizzard. It had been such a terrible time, but had also been the time for them.

During those quiet and frozen days, no one knew if anyone was alive at all and they had been so frightened. They had all been so frightened. So many had died, and so many were yet to be found, some of them frozen and clinging to one another, their eyes shut, the lashes black crystals, the blue children, the gray dogs. The wind was almost the same then, too. It was as if it would never stop blowing. It was as if the wind itself was a thing, an angry thing that wanted to destroy everything else. The winds kindled the fires and froze the town.

The cold had taken the preacher's ears and Anna Marbo's life and so many of the children. Nearly all. She'd heard that things were worse in the Ridges, but no one knew for sure. But Violet had seen with her own eyes the spidery spook clambering on the rooftops, its disgusting maw swallowing down the frozen and the living. She shuddered with the memory.

How could she have known that Bill would come back? Bill could have been just as dead as the others. How could she know what would happen when Huck found her, all that death and grief pent up inside him, all the fear that makes men and women cling to one another in the darkness. Her mind sunk into the moment, Huck's arms around her body, squeezing her to him.

Then her eyes opened. The wind beat against the sides of the house and once in a while she could hear another noise. A noise that sounded far away, like a person singing a bad song or calling out injured in the wind. When she became attentive to it, though, it died away again. It died away into the darkness until she could convince herself that she hadn't heard it. She hadn't heard it at all. She had only heard the wind through the ugly trees. Then, then it would come again. It came again closer and it was a voice, it was an unmistakable voice like a wailing.

She was sure now that it wasn't just part of her dreams or her imagination, and she could hear it more and more clearly now and in between the whirling gusts of wind. It called out to her. It was calling her name. It was Bill's voice, but it sounded somehow wrong.

In fact, it sounded garbled and strange, and as it got closer and closer it came not to sound like his voice at all.

There was a crash on the porch.

She got up now and ran to the front room meaning to grab the gun.

He burst into the front door, that hideous wind blowing and whirling behind him.

It looked like Bill, but worse. His eyes had gone all white and his skin had gone all white and he looked dead, but he wasn't.

"Violet!" he screamed and fell forward. His body was covered in dark blood. He fell right on the ground, and it looked as though his legs had suddenly gotten paralyzed. His mouth was so wide open, it was too wide open, and from inside what looked like black worms stretched themselves along the floor toward her toes.

"Violet!" he screamed again and blood spat out.

Violet was frozen at first. He lay in the doorway, clambering for her. Beside him, mounted up on the wall, was the gun. She couldn't get to it without him grasping her.

She turned and ran back into the kitchen and, picking up her little bag of powder and other things, she flew open the window and slid herself out into the night, carefully moving so that she did not tear her clothing. Then she ran. Behind her, in the night, in her home, she could hear her husband moaning and wailing.

Now she was exhausted, but too scared to shut her eyes.

She wasn't sure she had left him far behind, she couldn't hear him, but she was too scared to fall asleep now. She was hungry too, but not hungry enough to think of eating those awful leaves she had been sucking on.

Somewhere out here among these ugly trees she knew there was that stranger who might help her. She'd met him before. She couldn't remember the exact spot now, but she knew it was around here somewhere.

She was so tired, though, and she sat and rested under a tree, watching the shadows grow long and the sunlight crawling up over the hill. Soon the woods went quiet and still, the beating of her heart slowed, and the pulsing blood in her ear quieted. Now and again she could hear the chirping of some bird that was flitting among the branches.

She looked around in the gray and brown winter woods.

"Have I been out here all day?" she asked herself out loud.

She looked in her little bag. She had powder and some other things in there.

"I didn't get any rest last night at all," she said and thought again of the strange, pale skin of her husband and of the terror she felt when she saw him and how she was somehow sure that it was not really him somehow.

She thought that if she could close her eyes for just a few minutes she would be able to figure out what to do. She did have some choices. She could simply go back down into town from here. There was a clear stream that ran not too far from here that went straight back into town. She would have to find somewhere to go soon, even if it was up in this tree, because the wolves might be around. They'd disappeared for the whole day. In fact, the whole day had been totally quiet. She was sure that at some turn she would see her husband's gangly form romping through the woods behind her, but she hadn't. She was sure that as she rested here, she would hear the gentle rustling of leaves as the stranger came around the tree, but he hadn't come at all.

Sometime after the blizzard, the hooded stranger had come to her when she'd been out here. He lived out here, lived in the woods. Maybe there was a time when some people thought the stranger was a witch or a sorcerer or something of the sort. He knew the ways of the woods. He'd told her as much. He preferred to live on his own out here. Didn't say much else, other than the sayings. He seemed to know many of the sayings out the scripture. He'd given her the powder that helped her sleep and to think clear and sharp, but he wasn't coming today. He seemed to know somehow when she'd run out and he'd show up then.

Now what? To go back into town? To go running to Huck? To tell him that her husband turned into a monster and was chasing her? Another crazy story from Violet Hill, the weird wife of the town carpenter? She could go to the preacher's house. Maybe that was the thing to do. He would have to take her in. At least for a while. He would understand, maybe. How could they let her husband run off like that in such a state? Something was terribly wrong, and it made her sick to think of what it might be.

She looked at her bag again and looked around. She squinted her eyes, hoping to see the gray hood of the stranger peering around one of the trees near the horizon. She couldn't see a thing.

The woods were growing dim and clouds began to cover the sky and turn the same color as the gray, ugly trees around her. She looked at the tree she was sitting up against. Above her, climbing up the side of the tree were batches of thorns, like horrible nests, bunched and twisted in patterns along the bark. It might be worse climbing that than it would be to go and see the preacher.

She didn't want to go and see the preacher, though. The preacher and the preacher's brother and the preacher's sister-in-law had all come from up north. And they might be suspicious of her in some way. The people from up there were suspicious of everyone in some way for something; and she had heard that they would, if it suited their purposes, twist your words and your life around in some way that would make you seem evil. Even if you weren't.

Then again, the doctor might keep her safe too.

The clouds were very dark now and the thought of wolves grew in her head, the thought of the wolves followed by the spook. She decided that she would make her way to the creek and quickly follow the creek back into town and go see the doctor. He might have answers about Bill. She wasn't sure, but she was sure that she didn't want to wait through the night.

She got up from her spot on the ground under the tree and began making her way over the little ridge to where the creek was.

Just as she started coming up over the ridge she heard something behind her.

Violet stopped, but she turned slow and looked intensely around in the woods. Her face showed no fear. Her cheekbones were strong and the cold made her face white and her eyes sparkle in the dark of the woods. She wasn't afraid. She was looking. She was looking because what she saw would determine what she would do. She looked and for a while she didn't see anything, just the crooked trees and the cold wind blowing them around.

Then it seemed that there was something else out there, just beyond where she could see. Yes, she could see something solid and gray among the low branches, but it was tall, like a man. It wasn't an animal. It moved in and out of the shadows just beyond her vision. She squinted her green eyes trying to see. Yes, it was in the shape of a man, but something about it gave her a strange feeling. She was sure that whoever it was could see her, but whoever it was was only half hiding. Whoever it was was just staying where she could not see, but it seemed as if whoever it was was stepping just into the light enough where she could see. Whoever it was, she stood watching long enough to get the feeling that she didn't want to find out who it was.

She didn't get that feeling of comfort that came when the stranger came upon her. When the stranger had come upon her in the woods that time and offered his hand and showed her the way out of the woods, she had felt comforted. There was no feeling in this presence that waved in and out of the edge of her vision now. In fact, she noted now that when she glanced that way there was a certain kind of blankness that came into her senses. Almost a veil of sorts coming over her thoughts.

"What in the world could that be?" she thought and made swift steps over the little hill and toward the creek.

She got there and started through the gray forest along the creek down the hill and into Sparrow. Her mind flickered through the things that she had seen, and her heart began to skip beats as she ran. A cold sweat broke on her forehead. The faces of the frozen children kept coming up in her head. She stopped by the creek and listened as the water trickled and tinkled in the dwindling evening. She reached into her blouse and pulled the necklace and little jar of powder. It was almost empty. Her hands were shaking now and her left eye twitched maddeningly. She looked around. Behind her, just at the edge of the shadows, she saw the figure. This time she could see clearly the shape of a man—the shape of the man, but the head was not the shape of a man's head, and long, wild horns like branches twisted out from either side of the head.

Her heart thumped in her chest and she crouched down and went about her business with powder, quickly, quickly. The energy shot into her mind and heart. Her thoughts quickened and strength and color returned to her face.

She gathered herself up and tore off into Sparrow.

She ran straight for the doctor's house and got inside with the door slammed behind her.

Jim finished burying the husk of flesh that was once the preacher's arm. He got out the little book that he had kept his own writings in over the years. He flipped around in there. There was something in there about when the flesh was rotted by the touch of evil, but he couldn't remember where. He had a vague memory of talking with Spencer Barnhouse about it in connection with his father getting pulled into the hole.

He found it and started reading over the shallow grave of the arm with his head bowed slightly. He wished he could say for sure whether he believed in the power of these things or not. He knew there was a force in the world, some force that had taken his mother's life, taken his father to some other place through what looked like magic. But there were too many questions in his mind about it and no one seemed to know any kind of satisfactory answers. And he was so weak—weaker than he'd even imagined himself to be. Always on the run. Getting an old man in Hopestill even to steal the weapons for him. He'd known he didn't have the ability himself, especially as fuzzy as he'd got with the leaves and the whisky. There was no telling what would have become of him. And yet, he felt driven to try to help some way; he felt that so heavy, that he was supposed to help this town somehow, and that somehow this whole mess would lead him to his father.

But those wolves had dragged him around, ripped him up and whipped him around, taken part of his hand and his fingers. Maybe Bill Hill was right, what Bill Hill said. Maybe all Jim really knew was tricks after all; maybe he was a kind of trickster who had eventually tricked himself into believing that his tricks were not tricks, that they were real. Maybe there was something in that. Not directly, but indirectly, like a message, a message that he should leave Sparrow. What was he to do? Anything more than Spencer Barnhouse was able to do up in Hopestill? Barnhouse was one man who knew something and only something of the truth, and he stood against all those who were bought and controlled by some other mysterious man named Varney Mull. Varney Mull was supposed to be in league with the Evil One. If that were true, as he well expected it was, and as he suspected that this Doc Pritham suspected it was, and as he suspected that the preacher man, Vernon Mosely also suspected it was . . . if it were true that Varney Mull was in fact in league, what would any of them be able to do? The Evil One? Surely this was a power that was beyond him to rid out, maybe even beyond them all. On the other hand, he had just regenerated the arm of a preacher through the craft he had been taught by his father and Old Magic Woman. He wondered if he would ever see her again—if any of it was possible, or if he had only the bitterest hope of a child's dream.

He was leaning against a tree and thinking such thoughts as this when he saw the thing. He looked and he looked again and then he squeezed his hurt hand under the bandage. He did that because it would hurt and he needed the pain to tell him that he wasn't having some deep dream memory because of the doctor's medicine. It wasn't a dream or a memory.

It was tall and thin, and dead-looking antlers went out from either side of its head, which was like a cat's with no skin, but its body was as if someone had taken a man's body and beat all the innards out and stretched it upwards and fixed terrible claws on the end of the too-long arms. This looked not like the spook that he'd seen up in the woods behind the Hills', but he did recognize it. Yes, this was something other entirely, but not unknown to him. Its cat eyes beamed back and forth, stiff black hairs bristled on its body like quills. Its mouth was full of yellowish daggers, and what looked like tiny black snakes or worms wriggled and peered this way and that from its open mouth.

He remembered the old songs of the River People, the songs and singing that frightened him as a boy. The songs about Kitaman, who came from under the earth to eat the flesh of Eyabe's people, to eat the River People. These were the Katakayish people, the tribe which Old Magic Woman had come from. Could this be Kitaman in front of him now? Was this the earth demon of the tales of the people of this land, or was this something else, something older, more evil? Was this a creature sent by the Evil One? A true demon? Perhaps both.

It was creeping itself down into Sparrow, along the creek and down toward town where the doctor's house was. It stopped and seemed to hear or smell something. Its wicked head turned. It looked straight at him. He did the trick to make his mind go blank again. If he trained in on it with the jitters now, it would see him for sure. He blanked out his mind. He swerved his mind this way and that and brought up a bright memory of a field full of sunshine, then a snowfall, then a lightning storm.

It was just far enough off that he wasn't sure it could see him, but too he was sure that it looked at him and took notice of him there, but it did not seem to mind him there. Like an animal sizing him up to see if he was a threat or not and then deciding that he wasn't. The yellow eyes on him sent a cold and buzzing fear through his whole body. What would any of them be able to do if these were beasts the Evil One had sent along?

He watched it go by, its weird horns disappearing into the morning woods. He looked at his hand wrapped in the bandages and thought of his father. He thought of the doctor. He thought of

Violet and he thought of May Marbo. He watched the woods growing dim as storm clouds gathered. He started moving at a distance,
following that thing, allowing his thoughts to wander and go blank,
the way his father had taught him.

The doctor was sitting there with his head in his hands when
she slammed the door behind her. He popped up out of his chair
and drew his pistol and pointed it at her face.

John and Ruth Mosely were sitting at the table with him,
looking angry and suspicious with their arms crossed and their
eyebrows squinted in the same way.

When she looked into the doctor's eyes, she saw that he did not
mean to shoot her, but she did see that he was frightened, very
frightened.

"It's coming!" Violet said. "It followed me down from on top of
the hill. I don't know if it's behind me or not, but it was coming behind me."

"What's coming?" John Mosely said and stood up. Ruth looked
around and took a deep breath.

The doctor didn't ask any questions or answer any questions.
Violet's face told him everything. He went to the wall and pulled a
box off of the shelf. From inside the box he pulled another pistol
and loaded it with special lode and gave it to Violet.

"You know how to use it," he said with a kind of matter-of-fact
tone. "The special lode will make it stunned. It might even drop it
to the ground, but it won't kill it exactly. You will have to use all
the rounds and get them in it, and it will fall. Then we'll have to
take off the head and burn it."

"Burn it? Burn it?" John asked again. "Burn what?"

Ruth looked at him and said, "Shut your mouth, John. Can't
you be of any help?"

The doctor turned to them both and said, "Despite what the
two of you believe or don't believe about me or about the outlander, you'd better get in the back room."

"Why is she staying out here?" Ruth pointed at Violet.

"Because she knows how to shoot," the doctor said. "Now get back in the room with your brother!"

The two obeyed, though Ruth was making a sour face the whole time.

"Is the preacher here too?" Violet asked.

"I think we've got most of Sparrow back there at this point," the doctor said. "You aim straight for its head, the silver lode will do the rest, and then we'll have to take off the head and burn it."

Violet was looking at the big, weird pistol in her hand and back up at the doctor.

"You're talking about the spook, aren't you?" she asked.

"I don't know what I mean. The outlander gave me these weapons and those instructions."

"Jim Falk?" she asked.

"Yes," the doctor replied and moved to the window to look out into the growing darkness. The clouds had made a black swirl in the afternoon sky so that all appeared twilight.

"Where is Jim Falk?" Violet asked, coming up behind the doctor and looking over his shoulder out of the little window into the darkening afternoon.

"Now that I think of it, he might be out looking for you. He left," the doctor said. "Is he following you here?"

"No. It's not Falk, there is something evil out there," Violet said.

"The woods of Sparrow are no place to be out in," the doctor said.

"No, Doctor, you're right. The woods of Sparrow are no place to be out in night or day," Violet said.

They stood there as the sky grew darker.

They listened.

They could hear John and Vernon and Ruth whispering and grumbling about things in the other room.

They waited then together in the doctor's little house. The doctor and Violet. They waited for the thing to come running out the woods.

When Violet's hands started to tremble, the doctor felt bad for her. This pretty lady with so much trouble. Without taking his eyes off the window he backed up toward the table and, undoing the clasp on his bag, and reached in and plucked a blue bottle and lifted it out. He brought it to her and said, "Keep your eyes on the edge of the wood and open your mouth."

He gave her some heavy medicine to calm her, but she stayed awake, her eyes fixed on the edge of the woods through the window. She felt the medicine flow through her.

In her mind, Violet was sure that she could feel the force of the thing coming upon them now like a slow wind across a stream. The woods themselves appeared suddenly crisp, the lines of the crooked trees deep-etched against a smoky background of browning leaves. The sun, when it pierced through the black clouds, somehow seemed purposefully to cast longer, blacker shadows.

Violet was perched at the doc's window, one hand on the sill, the other holding the heavy silver gun in a trembling white hand. She felt cold, but she was not afraid.

The doctor looked her over from the side and glanced at her shaking hand.

No, he thought. That is not a tremor caused by fear. Her left hand is so relaxed. Her lips are a little blue, but they are not trembling. This is some kind of reaction in her muscles because of something her system needs that she does not have. This is caused by her not receiving the dose of whatever those powders are that she carries in her necklace. The stilling altha I gave her is not even enough; it must be something potent. I wonder where she got it.

The doctor glanced back at his bag again and wondered if he too should take something to calm him. The conversation with the Moselys had been almost as disturbing as the outlander telling him that there was a demon lurking about.

The whisky he had been sipping left a burn in his belly. There was that other feeling there too, the dismal worming around of fear. What was this thing? How could it be true? And when the only possible answer came to him, he said a prayer in the back of his mind that it might not be so.

Violet's eyes darted about and then stopped on a spot, her black pupils quivered in her green irises. Her mouth dropped open wide as she drew in a sharp, rattling gasp.

She whispered so carefully each word, "I see it, Doctor."

The doctor, who'd had his attention focused on Violet's face, snapped to and looked where she was looking out to the edge of the wood. Without a doubt, as if it had stepped out of a terrible painting, the thing came, sticking its twisted face out into a shaft of light and then recoiling quickly back. Seeing the rawness of the thing in the dim afternoon was somehow obscene; both the doctor and Violet felt as though they were watching some despicable act.

Its face had a jagged mouth and black, rolling eyes. There was an emptiness that ran in it deep. It was hollow and false, like some horrible mask. The light of humanity was not in its eyes, yet it did not seem animal either. It was something else entirely. Long, sharpened horns twisted out from either side of its bulbous head, and shiny black tubes stretched from its mouth like reaching worms.

The doctor said, "Save us."

Violet stood up and took a step back from the window. "That's not it," she said, raising her silver gun to the window. "That's not what I saw at night, or in the winter. That's not what attacked my . . ." She suddenly stopped speaking and her body deflated in her dress. She sobbed in great whelps and finally managed to whisper, ". . . husband." She never took her eyes off the monster.

The beast recoiled slowly into the darker woods, stepping backwards on its curving legs.

They waited with the heavy feeling that at any moment it might crash through the window.

"What's going on?" Ruth whispered harshly from the backroom.

Violet shushed her.

With a shaking arm, the doctor slowly creaked the window open and put his gun through, still pointed at the place in the woods where it had disappeared. Violet peered out, breathing shallow and quiet as she could. The woods and the clouds stood still so that the sunlight broke downward through the gray and dark clouds in white shafts.

And then the thing did come, marching straight out of the woods toward them as a cloud bank rolling overhead, dimming the scene to a dull purple. It came toward them. When its hulking form passed through shafts of light, a thin mist rose from its exposed flesh.

It was quick and all its movements were sharp and jerking.

Violet took a stance a few feet back from the open window. The thing's eyes were pinned on her. They were not like the spook's eyes, they were black with sparking yellow pupils in the center like little cracks with fire behind. They were fixed on Violet.

She raised her pistol at it and her hand did not shake.

"What is it?" the doctor asked and looked up to the ceiling. Then he raised, with both hands, his heavy revolver at the thing.

The thing made the distance faster than expected, and the two, Violet and the doctor, opened fire—the pistols cracking into the morning, both of them going deaf from the reports, the smoke stinging their nostrils.

Violet could see the thing slow down, its body jerking where the shots were landing, its face distorted, and it made a noise like a dry heave, but the volleys only worked to irritate the thing.

The doctor was yelling now and pulling his trigger again and again. He missed the mark, and he missed again, but Violet had a good eye and she landed three shots across the thing's shiny, black chest.

It was close enough now that she could see the sparkling quality of the coarse hair on the thing, and beneath its crooked collarbones another darker, glistening color that grew and spread downward as it lurched. "Yes," Violet whispered, "yes, you bleed."

The doctor's pistol was clicking empty. The thing staggered momentarily and then, with impossible speed, it was at the window, shrieking at them and reaching inside with its spade and spider hands. Violet snapped another round into its chest before one of its gripping claws dug deep into her left shoulder.

The doctor had taken a few steps and turned, rummaging for his ammo, when he felt his head jerk backward too quickly and the unmistakable force of the thing's claw on his head, the sting and gouge of the ragged nails in his temple. His left eye was blinded by his own blood. His revolver clacked onto the floor as he was raised up in the air.

He heard Violet scream. She wasn't screaming as if she was scared, though. She was screaming curses at the thing that had her. Both of them were dragged out through the broken window, and Violet was hurled against the house. Her back hit the wood hard and the back of her head smacked and she went out cold.

Now the thing gripped the doctor with both arms and raised the doctor all the way up over its head.

Violet's eyes fluttered open and she could see, dimly, the thing's jaw unlatching like a snake's, its maw growing ever wider and darker until the whole mouth seemed to overtake the thing, and it looked like nothing but a darkness surrounded by sharp, broken teeth. The tubes that were once worms whipped and curled about the doctor, thick and thorny. More arms came now, sticking up from behind like an insect's legs, ready to pack the doctor into its mouth and swallow him whole, once and for all.

The thing held the doctor up in the air a little higher to get a good angle on him for the swallow. His legs kicked weakly. The doc's eyes were wide with fear, but he couldn't make a noise. Suddenly, the thing shuddered in an odd way and a plume of black and purple smoke rose up from behind it and its arms lost their strength and it dropped Doc Pritham onto the green grass in front of it. There was another noise then, like a whistling and then a loud pop and a crackle, and Violet saw a bright yellow fire leap out of the beast's right flank and smoke and dark liquid sprayed out its side.

It fell on its other side as another whistle and explosion burst out of it, this time in its leg. The explosion sent the right leg whirling in three pieces across the grass. The mouth had collapsed like a bag; its eyes were rolling and rolling in pain.

Behind it, Violet saw a gray shadow dart from the woods and move across the hill toward them. The gray shadow was that of a man and the face in the middle was Jim Falk's.

He was on the thing. Straddling it, he used some kind of brace with his left hand, forcing its bellowing mouth closed. He had fastened a long, shining blade to his wounded right hand still wrapped in the bandages. He sliced at the thing's neck until the whole head was completely removed from the twitching, flailing body.

He stood up and for a moment held the hideous face with the horns twisting out at either side and the black tubes drooping. Then he walked a few paces from the body and dropped the head on a big rock. He made quick with a flagon from his pouch and began dousing the head.

Violet tried to stand, but she was too dizzy.

The thing's head was soon engulfed in a green ball of flames pouring oily smoke into the air, its eyes rolling.

The doctor was reeling, but he moved to his duties and, pulling a container from his own pouch, began dousing the separate body. The outlander joined him and in no time the sky was dark with the burning of the monster. Noises came from the thing's diminishing corpse, ugly sounds like the whispering of many people in pain and sorrow. As the burning continued, the whispering began to sound like faraway cries.

They all looked at one another.

Violet made an effort and was able to get up on her feet and soon found herself standing with the two men watching the flames. The strange, sad cries at once grew more desperate and terrible than before, so that standing there, the three of them felt that maybe they should put the flames out. The sounds of suffering were unbearable and now they could hear distinctly individual cries, voices, women, boys, men . . . so that as the smoke continued, any sense of comfort or victory or accomplishment in bringing the thing to its demise was completely removed from them. Only left with the three was the stark, empty feeling that they were power-less, and that thousands were suffering at the will of something impossibly terrible.

Jim looked around at Violet and the doctor.

He heard Ruth Mosely calling to the doctor from inside the house.

He looked at Violet again. "We have to find out what's hap-pened to your husband. Have you seen him?"

Violet looked at Jim Falk and said "No," but she meant yes.

## CHAPTER 14

Maybe he was alive, maybe he was dead, maybe he was both. After they burned the thing out in front of the doctor's house, the three of them had gone to Violet's place to see. To see if the dead and yet living Bill was in the house. Of course, he wasn't. There were pools and smears of blood and the table was shattered and the front door was removed and splintered. No Bill.

"I've been seeing that spook for years," Violet said after she'd got a little drink and sat at one of the chairs by the smashed table, the one that wasn't broken. "Just seeing it in the woods looking at me in the night, looking at our house, looking in the window . . . The folks around here and at church and all, they had me thinking I was crazy. For a long time it didn't seem to care about this place; it was like it was just watching." She fingered the locket around her neck. "They had me thinking I was crazy, and I thought that maybe I was crazy and that I had started seeing things." Her eyes began to focus on things around her—Jim standing in the busted doorway listening, the doctor looking into the other room, looking up at the ceiling and then looking back at Violet.

"Even during the blizzard, even when I saw it eating the dog and those kids . . . I rubbed my eyes and thought maybe I was seeing things. Maybe I was. Why did other people not see the same things?" She looked down at her lap and back up at Jim.

Jim pulled his little book from his belt and flipped the pages with his bandaged hand. "Violet," he said, "Violet, you said that the Starkey baby went missing."

Violet took a moment to come back from whatever vision was before her eyes and finally said, "That's right."

"How do you mean, missing?" Jim asked.

"I mean missing," Violet said. "Elsie said that the baby went missing."

"Missing," Jim said and made a frown.

"Missing," Violet said.

Jim looked at the doctor, who was looking at Violet. Violet's head was in her hands. She was looking at the floor through her fingers. She was trying to imagine what it would be like not to be afraid, she was trying to remember when she was a girl and wasn't afraid. She drew up images of a porch full of sunshine and her mother's hands on her shoulders, she saw Bill laughing as she tried to saw wood, she drank hot coffee in her mind. She thought of Bill again and her heart filled up with freezing water. She rubbed her chest.

Violet squeezed her eyes and opened them again. Jim was asking her about Elsie's baby. She looked up at Jim and said, "I don't remember her name. Elsie came in one day after the blizzard and things had started to warm a little and she said, 'I can't find her.' That was the last I saw of her. She doesn't get out of bed anymore from what I hear. From the grief. She doesn't want to die and she doesn't want to live."

Jim turned and looked out the front door and said, "That magician told me that the baby was dead, that it died from the freeze and that there was no spook."

Jim turned to the doctor. "Have you ever been up to visit Elsie in her bed?"

"No," the doctor said and opened his mouth a little and put his hand up to his mouth. "No, I've never been up to visit her."

"How long has she been in that bed?" Jim asked.

"It's been four years since the blizzard," Violet said.

The doctor and Jim walked out in front of the house and began talking in low voices. Violet gathered up some of her things in a pack and, walking through her home one last time, decided in her mind that she would never return here and that she had to think of her husband as dead. For a little moment, this relieved the pressure in her chest and the cold feeling of her hands. If she could think of her husband as dead, there were other things she might attend to. She thought of Huck Marbo, with his green eyes and his pretty daughter. She thought of all the sadness that had consumed him. She touched her necklace and wondered how the stranger in the woods played into all this.

Jim was interested in this fact about the baby, so he figured he ought to go and ask the preacher, because the preacher would know about deaths.

It had taken them all the dark day to rid out whatever it had been that had appeared in the woods, whatever it was that they'd burned out in front of the doctor's house. The whole day had been dark and now it was getting to dusk. The night was coming as dark as the day. Jim thought about the magician and the little baby missing and what had been happening.

He told the doctor to go and see Elsie Starkey and ask her once and for all about this baby and what had happened. Maybe Elsie had seen things the way Violet had and it made her crazy and lose hope. Maybe the magician, Simon, knew way more.

The preacher was having a dream. In the dream he saw a shiny black grasshopper and long blades of green, green grass. The grasshopper was bounding all around, its gold and black face twitching, its spiny, hard legs kicking. It spit dark brown, its mouth with those tiny, little arms working to spit the juice. The sunshine sparkling, a cold breeze blowing. Then there was more than just one grasshopper. All the blades of grass were the striped yellow and black bugs all clicking and whirring, rustling and fussing in the hot sun. There was a smell of burning and up ahead, as the preacher looked up and away from the ground, he could see his house and the church, like an arrow, rising up in front of a flat, gray sky. Then everything burst into fire and was covered up in dark smoke and glistening bugs.

"Thank God," he was saying to himself in his sleep.

Once he woke up and found his wife standing over him. He was sitting up straight in a chair.

"I want to see her. I want to see my little girl," he said. His face was moving now just as normal, his lips red. His right eye, though, still looked somehow broken with the veins. It looked as if it was dead, like a fish's eye.

"I want to see her," he said again.

Aline sighed and thought of her daughter. She remembered times not too long ago when the three of them sat around the table laughing and singing the old songs.

She helped him up. His mind was so fuzzy that all he really could feel was the deep, inside feeling of the urge to see his daughter—her face would tell him that everything was all right. Though somewhere in his head was the vaguest idea that she was in danger.

"Thank God," he said again, not sure why. His wife helped him up and helped him shuffle through the narrow hallway over to his daughter's little room.

He stood there for a while watching his daughter, Merla, sleep, her breath moving in and out. He didn't want to wake her. She had slept all through the whole night. His wife told him that she slept through all the commotion at the church.

He sat down on the little stool there beside her bed. He was so tired.

His eyes flickered and he wondered where his wife had gotten off to. He must have dozed on the stool. The room seemed so dark suddenly and the window even seemed to grow darker than the rest of the room. For a moment his heart started up fast and the blood rushed to his head.

He could hear his wife, though. She must be off in the kitchen. He could hear her clinking around in there. It calmed him. He realized that he didn't know what to tell her. Where had he been? He pushed around in his mind for a memory of anything, and nothing came. His body felt warm and there was a fuzzy, bubbly quality to everything he was seeing in front of him: his daughter's breathing, slow in, slow out; the blue and purples of the room around him growing and swaying as Merla breathed.

He suddenly remembered that a blade had been inserted into his shoulder and that the outlander had made off with his arm. But he had his arm.

He looked at his daughter. There she was, her chubby face with her mouth open sleeping, with her dark curls splashed out around her head on the pillow. He wanted to reach out and touch her curls, but he didn't want to wake her.

He remembered something of his arm being wrenched away from the shoulder and looked down into his lap. There, across his belly, was something that looked very much like his arm in his sleeve. At the end of it was what must be his own hand in a black glove. Pinned to the glove was a piece of paper with writing on it.

He picked up the paper with his good hand and read it. The paper read: "Do not touch or move the arm. Give medicine according to instructions in bag. Say your prayers."

The preacher's mind spun and there was a metal taste in his mouth.

His wife appeared in the doorway.

"Come on," she said, "I've let you look now. Come on, let's get you in your chair. I don't like it. It's what the doctor said to do. The doctor said so. We might as well do it."

"The chair?" Vernon asked and looked around, suddenly wondering why he was in his daughter's room. His throat was scratchy, his memories flushed away, but his voice sounded clear and deep to him. The sound of his own voice made him smile in the darkness.

His wife helped him into the next room and into his chair in front of the fireplace. She sat him down in the chair and got him comfortable.

She took the paper he was holding in his right hand and very gently pinned it back on the gloved hand that rested on his lap.

Vernon stared at the yellow and white and blue flames curling and flickering in the fireplace. Then he looked at the brick—the brick behind which he had hidden away the writings. As soon as he could, he would copy them again and again. He would spread the words when he could write again. But his arm, his arm, his arm . . .

As his eyes closed, the light continued to dance and it became the wings of grasshoppers, a thousand-thousand grasshoppers glittering and buzzing fatly through a smoky field. The sun was setting.

Jim didn't waste any time crossing the little town to get to Vernon Mosely's house. It was getting dark.

The house was around back behind the church. The preacher's wife was at the door when he knocked and she looked him over.

"John Mosely says you saved my husband's life, stranger," she said, "but that means nothing to me. I don't like you. Neither does John. Neither do most of the folk around here. They say you saved him with magic. We don't do magic down here in Sparrow." Her face was serious and blank.

Jim didn't say anything.

"He's in there," she said quietly and pointed to a room where a fire was going. "Don't you try anything."

Just off in the room, the preacher snored, his arm pinned to his shirt exactly the way the doctor had described, note and all.

Jim sat in the other chair and got out his little book and thumbed through the papers. His memory was terrible right now. If he didn't chew the leaves, his mind got scrambled. He was low: only a few small ones left, and they were turning brown. Sometimes his memory would come sharp and quick, but mostly it was wandering. Sometimes the wandering was good, as if an invisible shepherd was out there in front of the thoughts, drawing them along. Something seemed at times to be leading him through his own mind, as if there was something else inside him besides himself. He trusted it. He had learned to trust it, even if it provided more questions rather than answers. It was a bad situation. If he chewed the leaves, the shepherd wouldn't come at all, but if he didn't chew them, he had to rely almost completely on his little book as his own memory.

The preacher, Vernon Mosely, opened his eyes, and they fluttered for a moment and then landed on Jim. The minister's plump face almost turned up in a smile, but then fell into a heaviness; his eyes turned away from Jim and, glinting, looked deep into the fire.

Nothing was said between the two of them for a long while. Jim fiddled around in his little book.

The preacher coughed and then he said, "She let you in?"

"Your wife doesn't like me," Jim said.

The preacher adjusted himself in his chair a moment and looked back and forth from the stranger to the fire and back a few times. All kinds of worries were crossing over his face, and his fingers fidgeted on the note that was pinned to his once missing arm. He wasn't sure. This stranger, this outlander, had been the one who had removed and run off with this arm of his, but exactly why that was, and exactly what this strange man who claimed powers and carried a mysterious satchel and a book with writing in it, a man who made known in public that he was some kind of ridder of spirits, what this man was, the preacher didn't exactly know. He looked at the stranger's face. The man looked honest. Honest and good. His eyes, though hard, were kind, and there was something about the way he sat there that made the preacher feel certain that he meant no harm. Then again, that was what was to be feared.

The stranger was staring at him with wide, kind eyes. The preacher's mind started flashing and humming with all the events that had taken place, and suddenly, without meaning for it, the truth started coming out of his mouth and the stranger began scribbling in his little book.

"I've been to see the witch," the preacher said quietly, his eyes opening wide. "I've been to see the witch, Wylene, on the hill. The magician, Simon, he's the one helped me to find her. He gave me the token in a box. If you don't use it, you can't find the witch's place."

The preacher gave a long pause and then said, "I won't kill her."

Jim looked up from his book. "A witch, you say?"

The preacher continued: "I know the writings. I know what they say and I know what the people in the North are doing with them, but I won't do it. We're not the appointed judges of it, and I won't do it. I told her so. I told her that I wouldn't let her be brought to any harm, but that she had to show me, she had to help me."

Jim wanted to tell the preacher what he knew, but he wasn't at all sure if he should. What he knew was that if the preacher had been to see a real witch, he would have never returned. Witches were straight from the Evil One's world; there was never a human being that was helped by a witch, not a true witch.

The preacher's upper lip trembled a bit. "She showed me. She showed me the Evil One and told me things that I can't say and can't rightly remember." The preacher looked at Jim dead in the eye. "You see, at first I thought that maybe you had brought these things about. I figured maybe you was some kind of a witch-man, or maybe even a demon of some sort, or a conjurer, no. Then, too, I thought maybe it had been Simon all along. No. And that Violet Hill woman, she called you here by some power, but maybe that was a power outside her power, and that doesn't make her a witch. She wanted to do what was right. Somehow she had heard of you. Someone told her about you. A stranger in the woods told her about you and she could call you by visions. This is what the witch, Wylene, told me."

Jim Falk looked back into the preacher's eyes. He saw fear. But when he looked deeper, he saw there a conviction, and deeper than that, something solid and unchangeable seeming.

"Preacher," Jim said, "what do you think is happening here? This Evil One, as you call it. What is happening here? Tell me about this witch of Sparrow Creek."

Vernon Mosely looked back at the fire. "This evil, it's not the witch. She might not be a witch exactly, I don't think. She's just an old woman. She showed me. We are all in danger of death," he said. "They've been here a long time and they've had no reason to come out. They've been hiding in the hollows and in the forest. Sleeping. Waiting. Now they're awake. They woke up. They're coming around now because they're looking for something . . . maybe you or maybe me. Do you know what I am talking about?"

Jim knew. "I believe I know," he said. "They're after the ones who know the Waycraft and the writings. You know about the writings?"

"The Waycraft?" The preacher asked, but had heard clearly what the outlander was saying. He wondered what this stranger could know about it. He felt a bit of relief that someone else might know, but he also felt more fear.

"The Waycraft," Jim replied. "The writings."

The preacher's mouth dropped open and then shut. He said, "Some were not lost. Some have been found." And he couldn't help it, but he glanced toward the mantel of his fireplace and Jim followed his eyes.

They looked at each other for a moment and Jim looked back at the bricks behind the fireplace.

Jim raised his eyebrows and then he stood up and walked toward the mantel. "This witch, Wylene, how did she show you this?"

The preacher said, "Through her. She said she did nothing, but everything was shown through her. She said she was hollow."

"Hollow?" Jim asked and pointed to the mantel.

The preacher choked a little. "That's what she said."

Jim looked at the preacher in the little room. The fire in the fireplace lit up his body sitting there on the chair, all wrapped up in blankets. The note that the doctor had pinned to his arm was still pinned to his arm. The preacher was afraid. It was clear to Jim that whatever it was this witch had shown him had put a fear on the preacher awful.

Jim walked over to the fireplace and looked at everything that was over there. There wasn't much—a couple of candles and a dusty vase with no flowers in it. His eyes ran along the mantel and came to the one brick where the preacher had glanced. There was nothing different about it. It looked like all the others.

He reached out and plucked at it. Behind him the preacher drew in a deep breath. "Falk, Falk."

"What is this, preacher?" Jim whispered and removed the brick and then pulled the silver metal box from the hole. He opened it.

Inside were some old papers with writing on them, black ink on yellowing papers. The handwriting was different, by different people on different papers, and one was a little book not unlike his own. Jim read over some of the papers in the firelight. He read them more, he recognized a phrase "while you were in your blood," a sketch of a man coming out of a cave, and then a picture of a woman with wings holding a flaming sword on a mountainside.

He looked at the little book. He set down the metal box and pulled the little book out and opened it.

"I recognize these. These are like the writings that my father lost in the caves since before I was a boy, the spells, the Waycraft, the stories from the River People." He flipped the pages. "This is my father's book, but it's written by other people. How is that possible? Preacher, how is that possible?"

"I do not know, Falk. I do not know."

Falk flipped greedily through the pages. He wondered if there was anything in here at all that could help them. He hoped.

"This is what they are after?" he asked after a bit.

The preacher nodded. "I think that's a fair assumption."

"I need to find that witch."

The preacher pointed with his good arm toward the North. "She is hidden. You'll need to get that little box from Simon and what's inside," the preacher said.

Jim tipped his hat to the preacher. "What's inside?"

"A thumb."

"A thumb?"

"Her thumb."

"Where do you think Simon came across the little box?"

"He wouldn't say."

Jim scratched his chin.

"Preacher," Jim said, "whatever happened to that Starkey baby? What happened to that little girl?"

The preacher said, "No one knows what happened to the little baby Rebeccah."

Jim turned and left and the preacher watched him go, feeling his limp arm with his right hand.

⁂

"What is all this knowing or not knowing?" Benjamin Straddler asked Lane. He was smiling and looking at his face in the little mirror. He was smiling for real.

Lane was almost afraid to look anywhere but straight at her husband's mouth, afraid that if she blinked, that smile would disappear.

"You know something," he said, "or you don't know something. What does it do? Where does it end?"

Lane was close to him. His shirt was off and his hands were clean and his eyes were bright. The morning light was coming in through the windows in the kitchen, casting long shadows of the rickety chairs, making his eyes gleam with the sun's light.

He dried his hands on a rag and then grabbed her hands up in his hands. He pressed her open palms suddenly on his hairy chest.

She felt his heart in there, something like a big frog jumping against his bones.

"That's it!" he said and laughed. "That's what we know."

She put her arms around his neck and kissed his big face. She was looking at his mouth and the way he was smiling so wide. Then his mouth twisted a bit, but the smile stayed there.

Benjamin started sobbing, "My father, my father! I saw my father's face—it wasn't a dream, Lane. It made me know. It made me know just like this, like my heart thumping, it made me know."

The feeling Lane had in her chest turned inward on itself and, as she held him, a shiver of something passed through her mind. She thought of all these years she'd spent with him, taking care of him as he drank bottles and sobbed about his lost family, never listening to her talk about hope, him never changing, always arguing against it, some excuse, some memory blotting it out. She thought of her prayers nightly—prayers for his peace, for him to be sent peace. The shiver in her mind told her that God, if there was a God, had given him a peace here—even if it was the twisted peace of madness, it was peace.

Yet he'd not picked up a bottle since seeing the outlander lying there in the mud. He'd not done a thing but sleep, sleep and eat and smile with that weird light in his eyes. And now, here he was in front of her, getting ready to go out. She let go of him, feeling the shiver blossom in her stomach.

"I'm going to the Marbos'," he said.

Her heart went cold. She walked to the stove. This is what she had feared. "They're closed up," she said quietly. "They're closed up on account of what's been going on."

"What's been going on?" he asked.

"The happenings," she said, fearful. "Bill Hill gone. The chicken man gone. Both dead, probably. Says there's been demons around, spooks. Haven't you heard? Now what—you gonna go up and have a drink and see about it?"

"No," he said after a moment's thought. "No. I am not going to Huck's for a drink. I'm going over to the Marbos' house. I need to tell Huck and May too. I need to tell them what's happened to me and start setting some things right around here."

"What did you see?" Lane turned and looked at him. Her heart wanted this hope to be real, wanted her husband to be back and to be what she once thought he could be. But this tremor lay in her and a greater and more real-feeling fear mixed in her and soured the hope. He had gone out of his mind.

"What did you see, Benji?" she asked again as he didn't seem able at first to answer her.

Benjamin looked at his beautiful wife and saw that awful fear in her eyes. He stepped up to the table and pulled away a chair and sat on it.

"Come," he said.

"What?"

"Come and sit down. Sit down and we'll talk."

"About?"

He smiled again. "About what's happening, Lane."

"What's happened here?"

"Yes, I saw something that . . . well, I saw, yes, but it's more than that. It's more than that, Lane."

"What did you see, Benji? The stranger's face in the dark? With wolves all around and lightning flashing and whisky in your stomach? And you saw your father? That stranger is not your father."

"Lane, come and sit down."

She'd begun to cry a little bit.

"I want to tell you exactly," he said.

She started shaking her head no.

He looked at her for a long time, watching her shake her head and stare at the floor with her eyes wide, too many thoughts moving in her mind.

Benjamin wanted to speak, but he did not. He wanted to say something, but he did not.

More than anything he could feel that something somewhere inside of her had shut itself off from him. That this moment he'd wanted, where she would sit across from him and the words would come out of his mouth that would make her understand, that moment would not be.

She turned away from him and walked toward the side window, looking out.

Slowly he stood and thought of going to her, but again he felt that shut-off feeling coming from her and he stepped back toward the door.

"Yes," the voice said in Lane's mind. "There's no telling. There's no telling what he'll do."

"Lane," Benjamin said at last, "I'll be back and you'll see. I mean to set it right."

She did not turn around, and she felt it, too. She thought of him, but nothing happened in her heart. What about her? What was he going off to set right that didn't start right here? Here at this moment when she wanted to be able to turn to her husband and hope, she could feel nothing except a flatness. She looked out the window at the frost on the grass.

She heard the door slowly open and close behind her. She began to gather her things.

Benjamin Straddler walked through Sparrow in the early morning. The frost was on the grass and there was a clean, wet scent somewhere underneath everything, too. Benjamin thought there was something that smelled a bit like gunpowder.

Then he heard the reports, loud and clear, coming from down where the doctor lives.

He ran up the little hill to see if he could see. He got to the top and looked down toward the doctor's house. He could see figures moving about, but some kind of a fog had descended on the whole area down there so that he couldn't really see. He heard more reports then and saw figures running about. He could see something bigger than a man, something dark and much bigger than a man whirling around in the mist.

Benjamin patted his waist and his sides. He'd nothing with him, not even his knife. He thought about running down there to find out and help whoever was down there in the mist. He squinted and looked in again.

Behind him was the long road out to the Marbos' and the Hills' house. He could run home and get his gun. He stood there looking. Now a deeper thunder and crackle came, and the mist seemed to grow thicker. He took a few steps toward the mist to see if he could get a better view.

He heard a voice beside him. "Are you lookin' too?"

It was Hattie Jones and Samuel. Samuel's eyes looked keen and liquid down toward the noises.

"We've been hearin' the noise for a while," said Hattie. "It's like they got an animal down there. I think it might be one of them bears like a big black bear from somewhere down there, like one of them black bears mighta come out of the woods just like the other critters, the wolves, and the raccoons. You had any trouble with raccoons? We sure have. You know the woods have gone barren, they say. And worse than that. They say that there's places you get to where the trees turn to dust if you touch them."

Hattie Jones turned his eyes away from the mist as two more thuds came up from below. He looked at Benjamin.

"My gracious," he said, seeing Benjamin's face. "My gracious."

Benjamin looked back at Hattie; his old forehead was wrinkled up in some kind of wonder.

"Look at you!" Hattie said and smiled and kind of went back on his heels.

Benjamin smiled too. Knowing now that what he had seen in the mirror this morning wasn't just wishful thinking or that his hope and whatever this feeling was inside him just made him think that he looked that way. There really was something different, there really was some light in his eyes that hadn't been there.

Samuel's eyes were darting this way and that. He was looking into the mist, but his eyes seemed to be following some kind of movement down there.

It got quiet all of a sudden and the mist seemed to grow even darker, changing from a cloudy white gradually to an oily gray. There was no noise for a little piece and then all the wind died away.

Hattie whispered, "I heard some shots and came to see, but it seems like there's nothin' to see. I tried goin' down in there, but that gave me the shivers so bad I got dizzy. It's strange, isn't it? I couldn't see a thing in that fog, and the more I was in it, the more I felt like something else was in there with me. Strange, isn't it?"

Hattie reached out when he said this and grabbed onto Samuel's arm. "Come on, son, let's come away from this place."

Benjamin said, "Hattie Jones, you've known me for a long time. You've known all my story and you were there when the wolves killed my pa. I want you to know that you've been a good friend to me."

Hattie turned very slowly and said, "Are you dying?"

Benjamin paused a moment and thought about that because, to be honest, he felt that sounded right even though he wasn't really dying. "No," he said. "No. I am not. Not exactly."

Hattie Jones tipped his hat and looked back into the darkening mist and then to his left and his right and was not sure what to say. "Well, okay," he said and tromped off, his hand around Samuel's wrist.

Benjamin could hear him saying, "I'm done in this town. The devil take it."

# CHAPTER 15

Simon cried. The tears were all over his cheeks and his nose was running and he had to keep wiping his hands across his face. The fear had him.

He looked once more through the just cracked doorway into his mother's room. For a moment he froze and didn't breathe. His reddened eyes widened and his mouth parted, his breath stuck in his chest.

There it went.

Another black shadow danced along the inside of the door frame. The fire crackled and Simon walked quiet as he could to the door and closed it. When it was clicked shut, his breath came out in a sob.

On the table in the room lay the Book flipped open to pages covered in scrawl and spirals—he'd made some of these marks himself. He glanced over and his eyebrows came together and he put both hands up to his face. Out of his mouth came a quick bark of grief. He ran to the table and scooped at it wildly, to pick it up or to knock it onto the floor, he couldn't tell.

Then a noise came from inside his mother's room, a low, quiet chattering. Someone was talking, in a way, but trying to keep from being heard.

Simon grabbed up his books. He looked again at the door. His face was white and shone with sweat. He looked at the books on the floor and on the table and he kicked one of the books. "I didn't mean it," he whispered, but then he frowned and looked at the door and said it again louder, over the fire, "I didn't mean it! I take it back! I take it back!"

As in answer to him, a hissing came from his mother's room. A hiss and then a bump, and then a louder bump.

Simon looked at the Book and quickly grabbed up a sack. His hands and body moved fast; he suddenly caught up its weight and stuffed it in.

He heard another voice in the room now. His mother's voice. He heard Elsie Starkey's voice. She said, "Who are you? What do you want?"

He turned away from the door, yanking up the sack onto his back.

He heard his mother's trembling voice: "Who's here? Who is that? What do you want?"

Simon knew that they would come for her. Whatever they might be. They always came for their part. They had repeated that several times. He'd kept her as long as he could, which was as long as they said he could. He'd kept her there just as they said he could in exchange for little Rebeccah first. Now they'd come to take what belonged to them.

He could hear the struggling begin now behind the door, he heard the low rasping voices of the killers growling threats and curses in the forgotten language. Suddenly there came a thrashing form from the room and the thumping sound of fists against flesh. Simon put his hand on the latch of the front door, quietly, slowly, fearful to move, fearful not to move, or to distract the things from their task.

Just as he turned the latch, the door to his mother's room shattered and her body clumsily landed across the table.

"Simon!" Elsie shouted, her face was already swollen. "Simon!"

Simon shut tight his eyes, his right hand gripping the latch. He'd seen the things in the dark room, and they had seen him. For some reason, they had stopped their onslaught and were observing him. Waiting in the blackness of the room. Now and again, the fire flickering in the fireplace would reveal a swatch of the smooth gray skin, or cast a pale light across the sunken faces. In the reddish light, one could see that perhaps these were once men. Yes, they could be just men who'd become crooked and bent into their own evils—lost in the wilderness, wild and without mercy, their nails sharpened, their eyes quick and flashing as a dog's, but this was only in the light. As the shadows passed over them, or if they receded into the dark corners of the room, the figures grew ever more twisted and cruel, and then, rising from their backs stretched the webbings of long-fingered wings.

But later, in thinking back on the things, the mind could never be fully satisfied or convinced that it had seen anything more than a trick of the shadows and the wild men of the woods—perhaps a tribe of old natives from deep country.

Now those things held back, but they peered into the room where Simon and Elsie were.

Elsie began to recover, sitting up on the table. "I've been asleep?" she said. "How long? Was it a dream? Simon?"

Simon could feel Elsie's eyes on the back of his head. He turned the latch and disappeared into the night as behind him the things launched from Elsie's bedroom and onto her.

As he ran from his home he could hear crashing and gurgled screams coming from behind him. This was the end for her. But for him, for him, this was not the end at all.

He held the book tighter to his chest and ran down the main road into town. For a moment Elsie's face flashed up in his mind. He remembered that she had been there. Someone had taken him away from those people. There had been some blurred time of terror and a strange figure between those people and Elsie—those people who made him tired, screamed at him in a language he didn't understand, caged him. He remembered it as if it was some legend told to him by a storyteller, he remembered some cloaked man fighting with the people who had imprisoned him and then Elsie's warm hands hugging him close. What had he done?

The memories sickened him. Their softness began to sharpen and mix with the images of these dark things that came to him in the blizzard. They spoke of a power to get revenge on those slavers that took his real mother and killed his true father. They spoke of a power that would free him from his current life, bound to a hopeless mother, in nowhere Sparrow, fiddling with parlor tricks, searching, searching. The Way of the preachers and the church were empty tales told by hypocrites and farm hands. The dark things spoke of practicality, of wealth, of power.

But this mother, Elsie, she had been kind, bright as a flower in the moonlight, now . . . "We will show you these powers, but we will take our part. We always take our part."

He ran on. He was running in fear deep and true and he knew that now. The fear kept him going. On this night, the agreement between him and the dark things was ended. He had the Book now, though, but he would have to get away, far away. They could do as they pleased, as could he. He was no more protected from them anymore than the rest of the folks, but now he could try the powers.

On up ahead of him, he caught sight of a shape at the edge of the path. Out of breath as he was, he put on an extra burst of speed and cut hard away from the shape, thinking that this would get him by. But instead he found himself suddenly lying on his back and struggling for air.

Something had pounded his chest and dropped him hard into the cold mud, his satchel of books somewhere beside him.

"Simon Starkey," a man's voice said to him, "where are you headed in this night?"

Simon tried to get himself up, but Doc Pritham kept him down with a heavy thrust of his boot.

The doctor was looking at the house up there at the end of the path and something looked not quite right about it, but he couldn't quite figure out what.

"Where are you running off to?" the doctor asked.

Simon smiled up at the doctor. "Doc, you gotta let me up. Something terrible's happened."

The doctor let him up, but grabbed him tight by his elbow on the left arm and twisted a bit. He could see a blazing fire suddenly pouring upwards from the Starkey house and he could feel that Simon did not intend to stay put.

"The killers," Simon said in a harsh whisper and scrambled about. "The killers! Old Bendy's Men! Like from the old stories. They've come and they killed my ma! Elsie!"

Doc Pritham glanced up toward the Starkey house which was crumbling into flames and smoke.

"We'll see about this," the doctor said and, dragging Simon by his arm, began to head up toward the house. "Who set this fire? Who set this fire, magician?"

"No!" Simon shouted. "No! Doc! No! They'll kill us!"

"Kill us? Who's going to kill us?"

Simon spun hard to the right, but the doctor was heavy and his hand was strong—he tightened his grip on the kid's arm and Simon's wiry frame buckled and he went down on one knee in pain.

"Look, Doc," Simon was saying, glancing back down the road. Somewhere there in the mud and darkness was his leather satchel with the Book. "Doc, don't you know what those things are?"

The doctor shoved his face into Simon's face. "Why? Why would I know? You have some reason why I should know what these things are? Stories! Monsters from stories? You got a good reason for me to believe old spook stories, magician? Did you conjure them up? Or did you set fire to your own house? What I can believe, Simon Starkey, is that some kid is mixin' up with some kind of false magic, expecting dark miracles from old books, and now he's got blood on his hands and he's finding out that all them books and symbols aren't worth anything but a few card tricks!"

There was a poof noise and they were awash in a bright yellow glow followed by a crackling and snapping wind.

They both turned and felt the hot wind of the house fire roll over them.

"Elsie!" Simon shouted.

The flames were enormous now, reaching in a kind of column up into the night and then dwindling quickly into a smolder. Pieces of the little home flitted about and burned away here and there in a tree or landed in the soft mud still glowing red and orange embers with white tips, wide swatches of burning cloth flapped by the doctor's head. He grabbed his hat and held it tight on.

The doctor let go of Simon then and the two men stood there staring into the big, bright fire.

In the fire, they saw the outlines of what looked to be men, five of them. The dark silhouettes stood together and then, as if noticing they had been seen, they shifted, rose from the ground, and disappeared into the smoke.

The doctor looked at Simon.

Simon looked at the doctor.

Stubble covered most of the doctor's old face and neck. The wind blew hard and the house fire whipped the shadows around on his face.

Doc Pritham smiled a quick smile and said, "You're scared, aren't you? What are you scared of?"

Simon began to walk away.

The doctor looked at the house still licking flames into the night and then back at Simon. He could hear Simon picking up the pace, putting distance between the two of them.

"Simon!" the doctor called after him. "What happened? What happened to your little sister? What happened to Elsie's baby?"

Simon turned and looked at the doctor. The house blazed up again behind the doctor. He took a few steps back toward Doc Pritham so that the doc could see his face.

Simon pointed at the house. "They came during the blizzard! You know!"

Somewhere off in the sky, Simon thought he heard a whispering voice and he noticed that the night wasn't so dark, at least not in the road where his satchel lay with the book inside. He could see it up there in the road just behind the doctor. The doctor was keeping him from it.

"Who came?" the doctor asked.

Simon said, "Doc, you know who came. Men like us; we don't have to pretend. Men like us; we don't have to lie. We know what we know, Doc. Yes? Don't we? We know what we've seen. We know about the darkness. And I know that you know, or that you pretty much can guess where that little girl is."

Simon took a few more steps forward and felt a kind of heat coming at him from the bag that was over there in the mud. He saw an image in his mind of the doctor flailing and falling aside; in his mind he picked up the Book, gripped it, and as he did so, symbols floated up in black swirls. He saw a drawing of a kind of knife-fingered glove, he saw a conjuring circle sketched by a sharp pen with four triangles pointed to four directions. He felt his heart beating, beating. It was the Speaking Book that he'd been promised by the killers. It was speaking to him!

This old, fat doctor was not going to end his journey. In fact, no one could.

The doctor saw something in Simon's eyes and he moved his hand slowly down toward his belt where his gun was holstered.

A smile drew across Simon's face and his white teeth shone in the firelight. His voice grew louder. "The killers, Doc!" Simon laughed and raised his arms a little and took another step toward the doctor. "Isn't that what you call them? The killers? The Sons of Nod? The sons of Cain? Yes, yes! From the mountain of the angels? They survived what the others didn't! They survived the great flood waters! How did they do it? How did they do it?"

Simon drew his hands together like a prayer and something shifted in him, and he seemed momentarily to stumble as if a big wind blew him from behind, then his features grew dark and unseen and he rushed wildly at the doctor.

The crack of the doctor's pistol stopped Simon and he fell down in the cold mud. The doctor walked up to him and saw him sputtering and twisting there on his back. He gave him another round in the head to stop the pain.

"No friend of the Evil One," the doctor said, "is a friend of mine."

The doctor left Simon's body lying there in the mud in the night. By the light of the burning house, he could see where the magician's bag was plopped in the mud just down the path. He went and got the bag and closed it with the Book inside and took it with him. He didn't know what was in it, but he took it anyway. He headed back to find Jim and Violet.

Wylene, who was called by some a witch, and who was called Wylene by the people of Sparrow, lay in her broken cot in the center of the abandoned shed she called home. The darkness of night was disappearing, and gray and blue morning light seeped in through the slats. Long ago, her sense of smell had disappeared too, but somewhere back in her head the tiniest curl of a scent rolled up from her memory—the steely smell of frosted glass, the pines scratching the roof.

She placed her old hands in front of her face, studying her palms. The swirls and crisscrossed tattoos, the winged and arrow-ended circles and staffs—it was no longer possible to tell anymore which lines were drawn at birth and which had been stitched with ink and needle. She traced for a moment, with the index finger of her left hand, the nub where her right thumb once was. She remembered the woman who had taken it from her.

The pointed chin and thin lips were all she could see under the dark hood. They came in the night. Wylene rolled herself into a ball on her cot with the memory; the soft, serrated edges of the scars on her back tickled against her robes.

"You can't hide now," the woman's voice whispered harshly in her ear. "We'll hold you until they come for you and then we'll burn the whole lot of you. None of you will escape."

The figures in the square hoods behind her stood quietly by with whips and hatchets, the cloth hoods moving in and out with their breathing.

Wylene endured and was left naked and twisted on the dirt floor of this shed.

All these years, she'd wanted away. She'd wanted freedom and to run in the night again—to run free and not in fear. She wanted to be free again, but she'd not wanted revenge. These folks, scurrying through the night with their hoods and hatchets, their scriptures tucked away in a satchel, they simply did not know. How could they? They were animals who'd encountered a fire—standing, staring, or perhaps nestling close to get warm, none of them knowing where the fire came from, its power, its potential. The people of this world did not know that there were lightless fires that could freeze, and they certainly did not understand that mercy and goodness could come from strange faces with black eyes.

No, she'd never wanted revenge on these poor animals who could only be guided by fear, but freedom from their cruelty, yes. That would be enough.

As the morning light filled up the house, Wylene stood and walked to the back wall of the cabin, winding tight her black and gray wraps around her. She put her hands as close to the light as she could, but the spell with which the woman held her caused even the edges of the light to sting and bring smoke from her skin. She turned and shuffled back and lay in the small, dirty cot to sleep away the light.

She woke abruptly to see a long shadow fall onto the western wall of her cabin. Squinting into the light of the open door, she saw the outline form of the outlander with his long coat and beat-up hat. His hands held the little black box that the preacher had brought with him. Inside was her thumb. She shuddered. He had come in the day. Come at a time when he was here either to dispatch her for good or to force her through pain to a revelation. But men like this? She opened a black eye and peered at him. Men like this. She could see the green mist that shimmered around his body: he was a man of the Waycraft. If he thought she was a witch, a true witch, he would drag her into the light and she would burst into flame and die. She would not panic, though. These men were often weaker and more confused than their brashness projected; they were often fallen, too taken to drink and whoring, and their minds were often clouded and confused.

The witch unrolled the fabrics from her cowl and stood up like a black ghost. She pulled the dark veils over her face to protect her eyes from the pouring light that came from behind the outlander. To the outlander now, she appeared as only a black shape in the dark of the shed.

"Old woman," he said being cautious and formal, "stay at your bed."

"What do you want, outlander? Why have you disturbed an old woman's rest?" she hissed.

Jim took a step forward and, seeming to realize her discomfort with the light, used his foot to clap the door shut behind him.

Wylene did not relax.

He set the box down on a disintegrated stove.

"Old woman, the preacher told me that you were hollow," Jim said and raised an eyebrow. "I have not come here to rid you out."

The old woman didn't move.

"I have the power," Jim said, "to restore your hand."

The old woman didn't move.

"What is it that you want, James Falk?" she asked, a puff of her cold breath escaping from behind the dark veil she wore.

"You know that the old evil has awakened in the land," Jim said, trying to see her face behind the cloth.

She was quiet.

"I know that it was not your doing. I know that you have not brought this about."

"And what would you, child, know of such things?" she asked.

Jim didn't smile. "I was raised by the one they call the grandmother of the woods. Do you know her?"

Wylene's clawed fingers went limp when she heard the name. A heavy motion of some sort passed from her hips to her head, and she had to move her feet to stay standing.

Jim edged closer and closer to the dark figure standing near the cot.

"Woman, some think that you are a witch, but I know witches and you are not one," Jim said, and now knelt on one knee so that he could try to look behind the veil, directly at her face. "These powers that have awakened are stronger than I can face alone. You know what I am talking about. They are hiding some way. I cannot feel them as I once was able, or see where they've gone off to. They are too much in the darkness for my eyes. But maybe not for yours."

The witch's body slumped under the robes, and she turned her head away. "They will kill me," her voice croaked. "The rest of them are not like you. The others here in Sparrow. They are not what they seem either. They bound me here by way of some dark power that they do not know, but they will kill me as soon as the time comes—when the powers have grown full and their master comes from the North."

She sat back down on the edge of the little bed, searching in her mind for the reason for the feeling that she felt now, so foreign and heavy, and yet it felt like a cool water tingling and bubbling in her chest. She recalled suddenly finding a rabbit's den and the tiny ones bounding this way and that, and then she remembered this feeling. It was hope.

"No, old woman," Jim said. "They will not kill you, because I will not let them."

Jim stood and brought the box and set it in her lap. Kneeling in front of her now, Jim said, "I know the difference. Evil is evil only. You can't make it into good. You are not those things that you see, those visions, those voices. You are different somehow from those things, aren't you? You are hollow. Just as I am."

Jim opened the box in her lap and from it he drew the crooked piece of decayed flesh and bone.

"Give me your hand," Jim said.

"They will kill me," she said, but she almost sobbed with joy.

"No harm will come to you," Jim said strong and gruff. "They do not know evil. They cannot discern it because it has nearly consumed them."

From somewhere beneath the dark folds of cloth came the witch's wrinkled, tattooed, and thumbless right hand.

Jim united the thumb with the stump and covered it with his own two hands, his right still wrapped in the white bandages. Jim bowed his head over his hands and a stillness filled the little shed, then a cooling wind blew in through the cracks and Jim could smell the burning fire of the healing taking place as a pale gold light lit his face.

The witch felt a feeling in her hand, something like a tiny animal suddenly squirming and hot—and then the warmth of water cascaded over her whole body and behind her veil her eyes felt wet and there was a sudden moistness in her nostrils. She could smell something burning, and the light of the sun in the cracks of the cabin warmed and defined itself. Her muscles became lithe and itching, not just in her hand, in her whole self.

Jim stood back as she stood up and dropped back her hood and veil. Her black hair rolled in heavy curls from under her cowl, her face pale and sharp as a half-moon, the carved cheeks over pale, full lips.

Jim mumbled for the woman was young and beautiful.

Her eyes, though, were still without whites, black as oil in the sun and sparkling with dark rainbows.

The talons of her restored hands stuck out from her black sleeves. She stared at them momentarily and then stepped lightly to the boarded window. She tugged at the boards and allowed a wide blaze of green-tinted sunlight to fall on her hands and face. She curled and stretched her white, sharp-tipped fingers in the light, and they appeared beautiful and white and wicked.

She warmed her face in the light and then she smiled, revealing her perfectly sharp teeth.

She turned and her black eyes met Jim's blue eyes. In a clear low voice she said, "Old Bendy's Men they are. They must and can be lured. If we are to destroy them, we must draw them out from beyond the veil so that they might be burned. We can draw them out with a fresh corpse."

"The Starkey boy's been shot," Jim said.

"The magician?" she asked.

"The doctor's shot him. He's dead in the mud not far from here."

"They'll come in the night before dawn; we must move quickly," Wylene said and dropped the heavy outer portion of her black cloak to the ground, beneath which was a very thick black cape.

Jim and Wylene stepped out of the house and headed through the woods. Behind them a wind blew through the trees and the house quietly collapsed and slowly swirled away into a dusty wind and was no more.

As Jim looked at her and thought about what the preacher said—that she was hollow—a notion came to him. She was going to help him. She was going to help him rid out this evil. Whatever powers she had, without even blinking, she had already given him a key to drawing these creatures into the open so that he, so that *they* could finish them. Jim felt a strange warmth in his chest and recognized it as hope.

Wylene smiled at the sound of the little house collapsing, her sharp teeth glinting in the morning sun, but she did not turn back to look.

As they walked along, a cold wind blew through the tops of the trees and Wylene took a deep breath of the air and felt in her breath the tiny sparks of ice that meant snow was coming.

Jim came to the edge of the woods and looked down on the town. Snow was coming now, and it was dancing here and there in sunlight and clouds. Wylene had stepped into the trees behind him and he could not see her at all. He motioned for her to stay behind. Looking around and not wanting to whisper for her, he was pretty sure she was the shadow that looked a little too tall over by the crooked tree on the bank.

It was risky to bring her across through the open part of town and down around the bend to the doctor's place. It was risky for sure, but they were running out of time. Whatever the thing was that they'd killed out in front of the doctor's place, it was different from the others and it was stronger. It was stronger and stranger than anything that he'd ever seen. The other thing about the thing was that he couldn't shake the idea that it looked just like Kitaman. How could it be? It was one thing to understand that demons and spooks and witches were coming out of the woods, but it was another thing to consider that these old tales told by the old people of the woods and rivers were true too. It was too much to think about, and they were running out of time. But she was here now. This strange woman who was a witch or not a witch.

Jim had used the ancient words given to him by his father to restore her to her true form, and when she was restored she offered help.

He looked around again and squeezed his eyes and tried to clear out his mind so he could think of all the possibilities of what might happen if they started out of the woods and someone saw them. He felt around to see if anyone was standing about. Something in his mind told him that it was safe, but they had to go right now, right now, or else someone would come along. He waved at her to come with him and right away.

Wylene looked at him from her shadows. Here was this raggedy man in a beat-up hat who had for some reason restored her to herself. She wondered if he really even knew what he had done or how he had done it or why. Now, for some reason, he was leading her back into the town where she knew her captors from long ago were still lurking, still waiting. Yet there was something that was speaking to her through this broken-looking person. Something from long ago nudged her toward him, and she did move out of the shades and down the embankment toward Jim Falk. She wanted to help him.

There was a worn-out road that went up from what probably used to be a well just at the edge of the wood. Somewhere around here, long ago, might have been a house. They stuck to the edge of the clearing, making their way around the long way around.

The snow was still coming, and it made the clearing a silvery pink and white as it mixed with the morning sunshine. Wylene smiled underneath the veil that hid her face. Her eyes were hungry for the light: she yearned to take off the veil and run into the sunshine, it had been so long, so long.

Jim and Wylene came to a spot where they had to cross directly across the old road and then down into the little hollow where the doctor's house was. Wylene seemed to have no problem completely vanishing from sight while she stood along the tree line, but Jim was just a man after all. He looked left and right and right and left and squinted and looked and looked again. He couldn't see much but trees and snow swirling and the old, dirty road.

"Let's go," he whispered to her.

They crossed so quickly and vanished into the hollow so fast that anyone who wasn't staring straight at them would have only thought their eyes were playing tricks on them. But Merla Mosely, who was staring out the window and down the road and right at that spot, saw them both. She saw the shape of the outlander who had brought all the evil, Jim Falk, go across the road, and what she saw following behind him made her shudder. A moving shadow, a shadow that slinked and flickered across the road, following behind him, not pursuing him, but following the way a hound follows a master. Jim was leading a witch into town.

"It's snowing again," the doctor said. "It looks like it might get bad out."

The window was broken because of what the thing had done and the two of them shooting through it.

Violet stared into the doctor's little fire and wished that she had never called Falk. Violet wished that her husband was still alive. She wished that she could go back to a time when her husband was angry and a strange creature stared in her window. She was only frightened back then. There was part of her too that could still imagine the spook wasn't real. There was in those times something like a hope that the people in the little town of Sparrow were right after all and that her seeing the spook was on account of that she was crazy. But these were dreams of before, these things could no longer be.

"When will he be here? Why do we have to stay here? Could we not just meet at Huck's or in the town somewhere?" she asked, and her eyes dropped to her necklace and then back to the doctor.

"Violet, if there are more of those things out here . . ." The doctor stopped and crouched down beside her by the fireplace and stoked it a bit. He got up off his haunches and looked at her. "I have to ask you where you got what you have been taking out of that necklace. I don't mean to pry, but I do not think that the medicine I have been giving you has helped you as much as it could, and if I know . . ."

"I don't know. I don't know what it is," she snapped. "It was given to me by . . . by a stranger that lives out here in the woods. All I know is that when I take it, I don't feel afraid anymore."

At that moment they both turned their heads because they could hear someone coming along the path.

"Doctor, please tell me that's him and that's not something else," she said and tightened her jacket around her.

The doctor kept squinting and looking out the window. Beside him on the table lay the satchel with Simon's book.

He could hear two sets of steps coming too, tramping through the snow.

The doctor didn't like what he saw coming up the path. Jim was walking deliberately in front of a figure that the doctor couldn't make out much except that it appeared to be female, it was wrapped in a black cloak, and it made him uneasy.

Violet, sitting in the rocker, saw the doctor's hands fidgeting and heard his breath huffing as he tried to make decisions in his mind as to what it was that he saw. She stood up and came up beside him and looked through the busted-out window with him. The doctor, though he appeared soft and round, was more like a boulder than anything. She put her hand on his hard shoulder and asked him, "Who is that?"

Her other hand was raised now as she watched the two figures moving down to the door. Her hand went up to her neck and began fiddling with the empty locket that was hanging there.

A woman with her face veiled was walking behind Jim, her steps light and all her angles sharp. Violet knew why the doctor was huffing. She felt her skin go cold.

A witch.

Violet would not take her eyes off the witch. The witch didn't take any notice of Violet staring at her. They just came in the door together, like old friends.

The witch was busy studying the doctor's face and the flames in the fireplace.

"I can't understand you," the doctor said as the two stood there.

"Me?" Jim only half turned to look at the doctor with one eye.

"Yes, you. A witch like this killed your mother is what you said. What you told me. And now here you stand?"

The outlander smiled and looked at him and then at Violet. "You believe in all that, witches and such?"

The doctor smiled a bit too, a little amazed, and then looked at the outlander. "How can you trust this witch? Just let her come on in! Maybe she is the same one who killed your mother and knocked you on the head."

"This witch, as you say, she's not the same."

Violet eyed the witch. She was too scared to move, but she didn't want the witch to know that. "Not the same? The same as what?"

"I am not a witch," said the witch. "Call me what you like, but a witch is not what I am."

"See?" Jim said. "We don't have time for all this and we have business to do. Doctor, why don't you show me up there by the Starkey house? Tell me what happened, about you shooting that magician," Jim said and gestured over his shoulder as if back in the direction of the Starkey house.

The doctor squinted and tried to read the face of Jim Falk, but he couldn't. Jim just looked serious and normal.

Violet's eyes darted back and forth. "What? Where are you two going? You're just going to leave me here, with, with this?"

Jim turned and said, "Violet Hill, there is nothing to fear. We won't be long."

They left and closed the door.

"Nothing to fear?" she called after him. "Nothing to fear?" She turned in a half-circle away from the witch and picked up the bottle of the doctor's whisky and looked at the witch and took a big swig. "Nothing to fear."

The witch sat down on a chair near the fireplace and stretched her white hands toward the fire to warm them. Violet looked at the hands, covered in dark symbols ending in talons. She looked at Jim Falk and the doctor, took another drink, and flicked her eyes once and again toward the witch to try and catch a glimpse of the face hidden behind the veil. Despite the creature's weird clothing and the writing that covered her hands and even crawled up her wrists in places to her white elbows, what Violet felt coming through the veil was not fear—a deep, almost sleepy peace was coming from the witch.

Peace? Violet chased this thought away and put her hand into the sack on her lap and felt the cool, heavy handle of her pistol.

"You're a dreamer," the witch suddenly spoke from across the fire in a soft, deep tone.

Violet's eyes came slowly up and focused on that area of the veil where she thought the witch's mouth might be.

"You're a dreamer and you dream dreams, talking dreams and calling dreams. In the tales of the River People who live deep in the woods, there is a story like this. Calling Woman and Talking God. Have you heard the tale?" the witch said, and her voice sounded rich and somehow happy. She spread her hands wide and turned them to warm the backs of them.

"I don't take in stories that don't come from the church or a preacher," Violet said and gripped the pistol tighter. Jim she trusted, and the doctor, sure. Jim had said that the witch would not harm her, but she was in no mood to communicate with the thing.

"I think it's best if you and I just keep to our own business, don't you?" Violet said.

"Very well," the witch said and continued warming her weird hands.

It didn't take Jim and the doctor long to move their way up the winding path behind the doctor's house and over the hill to where he had last seen the magician.

Jim looked up the path to the collapsed house where a thin spiral of black smoke was still twisting up over the trees and into the gray sky.

"That's where the Starkey house was then, right?" Jim asked the doctor.

"Yes," Doc Pritham said and turned in a circle looking at the ground. His feet crunched the frozen mud.

Jim knelt down by the spot where the doctor told him that the body had been.

"How could I miss?" Doc Pritham stopped spinning and looked down where Jim was.

"You say you shot him in the head?" Jim asked, now reaching down and touching the indentation there in the hard ground of the path.

"Shot him right here, look!" The doctor turned and tapped the back of his own head just under his hat, indicating where he'd put the bullet in Simon—but he wasn't so sure now.

"Look here." Jim got up and walked a few paces away up toward the house. "Here's his feet coming down." He walked along with the feet. "Coming down." He pointed in a different place. "Here's you coming along."

Jim jogged back down toward the doctor a ways. "Here's where you stood and fired. It looks like he ran at you." The mud made it all easy.

The doctor said, "He was very interested, I think, in getting the contents of his sack."

Jim pondered this for a moment, rubbing his chin and looking into the doctor's eyes. He hadn't considered the sack. He hadn't heard a thing about the sack until just now. Something in his mind told him that the contents of the sack held a clue to where that little baby had disappeared to, a clue to what the preacher said about the witch's thumb. Somehow, Simon Starkey had gotten a hold of some things that belonged to someone else—someone who was a far piece more powerful than Simon may have understood.

Now Jim came right up to the doctor. "Yes, you shot at him up close, but look here," he said, ignoring the doctor's reference about the sack and its contents. "You should have brought the body with you."

"Yes, I relish the idea of dragging a dead magician through town in the middle of the night, wouldn't you?"

Jim ignored that and showed the doctor the black blood in the frosted mud and a round little hole a few inches away. "See here," Jim said crouching again and sticking his finger down into the little round hole. "Your bullet's down in there somewhere most likely. See where these feet go?" Jim pointed along the ground in a zigzag kind of way until he was pointing at the edge of the woods.

The doctor pulled up in his memory the final bullet that he had snapped off, he thought, into Simon's brain, but darkness was all he could see. His lips quivered and twisted and his hands curled at his sides. "That magician boy," the doctor said in a deeper voice and pointed to the smoldering home back up the trail. "He's in league."

"Is he now? Either way, we'll not find the killers by use of his corpse, since there is no corpse," Jim said, turning his mind on the witch or not a witch, Wylene.

Jim smiled a bit, but hid it from the doctor. He'd read the signs without the help of the leaves.

The two men stood for a while in the frost, listening and looking back and again at the woods and then at the smoking pile that was once a home. They turned and looked down at Sparrow. They needed to get back to Violet and the witch.

The sun was nearly all the way up now, but was only shown by the ever-gradual lightening of the color of the sky from a dim gray to a pale milk color. Snow came from different directions in fitful swirls down through the winding path into town. From here they could see the little church and Huck's place on the east side, back behind the church. Smoke rose here and there from the scattered little homes in the valley. They could just barely make out the little black spot of the chicken man's shattered cart. Nothing moved in the valley except the twirling columns of smoke from the chimneys.

"He's not gone back into town," Jim said.

"He's most likely run off," the doctor said.

"Or he might be looking for the book and his sack," Jim said.

The doctor didn't say anything.

Then they saw someone walking across the town toward the church. Then they saw two more. Jim was pretty sure one of them was May, standing in front of where the door had been busted. But there were other people holding rifles. They were looking left and looking right. Then they could make out the forms of Ruth Mosely and John Mosely headed up toward the church.

Jim said to the doctor. "If someone saw me . . ."

The two rushed back into the woods and through the path to the doctor's house as snow started dumping out of the sky and everything started to turn white.

Violet was chewing on some hard bread, still watching warily the witch on the other side of the fireplace, when the two men came through the door.

Jim said, "Grab up your things, Violet."

The doctor moved forward and picked up a bucket of dirt and threw it on the fire.

"We've got to move. Simon, the magician, is alive," the doctor said and picked up the sack of books that once belonged to Simon and rolled it up tight. "He's moving off to the west."

Jim watched the doctor pick up the sack.

"He's following after them," the witch said not moving from her rocker.

"Them?" the doctor asked.

"The ones he hates."

Jim said, "We don't have time for this. Something's going on down at the church. We saw some men with rifles and Ruth and John rushing up there."

A fit of snow burst suddenly into the broken window.

The four of them said nothing, but Violet gathered her things and the witch, Wylene, stood up.

# CHAPTER 16

Benjamin Straddler walked alongside Huck Marbo. May was behind them, looking this way and that. Each of them, their breath steaming, carried a bundle of wooden slats or tools, a heavy bag of nails jingled at Benjamin's side.

"Bill would have fixed this right up," Huck said, looking at Benjamin Straddler. Benjamin was looking at the sky.

"He sure would have," Benjamin said. "I'd like to see a blue sky sometime, wouldn't you?"

May nodded her head and Huck said, "Yes." The snow started.

The three of them got to the church in the center of town. Benjamin Straddler, with a wide smile on his face, took a long look up and down at the busted door on the front of the little church.

Huck got himself up the stairs and began studying the twisted hinges.

"I'd say that we can do a part fix today," Huck said. "At least get this part of the door back on, but we'll have to do more cutting and all to get this right—more than we can do. We'll have to ask Hattie, or get someone from outside Sparrow, to fashion a whole new door if we want it to look right again, seeing as how the man who made the door is the one that tore it down and I guess he's most likely dead now."

May thought about that. She thought about Bill and Violet and remembered back to when she was just a little girl. She remembered sitting in the pews at church between her ma and pa and

251

turning around in the little wooden pew while the preacher was talking. She remembered turning around and seeing Bill and Violet sitting there in the back, their faces looking bright as the sun came in the little windows along the side, the sunlight making Violet's red hair glow orange. Now what?

May looked at her pa and Benjamin Straddler and felt good to be with them. She felt something changing, but couldn't quite tell exactly what it was. Something was changing in Sparrow and maybe inside of her, but she wasn't sure if it was for the better. The sun seemed a little darker and the colors and shapes of things a little harsher. She looked back and forth.

Her father started in on some instructions, pointing and gesturing, but she couldn't pay attention.

"Alive!" she remembered Benjamin saying over breakfast. "I know it!"

May smiled and almost laughed remembering her pa's face all scrunched up and concerned and then across at Benjamin's face all wide open and young-looking, his eyes glittering. "Your Anna lives, Huck Marbo!"

But her pa was angry now. "You need to keep your religion to yourself, Benjamin Straddler! You may think certain things or see certain things. But that's not the way it is with all of us."

Benjamin turned his eyes down and looked at his eggs. He fumbled a bit as he talked about seeing his own father's face in the face of the outlander, and talking of how his bad dreams had gone, and how the fear in his heart had disappeared. A lot of what he said didn't make sense, not even to him, and Huck couldn't see where he was going with it or why he was even saying it. May couldn't piece it back together in her mind, but what she could see and what her father saw was that Benjamin Straddler, no matter how clumsy his words were, believed every word of what he was saying and that his eyes were shining.

May was smiling as she remembered and giggled a little at Benjamin's beaming face.

"What's funny?" her pa suddenly asked her.

"I don't know exactly," May said. And she didn't.

Then a man with a rifle was standing there on the steps of the church. She had seen him before at her pa's. His name she couldn't remember. But she remembered him being one of them men that drank and played cards and went home and didn't talk much.

"There's a witch," the man said. "The preacher's daughter seen her and she's in town. She's down with the doctor is what she said. She says that Falk brought the witch down into town just an hour ago or so and that he's fixing to turn her loose on what's left of the good folk of Sparrow. How can we stand for that? Marbo? You hear?"

Huck was standing there and he was listening, but this didn't make any sense. There were too many superstitions in this town, but this man was standing there with a rifle and Huck looked at May and then back at the man. "I hear."

May felt cold and she moved away from the man with the gun. Falk? A witch? It couldn't be right.

"What? You say that Falk brought the witch to town?" Benjamin Straddler asked the man.

"That's what Merla Mosely said, said she saw him come in here about an hour ago, that they must've been up, way up in the woods and come down near the hollow where the doctor's house is. I knew that doctor was no good. Well, I knew that outlander was no good, but I knew that that doctor was no good. I won't be a bit surprised to find out that that magician boy Simon ain't somehow wrapped up into all this with them either."

Then Ruth Mosely and John Mosely were coming up the path with Merla Mosely and her ma, Aline. Aline had a bruise on her face from where Ruth had smacked her last night. They were walking fast.

"Get the rest!" Ruth started shouting. "Get everybody! We've got a big problem!"

"Where's the preacher?" Benjamin asked Huck.

Ruth moved up the steps and didn't look at Benjamin or Huck or May and neither did John Mosely; they just went on by and went inside the church and so did Aline Mosely and Merla Mosely.

"Now what are we going to do?" they heard Ruth saying inside the church. "Well! Get in here!" she shouted now to the three who were standing outside. "This involves you too! Get in here!"

There were more people coming now, many of them May didn't recognize, but some she did. Some people were people whom she had only seen in the church and some people were ones whom no one really ever saw ever. But somehow, Ruth Mosely had drawn them all together here, and May could guess pretty easily that it was on account of Merla Mosely's report that Jim Falk had brought a witch to town.

Simon stumbled again and leaned against the cold tree in front of him. The morning light in his eyes only brightened the pain that ran hot and deep in his stomach. The doctor's bullet was in there somewhere. He was thirsty and his mind was cursing the doctor for not killing him.

It was hard for Simon to move his body at all without screaming. Now and again he would look up and see that he'd moved ahead or in some direction and that he was in a different place from where he was before. He found himself thinking only half-thoughts and seeing pictures of things that weren't there—his mother, strange animals—his memory was full of flashing holes.

He leaned on the cold tree and moved his other hand up to touch the sticky hair and the burning stripe of open skin that the doctor's second bullet made. The blood there was crisp and frozen, but at his belly it dribbled and sopped. He thought he could hear faint voices and the movement of feet crunching in the grass. Was that his own voice? His feet?

He staggered onward into the cold, white morning.

Then, with shaking legs, he was crossing over a frozen stream and then up a hard, little hill. Against a tree, he sat on the little knob of grass there at the top. Under him, down his sides, the hot blood was feeding the frosted ground.

He couldn't believe he was even alive. He raised up his hands in front of him to see if they were really his. The long, delicate fingers, so able to be quick and conceal and turn a card, now they were stained red and flopped toward him. His hands already looked dead. There wasn't even enough strength in them now to shake, and before his eyes, against the icy background of the woods, those hands looked unfamiliar to him, fake, like a bad trick. A shiver poured through his chest and legs that turned hot quick and then back to shivers. This happened over and over again, and soon he had forgotten what cold and hot were at all. He just felt warm and numb and sick and his thoughts raced away into the frozen sky.

It was then that he saw the shadow move suddenly from his right. A dark, hooded figure. He was sure he'd seen Death coming.

The figure leaned over him and whispered something. Whether it was to Simon, he could not tell, he could not even be afraid. He was too drained. His eyes rolled toward the spot where the figure's face should be under the hood, but there was only a flat darkness there. Many times in his life he had wondered what the end would be like.

"Who . . . who . . . who . . ." Simon managed to croak with cracked lips.

The dark figure in the hooded cloak knelt down now beside him and a little glass bottle came up to Simon's lips and he sucked at the lip not caring if it was poison or water. A taste like metal and a flood of relief came spreading through his veins. The nausea left him and the pain came back, quick and twisting into his stomach. He could hear again the wind through the bare trees and the rustling of the figure beside him. His ears were burning with cold. His vision sharpened and he saw the withered and strong, brown hands of this stranger working at Simon's naked belly, pressing something dark against the wound.

The pain of the sudden pressure was too much and he went out.

Simon woke up in a warm tent. There was a little fire some-where near him and he could feel someone close by.

"Don't try to move." The voice was hoarse and muffled, some-how far away.

His head, he could feel, was wrapped tightly with something that burned and itched and felt oily. The figure was suddenly over top of him, adjusting him roughly, fidgeting with his wrapped-up head.

Simon rolled his eyes around to take in the tent. It was made of animal skin and it was square, like one of the homes of the River People. One wall he could see looked to be made entirely of black-ish mud and rocks. At the same time he smelled it, he saw a man-gy-looking dog asleep on its side on the dirt floor. It was speckled with patches of bare skin, but it had bulging, coiled, almost cat-looking muscles. But it was a dog. It smelled like a dog. Was it a wolf?

The figure dropped Simon's head back down and moved away to sit on a stone by the fire. The wolf sprung up and meandered to the figure's side. Its big, pointed head had powerful jaws and bright silver eyes. It dropped and resumed its splayed position with a huff on the dirt floor beside its master.

The figure looked nothing more than a tall pile of dark rags be-side the animal. Then, a hoarse voice from the rags, "There were two men who came looking for you."

"Who are you?" Simon asked.

"What do you think they'll do if they find you?"

"I don't know."

"Do you think they'll kill you? Give you a trial maybe? Force you to say things that aren't true like they're doing in the North? They think you're in with the Evil One. What will they do when they open your book and see what's written in there?"

"You don't frighten me."

"I shouldn't. I am not the one you should be afraid of. You should only fear those who have powers to destroy both soul and body. Besides, I'm only here to help."

"Why?"

"Because you were dying there by that tree and I found you."

Simon was exhausted suddenly from talking. He took a deep breath that sent bolts of pain into his sides. Then he slept again and dreamed troubled dreams of being a boy in a cage surrounded by monster men.

Hattie stepped back from the drawing and turned in a little circle and looked at it again. He figured it might have disappeared if he looked away; or maybe if he looked away, when he looked back there would be some other picture there. Some other drawing that didn't have all those specifics in it, something that a boy should draw, but not this thing. But there it was, in curved and even elegant lines—a monster crouching over a heap of twisted and torn meat and bones that was once a horse. It was looking up right at Hattie, eyes wide in surprise as if Samuel had caught it there and frozen it somehow in that instant looking at him, pieces and parts of horse dangling and dribbling from the side of its weird mouth. Hattie looked closer at the drawing. Samuel drew the skin there with wrinkles all through it, wrinkles and pocks and scabs and cracks, so many lines. And worms or tubes like long leaches grabbed from inside its mouth, burrowing into the horse's hide.

The arms and legs looked like a man's, but they had been stretched long and they bent differently against the normal way and wherever they seemed to need to as if there were no bones in them at all. The face was what really got to him. It was not just one face, but looked to be the faces of many different animals and men all patchworked and layered and fitted somehow over a wedge-shaped skull that ended in that weird maw of broken, angular teeth. That mouth was ready to take whatever shape was necessary to fit whatever prey inside, pulled and bitten by the long, dark worms that twisted this way and that from the open mouth.

On its back were long, pointed quills that ended in what appeared to be little pointed hands or in some places like a bug's pincers. And its eyes were wide and empty and, more than menacing, they looked themselves to be frightened and pitiful like the eyes of someone in hopeless anguish.

Samuel sat over in the corner of the room now, rocking in place and humming to himself. Hattie didn't know what to do and he was tired of that feeling. He was tired of not knowing what to do. He was tired of thinking of leaving Sparrow altogether, but where would he go? This was his father's house and his father's house before him. Where would a Jones go, but Sparrow?

Hattie picked up the drawing and walked over to Samuel.

"Samuel," Hattie said and knelt down beside the boy, putting the drawing near his round, plain face. "Samuel, where did you see this?"

"No," Samuel answered, looking at Hattie with a sideways glance.

"Where did you see this?"

"No."

Hattie sighed and sat down on the floor. He looked at the picture and showed it again to Samuel.

"Horse," Samuel said.

"Right," Hattie said, and pointed to the mound of meat and bones. "Horse."

"No," Samuel said and shook his head and then extended a finger and put it on the thing's ugly face in the drawing. "Horse."

Hattie stood and rolled up the drawing and started getting things ready to go up to the church with the rest of them.

Tracks from every which way could be seen leading right up to the church. Hattie walked up the steps holding Samuel's hand.

They could hear the crowd that was gathered inside and when they got in the door they saw it was full of folk, full of folk from the whole of Sparrow. May and Huck were there, but many others were there too, many folk who were hardly seen or heard from, the ones who lived up on the ridge had even come in, the Osloes, Arnots, and the Dankirk brothers, Martha Mofat and her blind sister Annabelle. Clive Skiles, who used to help Bill Hill make wagon wheels, was holding a rifle. Marty Billowait was holding a rifle. John Bandy was holding a rifle.

Hattie felt like taking Samuel right back out the way he'd come in. But there was just enough room in the way back at the edge of the pew for Hattie and Samuel to squeeze in and kind of hide. The murmurs and whispers of the crowd grew clear and turned into understandable words like "up north," and "witch," and "snow spell."

Merla Mosely was talking loudly to Clive Skiles that she'd seen the witch at the edge of the wood dancing around a bucket of water before Jim Falk brought her into town. Immediately, heads turned with "whats" and "wheres" and "whens" and "the outlander with her?"

Ruth Mosely stood up from the crowd and walked up to beside the pulpit.

"Merla Mosely!" she shouted. "John!"

Her husband popped up and came to stand beside her, and Merla Mosely walked away from Clive Skiles and came and stood up there with them.

"Quiet!" Ruth shouted, and everybody went quiet. "Merla Mosely's got something to tell you all. Go ahead, Merla."

Merla looked around at all the faces. This must be what her pa sees on the days when he gives a lesson. "Good morning," she said.

"Good morning," the crowd said together.

"Just tell them!" Ruth whispered harshly at her.

"I saw Jim Falk bringing a witch to town . . ." Merla started to say, but before she could finish there were gasps and loud voices and some people stood up.

"Quiet!" Ruth shouted.

"Quiet!" John Mosely shouted. Everyone quieted down.

"Now go on, Merla," Ruth said again.

"Just at the edge of the wood they were. I couldn't really see what they were up to, but the witch seemed to be, well, dancing around a bucket. You know that's a spell they do to bring on the weather."

Many people nodded their heads.

"Then he took the witch down to the doctor's house and that's where they are right now!"

John spoke up now. "When Falk came to town, all these things started up again. If the snow continues as it is, we may be in a blizzard, but we're more prepared. Huck Marbo and some of us others have stored up quite a bit—enough to last a while for us all, a few weeks, maybe a month if we ration it out and if everyone is able to follow the rules. Enough time for someone to go up to Hopestill or over to Bowden and come back with more. But for the witch and Jim Falk . . ."

Ruth burst out impatiently, "Falk's to blame for all this! All of what's happened here, the chicken man getting killed, Bill Hill! The Starkey house burned down. Falk and the witch! The snow's coming! The snow is coming! Falk's brought the witch in here!"

Someone shouted, "Kill the witch! Kill Falk! Kill the outlander!"

May's eyes looked around at all the people of Sparrow and from up on the ridge and everyone who'd packed themselves up into the church.

The faces were pinched and eyebrows crooked, the mouths were open and twisted or closed and twisted and people were up suddenly on their feet with fists up in the air.

She looked up into her pa's face, but his eyes were cast down into his lap. They looked closed, but they weren't; they were looking down into his lap and his hands were there in his lap, clasped together.

"Pa," she whispered into his neck, "this isn't right."

Hattie Jones felt that this was all going in the wrong direction, so he shouted, "Where's the preacher? Why are we listening to you all anyway?"

Then Ruth snapped, "Silence!"

It was then that the preacher rose up. He had come in during the commotion. Vernon had woken up in his house to find that he was completely alone. Aline was gone, Merla was gone. He immediately ran to his fireplace and made sure his papers were safe in the spot. They were. He figured he should move them soon again, even though Falk was the only other person who knew where they were. He walked outside and noticed the snow coming down, but he noticed something else, too. He noticed that his arm was completely healed. He saw some people heading toward the church.

Now he stood and raised both his arms in the air to still the folks in the church, but now that he'd drawn attention to his arms and hand, many in the crowd took notice that his right hand was inside of a black glove, but his left hand was pink and exposed.

"Now," Vernon said again, and not being a man who was used to shouting, it was a little cracked in the middle. "Now! There's no use in this while the blizzard's coming! If there is any time we need to all stick together and not go accusing one another and judging one another, now is that time!"

He walked forward and stood down in front with Ruth and John and Merla Mosely all standing behind him.

Vernon looked over at his wife again and saw that not only was she not looking at him, but she was looking away and over at the wall of the little church. He looked over his shoulder to catch a glimpse of his brother's eyes, to see if there was any help there, but his brother was eagerly leaning his head up against Ruth's mouth as she, with a cupped hand, whispered and whispered into John's ear.

He looked at his wife again and now her eyes were open and on him burning and her brows were together. The conversation of the previous evening had shut her heart closed to him and her eyes said loud that he'd betrayed her. He shouldn't have told her. He was realizing this now. He shouldn't have said anything. Or at least, he should have said that he didn't know and that it was a snake probably that bit him was all and that all he remembered was waking up in the doctor's house and that the outlander had tried to help him but couldn't or some damned lie. He shouldn't have told her the truth, but he had.

At the sight of these eyes, Vernon's own heart burned with a sick and lonely fire. There came over and upon him a dizzying feeling that he'd never had; in his mind he saw a boat on a dim lake of silent, dark water. He looked at his wife and wondered about the truth that he told her the evening before and the truth about the stranger, about the witch, about his healing. Was it only overnight that all this had somehow twisted her against him? He looked at Ruth again. She was looking at him the same way, her white lips pressed together.

"Magic!" the word spit from Aline's pressed lips, and her right arm extended and at the end of it her hand curled, shaking and a finger pointed at her husband. "Witchcraft!"

Gasps came from the crowd.

"That's what's under the glove! Tell them, Vernon! You man of God! Tell them the truth!" Aline stood now and she was shaking with rage.

The people of Sparrow grew very still now and all who were standing took their seats.

"Yes," Ruth said. "Preacher, is there some truth that you need to tell us?"

May grabbed her father's hand.

John Mosely looked at his brother and said, "Brother?"

May whispered to her pa, "Pa," she said, "we know . . ."

"We don't know nothing, May. Quiet," he whispered quick back into her ear.

Ruth said, "Take off the glove and show us, Preacher! Show us the evil hand!"

Vernon stuttered, "Now, I . . . this is . . ."

"Yes," his wife muttered, "show them!"

Vernon cleared his throat and removed the glove. Beneath the glove, there was a hand, white and skinny as bones with purple fingernails, but a living hand nonetheless. The fingers wiggled. He rolled the rest of his sleeve and showed the church the rest of his arm, which was just as white and dead-looking as his hand, and yet it was shot through with blue veins and the muscles inside bulged a little as he turned it for the crowd.

"Yes, the outlander healed my arm, but not with magic or witchcraft, but with a kind of medicine and faith . . ."

"Liar!" his wife screeched. "You've gone to see the witch of the woods! He'd gone up to ask her for power over the spook! At least that's what he says! A spell of protection on Sparrow! But that's not what he got! Coming back from the witch's place he thought better of the whole deal and went to the church to ask forgiveness and it was walking in here that his arm was burned up with holy fire! The arm that he swore an oath to the witch with, God burned it up! Whatever it was that he asked that witch for, God saw fit to burn him up, but then he called on the outlander to heal him up! Now we know this Jim Falk is with the witch. They're all in league! You're in league too!" She turned to the crowd with tears in her eyes, her right hand still pointing at her husband. "My husband! Your preacher! Is in league with the Evil One!"

"God did not . . . I'm not . . ." Vernon started in, but it was too late.

Gasps and shouts rose from everywhere in the pews now and someone said, "Tie him up!"

"It was a demon that come in the church that twisted up my arm!" Vernon cried.

"Quiet! Servant of the Darkness!" Ruth Mosely's voice broke clear and hard over the din of the crowd.

Then several men from the front pews jumped up and rushed Vernon and they overcame him, their hands grabbing hard against him and fingernails digging into his neck as they grappled and dragged him away from the pulpit and against the back wall under the wood cross.

"Brother! Brother!" John was shouting and watching everything happen to his older brother, but there was nothing he could do. How could he come to his aid?

Then another sound was heard. Martha and Annabelle Mofat were screaming and then a cold wind blew up through the center aisle and there was the loud clap of the repaired doors of the church swinging open.

There, in the church door, stood James Falk, the outlander, and beside him under her dark veil, the witch.

"Let the preacher go!" Jim yelled at the men.

The men did not and the crowd got quiet and all exchanged glances.

"Let the preacher go," Jim said and took a step forward.

"Or else what?" someone in the crowd snarled.

"Preacher!" Falk yelled. "The whole town is against you!"

Violet came in with her pistol out. Her wide eyes met Vernon's and flickered. The doctor walked in with his pistol out.

Huck grabbed his daughter's hand and Huck and May Marbo rose up and May's face beamed out when she saw the outlander place his hand on the witch's shoulder, but whether in fear or in hope, May could not tell, as both were mixed inside her and both felt equally appealing. "Not the whole town."

The witch raised her hands to speak.

At this, a shot was fired, shattering the glass and causing the group to all jump but the witch.

Another shot came and splintered the ceiling somewhere in the corner. It came out of Clive Skiles's rifle. "I didn't have to miss," he said.

"Well, this is just fine," Violet said.

"It's me they want," Jim said.

"And me," the witch said.

"And me," the preacher said.

Huck Marbo produced his pistol and said to the crowd, "Do you know, before my family came into Sparrow, there was trouble? There's been trouble and tales of trouble for so many years going back, as I hear, before even us Joneses came to Sparrow, ain't that right, Hattie?"

Httie said, "That's right!"

Huck continued, "Why, I heard tell that even one of the first families here in the area, the Ingerfells, bore three sons and that the third was a devil with wings and horns, but with a horse's head and hooves. That it lurked here in these woods and made offspring so as all the horses around here were once feared to be the offspring of this devil. So that sometimes, in the night, you might hear a whinny or a neighing and you'd freeze up wondering if the thing was coming to catch you up. See, this ain't no kind of news to me about demons and spooks crawling around in the woods around here. These people brought nothing. Well, I don't know about that exactly," Huck said, indicating the witch.

Benjamin Straddler stood up and was about to speak when everyone noticed that John Mosely was muttering to himself. He had a pistol of his own and it was pointing at the witch. Tears were dripping from him, and he was muttering, "Evil. Evil. Evil. Evil."

John Mosely fired and his blast hit the witch and she fell straight back against the floor as if she'd been a sack of rocks.

But John Mosely never saw what happened after that because his own head was whipped back with a burning force and a crack of light. He tumbled down from beside the pew and everyone was running in every direction suddenly.

John flailed, clutching at the empty space where his nose and eyes once were. White smoke filtered from Falk's Dracon pistol. May was holding her ears and Jim and the doctor rushed to the fallen witch.

The people fled the building, Ruth running, Clive Skiles bounding along the pews, Hattie running with Samuel, the crowd screaming and pushing and falling and kicking out the broken door.

A man's voice from outside rang clear. "They've killed John Mosely! They've killed the preacher's brother!"

"John!" Vernon cried and fell to his knees and hot tears formed in his eyes. "My own brother! No!"

Jim and the doctor looked at the witch. Her body lay still and her right hand was in a tight fist over her chest and smoke curled from beneath the white fist.

"Alive?" Jim asked the doctor.

The doctor grabbed at her hand to feel her wrist, and as he did the hand fell open and inside was a bloody and smoking lump of black lead. The witch's face moved and beneath that thin, dark veil, the doctor and Jim were sure they saw a smirk that revealed the white curving teeth behind red lips. Then the witch, Wylene, cackled in high, sharp bursts, gleeful and wild, and got all too quickly to her feet. She dropped the smoking shot to the floor and cackled again, shrill and climbing ever higher into the rafters of the little church, ringing like silver knives in the air.

"We must leave this place," she said. "I've heard their thoughts. They mean to shut us up in here and burn us all alive."

The witch turned to Huck and May, "All of us."

When they turned to the doorway it was dark and hammers could be heard hammering in the nails. Then the windows went dark too.

The next dawn, the church still burned and burned, bright against the gray light of the morning. There were still a few folks about watching the blaze. The snow had stopped completely and when the church went on burning into the afternoon, many thought that the whispers about the unholy fire might be true.

"How come the church is on fire?" Hattie Jones asked one of the men from up at the ridge who'd come down when the snow got bad. He didn't recognize the man for sure, but he looked, he thought, like Clive Skiles.

"There was a witch inside," said Clive Skiles.

Hattie nodded. "You saw that witch in the church?"

"Yessir, and that outlander, and a crew he'd formed I guess with the doctor and all. You was there."

"Yeah, but I got out quick. What's the preacher say about all this?"

"Preacher was inside too when they boarded them up. As far as I hear tell, he'd gone over to their side! He was one of them, *in league,* as they say. And they shot and killed John Mosely, yessir. Ruth, his wife, put a gun in his hand and whispered to him to kill the witch, told him that if he killed the witch, the others might come out from under the spell that had come over them or something as such. Yessir, I was on my way out the door, but then I got involved! All I seen was people running this way and that and John shot at the witch and the witch goes down! And then, bang! He comes falling down and he's got no more face at all, and he fell right down right there and he was just dead."

The burning church crackled.

"So that's what they did, then? They closed it all up and burned it down."

"Yessir, they were all still inside, some said they could hear 'em all screaming as the flames got to them," Clive said.

"It sure has been burning a long time," Hattie said.

"You know," Clive whispered, "some say it's a special fire that God caused to happen so as to burn up all the evil inside the church."

# CHAPTER 17

The snow flew against their faces and the outlander and the witch led the way. Behind her, May thought she could still hear the hollering and yelling of the men who'd set about to burning the church. Hadn't they?

She held tight to her pa's hand and he held tight to hers as they rushed along behind Jim and the witch. Jim's cool blue eyes glinted at her as no Sparrow boy's ever had when she'd handed him the doctor's medicine. But now, how could this be? Rushing along suddenly in the night. At one moment they had been in the church and then . . . had she imagined all that?

Her right foot slipped and she almost went down, but her pa's arm tightened and he said, "Watch!" harsh under his breath.

She knew he couldn't like the situation they were suddenly in. But they didn't seem to have a choice now. Somehow, Ruth Mosely got the whole town up and against them. That made less sense to her than following a witch through the dark woods in the snow. Up ahead, May saw the black shape of the witch passing back and forth among the trees. Had she saved them all from the flames of the burning church? Between the smoke and the snow, May couldn't remember.

There was heat and smoke, choking, running, and then darkness. Darkness for a long time and then the cool wind and the stars and the trees and the snow.

Ahead of her, they moved and she could hear Jim whispering to the witch and the witch whispering back. She could make out the tall shape of the Hill woman walking ahead of her. Around her, the other folk were moving along with them through the snow and darkness. The poor preacher and the doctor too struggling up the side of a rocky hill. The way was growing steeper and steeper. She guessed they might be headed up into the Ridges, where she'd never been. She'd heard of them, she'd seen the folk come down to the church at times and knew that they built good houses, almost as good as the ones that Bill Hill used to. She watched the back of Violet's head for a moment against the sky and then dip down with the effort of getting up through the rocks.

These people from the Ridges came down once in every so often, mostly when something big was happening. That's why they'd been down to Sparrow when everyone was at the church. May wondered if anyone from up on the Ridges had seen a spook, or knew about the witch. She'd heard that long ago the people of Sparrow, before it was called Sparrow, had it out over something religious and that those who lost out had moved on up to the Ridges. Whatever it was that had driven them apart, the power of it had faded over the years to the point where someone might come down once in a while. Some of the older people in Sparrow still gave the folk at the Ridges a sidelong glance when they showed up.

Her pa was pulling her up now, and she was climbing then along with the rest of them, using her hands and grasping cold rocks and slippery weeds and brambles in snow, dulled and crisped by the wetting of winter. At last she smelled the crispness of open air, and a strong wind blew across her face and whipped her hair and snow all about.

The sky opened up over her head and dark shadows of crooked rocks stood up in the starlight. Then the clouds closed the hole. But she saw clearly now the figures around her in the darkness and could see their faces in gray and blue shades.

It was dusk and they had come up along the crest of the western side of the hill. In a little line, they stood for a while and watched as the sun, just at the very edge of another row of darkening hills, burned a pink circle behind the veil of the white sky. It was going down.

Jim and the witch had led them the whole way here, but now, as the sun began to set, Jim's face bowed down and up again. His left hand went to his hip and then up to his head. He took off his hat. He put it back on. He crouched and turned and picked up snow and dirt and turned again.

Watching all this from a little distance away, the doctor turned and looked at Violet, who was standing high up on a rock as if to try and keep off the same spot where the witch was. The witch stood straight and motionless beside a straight and motionless tree.

The doctor looked back at Violet's face. She looked better. She was better. Different already from the blue-looking woman he had seen, her trembling lips talking about her Bill, her hands steadily firing shots into that thing that picked him up and tried to eat him alive. The sun, disappearing behind the hills, cast a pink light across her face, filling in all the shadows of her angles—her face was full and her cheeks soft and her eyes shone green. But she was thinking of some memory that pained her, and her gaze drifted toward the witch and her feet moved in her brown shoes to keep their footing on the snowy rock where she stood.

The doctor wanted to comfort her, but he couldn't.

They were all looking down at Sparrow from the big hill in the dark. Down in Sparrow, they could see the flames shooting up to the sky. The church was still burning. Still.

"We should be dead," Violet said and looked at the doctor's face looking up at her. "What will we do?" She glanced at the witch, who stood stiff and still as the tree she stood by.

"What is it that happened?" Violet said. "We're going to need food. Where will we go?"

"The sun is going down," Jim Falk said. "We need to find shelter and find it quick."

As if it had heard the thing that Jim said and wanted to make the point, a wolf howled. It wasn't from far away. It was close. The group shrunk together. May, Huck, Doc Pritham, the preacher, Violet, Jim, and the witch, all of them made a little circle.

There was another howl and a yip. May sniffled a bit and reached out for her pa's hand and found his arm. She squeezed close to him.

"I won't let them get you, May," he said. "No matter what."

"There is a cave near here," Violet said. "I remember it being near here. I've been up here before. If we can just make it along up that way." She pointed and waved her hand so that they could all see where she was pointing to.

Jim Falk said, "She's right. It's up over that crest. If we can move."

There were little snarls from in the woods near them.

"It's too late," Vernon Mosely said. "They are upon us!"

When Mosely said that, a group of wolves sauntered into the open, blocking the way to the hill beyond where the cave was, just as if they knew that was where the group was headed.

May whimpered. She had never seen a wolf and she had never smelled one before, but now here they were, right from a nightmare, and they smelled bad.

"Stay in a circle," the witch said. She looked at Jim. "I am weak from making the tunnel. I don't know what I can do, but I will do what I can."

They all wondered, the *tunnel?*

But Jim was quick and angry. He grabbed the doctor and pulled him forward. "We'll take them!" he shouted. "Run! Follow Violet! Run!"

Violet ran fast up toward the trees, and the rest followed her as Jim's gun cracked and the doctor's gun cracked and flashed and lit up the night. They heard the barking and the yowling of the wolves, they heard Jim shouting and the doctor shouting.

"This way!" Violet called.

May and Huck followed close behind, but May could see out the corner of her eyes that there were dark forms rushing along beside of them. She glimpsed the shadowy shapes of their pointed noses and their sharp ears and heard them panting. She could hear the guns of the doctor and the outlander banging and the flashes from their guns lighting up the woods with green and yellow lightning.

Her pa fired his rifle into the bushes and May shrieked and three wolves scurried. "Stay close, May, stay as close as you can. Don't look anywhere but straight ahead!"

He was struggling with his leg. She wasn't sure how long he would be able to keep up with Violet, but she also knew that he was strong. He squeezed her hand hard.

The wind and the darkness moved against them. The gunshots rang in their ears. The wolves that ran to the right and left of them only scattered momentarily. They came right back. One of them rushed across the path in front of them. As Huck ran, which was not very fast with his leg, he let go her hand and struggled to reload his weapon.

"Stay close, May, stay close," he said again.

The witch and Violet were getting farther and farther away so that May could barely see them against the trees. May shut her eyes tight and opened them at any movement expecting those slavering teeth to clamp down on her leg or her neck. Another wolf rushed out into the path in front of them, and this time it stopped cold and another appeared behind it.

They snarled and lowered their heads and bristled their backs in the snow and wind and blackness. May could see their teeth and the little wisps of their breath like smoke puffing out.

Huck was fidgeting and trying to get his cold fingers to get the bullets in the chamber.

Then a black shadow fell on the wolves and their bodies twirled and spun and yipped. The black shadow spun with them and one of the wolves flew off into the brush. Another went suddenly limping and running wildly in the other direction.

The witch's voice called to them, "Come on! The cave is just ahead."

Huck managed to get his gun loaded.

They came into a place where she thought she could hear water, and she saw the shape of Violet move into a blackness and then return and wave them onward.

Jim and the doctor were able to clear away the wolves with gunfire quickly and head up toward the cave, but as the doctor turned and looked back at the clearing where they had been, he saw something that sent a freezing fear into his heart.

There was a huge wolf, at least twice the size of a normal one. It had come into the clearing with many, many other wolves. It was standing there nearly as if it was talking to them, giving orders of some kind.

"Falk! Look!" he said.

The clearing was filled with wolves now. Jim counted twenty before he stopped counting. They were not moving up the hill toward Jim and the group, though. They all started heading in the other direction, to Sparrow!

"They're heading to Sparrow! Falk!"

"I can see that," Jim said as the two men headed up the hill and into the cave. "Who knows how many more of them there are?"

The cave had a small entrance but a large den. Huck and May and the preacher got to work right away on making a fire.

"How did you do it, witch?" the preacher asked. "How did we escape the fire? Where were we? How did we get here?"

Wylene leaned against the wall of the cave and heaved a heavy sigh. "I saved us," she groaned. "What does it matter?"

Jim said, "The people of Sparrow may be in grave danger. Those wolves are some way not natural and are heading back into the town."

Violet was grumbling at Huck as they tended a small fire in the back of the cave. The doctor had come in and told them to move the fire, to put it out, and if they had to start it again to move it to the back of the cave. Then there was a lot of fussing around for a while between Huck and Violet. The preacher had started into talking about his daughter—his daughter and his wife. He was worried. He was worried about what would happen to his daughter if his wife had turned against him. There was no telling what was happening down in his town now. He told the group how much he loved everyone in the town—that they were all like children to him.

Violet said, "Bring those rocks back here, Preacher, and put them around the fire."

The preacher stood. He looked at Huck Marbo and saw in Huck Marbo's eyes a dead seriousness, but he saw too that Marbo's eyes flickered back and forth from Wylene to May and then to Violet. He saw that when Marbo's glance happened on Violet she could feel his glance, but Violet never took her eyes off the witch, who was crouched at the cave entrance. The preacher started getting some rocks to put around the fire.

May looked up when the witch groaned. This witch had saved her life. Witches were supposed to eat children. Just then the fire cracked and a big flame came up. She could see the witch leaning on the wall holding her side. She had been injured in the fight with the wolves.

The witch looked small. The witch looked skinny and helpless and her clothes looked like a black sack on her. May thought of a sudden that there was nothing scary at all about the witch. If she even was a witch. She was not like any witch that May had ever heard of. She did have weird fingers with sharp hooks on the end, like a bird's claws, and those black, black eyes and sharp teeth, but the witch was more like some pretty animal than an old evil witch from a story.

"We're needing to decide what to do here," Jim said.

They all started talking around the fire, making plans and ideas about what had happened and what should be done about the wolves, but May wasn't really listening to all that going on. She had wandered away, taking steps closer to the cave's entrance where the figure of the witch leaned against the wall in the cave. Wylene wasn't talking to the others either. She was fixed on something else and holding her stomach.

When she was just a girl in Sparrow, May heard that there was a witch in the woods. The witch was out there, the stories went, and once, long ago, she had come into Sparrow and taken children or a family, which, May supposed, is what most witches do. They take away children and innocents and do awful things in the name of the Evil One. That's what witches do.

One night, when her ma was still alive, the men were drinking and talking and May heard about it. She heard about a lot of things that way.

The men were all sitting around at the bar and they were talking about the old days.

"Back then, there was a lot of strange folk in the woods," Walter Chimley said and scratched his fuzzy red beard and took a big drink of his beer. Walter would come down from time to time, down from the Ridges, to help out with building things. He was one of the very few people who ever came down from the Ridges and back to Sparrow. "There was always the River People, sure, but there was some strange folk on top of that. Them River People been around here since before God, but them weird folk, them that live in the hollers and in the dark places of the woods . . ." He started coughing a lot and couldn't finish.

Benjamin Straddler looked at Walter Chimley. Benjamin poured more whisky into his own cup and drank it down quick and licked his lips. "You go on talkin' that way as long as you want. Them legends and tales is legends and tales. People just tell 'em. People remember 'em on account of they're memorable. Just 'cause they're memorable don't make 'em true."

Arthur McKee said, "Yeah, old Benji's got a tale of his own that's memorable."

Hattie Jones said, "McKee! You be quiet now!"

Benjamin Straddler didn't smile a bit, but he liked it that old Hattie seemed to be trying to come to his rescue. Arthur McKee didn't smile either. What was between McKee and Straddler in those days was more than legends and tales; it was a woman named Lane McKee that was between them.

They both were about to say something more on the subject when Hattie broke in, "I'll tell you both! I'll tell all of you! Chimley tells the truth! Strange folk in the woods. River People, sure, but these were even against the River People. The River People had to fight against 'em as well as we had to. We were together with the River People from around here. Fightin' against these weird folk. Many of us even saw that there was a witch still in the woods who, a few years, not long ago, came down and into Sparrow. Some say she came to take the kids, and that's why there's not many has kids in Sparrow anymore—for fear that she'll come back to take 'em. But what we saw, what we saw, we couldn't see what her purpose was. Movin' from house to house in some strange way."

Benjamin Straddler smiled. "You fought against these weird folk, old man? Back in the times?" He laughed a little and looked around to see if anyone else was understanding. "Things happen," Benjamin Straddler said. "Some folks die, move away, get sick, dead babies, disappeared kids, and they tell stories is all. Some folks get swept up by rivers or eaten by wolves. That don't mean witches come and steal 'em away or that the woods is haunted by spooks."

Huck Marbo said, "Spooks."

But that was all in May's memory and this was in the here and the now. May stopped just short of Wylene.

The witch turned and looked at May. May didn't say anything, but her mouth came open a little bit. The witch was looking at May from behind the veil that still covered the white face and black eyes. May's face was so different from the witch's—round, flat nose, square teeth. From under the veil, the witch's eyes glittered and caught some firelight.

The witch thought about May's round face and her big eyes and flat nose. May's father may be a pale-skinned man with red hair from across the sea, but Wylene could see deeper than that. Wylene could see the faces of the Old People in May's face.

May squinted to try to see through the veil.

The witch lifted her veil and gave May a little close-mouthed smile. "You should not be afraid of me, young one."

May looked down at the witch's sharp fingers. One of her hands was clutching her side.

"You're hurt?"

"Yes," the witch said, "I am."

May looked away from where the wound was and up at the witch's face. The witch blinked her black eyes. May couldn't help but gasp.

"Yes," the witch said, "I came into the world this way. Like a cat, I suppose. My eyes. My teeth." She chomped them neatly behind her lips. Wylene lifted her other hand and spread out her fingers. "You can touch them," the witch said, and tilted her head, looking at her own hands.

May's eyes went wide and then she turned quick around to see what her pa was doing. He was crouched down with the preacher; they were drawing something in the dirt around the fire, talking and pointing and serious. Violet was pacing with her arms crossed.

May looked back around then at Wylene. May's right hand started to come up from where it had been near her waist, but she didn't look at Wylene's dangling hand, she kept looking into the witch's eyes—something there, a shadowy light, the little fire in the cave reflected in there, in the witch's eyes like black mirrors shining. They were wet and they glimmered, but there was too a kind of shyness in the pointed little lashes. May could see crinkles at the corners in the white skin. Then May started to see colors in those eyes, dragonfly wings and oil, dark rainbows turning.

When May touched her hand to the witch's hand she felt a heat. The witch's hand was soft and smooth, but May felt something warm like water move from the witch's hand and down into her own finger bones and then up her arm, spreading a sleepy warmth. Like a drink of her pa's whisky, it spread deep through her body.

And then May thought her eyes must have closed, because she felt of a sudden that she was waking up in bright daylight and there was the witch, Wylene—seated on a flat rock in brightest sunlight and around her, big, flat stones, bigger than May and bigger than her pa, covered in green mosses and long, twirling vines.

Wylene wasn't dressed in her dark veil or cloak; in fact, her skin was more bare than not and white and shining in the sun where it wasn't painted with swirls of black and red. Wylene's face was painted gold and red with almonds of bright yellow around her black eyes. Her hands were covered in symbols. May could see now that Wylene had been painted to look like a fierce cat. The teeth, so sharp and white in the sunlight, looked almost blue, glowing strangely from the witch's face over the rocks and leaves, outshining the yellow sun.

She heard a voice, and then the light disappeared and the mute darkness of the cave swirled over her. "May! Come away from her!"

It was her pa.

"Get over here! You come away from that witch! Witch! You stay away from my daughter!" But Huck's eyes darted this way and that when he spoke to the witch, and then he kind of nodded to Wylene after he'd hollered at her and blew out a sigh as May came back to his side. Even though the witch had come through the darkness and fought off the wolves to save May, he didn't feel right trusting her. It just didn't feel like the right thing to do to trust a witch.

May came toward him and he looked over at the preacher. Huck didn't know what to say to the preacher either, but the two of them had passed looks and it seemed to Huck that the preacher had understood in some way, maybe even more than Huck understood, how it would be that they would come to trust a witch. The other thing was that there was another strange kind of look in the preacher's eye when Huck looked at him, a look almost as if the preacher was sorry, that the preacher understood and that he was sorry. Not sorry that his brother died, but sorry that somehow he'd caused his brother to die. The preacher looked as if he was about to say something, but then he would just wipe his eyes with his thumb and fingers. Jim didn't like watching the preacher cry.

Violet crossed her arms and looked at the witch with a squinted eye, but she moved around the fire toward Huck a little, keeping her eyes on Wylene.

"She's hurt," May said.

The doctor looked over at the witch, who was now bent in some kind of pain, but her face was turned away from all of them.

"What, you can catch bullets and make magical tunnels through the earth to escape fire, but you can't get bit by a wolf?"

The witch turned to the doctor. "That's exactly right, Doctor. The wolf tore into my side with its teeth. It's not a wound I can bear very easily. I am sure you would have difficulty too."

The doctor's eyebrows rose and his mouth slowly closed up as he watched her reveal the jagged bite. In the firelight, it looked more black than red. He suddenly wondered at the creature he had just seen in the clearing, the huge wolf who had seemed as though it were giving orders to the others. He wondered if the medicine and treatment that he'd given Jim Falk hadn't warded off the same greater evil from Jim's blood after all—an evil that could turn men to beasts. If this witch, or creature, or whatever it was that Wylene was, could be harmed by the bite of this wolf . . .

Jim said, "Doc, are you able to help her?"

"What about the town?" the preacher almost shouted. "What about our homes? Who will save my wife and my daughter from those animals?"

"Benjamin Straddler is there. There are other men of the town," the doctor said, looking back in the direction of the witch and fumbling around in his bag.

"Not many," Violet said. "And not enough. Not with courage. They'll run. Sparrow is full of cowards and hermits shut up in their houses to come out on Sunday and sit silent in the pews, their cold eyes on the back of each other's heads." Violet had a sudden thought that the spook and these killers might be agents come to rid out just these kinds of people. She twirled her red hair around her finger and wondered what would become of all those quiet, frowning folk. She pulled the strand of hair hard and thought about the powder.

"Yes," the doctor said. "Yes, the people are scared. But they'll fight."

"Will they?" Violet asked. "And what if we were to help? Will they come to our aid, Doctor, or will we all find ourselves tied to a post in the middle of another fire? Will they be brave and fight against the monsters or will they be cowards who burn women?"

Jim walked over to them and, looking at each of them in the eyes before he spoke, he said, "This isn't just another town. Violet, this is your town. This is Huck's town. These things, the killers, Old Bendy's Men, they've woken up."

The preacher stood up. "Yes, that's right. They've woken up to find something." He looked toward the witch. "It's what she told me!"

The doctor was at the witch's side now. He gave her a drink from a green bottle and then a drink from a brown one. She sat down.

"They're not going to stop with Sparrow," Wylene said and choked a little on the medicine. "They will ruin every town that has a good preacher and has good people. People who follow the teachings of the Way." She pointed at Jim Falk and said, "And people who know the Waycraft."

Jim Falk couldn't help but to draw in a breath. He looked at Wylene's face. How could she know?

"Where do you know that word from?" Jim asked her, stepping forward.

"I am old," said Wylene, and a sputtering laugh came from her.

The doctor said, "May Marbo, I need you to come here and help me."

Huck said, "Help you what?"

"I need her to help me help this woman. She has a wound and I need May's help."

Violet nearly stopped May from going over, but Huck made a quick glance at Violet. She could hear the doctor's desperation, and he pointed where the wound was and the area was bleeding heavily now.

May jumped up and soon they had moved the witch closer to the entrance where it was cool and away from the fire. The doctor gave May a rag and told her to fill it with snow and wipe her forehead and talk to her. He tore open the witch's shirt below her breast where the wound was weeping and giving off a strange smell. The witch also had some bad punctures on the right arm that had a similar quality. Her blood was very dark and gave off an oily shimmer in the firelight.

The doctor said, "I'm going to make a guess at something." He took out several metal tools from his bag and placed them on a rock.

"That doesn't comfort me," Wylene said and looked at the tools.

May went out of the cave in the dark night and grabbed up some snow. Branches in the trees around them crackled as a wind blew, and then the woods dimmed and a heavy snow came filtering down through the trees. In the distance she heard the howling and barking. The trees were shaking in the wind.

She came back and saw the doctor crouched there beside the witch.

"Press that cold rag with the snow inside to her forehead," the doctor instructed and picked up some tools and went off to heat them in the fire.

Jim said, "We need to go back. We don't have food or proper trappings for us all to stay anyway. The witch . . ."—Jim corrected himself—"Wylene is right. They will not stop at Sparrow. They will come for us whether we save Sparrow or not."

"Also, I could use a bath," Huck said.

May put the cold rag to the witch's head. She was sure that, underneath her veil, she saw the witch's lips curl into a smile at Huck's comment or maybe at the cool rag.

The doctor returned and said, "I am guessing that, for some reason I can't really say, you are not hurt by lead bullets, but you are hurt by the organic bite of a wolf. In my book that means that your makeup is quite special, but not completely unknown to medicine. Especially to my medicine. Drink this," he said and gave her a bottle. She did so. "Open your mouth," he told the witch.

He picked out a leathern bit and placed it in her teeth quickly and moved his fingers away, trying to ignore the fact that her mouth was full of neat white points and fangs.

"Do you want me to hold your hand?" May asked her.

Wylene reached her clawed hand to May and the two held tight. May was surprised that she did not feel the pinch of the witch's talons. May was waiting for the strange feelings and the visions to come again. May closed her eyes, but all she could hear was the witch trying to catch her breath.

The doctor's hands moved fast, but Wylene curled with the pain of the healing; and with her teeth she sheared the leathern bit into three pieces.

May and the doctor worked for a few minutes to bind up her wounds while the witch seemed to doze, whether from the shock of the pain or from the doctor's medicine, May did not know. Very soon, though, she blinked her black eyes and started up alert.

"You are a good doctor," Wylene said, "and you're probably right about my special qualities."

They looked over and noticed the group was staring at them.

"We have to go back now," the preacher said. "My wife, my daughter."

They all were looking outside of the cave now and into the snowy night. Far off, they could still hear the animals in the darkness crying out to one another. Were there more wolves nearby? What else was out there in the night? Already the snow, even through the trees, had managed a thick dusting of the ground.

"If we do go back, she can't come with us," Violet said, pointing at the witch, Wylene. "She can't come with us. They'll just hang us up and burn us."

"Who will?" Jim asked, turning to Violet.

"It's not everyone in town we need to fear," the witch who was not a witch said, standing up. "It's this preacher's brother's wife. The woman called Ruth Mosely. She means to kill you too, Jim Falk. Violet is right. The people of Sparrow are scared, but some of them don't believe in spooks or demons quite as much as they believe in punishment and power."

Wylene's voice grew deeper and trembled when she spoke the word "punishment." Violet felt something inside her heart slide in the witch's direction. She looked at the witch's hands and at the tips of the witch's fingers. The fingernails there were sharp and white and pointed, hooked something like a bird's toe. But where they grew out of the finger was soft and lined and vulnerable-looking.

"Ruth Mosely was the one who took my thumb," the witch said. "Before she came to live in Sparrow. Before she married the preacher's brother. She came with"—the witch swallowed—"helpers, and they took my thumb and they cursed me. They made me old and weak but kept me from death because they feared my spirit being free in these woods even more than they did my living body. And they were right to fear. But I am not a witch."

The witch lifted her veil so they could see her black eyes and her young, white face, and her mouth was filled with sharp teeth. "You see," she said, "Ruth Mosely is the one who is in league. She's the one with the old books and the powers. She's the one that you might call a witch. Not me. I was born like this, not because I am a witch, but because I am the daughter of two very different parents. One parent from the earth and the other from the sky. In the tongue of the River People, my name, Wylene, means . . ."

"Daughter of Earth and Sky," Jim said suddenly, his mind putting the syllables together for the first time, and when he said it his heart jumped. He felt that warm and sweet feeling of the presence of Old Magic Woman. He felt the nearness of his father and saw the sun rising over his old home. He had heard Old Magic Woman speak the name of Daughter of Earth and Sky in her stories. Jim's chest got warm. What if he were closer than he thought to finding his father? If the Daughter of Earth and Sky was *hollow* as she'd said to the preacher, and if she had brought them through that strange, cold dark tunnel, perhaps she had this power to walk between two worlds. He could hardly believe what might be.

Jim looked away from the little circle of people in the cave and remembered Spencer Barnhouse pulling him up off the floor of his home so long ago. Spencer had pulled him out of the darkness and dreams of grief and heavy drink and given him things to do with himself. But books and shelves weren't things that interested Falk much in those days. He'd wandered. He'd wandered far off the path.

When the visions started, he'd come back to Barnhouse, needed things again. He followed the strange call that came to him in the vision he got from this woman, this Violet Hill, who stood now with the tiny flakes of snow glittering on her cheeks. She stood there beside this Daughter of Earth and Sky, Wylene. He looked at the doctor and the preacher and May and Huck and wondered suddenly how it could be that all these people were here with him. When Barnhouse found him that day so long ago, it seemed Falk was little more than a ghost of himself, terrorized by the grief of losing his mother and father, drowning in whisky and the special magic world of the leaves that he'd eaten. Too many and too fast. Now he stood inside a cave near this town that was about to be torn apart.

And all these people.

They had somehow been gathered together with him, and now he had to help them. The evil that was here in Sparrow was something larger and darker than he'd ever imagined. He closed his eyes and bowed his head, searching in there for even the slightest hint of the jitters, anything he could grasp onto, to help him know the future, to help him know where these things were hiding, what their weaknesses were, or what they were planning. He was so close. He looked at Wylene, the Daughter of Earth and Sky, and wondered, he wondered by what power she had saved them all from the fire and where it had been when they had walked through that strange, cold, and dark tunnel. *Hollow.*

He knelt and opened his bag. He unrolled the little cloth that held the two leaves that he had left. He picked them up and turned to the little group of people. Jim put the leaves in his mouth and began to chew them.

"Are those leaves going to help us?" Violet asked him and breathed a sigh.

"He's going to try to pick up the trail of the things that are in the woods other than the wolves," the doctor said.

Jim took a few steps out into the night and, slowly, each of them followed until the whole crew of them stood outside of the cave looking this way and that, waiting. But for what they did not know. The snow fell.

"They're gone, mostly," Wylene said, rubbing the place where the doctor and May had patched up the wound. "There is something, but it's weak and it's hard to see."

"The other side?" Violet's eyes opened wide. "What are we talking about? What are we talking about?"

"Violet," Jim said, "you were right about that spook and you were right to call me here, but I can't rid these things out on my own. What the witch"—Jim corrected himself again—"what Wylene is saying, is that these things have a way to come between our world and the other world. Isn't that right?"

Wylene nodded.

Violet was not sure what to say next. "A way of traveling? What are we talking about? So what do we do? Go back to Sparrow now? We go up in there, where there's a whole town of people waiting to kill a witch and hang an outlander? We go back there to try and save them from some spook they don't even believe in? You can be guaranteed that Ruth Mosely's got 'em all rounded up somewhere. She's explaining to them all about the witch, about you," she said, pointing at Wylene. "See? They believe in monsters, in real monsters and evil, and witches, and we're it! At least Ruth Mosely believes that! And Ruth knows more than the rest of them. Apparently she knows some truth."

"What truth?" Huck asked. "You yourself don't even know the truth."

"And you do?" the preacher asked.

"Listen," Jim shushed them, putting his hand out in front of him. They stood quiet a moment and then they heard it too, a crackling like sticks and a steady crunching noise. Something was moving and then stopped.

"It's the snow," the doctor said. "Look."

Around them, the snow fell in sheets, already up to their ankles.

The noise came again, crashing now.

"That's not the snow," the doctor said.

Jim searched his mind and squinted in the direction of the sound, but he was blind to what it was, or what its intentions may be. The couple of leaves that he'd chewed just didn't work. He needed more and besides, it was as if something was blocking his senses. He couldn't pick up on the jitters at all. In fact, he felt empty. Only Wylene glowed a faint green.

The doctor and Violet pulled their weapons, Jim pulled his pepperbox with his left hand, and Wylene stepped slowly up onto the rock in the center of the group, still nursing her side. They heard a moan. Then, they saw it.

It stumbled out of the dark woods and swayed left and right. It looked so pitiful that no one really knew what to do. So they stared.

Whatever it was, it may have once been a man, but it looked torn apart and put back together again, and where the mouth should be was a black tube of some kind that sucked at the air as if it were drowning.

"What is this?" Violet shouted, her pointed finger curling up with the rest of her hand into a pink fist.

May hid behind Huck. The preacher gasped and said, "Oh no."

It moaned and extended an arm and pointed at Jim and moaned again, a louder, high-pitched, rattling noise, and its eyes rolled this way and that. It was something in the voice, possibly, or possibly something in the wet flap of yellow hair that stuck out at the top of its head that made them all realize that this thing that stumbled and leered in front of them had been, at one time, the chicken man. It stood there dumbly.

Violet marched up to Jim, her finger stuck out at the thing. "Is this what is happening to people? Are they turning into this? My husband is dead!" Her face was in a knot. "Is this what happened? Is this what happened to my husband? He was still alive and turned into what, a monster? Maybe that monster we burned back in front of Pritham's was my husband? A demon? I called you into this town to rid out these things, to get rid of that thing that looked in my window and to get rid of the fear that lived in the woods and in the people. But what's happened? There's more and more! Look at that! What is that? We killed something—was it the spook? Was it my husband? Is that what we burned to smoke out in front of the doctor's? I thought you'd already killed the spook, James Falk! Out in the woods and you brought its head and dropped it down in my lawn."

The thing moaned again louder and gestured at Jim again.

Violet took in a deep breath and staggered a little. She looked back at the thing. She looked at the doctor, whose face was wide and whose eyes were glancing back and forth between Jim and Violet, his mouth open and quivering as if at any moment he would start talking. The witch, of course, her face hidden behind the veil, stood stiff and silent.

Violet steadied herself. The snow was filling up the open spaces now, filtering down through the woods and turning everything white. Why had she called Jim Falk? What were they going to do now—shoot demons? How can you shoot a demon? These things are of the Evil One. She felt light-headed; a dizziness came over her and a sudden thirst.

"What are you going to do about all this evil?" she heard herself shriek at James Falk.

Violet looked at Wylene, the witch, or whatever it was. "There is a witch standing right next to you and a demon swaying in the breeze, but what are you doing? Chewing on leaves and staring at the snow!"

"Violet," Huck said.

She locked her eyes on Huck Marbo. "I can't go back to that house. We can't go back to Sparrow," she said plainly.

"Then what?" Huck asked, slowly stepping toward her. "Then what, Violet Hill? If we don't have Sparrow, what will we do? Wander in the woods with the leaf-eater, James Falk? What will we do? May and I? How will we live?"

The thing let out a wet sigh and Jim moved in on it. Its face slackened and something like worms swirled out of its tube-mouth and reached toward Jim. Jim looked at its face, or what was supposed to be its face.

"They must use them, the bodies, and wear them like skin," Jim said and looked at the doctor and then at the witch.

"Why is this one so weak?" the doctor asked.

"Well, I don't know," Jim said. "Maybe something happened and it's starting to kill off all the evil. Maybe something happened when we got rid of the big one down by your house. Sometimes it can happen that way."

"Kill all the evil?" Violet pulled the silver pistol from her side and pointed it at the witch. "You want to kill evil?"

"Violet, no," Huck whispered.

"You want to kill evil?" Violet took a step toward Wylene and leveled the gun at the witch's face. The witch did not move.

"She probably used whatever powers she has to lead this weird thing here to find us out and tell the others. James Falk, do you even know what she does? A witch? Do you know what a witch does with the Evil One? They bathe in the blood of babies and eat their hearts for power! Did you ask her where the little baby Starkey is?"

At this, the preacher knelt down in the snow and clasped his hands together and started to shake them in the direction of the sky.

Violet's eyes moved from Jim to look at the witch. "If you all can't do anything about evil, I certainly can! Take off that veil," Violet said to the witch. "Take it off. I want to see the face of a woman who's eaten up a baby's heart before I send you back to hell."

Quietly, the witch reached up and pulled the veil back from her face. Wylene did not smile, she kept her mouth shut, and her eyes were closed and her head was bowed.

"Open your eyes. Let's see if you can catch this bullet," Violet said, her hands shaking.

Wylene opened her eyes and Violet saw those eyes, black and shining pools of oil in the witch's white face. Violet squinted for a moment and positioned her hand a bit, getting the aim right for the shot. Then she looked down the barrel at the witch's face. The witch was young, her skin was not cracked and lined, and her nose was not crooked and weird. Violet had heard tell, though, of these young witches too and what their powers were over men and what they could do. The witch's eyes were black, yes, but there was no denying that there was a softness about them, a softness that even Violet couldn't quite put her finger on.

It was then that the thing came bounding from the edge of the wood and toward Violet. It was so slow and had so much trouble getting itself moving that it was almost comical to see it blundering along and hollering at Violet. Violet turned away from the witch with her gun.

"I think it's trying to tell us something," the witch said. "Nevertheless. Evil is evil."

Violet's gun exploded in the night and the thing toppled backwards. It dropped to the ground, but its head fell in a different place. Jim had lunged from behind it, his hatchet cutting clean through its neck in one blow. Then Wylene moved from the rock and made a waving motion with her hands, and the two separate pieces of the thing burst into green flames and spewed a black smoke into the air until there were only ashes and melted snow. Wylene panted.

They all looked at the pile of ashes, then they looked at the witch, and then they looked at Violet. She was looking at the pile of ashes too and her mouth quivered and her eyes were watery. The snow was coming down around her red hair and she was crouched on the ground, bunched up there, sobbing now.

"Violet," Jim said, "I am sorry about your husband, about Bill."

Violet waved her hand at them as if her hand would make them all disappear. She threw her gun into the snow. She turned and didn't look at them. Picking up her skirts, she began trudging through the snow back in the direction of Sparrow.

Huck shouted after her: "Violet! Violet!" He looked at May with wide eyes.

Huck looked at Violet walking off and looked at May again and then ran into the woods after Violet. May took a few steps closer to Jim Falk and Jim looked down at her face.

"What was that thing?" the doctor asked Jim.

"I don't know," Jim said.

"Why did it look like that? Like the chicken man?" the doctor asked.

The witch pulled her veil back down over her face and grasped at her side again and sat down. "That *thing* was very likely an eye."

"An eye?" the doctor said.

"A way for them to watch us," Wylene said.

Jim looked around but couldn't see or sense anything at all. Even with the leaves, the last of the leaves running in him, he couldn't sense a trace of the killers or even feel the slightest vibration of the jitters. He hadn't felt much when the 'eye' had arrived, or now. He wasn't sure how much use he was going to be against these things if they came in force.

"There's nothing else here," Jim said.

"No," Wylene said, "but someone is watching us. Someone has likely been watching you since you came down here from the North. He will come soon."

"He?" Jim asked wondering if Wylene knew anything of Varney Mull or anything of Hopestill.

"Yes. He will come to establish his ways in the little town," she said.

The doctor looked down at his boots.

"James Falk, maybe it's not my place, but my pa, Violet, you're going after them, right?" May asked.

Jim didn't answer, but kept looking into the woods as the wolves yipped and yipped here and there.

"Witch . . . Wylene," Jim said, correcting himself, "take the preacher and May Marbo and get them back into the cave. Keep that fire going, but keep it small. We'll go after those two."

Wylene stood and the three started making their way up the hillside, May holding onto the preacher, the preacher with panic on his face. They were all looking this way and that, listening, waiting for something to lunge at them from the darkness.

After she had run off, Violet had not got very far before Huck had caught up with her. She didn't turn to look at him right away. She just asked him, "Why are you following me, Huck?"

Her voice sounded scratchy and she sniffled. She didn't slow down.

Huck came up alongside of her. They both had to pick their feet way up high in order to get through the snow that had already piled itself up to their shins.

Her face was wet and her eyes were bright with red around them and Huck could see that there were still tears coming down.

"What do you want with me?" she asked him.

"Violet," Huck said in a soft way, "there's nothing that I want from you. I want you to be safe. Falk does. I do. We all do. That's what we want. You can't run off into the snow and the dark by yourself."

Then there were no words for a long while, just the muted noise of the two of them stepping through the snow, and then she said, "You know I loved him. He made every stick of furniture in that house. Everything except that table that his granddad made. The house itself. You know, he built probably half the houses in Sparrow. He was a good man and I loved him."

"Of course you did," Huck said, "and I loved Anna."

They were quiet with each other then.

Now and again, Violet began to glance over at Huck's face, watching his clear, green eyes searching out in front of them, looking into the snow and sticks and bushes to find a place for his wooden leg to stick. It was hard for Huck. It was hard, but he was doing it anyway. She felt something warm in her heart, but as soon as it came it went. Her husband was dead, gone, and beyond any of this now. She was sure of it, and she cried hard for him as they tramped through the snow. But even as she cried herself blind in the snow and in the dark, she couldn't quite get her mind clean of Huck and his strong arms around her—that night those years ago—the two of them trapped and never thinking they'd see the light again. No one knew and how could anyone ever know and how could anyone ever understand? Only Violet could work it in her mind to the point that she was convinced that anyone else would have done just the same.

The woods got darker and darker. At some point along the way, whatever little light of the moon had come blue and dim through the trees had disappeared. Whatever clouds that brought the heavy snow had darkened the sky and dropped heavier flakes, and wind came so strong that it cut through the trees and blew hard against the two. The wind was loud and cold and it forced them together.

"This is a bad storm!" Huck shouted. "We should have stayed! You should not have run off!"

She pushed herself against him and folded her arms into his chest as he opened his coat and wrapped her into it.

"I am so afraid," she said in his ear. "I am so sad and I am so afraid."

"We've made it through this before, Violet Hill. We will make it through again."

Huck did not stop walking. He kept the two of them moving along with his one good leg and using the peg on his other as a sticking point to keep him from slipping in the cold. It was very slow movement, but it was steady and sturdy, and Violet could feel the warmth of Huck's chest heating her arms and his breath on her neck as they struggled together in the frozen darkness. They could not tell which direction they were going in any longer. They could not see the sky or the trees. They could not tell anything much except that they were moving.

When they saw the little lights ahead, they did not speak, each of them hoping that they were already seeing the windows of somebody's house on the outlying edge of Sparrow. But they knew in their hearts that they had not traveled far enough for that to be so.

"What?" Violet whispered, her voice shaking with the cold.

The little lights moved when Violet spoke—two little sparks that disappeared off into the darkness and then reappeared slowly, one at a time. The little lights were green and white and they blinked.

Then they saw two more of the lights join the first two, side by side. The lights slowly moved toward Huck and Violet. Huck's cold fingers grabbed at his shotgun and Violet stepped behind him and pulled her pistol from its holster. Huck wondered to himself how an eye could shine with its own light in such a dark wood, but he was too afraid of the right answer.

From over the hill and down where Sparrow was in between the hills and alongside of the creek came the deep and hollow sound of a big wolf howling. The howl was answered from everywhere.

Jim peered out into the hills dark with night. The moon was near full and, when the clouds parted here and there, it sharpened up all the shapes of everything. He could see the deep, dark of the woods that flowed into the valley below, the long twist of the black river, the thin patch where some road had been beaten by the years and, down there in the valley, a yellow light dancing by a crook in the creek. The church still burned. A cool wind came through the trees, and he could just make out the shapes of Violet and Huck moving along the pocket of the hill.

The doctor and Jim headed down the hillside. The doctor walked behind him whispering, "Why did you come here? Why did you talk like that to us? That woman, Violet, she says that she called you?"

Jim turned a little toward him. "Doc, you know me in some way. You have an idea of who I am and why I am here. I can hear it in your voice and see it in your eyes. How is it that you know me?"

"Tales," the doctor said, and even though they were in the dark, in the night, and wolves prowled, he smiled a little. "Tales that folks tell all over. I haven't always been a doctor just in Sparrow, you know."

"Tales?" Jim asked.

"Well," the doctor said and tried to look over at Jim. The snow and the darkness covered Jim's figure and whirled around him; the moonlight only cut dimly here and there the shape of the outlander against the drifting gray. "I can't tell from the stories who they are about exactly. Someone who fits you, though. Maybe they are about you, maybe they are about your father." He watched Jim's eyes and face for a reaction, but there was none. "Maybe the stories—they're about your grandfather's grandfather. Who can tell? Maybe the stories are about all of you at once."

The doctor crunched along in the snow, lifting his big legs and moving his arms this way and that to keep his balance. "Some of the stories are pretty interesting: shadowmen, tree spirits . . . witches."

The clouds broke and the moon shown down across the hills. The snow was already so deep. It was up to their knees, but it really didn't seem as if it had snowed enough for the snow to be that deep already. They came down where there was a little offshoot of Sparrow Creek, and now could see Violet Hill and Huck Marbo tramping through heavy snow out ahead of them. Violet and Huck were leaving a messy trail behind them, enough for anyone to follow, but it was being filled in fast.

Jim called out to them, but they didn't stop or even turn and wave. Could they not hear him? He yelled at them a few times, but they didn't do anything to show that they could hear.

Then, Huck and Violet pointed and gestured with each other and moved into a darker set of trees and could no longer be seen from where the doctor and Jim were.

"We better hurry," Jim said. "Maybe the wind is taking our voices away."

Jim looked at the doctor. The doctor looked back at him and asked again, "Why did you come here, James Falk?"

Jim's face was blank for a moment. The shadows of the night seemed to rush in and cover his face so that only the tiny sparks of his eyes twinkled in the dark patch under his beat-up hat. Then he tilted his head just a bit to the left so the moonlight came in under the brim and gave a blue light to his sharp features and he said, "I saw a darkness in my mind—a darkness of the same shade as what took away my father. It was there, moving in my vision." Jim looked forward, indicating Huck and Violet up ahead. "The Hill woman, Violet, she was in the dream too. Or at least a figure that looked like Violet. I would wake from the visions and feel in my bones a direction and so I would move. When I slept, more dreams. I dreamed all along the way to Sparrow, but I can't remember anymore. I knew evil awaited me here and that this path would lead to my father. More than that, I couldn't know."

The closer that they got to the grove of dark trees, the louder the noise of the wind was, but there was no wind where they were.

"Did dreams lead you along a path to Hopestill as well?"

Jim recoiled and stopped. The two were close together in the deep snow.

"Pritham," Jim said under his breath, "what are you at?"

Doc Pritham didn't move. His lips barely moved, his body didn't move, but he said, "Well, I ain't sent for you if that's what you're thinkin'."

"I know you're not sent for me, elsewise you would've poisoned me in your little doctor house with potions. Now tell me what your business is, Pritham. There's other kinds of business to be had. Especially from those up north. Those who are working with Varney Mull."

The doctor puffed at the pipe that stuck out of his mouth and said, "So you've heard of him too. Look, Falk, just a few days before you got in to Sparrow, a young man called William Wade came through here down from Hopestill. Not because he was looking for you, Jim Falk, but because I'd ordered a batch of healing herbs and some other ointments and such a few weeks prior. Wade's a runner for me and for someone I think you know. He brings me things from about for a wage. He moves around, but he'd been stayin' up a while in Hopestill. He said there'd been some kind of trouble up there that had to do with a witch man who'd stolen weapons from a ship and had poisoned a man called Spencer Barnhouse."

"Doc," Jim whispered, "do you think I did this thing? Do you think that I am, as you say, a witch man? You think I killed Barnhouse? Or do you think I'm some fiend? Why'd you patch my hand then, why give me medicine and help me live?"

Pritham sighed and smiled some. "Other tales. Other tales that rang truer than those. Wade said that he'd also heard around the edges and in the public houses that the culprit, the one they called a witch, was a man who was on the run and it wasn't the right man. That they'd pinned a queer murder on an outlander so someone in a high place might go free. More than tales, though, Falk, I just had a feeling about you."

"Barnhouse was poisoned?" Jim asked and turned and looked back out over the valley and down toward the little flickering flame that must be the church in Sparrow.

"It's what Wade told me."

"William Wade. I have not met him, but I'd seen his name enough times on Barnhouse's books. They're after me, Doc, sure, but they're after us all," Jim said. "Whatever story comes along with them will only add fuel to that Ruth Mosely's fire."

They started moving again toward where they thought Violet and Huck had gone off to. It was hard to tell. It looked as if down where they went everything was dark now and a wind was starting in the trees.

"Spencer Barnhouse is a good man. I don't know why anyone would want anything evil to befall that man," the doctor said.

Jim nodded. He thought of the man who had helped him so often, the man who had helped his pa, who had saved so much of what his pa had worked so hard for. He thought too of Barnhouse's little girl, of Emily, and wondered if Barnhouse had been murdered, what would become of her.

"What do you know of this Ruth Mosely?" Jim asked the doctor.

"Little," the doctor said. "She's from the North, though, that I know."

Jim turned to the doctor. "The witch said that Ruth Mosely put a bind on her. It was true, Doc. True that she was bound and weakened to near death. An old spell, the spell of the Witch's Thumb, or some call it the Wastrel."

The doctor rubbed his chin. "The Wastrel? Ain't that a twist."

The doctor glanced away and back over his shoulder toward the cave. "The preacher will know more about Ruth Mosely."

Up ahead of them, there was noise now and they stopped. The trees in the little dip of the woods where Violet and Huck had headed off to were bending with such a force it looked as if someone was pulling on them.

"Is that wind?" the doctor asked, and then darkness moved over them. Whatever sky or moonlight had been lighting the woods disappeared, and snow rushed down from the sky and all about them.

"We're going to lose them in this!" Jim heard himself shouting at the blurred form of the doctor standing there. They were in a clearing, and so Jim figured maybe there was some more cover in and under the trees. "Let's get in there and find them!"

Jim grabbed hold of the doctor and started pulling him along with him. They had to take great big steps to get through the deepening snow. There was another noise that came from all around them. Jim knew that it wasn't the wind.

"Wolves?" the doctor shouted the question. "More wolves?"

"Let's hope that's all!" Jim yelled back.

They moved into the deep, cold darkness of the trees. Here there was no moonlight and there was only noise around them, the noise of the wind whipping this way and that. There might be shapes moving, but whether it was Huck and Violet, wolves, killers, or trees moving about them, neither of them could tell.

Jim started shouting at the doctor: "Go back! Go back to the cave! It's too much here! It's too dark!"

He was shouting and pulling on the doctor's coat, and then the coat went limp and came off in his hand. He felt something heavy brush against his face, but whether it was the doctor moving off into the wind, or a tree limb, or something else, he couldn't tell. How he wished he hadn't taken too many of leaves now: the power of them would have helped him to see in the torrent of darkness that swarmed at him now.

"Doc!" he shouted, but the wind was harsh and took away his words.

He fumbled around until he got his footing, the wind knocking him this way and that. He pulled his hatchet and looked around squinting and whirling in the wind.

He started to make out some light, but he couldn't tell what was making the light. It looked as if stars moving in the darkness.

Then it was upon him. The jagged fingers were cold and hard and scraped at the skin of his throat. Its face was in his face, the crooked, smashed-looking face. These creatures were somehow using the bodies of dead men. Whatever was inside the mouth, those long worms that reached out, wrapped themselves around his neck. He wondered if the doctor had met a similar fate. Jim chopped upward with his father's ax, slicing the black worms and breaking the jaw of the thing. It slipped away from him almost immediately, shrieking into the blackness and wind.

The doctor saw the wild shape of Violet's hair whirling up around her in the wind and the blue light of the moon through the snow and made his way toward her. He figured that must be Huck standing by her, each of them holding onto the other. Then something else moved—a dark, dark shadow that jumped into the way. It started toward Huck and Violet, but the doctor drew and blasted straight at it.

At once he tripped and fell into deep snow and tasted his own blood as the wounds on his face and neck bled hot and then began to freeze closed. Something underneath him wriggled, and he found that he was holding onto a thin frame. There was a flash and a pistol thump, but not his own. He felt hot blood again on his fingers, but it was not his own. There was more shrieking, and something grasped his ankle in the dark. He felt those claws punch into his muscle and brought his hatchet down in that direction, connecting it with a crunch.

The wind slowed and then was gone. He could hear breathing and panting and someone saying, "Violet, Violet."

"Who's there?" the doctor shouted hoarsely.

"This is Jim Falk! Who's there?"

The doctor tried to answer Jim, but suddenly felt no strength in himself. He thought he could feel heat sliding out of his body.

"Huck Marbo!" Huck shouted, answering the doctor and Jim. "I've got Violet, she's okay. I think she's hurt, but she's okay."

The trees went calm and moonlight filtered again through the pines. Jim could see now Huck Marbo leaning over Violet and Violet was holding her gun and there was a dead killer on the ground beside them and another below Jim with a smashed head. But there was another lump in the middle. The doctor.

Jim ran, pushing his legs through the deep snow. He grabbed the doctor and rolled him over, but the doctor's face was stone, his eyes fixed on something far, far away. His neck was severed and his chest and arms had been clawed to tatters.

Jim looked this way and that, looking to see if any more killers remained in the clearing.

"We need to get back to the cave!" he shouted to Violet and to Huck. "It's not safe here and it's not safe to go back to Sparrow."

He looked at the good doctor's face. "Why did you come here, Doctor? Of all the places, of all the towns here in the South. Why did you have to come here?"

Around them, they could hear wolves howling.

"Get on!" Jim yelled at Huck and Violet now. "Get yourselves back up in there! Hurry, run! They're coming!"

Violet and Huck did not need to be told again. They started moving back toward the cave, up the hill. They looked over at Jim attending to the doctor's body, and Violet tucked her face into Huck's shoulder.

"Doc," Jim said to the doctor's body, "I am so sorry, Doc. I didn't mean for you to get into all this."

Jim grabbed the doctor's pack and slung it over his shoulder. Then he noticed that the doctor had another pack. It didn't look like a pack that the doctor would have. It was heavy. He put that over his shoulder too. When he did, he felt weak.

Then he tried to lift the doctor's body and couldn't. He heard the wolves bawling here and there around in the trees. Jim thought of what the doctor had said about Barnhouse again. Was it going to be that whoever he came into contact with would eventually find some evil end? His mother? His father? Bill Hill? The chicken man? He looked at the doctor's face in the moonlight. The doctor didn't look afraid. He wondered if somewhere the doctor's wife or children or even the doctor's parents might be waiting and wondering.

"Why did you come here, Doc? Why did you come to Sparrow?"

He heaved again, and this time the doctor's frame came up and Jim meant to drag the corpse off and up the hill to find a suitable grave, but he heard a voice.

"Wait," the doctor said and feebly reached out and put his torn-up hand on Jim Falk's shoulder. Jim stopped and knelt down with the doc over his knee.

For a little moment the doctor passed his eyes back and forth between Jim's face and the shadowy trees above.

"What is it, Doc?"

The doctor motioned with his hand to Jim and pointed to the heavy bag Jim had just put on. Jim handed it to him. The doctor reached into the satchel and removed a large square object that was wrapped in a cloth. He handed it to Jim.

"What's this, Doctor?" Jim flipped it over in his hands and the cloth wrapping came off and showed Simon's book.

"Witchwords?" Jim said.

The doctor's bushy eyebrows came together. "I couldn't open it. The Starkey kid, Simon. He dropped it in the mud before. It's his bag. I picked it up."

"Did you open it up? Did you try to read it?" Jim's blue eyes flashed in the moonlight.

The doctor said nothing. He coughed and blood came out. Jim wiped it away. Then Jim wrapped the book back up fast and dropped it back in the satchel and quickly pulled out the doctor's bag.

"What can I use in here?" Jim asked and began fumbling around in the bottles.

The doctor reached out and grabbed Jim's arm. "I'm past all that. I'm past all that, outlander."

"You're not. Show me what to do, old man! Show me what to do!" Jim was nearly yelling at him.

The doctor was calm. The thing that grabbed his chest was powerful and its hands were hot like fire against his skin. The wound, he knew, was so deep that it was bleeding inside and out. There was nothing Jim could do, but the doctor said, "Get the blue bottle with the square stopper and give me that."

Jim did so immediately, and the doctor drank. Jim grabbed a long, wide bandage and began pressing it onto the doctor's chest.

"What did you see in the pages? Did anything happen?" Jim asked quick.

They could hear again the wolves howling somewhere in the night.

The doctor looked at Jim and said, "Scribbles, shapes, nothing. There was nothing. It looked like a book full of spirals and blotches. But it gave me a chill when I opened it."

"You saw no words or pictures?" Jim asked. He pressed the bandages into the doctor's chest. There was too much blood.

"Words? No words."

"Good," Jim said, and the doctor looked at him with eyes wide and his mouth half parted and Jim took in a short breath. "You don't know what it is, do you, Doctor?"

The doctor coughed, "No."

"This is a very old thing, Doctor. A book of Witchwords and it must be destroyed. That you looked inside is bad enough. We'll have to destroy it soon as we can."

The doctor's eyes were wide. He thought about Simon. He thought about Simon's strange card trick—the moving hole.

"Jim, when you go back to the others, I don't want you to hide anymore. The time for hiding and for fear is over."

"Fear?" Jim asked and kept the bandage tight over the doctor's heart.

"Can you read that book, Falk?" the doctor suddenly asked.

"No one should read a book such as this," Jim said angrily. "It must be prepared and burned up."

Jim could feel that the doctor wasn't breathing right, but whatever medicine Jim had given him had brightened the doctor's voice a little.

"Jim, those people back in Sparrow will need you. May Marbo, the Straddlers, all of them. They need you."

"Doc, we're not going to get out of this without you. What will we do without the medicine? Without the healing ways?"

The doctor didn't answer. His eyes were open, but he did not see anymore.

Jim was telling the preacher about the evil book. "There's words you must say over it, Preacher, to bind it. Certain words. Then burned and washed away in a river or a creek. That's all. My father had gotten rid of books like this before. It takes some doing to get it gone."

"Doing?"

"Preacher, you could tear this book to shreds and throw some of the pieces in Sparrow creek and some of the pieces off the mountain. Those little bits would find each other and rebind to the binding. There's a certain way to rid the evil out of the book, and it appears that I'm the only one who knows how around here. Others who once may have known are absent from our company."

The preacher didn't understand exactly what Jim meant. He looked at his hand and his arm, which Jim and the doctor had restored to his body. He thought again of that night when the witch had showed him the terrible thing on the other side of the darkness. She was young now and Jim was telling everyone that she wasn't what she appeared to be. Then his mind went to his sister-in-law.

Jim looked back toward the preacher, who was standing there looking scared, this way and that. Jim whispered to him, "Preacher, I know this time is hard for you. We're all sorry for the loss of your brother. We can't know why things happened the way they did. We need to know about his wife, though. We need to know about Ruth Mosely."

Vernon stepped toward Jim, quietly, wanting not to awaken anyone and looking cautiously toward the witch, who seemed not to hear them. He was still wringing his hands together. He said, "Some men that had gone out into the mountains for game had found her and brought her back. Just alone out there, coming down a steep mountain way with a hungry horse. She told us many had died. She told us that it was a sickness come and killed her two brothers and everyone else. She was all there was left, as she told it, and warned the men against going up any farther along that way on account of a sickness that was in the water. She warned them against drinking the water. We took her in, even though people thought we ought not. My brother, John, he took to taking care of her because she was skinny and seemed like she might be sick her-self. We kept her off from the rest of the people a long while. Only John would go see her and take care of her." When he spoke the name of his brother, the preacher paused and his eyes wiggled and got wet. He swallowed and looked down, rubbing his eyes with his right hand, took a deep breath and continued on. "I guess that's when him and Ruth became fond of each other."

"A village up in the mountains?" Jim asked.

"Yes. The name I don't remember, River Den or River Top, something like that, but the men knew about it. The men that brought her in were familiar with the name of the town."

"River's End? I've heard of that. There was a terrible sickness up there. She was the only one who lived? Is that what she said?"

"That's the way she told it. You could see it in her eyes at the time that she'd seen something terrible and she'd near starved to death. She looked it."

"You know nothing more than that?" Jim asked.

The preacher shook his head, but didn't look at Jim. His hand curled into a little fist and he shuffled his feet and then looked at Jim. "It doesn't make sense to me," the preacher said. "It doesn't make sense at all for my brother's wife to turn against the teachings like that and for her to turn against me. There's something in me that tells me"—the preacher again had to pause and take a deep breath—"something says that she might of even used some kind of power over my wife. My little brother. I don't know, I really don't know. I just can't make any sense of it."

Jim reached out and tried to put his hand on the preacher's shoulder, but the preacher backed away.

"I don't know why or how that witch saved us. I don't know why you killed my brother." He started to cry.

"Preacher," Jim said, "there are things at work here that are greater than all of us."

"I know that you're right," the preacher said. "It may be those papers. Those writings that they're after. I fear that it is. I fear that somehow, this whole time, Ruth has been seeking them out. Not only Ruth, but that somehow the wolves, the creatures that Violet Hill saw, all these things, somehow they've been trying to get at me, at these things, and now I am so afraid for my wife and my little daughter! They're in danger, Falk!"

Jim reached out again, and this time he succeeded in patting Vernon Mosely a little on the back. Vernon looked toward the front of the cave and drew a quick breath. Wylene had moved while they were talking and was now standing on the opposite side, crouched down strangely and looking at her arms.

Jim turned to see what the preacher was looking at and then turned back, still whispering to the preacher. "She's not a witch. She can't be, although, as you know, the fiends can take on many forms."

"You've said that, but it's hard to take—fangs . . . claws . . ." the preacher asked.

"A witch would not have helped us. A witch would not have saved May Marbo from a wolf. A witch would have torn her bones out and drank up her blood," Jim said and looked at the preacher and then toward Wylene who ignored them.

"Hmph," the preacher said.

"This Wylene, Daughter of Earth and Sky, whatever her name is and whatever it is that she might be, she doesn't cast spells like a witch. She doesn't give out curses. She doesn't use the Witchwords." When Jim said "Witchwords," the preacher raised an eyebrow and took a sidelong glance at Jim. "She's not decrepit, or decayed. Her body isn't beat down with the Evil One's emptiness . . . the way a witch's body would be. And I was able to restore her from a curse. Do you see? She herself had a curse put on her that she herself was not able to undo. She claims it was the Mosely woman that did that." Jim paused and fiddled with something in his jacket pocket then said, "She's got a strange look about her, a look akin to how the killers look, but she's not exactly a killer neither. She said she's from different things, two different parents. And, as far as I can see, she's not in league. There's no pact or covenant made between her and the Evil One. As far as I can see. Of course, my way of seeing doesn't always see all the way."

"You just have a good feeling about her."

"I suppose so. But it's more than that."

"I am familiar with the scriptures, Jim Falk, and I do believe that I do know what you're referring to."

"If what Wylene says is true about this Ruth Mosely, and that Ruth Mosely is the witch at Sparrow Creek, then Ruth may be the one who has called these wolves and she may be in communication with the killers up here in the woods. They've burned the church down toward whatever purposes they're bent to do. Next, they may mean to have these wolves to rid out what's left of any of the good folk of Sparrow. If that is the case, which very well may be, then there are only a few who are left that can defend against these creatures in the town, and it would be up to us to prevent her from achieving her end."

"I'm not sure, Falk. I'm not sure. You healed me, but my brother is dead now. What is my sister-in-law doing? What is Ruth Mosely doing here in Sparrow?" the preacher asked Jim and rubbed his hands together. He looked over at the fire and at May Marbo, who was sleeping there. He did not want to wake her up. Huck and

Violet were curled up one on the other and their eyes were closed too, but he didn't think they were asleep. What would May think when she woke to find the doctor was gone?

He glanced at the witch at the front of the cave looking out into the night and thought of his sister-in-law again. Thought of her past.

He asked Jim a second time, "What is Ruth Mosely doing in Sparrow?"

"Preacher, whatever questions you have for Ruth, and whatever you need to talk to the preacher about, you don't speak a word of this book to anyone. Now I'm going off to make quick work of it. I'll be back."

Now Jim was alone with this book in the moonlight and trees. He looked at the wrapped-up book in the woven blanket. Somewhere along the way, the doctor had got himself one of these woven blankets, almost just the same as he'd got from Old Magic Woman a long time ago. Jim hunkered down by a tree and looked out into the dark woods. Just for a moment he thought he could see something like a mist moving out there in the woods, but he squinted and saw it no longer. He glanced over his shoulder and back up the side of the hill to see if he could see the front of the cave. He couldn't. Here, in his hands, he held one of those old books, those books that contained the Witchwords.

Ithacus had taught him to read these words. His pa could write in them when he needed to, which wasn't often.

"How'd you learn those words, Pa?"

His pa would say nothing.

There was only a single time that Jim could remember his father ever having need of using the words. It was a strange issue of something that had got caught in John Goodwater's barn. Ithacus knew Ways that Jim never got to learn from him before he disappeared. His pa could fashion special wood boxes or boxes of metal to trap certain kinds of things in, but it was so seldom that he had to do it and Jim wasn't sure that the craft for making these things was something he would ever have to learn. But that time, when

John Goodwater had that thing down in his barn, Jim's pa had to take one of those special boxes and write Witchwords all around the outside of it.

After the deed was done, Goodwater always brought around food and lots of it, but his pa had been sick for months and his hands had taken on a kind of gray color and the fingernails turned black. It wasn't too different from the way the preacher's hand and arm had looked before they had restored it to him.

Jim unwrapped the book. However much or little the old doctor knew of Waycraft, he'd known enough or been told enough to keep the book wrapped up in an old magic blanket.

"The weave," Old Magic Woman told him, "the weave shuts out the shadows. Or shuts them in."

Jim kept a small collection of woven blankets of this type in his satchel and one he always carried slung over his shoulder, and a group of them were sown into the lining of his jacket. Old Magic Woman spent much time weaving. Some of the older blankets he had come to have a strange feeling about when he held them, like a noiseless humming about the fabric. This one that held Simon's book had that same feel about it. It was old.

He wished he could ask Old Magic Woman about the blanket. He wished he could ask his pa what to do. They were gone now. Faded into the forests.

"It is one thing," Old Magic Woman said to him back then, "it is one thing to know the trees, the forests, and the mosses, to know when the bees honey, and how to make the Leaves in warm darkness. It is another thing to know the Way and it is yet another to walk the Way."

In his memory, Jim watched her wading in the sparkling stream. The water moved around her robes and carried them here and there, the sun shining on her dark eyelashes, the old skin of her hands dipping here and there at a fish, maybe. They had been out in the water all morning, fishing like that. Catching nothing, but talking.

Jim looked away from his memory and down at the unwrapped book that was now starting to catch flakes of snow. Over the years there had been times when his mind had turned over learning the things contained in one of these books and how his pa had come to be able to read the words inside.

The leather of the cover was thick and felt somehow smoother than it should. Jim shuddered to think what hide covered the book. Wild carvings and scratches covered the surface, as if some kid had tried to draw monsters on it. Mean, horned faces bunched together and overlapping, hooves, fangs, and lizard tails. None of the faces were as ugly or awful as those real faces—like the one he and the doctor saw outside the church that night.

Jim wondered if maybe he too could read the Witchwords the way his pa could. The doctor had said that he'd only seen scribbles. But Jim knew since he was young that there was something about him having a knack for the Waycraft and other things that others didn't have. Maybe his own pa never had to learn to read the Witchwords because he'd always known how. Maybe Jim could open up this book and get the secrets. Maybe the secrets would help him rid the land of whatever was left of the killers.

# CHAPTER 18

"It's gone quiet," Benjamin Straddler said.

"Quiet, sure. But them wolves only get quiet when they're busy," Hattie Jones said. Hattie Jones sat there in Huck's place, which was empty except for Hattie Jones, Benjamin Straddler, and Samuel, who sat in a corner poking at the floor.

"Seems to me like there's been some kind of a noise going off in my head starting around about the time that that outlander showed up." Benjamin Straddler took a sip of strong coffee from his little mug.

Hattie got up from the bar stool and went over to the fireplace in the wall and messed around in there for a while with the wood and embers. Soon the fire was crackling again. Benjamin started thinking about the church and how he and Lane had looked at it burning out their window and seen the form of Ruth passing here and there in the smoke. Sparrow was very quiet now, though.

"That dang church is still on fire. Little church like that shouldn't burn so long. And with all that snow coming down? Way I figure is, we'll have another blizzard here and all kinds of trouble and death."

Hattie came away from the fire and glanced at Samuel over in the corner and then came back and sat on a stool by Benjamin and took a swig of the hot coffee.

"In terms of supplies," Benjamin said and glanced around, "what do you think we'll need?"

"Well, you might as well leave it here, unless you're planning to take it all for yourself. And you won't need to worry about an old man like me. No, sir. Samuel and I are fixin' to move outta here for good."

"Where you going to move to?"

"We're fixin' to head somewhere, south, maybe north, but maybe west, but probably most likely south. We're through with winters and spooks."

Benjamin took another drink of the coffee and said, "Medicine, bandages, ropes, candles, shovels. If we're going to be digging through the snow, we're going to need shovels. There's probably a whole set of other things around here."

"With Vernon and John both crossed over, there's gotta be someone to stand up and take the leadership as well. If a man don't step up to do it, you can be sure as sure that that Ruth Mosely is going to start giving orders."

Benjamin looked around the place. "There's no one left, Hattie. You and I are just as well in line to head up this town as anybody else." Benjamin made a terrible face and his eyes got wide.

There was a long time of quiet between them. Somewhere they could begin to hear a sound like metal hitting on rock.

Benjamin mumbled, "That church burning and burning like that is some kind of a sign. They got men digging a grave for John Mosely, but Ruth seems bent on occupying herself with looking for the burned-up pieces of Huck Marbo and the outlander and all the rest of them was in the church."

"You think that was a witch that came in there? A real witch?" Hattie asked and looked at the floor. Then Benjamin Straddler got out a cigar and chewed off one end and lit it up.

"I don't know how to figure it. We seen a witch when I was a boy, but it was way worse looking than that lady in black. The witch we seen was like a demon or a shadow. I hate to even remember it."

Hattie said, after he watched Benjamin puff a few times, "Thing about this thing is whether it was a witch or not, I can't tell how a fire like that even got started in the first place with the church.

When I talked to one of them Ving brothers from up on the ridge, he said that he thought he saw the church lit like a candle. That the roof shot out a flame."

"Can't be right," Benjamin said. "Them Ving brothers always have something to say even when it's nothing."

"No," Hattie Jones said and got out his pipe. "No, you're right. It can't be right."

There was a quiet over Sparrow so that, even inside Huck's store, you could hear a few folks talking and mulling around the ashes of the church still. Once in a while too, they could hear the voice of Ruth quacking around in the night air. From somewhere else came the sound of the men digging John Mosely's grave.

"I figure on more graves," said Hattie and lit his pipe up and took a long puff.

"Yeah," Benjamin said, "I figure on more graves." And his eyes wandered along the bar and rested on the glass bottles full of brown whisky.

How long had he been asleep? He'd dreamed of her again. Some nights he saw her among the gray figures. There they went, disappearing into the dark hills, the men in the long gray coats leading them away. He heard a woman's voice calling to him, maybe his mother's voice. He could not know. A word, over and over. He couldn't understand, some sharp-sounding word. The woman's square, white hand with neat little nails thrusting out suddenly from between the dark coats, the voice calling, calling—calling his name. Yes, it was his name! His real name. His real mother. The things that he never knew. Some nights he would dream this dream and wake up in his little cabin having forgotten the truth just for a moment, and just for that moment before looking at the dwindling fire, he would feel light as though a wind blew in his heart. And then the fire, and then Dan Starkey's coat, where it had hung since he disappeared, and then the raspy breathing of his other mother in the room, the door closed.

This time he woke in the stranger's hut with his ears almost aching, as if in the silent dark of his dreams his ears could somehow stretch back to the sound. To know the sound of his real name on his real mother's tongue.

That long, deep burn of the doctor's bullet stung like a line of hot fire. It itched and he wanted to dig at it.

The smell of fish in the hut and the firelight dancing around made him sit up.

That weird wolf dog slumped next to the hooded figure licking its chops and watching with its black eyes the burning filets in the iron pan.

The stranger turned his darkened face toward Simon. "Come and eat. Come sit by the fire."

Simon moved slow off the cot, an itchy blanket wrapped around him, remembering the stranger's last words, "the Waycraft." He went over to the fire in his bare feet. The stranger rose and pulled the two small fish out of the fire and set them somewhere near to him where Simon couldn't see.

The wolf's eyes went wherever the fish went, but the snout stayed, resting on the pointed paws. The wolf chuffed in disappointment when the fish didn't slide down off the plate and land in front of him.

Simon hadn't been this close to this kind of an animal before. Now that he could see the thing's eyes, he wondered if the poor animal was blind or diseased or both. The eyes seemed shattered in the center. The wolf's pupils, like tiny pieces of dark, broken glass in golden water, floated around inside.

The more he studied the thing, the less it looked like a wolf and the more the shape of the thing looked like pictures he remembered as a boy carved into the handles of knives and swords that his father kept. Winding serpent's tails etched and lengthening into jagged mouths with flaming swirls of tongue.

Then a hot plate of fish was in his hands. The stranger's face hidden in the darkness of the hood hovering behind the brazen and steaming stack of filets. Simon, overcome by his hunger, stuffed the flaking pieces of steamy fish into his mouth.

"Slow down," the stranger said from the darkness beneath the hood.

It was the first time Simon had got anything solid into his belly since that damned doctor shot him.

Even now, the memories of that night flitted about in his mind. Those ugly things in Elsie's room.

"Slow down," the stranger said again. "You'll be sorry."

Simon felt the tightness rumble in his stomach and bowels. He had been standing straight up by the little fire and the stranger, but now he sat back on his cot and held his stomach and touched at his bandaged head.

The stranger reached over and took the plate from Simon's hand and set it on a little shelf and then handed Simon another cup of hot medicine.

"All of it," the stranger said.

Simon took the cup. The wolf's weird eyes looked from the plate to the darkness under his master's hood. So it was not blind.

Simon swallowed down the medicine. Its smell cleared his nose as it warmed up his belly and blood. A twinkle came then in his eye and his mind started moving faster.

"What kind of a dog is that supposed to be? Is that a wolf?" he asked the stranger, taking another big swig of the stinging brew.

"Because it looks more like a dragon to you?" the stranger asked. His voice was quiet, hoarse, but somehow a sweetness had come into it.

Simon squinted his eyes and tried to see the stranger's face under the hood. "Yes," Simon said, "that's right."

The stranger flipped a piece of fish at the dragon wolf, and its mouth flashed open red and then shut with a clomp.

"Yes," the stranger said, "Fenny does look like a dragon, doesn't he?"

Simon looked back at the dragon wolf. The floating black shapes in the wolf's eyes now seemed to come together and form a slit down the center like a snake's eyes. Its back arched and Simon thought he could see the long, hard bones and lines of webbed muscle that would rise and flap like wings lining the dog's back.

The stranger said, "Fenny looks in a way like a cat, though, doesn't he?"

Simon looked back at the stranger and then to the dragon wolf again. He saw the pointed ears and whiskers and the long pink tongue lolling and licking the black, diamond-shaped nose.

Simon sipped again the tangy medicine and felt a heavy spin in his head. He was sure now that the stranger's medicine was doing the tricks, making him see strange shapes in the flickers of fire and shadow in the hut.

The fish had tasted good, though, and he wanted more.

"You can have more fish after your medicine's gone," the stranger said.

"How long have I been asleep?" he asked.

"Only a few hours," the stranger said and turned to pour boiling water into a cup and pinch in some dark powders and dried leaves. Simon watched the stranger's wrinkled, brown hands do the job. The hands were strong, but somehow delicate and careful.

"Who are you?" Simon asked. "Why are you out here and why are you helping me?"

"I've told you," the stranger said.

Simon said, "Tell me again."

The stranger shook his head. "You've made a pact with Old Bendy's Men." The stranger stirred the brew with a wooden spoon. "The pact's gone bad, Simon Starkey. They've claimed all and left you with nothing. Left you for dead. As they do. Their kind only comes to steal and to destroy."

How could this man know so much about what he barely knew himself? How could this crooked old man in a hut know?

He thought again of his dream. He saw the figures carrying away his real mother to the woods. He saw Dan Starkey's hand reaching into the cage to pull him out. He smelled the thick smell of Elsie's stew and saw her belly grow with Dan's baby. The boys of

Sparrow prodding him and laughing—then the dark whispers in the night . . . Power, they told him, "power beyond imagining."

"Everything," Simon said, and his face went blank. He clasped his hands together and brought them up to his forehead and let out a long breath.

"You learned some tricks, some cheap sorcery. You got your reward."

Just a few pages of that cursed book of Witchwords was all he'd been able to read after four years—a stupid card trick, some special seeing, hardly even a beginner's beginning.

Simon didn't say anything. He looked at the fire.

"They wanted you to think that you had no choices, that you were powerless and without choices."

"When they took the little one, Rebeccah . . . I thought if I learned enough, one day I would be powerful, one day I could turn those powers against them. Make them pay."

Simon swallowed hard and squeezed his face with his hand so that he wouldn't cry. Any movement of his head hurt.

"What is it that you want, Simon Starkey?"

"I don't want to be afraid anymore," Simon whispered.

"The Waycraft," the stranger said, "the Waycraft will make you strong against them. I can show you." The stranger finished up whatever he'd been brewing and brought it to where his lips must have been under the dark hood. "You can't use the same powers they showed you to fight against them. There is only the Way."

"Those are stories."

The stranger lifted the cup up again to the darkness under the hood. "So they are, so they are," the stranger said, "but some stories are true. They've burned down the church."

The agony that had been churning in Simon's stomach was only a dull throb now, and when he swallowed more fish the pain flared again, but the medicine brought a strength back to his eager body and a certain shine back to his dull eyes.

"They thought that the witch and the outlander were trapped inside the church, and so they burned it down."

"The witch?" Simon asked and tried to see the face under the cloak.

"Yes," the stranger said. "Old Lady Wylene's grown young again and strong and has sprung from whatever spell that held her in her home. I guess she'd made friends of a kind with that outlander. They used that little token you gave to them."

"They're dead now? Why do you know so much about it?" Simon asked.

"Sparrow is a small place, Simon Starkey. There are not many secrets here. You may think that there are, but many things are known about this little town. I doubt that they have achieved what they think they have. It's something to trap and kill a witch. It takes more than fires and churches."

"They're alive?"

The stranger turned toward the little fire in the tent. "I saw them making their way up to the Ridges. More than just the witch and the outlander. A doctor, a preacher, a peg-leg, a young girl . . ."

"The Marbos?" Simon said to himself.

"And a red-headed woman. I saw the whole lot of them moving through the woods and then out past the Ridges and on into the mountains."

Simon used his arms and slid himself down off the little cot and he stood on his own legs and limped closer to the fire and the stranger. His legs felt strong, like they were his own.

Then the stranger raised his cloaked and musty-smelling arm and put his hand on Simon's shoulder. "You're safe here," the stranger said. "You can stay with me until you're well. We'll keep an eye on this town a while longer. They may need you soon."

"And what do you want from me?"

"Let me teach you."

"Teach me?" Simon tried again to see into the darkness under the hood.

"You think, if you chase these monsters down, these creatures that took your little sister and took your mother, that you'll be able to destroy them somehow? That you'll be able to get revenge?"

Simon looked down at his hands.

"Do you think, if you are able to recover your book of spells from whoever may have taken it from you, that you will be able to learn the dark ways and that the dark ways will help you get revenge?"

Simon said nothing for a long while. A hum started in his head and he thought he could hear music, a kind of tinkling bell music. He felt sleepy again and he felt all his pain lifting away. He sat quietly on the little cot while the stranger worked at the long wooden table with the shelves over the top of it filled with odd-shaped bottles and jars of dark stuff. Every so often, the stranger would stop and hum for a while something that sounded like the song that played in Simon's head—a crooning, rising and falling song of bells and wind. Simon never heard a song like that again and could never remember it after.

"What's that you're doing?" Simon asked.

"Medicine," the stranger said, "making medicine."

Simon hadn't any idea how long he'd been staring at this stranger without a face. He thought it was a few days, but considering he'd been shot in the head, he wasn't sure he could be so healed in only a few days. The soft brown walls of the hut seemed to move in and out with his breath. At times he couldn't tell whether he was thinking things or saying them out loud. The wild dog, Fenny, was flickering with the strange shadows around the fire.

"I'd like to go outside," Simon said, a fear growing in his gut.

The stranger turned his hooded head a little to the side. "Outside?"

"I think I need some air."

The stranger lifted a hand and in his hand there was a bright silver knife, long and ornamented with an odd, twisted blade.

"Take this with you in case there's something out there. I've heard wolves howling tonight."

Simon looked at the sleeping dog and back at the man in the robe. He slowly got up off the cot and walked toward the man.

"Something you want to talk about?" the faceless man asked. Simon looked at the knife that the stranger was holding. He concentrated on the blade. At first he thought that etched along its handle he could see the face of the dog that was by the fire, but then he pinched his forehead and looked again. There were dragons on it—dragons that twisted and curled up and down the hilt, dragons in a maze of dragons. The blade twisted too, like a slow corkscrew, to a spaded tip. In fact, it looked less like a knife and more like the tail of one of the silver creatures twisted around the hilt. He recognized it. It almost spoke to him.

"Where did you get that knife?" Simon asked.

"Does it matter?" the stranger asked without turning his head. "I am giving it to you now." The stranger said and set the knife there on the table.

Simon walked slowly toward the faceless man and his knife. This knife was very familiar to Simon. In fact, it looked just like the knife that he remembered from his dream, the knife his father had slung on his belt. It was one of the few memories that had stayed together in his dreams from when he even knew his parents at all. It was a true memory now, flashing forward from his deeper mind: his father's dragon knife bouncing in front of him as they walked along a path by a river somewhere in Simon's past. In fact—and he knew it now—this was his father's knife.

Simon reached for the knife, but did not grab it. He yanked the hood and yanked it hard.

The back of the stranger's head was gnarled and the long black hairs that swirled there against the brown and gray skin were thick and almost bright. Something came off of the head like a wave and hit Simon in the face. At first that's what it felt like. It felt as if something hit him in the face, but that wasn't quite right. Whatever was coming off of the back of the stranger's head was more like light or wind or something that pushed at him like heavy water. Simon's desire to see the face of the stranger left him as a kind of hum pushed into his mind. His stomach curled and his head went dizzy. He was sure that suddenly he could hear voices, forbidding voices. He looked away from the back of the stranger's head and to the knife. He was sure that it was his father's dagger.

Quietly, the stranger turned to face him. Simon almost fell backward into the fire. It was a woman—an old woman with a kind smile and bright eyes.

"Where did you get that knife?" Simon asked, holding his head and curling his lips.

"You know this knife, Simon Starkey," she said. "This knife once belonged to your father. Your real father."

"My real father is dead."

"And so your real mother."

"Did you kill them? Is that what you're telling me? I could end your life right now, old woman."

"Could you? Perhaps. But then you would never know what it means to live a life without fear. You would never know how to live a life in which you could see them again. You've lived so long with fear. It is a part of you now."

Simon sighed.

"I can show you that. A life without fear. I can show you much more than that, though. I can let you see your father again, and your mother. I can show you the Waycraft."

"They'll come after me and kill me for sure then. The Waycraft. What you're talking about. That's what they're out to destroy. You know that. It's a weak way. It's a way of herbs and prayers. They'll come for me for sure."

The stranger turned. "They'll come after you anyway."

The stranger handed Simon the knife.

Simon took it and held it in both hands. He looked at it quietly. Every strange twist and curve of the blade brought odd, hacked bits of memory into his mind's eye: his father's brown hands, his mother's coat coming over him in a snowstorm.

"What do I do?"

"You must trust me. First you must decide to trust me. Because I might tell you to do things that aren't going to make any sense to you. Things that won't make any sense at all."

"I need to think about this."

"Then go. Take the knife. You are free to go."

"Go?" Simon asked. "Go where? My home is burned and they are sure to come for me. The outlander and the doctor will hunt me for a witch."

Simon looked at the stranger's kind face. Then he slid the knife into his jacket and walked out of the little hut and into the cold night.

He stood in the darkness outside of the tent and pulled the knife out of his jacket and looked at it. He listened to the wolves baying in the distance.

The air was crisp and he felt the strength in his legs and in his arms. He went to the edge of the hill next to the little valley where the stranger's hut was. On top of the hill he saw the deeper valley below. This was not a small hill. The stranger had brought him up to the top of a tall mountain. Far below him in the valley, he could see a brown and orange thing rising from a patch of brown, a long gray string of smoke twirled up into the sky. It was the church. The church was burning.

He mumbled to himself, "This is what they wanted."

He looked back at the stranger's hut and saw that the big gray wolf, Fenny, had stepped out into the darkness too. It had a great, wide, hairy back and the light from inside the hut passed around it, making a moving shadow of its form. The old wolf wandered lazily through the snowy hillside and came up beside him looking down into the valley below and panting. Simon looked at the knife again. Could he? She was offering him something that he'd never dreamed to be offered. He thought of his real mother disappearing into the hands and cloaks of those evil men when he was young, and then he thought of Elsie. Hadn't he done the same to her and worse? Hadn't he given her over to a worse evil than even his real mother? It had been his own hand that handed her over—and now this old woman was offering him a way. A way. Before he had only wanted power, but now he felt there was something beyond power, something different, and he felt something in him shift and lean.

The sky was darkened by racing clouds. Here and again the moon would suddenly shine big and bright and round through a hole in the clouds that moved along. There were barks in the distance and then a whooping and a howl. Another long and low howl answered from the valley.

Fenny didn't seem to mind and he didn't answer. He looked along in the valley and then back up at Simon. Something grew warm inside of him as he looked down across the valley.

Simon was thinking that the killers had spent years trying to destroy this town, this little town of Sparrow that was miles from anywhere except the Ridges where the people that didn't believe like the people in Sparrow went to live.

The killers had nothing to do with the folks at the Ridges as far as Simon had heard. Each time a spook had shown up, it followed just after the wolves had come down off of the mountain. It might be this very mountain here that the spook lived upon and fed on what was about until the wolves were run out of their own territory. These things were old. Many people had stopped believing in them. There were three places where Simon had read about things that were like the killers and were like these creatures that the folks called spooks or demons. One place was in the books that the killers had given him to study the evil way, one was in the scriptures, and the other was in Sparrow.

He looked back at the tent. Whether he followed the Way or wandered the forests, there would be no peace for him. He was made to live in a time of hatred and fire and slavery and men who murdered parents. He was made to live in a time when demons hunted the living. This old woman was offering him something, but who was she? She might herself be a kind of witch. But she was offering him something different.

He looked at the animal that sat neatly beside him on the cliff as more howls were answered in the valley. This wolf seemed to be studying the situation just as he was. The animal seemed thoughtful and it wasn't snarling or growling at him. In fact, it pushed its nuzzle up under Simon's hand and nudged his palm.

He patted Fenny's head and Fenny butted his muzzle into Simon's hand. He watched the smoke of the far-off church twist around and back and forth in the wind. The killers had wanted this all along, but maybe couldn't find a way to do it themselves. Maybe they had needed help somehow from the people of Sparrow. Maybe Simon himself had somehow become trapped in this scheme. Perhaps he was never meant to survive. His mind started to put the pieces together of a very strange puzzle as he scratched the wolf's head.

# CHAPTER 19

As was regular in her preparations, Ruth Mosely walked backwards in a slow circle around the table sprinkling some dark powder from a pouch as she went. She mumbled to herself and looked up toward the ceiling, showing the whites of her eyes. She went this way around the little table three times. Then she got into another sack that she had on her and produced some long candles and stands and set five around on the table. She moved some chairs around, adjusting them here and there, and then she stopped all her fidgeting, went slow to her knees, and cried.

Ruth cried hard, hard enough that a wail came up from inside of her belly and out of her mouth. She couldn't stop it. John Mosely was dead. He'd been shot in the face by the outlander whose ashes were now black and blowing in the snow and wind over the cinders of the church. But they'd killed John. Shot him in the face. She wondered if John had known before he'd crossed over that his face was gone—or if he'd only felt a heat and then . . .

She sobbed again, but started to get to her feet. In her mind, she cursed the day she'd made the pact. She'd paid along the way for her power. Paid in shades and forms that she'd pushed down inside her mind never again to be uncovered, but the life of her husband John Mosely was a heavy toll. It hurt her heart, surely, but it might also hurt her plans. It hurt the truth that she stood for, but at the same time, too, it might help her. This brother of his, Vernon the preacher, had got himself tangled up somehow in the business of talking to known witches, like Wylene.

Ruth's eyes went into a dark squint. Somehow that Wylene, the one they'd called another name long ago, the one who'd somehow crawled up from the beforetimes, had regained her strength.

In the ultimate scheme, tying in the preacher of the Way with a known witch would serve her well. It would serve her well and Varney Mull would hear of it today. The two of them had shut Wylene away, shut her down with the Wastrel, and she didn't know how it was that the creature had escaped the powerful spell. The turnkey, which was the witch's thumb, had come up missing, and she was sure it had something to do with that Jim Falk. She thought about that man for a moment, that outlander, his strange blue eyes, the packs and satchels around him, the beat-up hat. She recognized the feel of him from tales of old.

Even though the killers and others, like Varney Mull, had spent ages removing the bloodlines from the earth, there were always rumors that there would be another, another like the first, and that he would come again and again until his stories were remembered as true. She shuddered and cleared her head. Varney Mull was coming with his men, if they were men. Even if, as she thought, this James Falk was one of these ancient hunters, it was over now anyway and Varney Mull would pay her handsomely for her deeds, in money or powers or both. Falk had been burned to ashes along with his witch prey and a preacher and the rest of that troublesome lot that had formed up around him.

Ruth mumbled some quick and strange words to herself and stood up and started lighting the candles. Soon after the room was washed in the yellow light, the knocks came at the wood door to the cellar.

Then they came, creaking down the narrow stairs. One by one the faces came out of the dark opening of the stairwell into the candlelight. Down came the faces to sit around the table and the candles, each face solemn, the eyes half closed and twinkling in the candle flames. Men and women of Sparrow, some from the Ridges, but not many. Not many yet. Just enough to fill this little dark room.

Why the men and women of River's End resisted, Ruth couldn't say. She held her body tight, preventing the shudder she felt as she saw the faces of her brothers being swallowed up in the dark maw of the thing Varney sent. The Waycraft. Those two words poisoned her mind. The simple people who followed the Waycraft and its supposed healing power, its kind-hearted magic, its total lies. Her brothers were among the folk that believed. Even when the beasts came, they couldn't summon the wisdom to see through the falseness of old stories and join her cause. They resisted and they died.

She and John had discovered this room the day after they'd put their stuff about in the little house. There had been an odd, dark-smelling smell, and Ruth and John came down to see what it was and to try to clean it out. The place hadn't been put to any kind of use in a long time, though, maybe years, maybe more than years. There were worms and fat trap spiders that must have been feeding on thick beetles in the spring and summer and spent their lives in some strange, frozen wakefulness through the winters. The black, scurrying bodies were quick out of the holes, but Ruth was quicker and her heels came down again and again to smash them—her own eyes darting in the cellar, John hollering now and again as another black shadow would shoot along the edge of his vision.

No more of them, though. And no more of him. Ruth and John had cleaned this space out good and put in a table and shelves, had packed the dirt hard in places and dug away other walls until they hit the bare side of a rock wall that must have been the original walls of the cellar. That had got them digging and digging until they were able to find three walls, or what was left of them. The fourth wall they could not get to, at least where they thought it was, because the dirt had got too hard on that end.

Now the faces hovered in the candlelight around the little table and Ruth put her hands on the table and the others put their hands on the table so that all the hands touched one another but didn't overlap and didn't touch the candles. Each of the faces with eyes down-turned seemed so solemn and so still that they might have been sleeping. Ruth took a small breath and started reciting the words that the killers taught her.

The men and women who were with her joined in the dark, chanting the deep song with its terrible words. Soon they were joined by voices. Not voices from within the dank cellar, but voices from outside, the voices of the wolves in the mountains. The baying of the wolves.

Jim felt the jitters.

He crouched down in the dark woods and, real slow, wrapped the ugly book back up and hid it somewhere in his long coat. Then he got out his strange ax.

Jim squinted his eyes in the moonlight. The witch at the edge of the cave whispered to him again, but he gave no answer. Doubtless, she'd picked up on what Jim had picked up on. Now he could see movements coming along the path up the hillside. Jim gripped his ax in his left hand. His right still wrapped in the bandages. He could see the wicked heads move off the path and shift from tree to tree. He wished for Leaves to help him see in the dark. Too, he wished for his fingers back.

The killers moved across the hillside with their desperate way of running and leaping crookedly into moon-shade, flicking their gangly bodies from tree to tree, whipping thin shadows along the snow. They were close to Jim fast and his heart thumped too hard. Without those Leaves, he couldn't stay as calm as he needed and he couldn't get his mind as blank as normal. They could hear his thoughts, or something of them, for sure, and that's how they moved right at him.

Jim was sure they would be on him. Quietly he unscrewed his little silver flask and drained it down his throat. His nerves weren't trained enough without the Leaves to keep his hands steady when the jitters were strong as they were now. When the warmth of the whisky spread through his body, the thing hit him hard from his right side and sent him toppling downhill through the brambles so hard and so fast that he was sure that he'd left part of his nose and an ear up at the top of the hillside.

When he stopped, the thing came crashing against him, but his left hand was quick with the curved ax blade and it struck deep and sure across the wilted face of the killer. Yowling and flailing backward now, Jim changed the direction of his ax and cracked the backside of the ax against its jaw and felt it crush upwards into the killer's face. Jim stomped down hard on its chest, forcing it back into the brambles. He got it down and stomped its head into the tangled thorns. Then, panting, he drove the spike-staved ax handle into its throat and it gurgled.

Another shadow shot past him toward the cave entrance. But before he pursued, he doused the flailing body with oil and struck the tinder. The oily blaze gave out a thick smoke. Jim scrambled through the thorny bushes and caught the other one just as it dived out of the trees and toward the cave, but it whirled about and scampered out of his reach.

It was then that Wylene stepped from the mouth of the cave and into the moonlit patch of snowy rocks. The three of them stood in the clearing.

The killer heaved and stared at the witch, Wylene.

The moonlight came bright across the clearing and, where the killer's features were caught in the light, they looked man enough. Here and there, though, its body bled into twisted, sharp forms in the shadows. From behind, Jim saw only the thing's shadow shape, its jagged claws and twisted wings and pointed ears. Wylene only saw something of a wild man blinking at her in the moonlight.

It stepped toward her and spoke.

"What are you?" it said.

It might have said something more, but Wylene raised her arms in front of her in a crooked way and pointed her sharp fingers and thumbs toward the killer. She stomped with one leg forward, and the killer got shaky.

Wylene whispered to the thing, "Go back into the Wydder."

Had Jim heard her right? *The Wydder?*

Noiselessly, the thing shriveled into the middle of the air—a tattered, black rag, stuffed into a tiny floating hole. Jim's eyes flashed from where the thing was to Wylene's eyes. Wylene's mouth was open almost as if what she just did shocked her the way it shocked Jim. But it wasn't fear that was in Falk's eyes; it was hope. In that moment he saw that there was one who could open that door for him. If this Wylene-who-was-not-a-witch could send these creatures to the other side, then maybe, just maybe, she could bring things back through. Elseways, maybe she could send him through to find his father.

Huck Marbo stepped into the clearing and the preacher was behind him and Violet came out pointing her gun this way and that. May stayed at the edge of the cave.

All of them were hungry. All of them wanted to sleep. All of them wondered what would become of the town they lived in and the homes they once knew.

May said, "We're hungry, Jim Falk." She was looking around this way and that. She was counting heads.

Jim looked at Wylene, who'd sunken herself backward into the dark rocks at the edge of the cave.

They hadn't noticed or they hadn't seen or they didn't care to say. No one but Jim appeared to have seen what Wylene did to the killer. Jim scratched his chin and looked at May.

"Hungry?" he asked and smiled a bit. "You'd think you'd be happy just to be alive. There's a little bread. I've got some. Early in the morning, maybe the preacher and I will go down to the other end of the creek and bring us in some fish." Jim took a glance at May and then over to the preacher, who was just sitting in the cave blinking and looking about as if he were looking for someone. "Once we eat in the morning, that will be the time to make decisions."

"Decisions?" Violet asked.

"On who stays and who goes," Jim said, "and who goes back to Sparrow to take it back."

Jim fiddled around in his sack and drew them into the cave. He started handing out the pieces of hard bread. Small pieces.

"Back?" the preacher asked, gnawing on the chewy chunk Jim gave him. "What do you mean, take back Sparrow?"

"Way I figure it," Jim said, "your dead brother's wife's fixin' to take hold of Sparrow as a stronghold for the Evil One. Somehow she got hold of a good family and now she's in league. She's gonna take the town and make it into whatever she wants, or perhaps what another is telling her to make it. This is just as long as the killers don't come and take her sooner. That's what I can figure. That's why they're comin' around here."

Wylene did not eat any bread. She looked at Jim, though. She wanted to tell him something.

"What did you do?" Jim stepped a few steps in the dark toward Wylene.

All the rest of them were in the cave entrance looking out. May Marbo was standing a little more in front of the rest of them, and Violet had her hands on May's shoulders as if she was trying to keep her from running out into the middle of the field where strange men, probably demons, had just killed the doctor. Huck stood behind Violet with one hand on Violet's shoulder and his other hand holding his shotgun. The preacher was standing there with his arms crossed. His mind was full of questions.

"What did you just do? How did you do that?" Jim asked her again.

"I came into the world with the power to open and close doors into the splitways." Wylene said and then slowly dropped to one knee. "It makes me tired, though."

"You can open the holes?"

"Yes."

"Where do they go?"

"The otherside. There are only so many ways to open them and only so much you can do."

"Can you travel through them?" Jim asked, taking another step toward the dark figure of Wylene.

"Why are they coming?" The preacher suddenly yelled from the entrance to the cave. "What do they want? What do they want? Why can't they leave us alone?"

Jim Falk looked over at the witch who was not a witch. She stood slowly and lifted her veil in the night and looked at Falk. She turned her head then to the preacher and pointed the sharp index finger of her right hand at the preacher.

"Preacher," she said, "the scripture you carry in your sack, the memories in your head, the stories that you tell that people are beginning to believe are only legends and tales. This is what she's come to destroy, this is what she's called them for, for the destruction of the history of the Waycraft."

"It is as I feared, then," Jim said and turned to the little crowd of folk in the cave. "There's a man in the North who's in league with the Evil One. The way I figure it, he's got some kind of hold over Ruth Mosely and who knows who all else in Sparrow. What they're out to do is to stop the followers of the Way. They want to destroy the writings and they want to take over the churches. They want to reestablish the Evil One here."

"The Evil One?" the preacher said. "What are you saying, Falk?"

"There's no time anymore to figure out riddles and mysteries. We've got to go back to Sparrow and rid out the evil that's come along with the Mosely woman. We've got to get rid of Ruth Mosely and whoever else has fallen under her spell."

"This outlander speaks the truth," Wylene said. "This is only the beginning. Sparrow is only one of a hundred different settlements that are likely under his attack now."

"Other towns, other churches, other preachers," the preacher mumbled to himself.

May and Violet looked at the ground at the same time. Violet thought about Bill, her husband, the wild things that had taken place behind their home, in their home. She thought of a clear spring morning when Bill Hill had brought home rabbits and the evening they'd spent putting together the table that had sat for so long in the front room of their little house. The way he'd looked at her with his eyes shining clear and full of life, the way he'd worried over her when she seemed to be the only one in the little town of Sparrow who was seeing creatures and having nightmares. The strange man who'd come from the woods and given her something that he'd said would help her sleep, and it did help her sleep. That green and yellow powder that she'd breathed and smoked in cigarettes. Yes, it had helped her remain calm and quiet and pushed the nightmares to the back of her mind when it seemed that she would split in two with fear, but she was awake too, awake in her dreams, wandering through the woods. Calling, calling out for help. She'd seen in her mind a man, a man with a beat-up hat, a man with strange blue eyes, resting by a gnarled tree in a gray forest. She'd seen this outlander in her dreams and called out to him for help. Come down from the North, she'd called to him. Come down to Sparrow. It wasn't her that had brought this about exactly, she didn't know what she'd wanted, she'd only wanted an end to monsters and nightmares and madness—how did that Stranger know? How did some strange man in the woods know that she was in turmoil? Why hadn't he stopped them from getting Bill? Why had this outlander been called here only to bring an explosion of evil, demons, and burning churches, and now in league with a witch and talking some nonsense about Ruth Mosely trying to destroy some old legends?

Yet, when the outlander mentioned the man in the North, an odd feeling had come over her. Something in the back of her mind seemed to be suddenly looking at her, listening to her thoughts. There was something that tingled there in her mind when that outsider was mentioned.

"Varney Mull," Jim said and looked at Violet and the group as if he'd heard Violet's thoughts, "Varney Mull is the name of the man in the North who's in league. I came through Sparrow to hunt down the last of his men. If you can call them men."

"Then all the teachings are true?" the preacher asked.

"Strange question to be coming from the preacher," Huck said. "I've never heard of some Varney Mull. I've never believed in none of those stories, but I can tell you this—something is happening here. I am not going to leave my shop, my house, and everything I've ever worked for in the hands of some woman who's burned down Sparrow church and plans on taking over my hometown."

"She has the Evil One on her side now," Jim said. "It's not just a question of wandering into town and asking to get the town back. We'll have to kill her. We'll likely have to kill her and anyone who's in league with her. The kind of evil she spreads is worse than any kind of spell or hold that a witch could put on someone. She's spreading belief. They'll be men and women of Sparrow who believe she's the one looking out for them. They'll be willing to put their lives on the line for her. Because the alternative she's presented them with is too frightening."

"The doctor?" May said suddenly from the entrance of the cave. Violet squeezed May's shoulders again, "Where is the doctor? Jim Falk, where is the doctor?"

Benjamin Straddler had been thinking hard at Huck's bar. It was all empty now and he was all by himself. Just the pictures on the wall were there. Just the bottles of booze behind the counter. Just Benjamin Straddler was there. There he was, sitting there with a bottle of booze in his hand. He hadn't drunk any of it, though. He was just looking at it. He was making a choice. He'd been listening to the wolves again and he was making a choice.

Hattie Jones had gone out of there a while ago. He'd said three days in a row that he and that boy of his, Samuel, were going to leave Sparrow, leave Sparrow and never come back. Maybe that's what he went to do. Though he'd been saying that was what he was going to do three days in a row. Hattie had managed to stick around to watch all the things happen—the church burning down and everything else. Hattie was right about one thing, though. That Mosely woman did seem to all of a sudden have a lot of people running to and fro doing whatever it was she wanted done. Benjamin sat there and chewed on his cigar and looked at the brown bottle of whisky in his hand. He thought about Lane. He thought about Dandy, that little horse, he thought about his pa. He knew that he would see his pa again. He thought about all the stories that he'd heard in the church growing up. He felt something warm and far away, but close too, in his chest. He could almost smell those old warm days sitting in the wooden benches at the church. Listening to one of the men tell the story of how a great leader would come one day to earth to rid out all the demons and set people free from their slavery. Those were old stories, though, and who knew if they were true or not? All Benjamin Straddler knew was that when he'd picked that outlander off the ground and saw his face, it wasn't the outlander's face. It was the face of his father, somehow reaching out to him, reaching back from wherever he was, saying, "You will see me."

Now he had a decision to make. What would he do about this little town and about his wife and about the people who were so desperate to hang on to life?

Dawn was coming. The wolves had stopped baying some hours ago. Whatever happened in Sparrow that night, if the wolves had killed them all, they would know soon enough.

Wylene looked from the mouth of the cave and down into the valley below. As the dark turned gray with the rising sun, she could make out the trail of smoke that still went up into the sky from the burned-down church, but there was another. Too, there was a foul smell that blended in the wind. What had become of this little town?

Wylene had seen them come and build this place. She had watched from the trees and the caves and the riversides as the people of Sparrow had moved in from the West. Watched them live and die and sing and fear. She'd seen the way the killers moved in not long after they did. Indeed, she'd fought alongside many of the Katakayish people when their numbers had been larger in those early times, when they had fought together against the killers. Her hope had always been to rid them entirely from this land and to let the Katakayish people, the River People, grow strong again. And to let these new people grow strong, these new people who had come so far because there was no place for them in this world—wandering and superstitious men and women who built sturdy houses and had laughing children.

But the evil was old and the evil was strong in the land. When Ithacus Falk came here, to the West, he'd done much to rid many of the evils along with the one they called Old Magic Woman, but they had not done enough. While Wylene had been under the Wastrel spell of Ruth Mosely, it had grown up again. What would become of this little town? What would become of the people of Sparrow? Wylene knew of towns that had been completely wiped away by the Evil One and the killers.

Jim Falk appeared beside her in the dim light.

"Have you buried him?" she asked.

From inside the cave, they could both hear May weeping and Violet trying to comfort her.

"I can hardly call it a burial. When this is over, we'll do it proper," Jim said and held up the doctor's bag and jingled it a little. "Do you know what to do with these?"

"I know very little about those kinds of medicines. I do not know how to make specials and elixirs and I do not know how to use them properly," Wylene said in a flat voice.

"Neither do I," Jim said. "There is a man in Hopestill by the name of Spencer Barnhouse who may be able to help with them. If he's still alive. And there is another who may be able to help us, but I have not seen her for many years and I do not know if she still lives."

"She?" Wylene asked.

"Yes," Jim said. "She was one of the magic women of the River People. She taught my father the Waycraft and they both tried to teach it to me too. But I was not a good student and she left me alone. She said that she could not stand by a son who had so much fear that . . ." Jim spoke no more, but looked over toward the piled-up rocks that marked where the doctor's body was.

"Perhaps this magic woman still lives, Jim Falk," Wylene said and turned her eyes away from him.

"What do you know of her?" Jim asked.

"I am not sure that I do, but I do not think that you should give up hope," Wylene said.

Jim nodded. "We've got to get back down to Sparrow and see what's been done. If it's still there and we need to deal with Ruth Mosely."

The preacher came out of the cave, followed by Violet and May and Huck Marbo. The snow was still coming out of the sky. It sputtered this way and that in the hard winds against the rocks and cold trees around them. The sunlight was coming, but it was grayer than white. It was coming slowly and May was rubbing her eyes. She could not stop sobbing.

"There, there, little one," her pa said to her and pulled her close to him again.

"There is too much death in life," Huck said to Jim, looking him in the eye and then looking back down at his daughter's head and her brown hair.

Jim looked down into the valley and nodded to Huck. "There will be more and more death if we do not do something."

"What will we do?" the preacher asked. "What about my wife and my daughter?"

"We will see," Jim said. "Huck, you might want to take May and get her safe up in your house. Violet, you too, you may want to stay safe with the preacher as well. Do you think that you can all make it to Huck's house?"

"I've only got a few more shots with this," Huck said, raising his shotgun.

Violet said, "I've got enough in here and in my pockets to get us there. I'm a good shot."

Jim reached into his pack and pulled his Dracon pistol and loaded it and gave it to the preacher. "It's only going to fire once, Preach, but that will do the trick. You gotta wait until they get real close and then pull the trigger. Wait until they're right up on you and then aim right at the face and pull this trigger. Aim at the face."

The preacher held the gun and made a frown. He pointed it out in front of him as if he were pointing it at an enemy and frowned again. "Yessir."

"If we head down along the southern trail and up toward the back way," Huck said, "we should be able to avoid anyone from the town until we're right up on the town and in back of our house. Stay close, Preacher, Violet. Here we go."

"Take this," Jim said and handed over the doctor's pack of medicine, unctions, and specials to Huck. Huck looked at it and handed it to Violet. Violet looked at it and handed it to May.

"May, you've used some of those before haven't you?" May nodded, but tears were splotched around her eyes. She clutched the bag.

They headed down the mountainside. Huck was in the front and Violet was in the back. May looked over her shoulder at Jim Falk and the witch until they were beyond the first ridge. May still couldn't quit crying. Her nose was red and her face was red. She thought about the doctor and squeezed the bag, his hands, the way they moved so fast to help. She squeezed at the bag in her arms and wondered if her hands could ever do the same.

After they were out of sight, Wylene looked at Jim Falk and Jim Falk looked at Wylene. The two looked at each other for a long time. Wylene lifted her veil and removed it from her head and walked over to the large pile of stones beneath which lay the body of Dr. Isham Pritham. She put the veil on the two sticks that Jim had drawn together to symbolize the meeting of heaven and earth, the crossway, the splitway. She spread her veil across the two crooked sticks like a web.

Then these two walked together down the crooked way that wound along from the cave to Sparrow by way of Sparrow Creek as the sun rose.

The snow had fallen so heavily in the night that it had come down through the trees and even piled up in big patches along the beaten paths that led along the creek and back into Sparrow. Jim and Wylene made their way as quickly as they could, but the snow was deep and cold and the wind cut through the trees and many branches scratched at their faces. Too, the sun was rising so bright and white that they were squinting and seeing orange and red and huffing along. It was hard going.

Since Wylene had taken the veil away and put it on the grave of the doctor, Jim could see her face in the sunlight. Each time he had looked over at it, it seemed to be a little brighter, fuller, younger. She looked as if she was healing and growing young right before his eyes in the sun and snow.

"What was that medicine that the doctor gave you?" Jim huffed at her.

"I do not know," she said. "If you saw the big wolf and the way the other wolves followed the big wolf, as I am sure you did, you know that the doctor may have feared that the bite of a wolf such as that could turn someone."

Jim said, "That doesn't happen anymore, does it?"

Wylene said, "Well, at least not to you and not to me."

They pushed on through the snow, and time and again Jim wondered how the preacher and Huck and Violet and May might be getting on, if they had the same difficulty getting up and around on that side of Sparrow. Jim thought they might be better off in that part of the wood where the pines were thicker and the paths were less brambled.

After many slips and cuts and twists, the two found themselves at the treeline where they could see the pile of wood and ashes that still glowed where the church once sat. The place they crouched down in was a low dip where some logs and broken trees had fallen. Here and there were dark holes where the snow didn't fall and the sun didn't reach. It was still here, and the snapping and crackling of the burning church was the only sound that penetrated the trees.

The fire had not gone completely out even now, and a blue and black smoke went up from the center of it looking like a wide rope twirling into the clouds. They both looked at each other. It might have stopped snowing, but there was so much snow that the wind was blowing around that they couldn't really tell for sure.

Wylene said, "I am still very tired. Very weak from the healing that is happening and from opening the tunnel."

"Yeah," Jim said. "the tunnel. You're going to have to tell me about that when all this is over."

Wylene smiled. It was genuinely pretty, even with her sharp teeth. "Over?"

Then they heard a shout. Then they heard a snort and a yammer and a yipe. Then more shouting. There was another fire burning somewhere, and the yammering that they heard was of wolves. Jim got out his rifle fast and laid it out on a bare log there and unrolled it from its case. He put it together quick and slick and loaded it with silverlode.

Then there was another noise beside them, like a whisper, and the killers sprang up from somewhere in the bank of snow. Jim quickly counted four of them, but they looked like messy brown shadows in the light and there could be more. Without the special power that the Leaves gave him, he was at a loss to be able to see or feel them. He wished he were more like his father, who could feel the jitters without the Leaves. He wished he had listened to them.

Jim fired his long gun at the head of one; the rifle snuffed and the killer dropped fast into the snow and rolled down the hill. He didn't want to lose too much ammo in a fight he might be able to fight with his hatchet, so he slung his gun and pulled his ax and then saw the black cloaks of Wylene flying down the embankment toward the group of others who were rushing at her. Wylene was rushing straight for them, with a growl.

He jumped a couple of logs and rushed in beside her, taking them on the flank side. His ax was quick to and fro, but Wylene's claws were faster and heads and limbs went whirling into the snowy banks and dark blood splashed and steamed in the snow. All was quiet again.

Wylene's breath came out in a white cloud and she looked around with her black eyes. When she was satisfied, she crouched down and cleaned her hands in the sparkling snow.

"I can see why they kept you weak," Jim said.

Wylene smiled again and flexed her arm. "I am still not completely healed."

Jim smiled back at her.

It stayed quiet and they lurked toward the church and looked around. The church was completely burned to a pile. There was no way anyone was going to be able to fix it.

"How did you get us out of this?" Jim asked.

Then they heard shots coming from down over the hill where the doctor's house was.

They ran along the edge of the hill and could see that Ruth Mosely was standing in the field where Jim had killed one of the spooks in front of the doctor's house. Below them lay the steep, rocky bank that led down toward the doctor's house. Some of the rocks were so big that they still poked through all the snow.

Beyond this, in the white clearing, Ruth was not alone. The wolves pattered this way and that way around her, barking now and again. And dotted all about them were the black splotches and paw prints. The wolves snorted and growled, not at Ruth, but at the doctor's house. Then they saw the big wolf come from somewhere in the trees along with two killers at either side of him, looking something like wildmen in the sunlight. Jim saw that the big wolf had something on its head that glittered like black jewels.

He whispered to Wylene, "What's on its head?"

"Many eyes," Wylene said.

"Come out!" Ruth shouted, and the boom of another shotgun shot came from the doctor's house.

"You stay away, you old witch!" Jim recognized the voice of Benjamin Straddler. "You won't take Sparrow for the Evil One's work! I'll see your brains in the snow!"

Jim wondered what to do and who was in the doctor's old house with him.

Now he could see that there were dead wolves on the porch, three of them splayed and curled. There was even a dead wolf up on the roof. Benjamin had been busy.

"The big one is very strong," Wylene said. "He is from the Wydder, from the other side, and will not die, even with the silver-lode in your gun. Even your specials won't kill him. Even if we cut off his head and try to burn him, it will not kill him. What he truly is, that part will go back to the Wydder."

There was the word again. Jim knew exactly what she was talking about because this was the thing that his father had talked about and had written about in his journals, but that no one believed. Now, here was this Wylene, who was not a witch, talking about it plain as day. And she had brought them through that strange, cold tunnel to come out in the woods to safety. Had she made a hole through the Wydder? It was too much for Jim to take in now.

"What about her?" Jim asked, meaning Ruth Mosely.

"She is just an old woman who thinks that the Evil One is going to make her live forever and give her power. If you can get a shot from here, you can put a hole in her head."

Jim didn't like this idea too very much. It was one thing to lop the head off a bad killer or to rip off a demon's head. Even killing John Mosely seemed something of a wrong move. Still, it was a whole other thing to ask a man to kill a woman. What had this woman gotten herself into anyhow? Trying to take over towns for the Evil One. He thought of Doc Pritham and the evil book that he'd handed over. Jim wished he'd destroyed the book back at the cave, while he'd had time. But it sat, wrapped in the woven blanket, in his satchel.

Jim looked at Wylene and remembered what she had said about Ruth and her posse coming in the nighttime and beating her and cutting off her thumb. He wondered if he could have done the same thing to her if he had thought it were true, that Wylene was a witch. Could he have done the same thing? Too, he wondered if somehow Ruth Mosely didn't think that what she was doing was somehow in the right, but how could she? Here she was destroying this whole town just because there were people in it who believed that there was hope in the future, people who believed in the Way and that there would come a day when heaven and earth would meet. But there she stood, surrounded by dirty wolves and killers, and whatever the wolf-thing was that had come from the Wydder.

There she was, shouting back at Benjamin Straddler: "Come out of there! Come out and we'll let you live! Come out and be with us!"

Wylene nudged him and whispered, "Now! Now!"

Jim raised the rifle and put her head in the thin crosshairs.

"Where did the big one go?" Wylene asked.

Jim saw the white of Ruth's face through his crosshairs as it suddenly turned toward him and he pulled the trigger, but something slammed against his body just as the bullet left the muzzle. His side felt burst and he rolled down a steep bank as his coat grew hot with blood. As he rolled he saw the huge black shape of the wolf-thing bristling and whirling in the snow. It was fighting Wylene. He heard his rifle go clattering away along the snow and rocks below them, and his head felt light as he rolled and rolled again.

He could hear shouting below him and shouting above him and the barking and growling all around. He tried to pull himself up, but found his arms were weak. He saw Wylene go tumbling as well. Down, down, down.

He felt the hot breath of the animals around him and when he looked up, he saw Ruth's face with them, her face among the wicked faces of the starving wolves.

"They are hungry for you, outlander," Ruth said and she started laughing. Her laugh was high and broken and reminded Jim of the sound of cracking ice on a frozen lake. He tried to get up again, but his vision was getting dim and he felt something grab him and his body began sliding.

When he woke up, his head hurt and it was dark and very cold. He heard someone cracking something nearby, but could not see because it was so dark. The animal smell of the wolves was still strong in his nose, but there was another smell of wood and something strong and rancid.

When he breathed, his chest ached, his sides ached, and his hands were twisted in back of him. In a moment, his eyes adjusted to the scene. He realized that he was strapped to a post and that shadowy figures were stacking firewood at his legs. He glanced over and saw Wylene in the same situation. Were they to be burned alive? What of Benjamin Straddler?

The sky was clear and purple and the half-moon shone clear and bright into the little valley where the doctor's house was. The snow had stopped and the stars twinkled.

"Wylene . . ." he tried to call out, but he was so weak, his voice was so dry, that he couldn't make a noise. On the other side of her, he could see orange light jumping. Then he realized that the hillside sloped downward to the doctor's house, which was surrounded by people carrying torches. Ruth Mosely, he supposed, had decided to mount them up on the hill and burn them as a threat to try to get Straddler and whoever else of Sparrow that was in there with them to come out. Why she didn't just burn the place to the ground, he didn't know. Maybe she was looking for the book that Jim had in his pack, but that was gone now too.

Jim thought of the old story as they stacked the kindling about him. He thought about Old Magic Woman's tale of Eyabé and that, before Eyabé came to the mountain to fight Kitaman, he had to pass through the Fire Door. Anger burned within him. If he died in flames here on this hill in this little town, he would never see his father. All because of this old witch Ruth's false beliefs in the promises of the Evil One. Ruth did not yet know it, but she too would burn one day at his hands and he and the killers would feast on her bones.

He pulled again at the ropes, but they were strong and he was weak. He tried again to call out for Wylene, but his voice was too hoarse. He could see her head moving, but she was not looking his way, she was looking down toward the doctor's house.

Now he could hear Benjamin yelling, "Instead of burning them two, why don't you come on in here, you old bitch! I've got something you'll like!"

If it weren't for the pain coursing in his chest, Jim would have laughed. He thought of May Marbo and wondered what had become of her and the others during the time that he'd been knocked out by that wolf creature. He tugged at the ropes again.

"Wylene!" his voice finally came clear. "Wylene, can you hear me?"

She didn't react, she looked to have fallen asleep again.

Then he saw the beast and Ruth coming up the hill together. Ruth's mouth was moving and the beast's head was swaying toward her as if it were listening to her words. There were some wolves coming too, and the killers came along with the rest of them. In the half-moonlight, it was clear what they were. They barely looked like men at all—their noses gone, the black teeth shining, strange antlers poking this way and that from their backs. They were the killers for sure and they had come to kill. Jim pulled again. If the fire started and the ropes weren't thick enough, he may be able to pull away, but by that time his legs might be completely burned to stumps.

"Wylene!" he shouted again. Maybe if she could wake up, if she was even still alive, maybe she was strong enough to open another tunnel, to do whatever it was that she did before that had let them all escape into the woods. He thought again of his father, of Ithacus. What would his pa do? He wriggled despite the pain.

"Falk!" Ruth was suddenly shouting in his face. "I will let you go if you can tell me which one of these wretched people has those false scriptures. Which one of you is hiding the damned writings?"

The false scriptures? Did she not have the book that had been in his satchel? He remembered the papers that Barnhouse and the preacher had stowed away. Was she talking about those papers? His father's journal? He wasn't in for this game.

"If you're going to kill me, Ruth Mosely, just kill me. I wouldn't tell you a thing, even if I did know. He'll kill you too, you know."

"Who, who will kill me?" Ruth asked.

"The Evil One, or whoever he's working through. They will not let you live. They have no promises. They have no hope."

"Hope?" Ruth cackled and looked at the wolf beast with many eyes. "What is hope?"

One of the wolves darted to the left and another went with it. The wolf-thing made a snarl that sounded too much like words not to be words, but Jim didn't quite catch what it was. What was she after? Didn't she already have the book?

The killers spoke something to one another in a snarled way, and Jim couldn't hear it either. Then Ruth's eyes went wide and the wolf-creature's hairs bristled and it lowered itself and roared. From behind him, Jim saw another wolf leap into the moonlight, a larger, gray wolf, with a healthy-looking flank. It turned and growled at Jim as if in warning. Jim thought for a moment that he might have already died and some of those who were already dead before him were beginning to break the barrier and come to his side, because he recognized the wolf. It was Fenny, Old Magic Woman's friend and the friend of his father.

But before Jim could get a better look, the gray wolf was raging and snapping in a terrible battle with the beast. Even for the size of the thing, the gray wolf was not losing; it sped this way and that, first chomping on a forepaw and then biting at the thing's underbelly, knocking it back and down the hill. Jim saw a killer running away from the site too, one of its arms missing. It scrambled and whirled and dropped to the ground as it ran, howling.

He felt the ropes behind him being cut and dropped to his knees when a strange man's voice said to him, "If you can move, get to the trees. She will be able to heal you." The figure that cut him free moved along the treeline to Wylene and crouched and began to cut her from her ropes as well. She looked limp as she crumpled into his arms.

The man picked Wylene up and walked toward Jim. Jim was on the ground and trying to stand when Ruth Mosely rushed toward him.

"No! No!" she was shouting. "You stay put! You're going to ruin everything!"

Jim tried to get up, but his sides were beaten and he had no strength. He crawled backwards away from her.

The man holding Wylene shouted, "Stop! Ruth Mosely!" but she ignored him and bent down and thrust her cold hands around Jim Falk's throat.

The man put down Wylene and ran to Jim, but before he got there Ruth toppled backward and a cloaked figure that had appeared from somewhere in the treeline grappled with her until Ruth was still beneath the cloak.

The cloaked figure stood up slowly and turned. Jim could see nothing beneath the hood, but he felt a presence, a peace, and his heart beat in his chest. Her brown and old hands reached for his and he put them into hers.

"Am I dead? Have I already died?" Jim asked. "I did not want to die before I saw my father again."

"Indeed, little one, you may see him again yet," Old Magic Woman said and pulled her hood down so that he could see her face. "But you have much healing to do before you chase after him on the other side."

Jim could not help but feel suddenly strong enough to stand when her hands touched his. He looked at the man who held Wylene again in his arms.

"Simon?" Jim Falk asked.

"She helped me," Simon Starkey said. "Matishne, the one you call Old Magic Woman."

They all turned to see that Ruth Mosely had got to her feet and was scurrying down the hillside.

"She is strong with the evil," Old Magic Woman said.

"She has your book, Simon Starkey, she has the book of Witchwords."

"We must stop her," Simon said.

Old Magic Woman brought some wrappings out of somewhere in her cloak and unrolled them. Jim's eyes grew wide because he saw that she had the Leaves. She gave them to him and he ate them and his pain disappeared. Wylene did the same and soon was up and feeling bright.

"Go," Old Magic Woman said to the three. "Go and put an end to her."

Jim Falk felt at his side where the wolf-thing had bit him. It was still sore and open, but the bleeding had stopped and there was a buzzing feeling about it. It was the Leaves. Soon the smells of the night filled his nostrils, and he could see the glowing light of Old Magic Woman and the strange green fire that moved around Wylene. Simon Starkey held a bright knife almost as long as his forearm, and his wise eyes met Jim's as the three of them ran down the hill and toward the doctor's house.

Ruth was limping around in the field with the book of Witch-words in her hand, walking in an odd circle and making motions with her other hand.

"Stop! Stop!" Wylene yelled at her, but she was not stopping.

The wolf-thing was heaving and spots of its blood were pooling below it; it was very badly wounded. Jim also saw the life inside of it flickering like a pale red flame. It surely looked to be dying. Fenny must have struck some mortal wound into it that only a wolf could strike into a wolf.

"I thought you said we couldn't kill that thing," Jim said.

"It's not dead, is it?" Wylene said back.

Fenny appeared beside them, almost completely unharmed. He barked at Jim and jumped at him, his tail wagging hard.

Then something black opened in front of them near where Ruth Mosely had been chanting. It was darker than all the night and shaped like a circle.

It was the same thing that Jim had seen his father disappear into so long ago. The black hole that led to the otherside. The black gate that opened into the Wydder.

Ruth went through without looking back at them standing there, and the wolf-thing with the many eyes followed her and the gate closed.

Killers ran from the hills toward where the hole had been as if they too could find a way through. Jim went this way and Wylene went that and Simon Starkey swung his blade and soon they had dealt with these few and were alone in the field, surrounded by the dead creatures, but Ruth Mosely was gone. Gone through the gate.

"Is that you, outlander?" Benjamin Straddler called from inside the doctor's house. "Who's all them people with you? You all survived that fire?"

Hattie Jones stepped slowly out on the porch of the doctor's house looking around in the night.

Jim went down on one knee. He was exhausted and the Leaves were wearing off. He suddenly realized that the Leaves were wearing off and remembered that she had given them to him, Old Magic Woman! He looked up the long bank in the dark and the moonlight shone on the small figure of the hooded woman standing just at the edge of the trees. Why had she come back after all this time? He had been sure she was dead, but there she was and she was walking along with her good friend, the little trickster, Fenny. It was like something from one of his visions, except that it was not one of his visions at all.

Hattie said, "You all here, I guess, to take care of them demons and spooks and that witch woman, Mosely. She did a terrible thing here in Sparrow. A lotta folk got killed last night by them wolves and them ugly men that were with her. It was bad. It was real bad. But you know what, Benjamin Straddler's got something in him that he ain't had before. He got up nerve and started fighting back and we all ended up down here at the doc's house on account of we knew that that's where we could find medicine and ammunition and other things that we needed. But then, that old witch, Ruth Mosely, got to thinking that the doctor had something important in here. Some kind of papers that she kept calling the false scriptures. I don't know if they're in there or not, outlander, but we were in there. We were in there. Me and Samuel and Lane Straddler and Benjamin Straddler and the preacher's wife and daughter and others too, I don't know who all. But Straddler had guns and he gave 'em out to everyone and we were able to hold him back. Old Benji stepped forward of a sudden, seemed like he wanted to lead us on! I think it done Benji some good to kill some of those bad dirty wolves."

Hattie was talking and then he stopped and his eyes went open wide because he saw Wylene standing there. He saw her white skin and her black eyes and her sharp teeth. "Outlander, you ain't in with the Evil One too, are ya?" Hattie asked.

"She is not what you might think," Jim said.

"Where did they go?" Hattie asked, meaning Ruth Mosely and the monstrous wolf.

"To the otherside," Wylene said and looked at the empty space where the hole used to be. "They've gone into the Wydder."

"The Wydder!" Hattie yelled. "That's all just stories and tales!"

"Yes," Simon said and smiled a little, "but some stories are true."

Old Magic Woman joined the little circle and looked at Wylene and nodded to her in recognition. Wylene bowed her head somberly to Old Magic Woman and Jim grinned and grinned.

# CHAPTER 20

It was not snowing and the sun was shining in the windows at Huck's house. May and Violet and Huck sat at the kitchen table in her pa's house. Her pa was making eggs and coffee.

Violet said, "I hear Falk's going to try to follow Mosely and the creature through to the otherside."

May said, "They say that the witch, Wylene, has a power to open the gate."

Huck turned and put eggs on everyone's plate and then poured hot coffee for each of them into their little white cups. "We don't need to fool or inquire in those things anymore. What we need to concentrate on is helping Vernon and Benjamin rebuild those houses on the west side that got destroyed and to help them rebuild the church, too."

He sat down and they all started eating their eggs and their eggs were very good.

"They're supposed to try it today, whatever it is that they're going to do, a spell or whatever it might be, to go to the otherside," May said between bites.

"I told you, May. We don't need to worry about them and that. We're going to have enough to worry about and more trying to build this place back up."

"But if it works, I thought that we should go and see and see them off."

Violet looked across the table at Huck Marbo, looked deep into his green eyes, and he looked back at her and looked even deeper into her green eyes. Huck huffed and then looked at May.

"Pa, I wouldn't be here if it weren't for . . ."

"We'll go," Huck said. "We'll go and see them off. They say that they're leaving right when the sun is directly overhead. So let's eat and get a move on. We've got stuff to take into town anyway and get the shop set up. We've got a lot to clean up."

Violet smiled in a funny way at Huck and they finished their plates.

Wylene was sitting on the doctor's porch and looking out into the sunshine. "You don't really know what sunshine is until you haven't felt it for so long. You don't realize that it gives you a kind of energy that you can't get from anything else.'"

"I suppose so," Jim said to her. He was cleaning his rifle. On the wooden table in front of him was his shining ax and his Dracon pistol that the preacher had given back to him. Jim was trying to say as little as possible because he was inwardly so excited that he thought he might burst into laughter if too many words came from his mouth. He thought he might lose control. After they'd talked with Hattie and Straddler and the rest the night before, it came out that Wylene had the ability to open these gates, but that she need-ed to rest up and gain energy and that she could only do it at cer-tain times and in certain ways. But she felt that if she got good enough rest and healing herbs she might be able to open one in the morning.

Old Magic Woman, or Matishne, as Wylene called her, did know how to use just about everything that had been on the doc-tor's shelves and in his bags. With those items, she packed as much medicine on and into Jim and Wylene as she possibly could, and the two had slept soundly through the night.

Early that morning, it was decided.

Matishne said, "Sparrow is not beyond repair. Simon Starkey and I will stay behind here with Benjamin and the preacher. We can make this town strong again. Should Old Bendy's Men come this way, we will stand together with the men and women of Sparrow against them. But you must go, James Falk, you must go to find your father."

"And I will go with him," Wylene had said immediately. "I have business of old in the Wydder, and James will need my help."

"So it will be," Matishne said.

When the sun was overhead and blazing, Hattie and Samuel, Violet and Huck and May, Benjamin, Simon, and Matishne stood watching as Wylene moved her arms slowly and spoke sharp words into the air.

Soon her arms were stretched out and her palms were open with the sunlight glowing in them. Then there was a noise like a pop and everyone heard a whining sound. Across from Wylene in the snowy grass, a rock split open and a cold wind came from the darkness behind the rock. Soon the darkness grew into a patchy looking shadow and then into a shimmering, black emptiness.

"It's open," Wylene said.

Jim turned and looked at each of them standing there. He looked at Fenny's bright eyes and perked ears, he looked at Hattie's old face. He looked them all in the eye. His eyes finally rested on Old Magic Woman.

"We will see each other again, little Jim," she said.

Packed with medicines and ammunitions, specials and elixirs, and other stuff that Matishne had given them, the two moved through the black gate. It slowly, but surely, disappeared, leaving only the sunny field and the good people of Sparrow.

# EPILOGUE

He walked in.

"They are in the den," the preacher said to the man wearing the broken glasses.

"And no one else knows?" Spencer Barnhouse asked the preacher.

"Only Falk knew that I had them and now he is on the other-side."

"The other side?" Spencer asked him, stepping toward the old fireplace in the preacher's home.

"He went through to the place they call," and the preacher whispered this word, "the Wydder."

Spencer Barnhouse said, "Hmph. Show me the papers."

The preacher went to the mantelpiece and moved the stone just so, and the stone opened up. He reached inside and slid out the shiny metal box. He handed it to Spencer Barnhouse.

The two men sat down in the chairs.

"Your wife is not here? There is no one in the house but you and me, right?"

"No one."

Barnhouse slid the lid to the box open and inside were the several sheafs of paper. His hands fidgeted with excitement. He could barely bring himself to touch them.

"But these are not copies," Spencer said. "These are the original papers, these are Falk's original journals and the scriptures." Spencer gasped. "Where did you get these?"

"There is a cave in the hills. It is the same cave where that witch-woman, Wylene, took us when we escaped the burning church. That's where I found these. Near where they buried the body of Isham Pritham, the doctor."

"What happened to the copies that I gave you?"

"I do not know. When I got home from the cave, they were gone."

"Who else knew about them?"

"As I said, only Falk knew. Only Jim Falk knew about the copies. But he doesn't know about the originals."

Spencer Barnhouse raised his eyes after reading a few pages of the scribblings. "Take me to this cave, Preacher."

THE END

CPSIA information can be obtained
at www.ICGtesting.com
Printed in the USA
LVOW01s1448140116

470662LV00019B/1143/P